MW01242651

# THE MESMERIST

## CLAIRE LUANA

LIVE EDGE
PUBLISHING

*Desire never lies...*

Someone is killing the Adrjssian royal family one by one. When the queen is pushed to her death, suspicion lands on 17-year-old Adrijana Mironacht, a village girl new to court. Determined to clear her name, Adrijana enlists the aid of the compelling and enigmatic Dragan Vulpe, one of the royal Mesmers—magicians with the ability to read and manipulate the thoughts and emotions of those around them.

As the royal body count grows and the hostile Vruk army gathers at the border, ready to capitalize on Adrjssian instability, Adrijana homes in on the Vruk ambassadors as the most likely suspects. But when she uncovers evidence of Mesmer help, she begins to second-guess both her instincts and the loyalties of those around her. Tangled in a web of half-truths and pretty lies, it will take all of Adrijana's cunning to unmask the true killer.

**From the author of the *Confectioner Chronicles* comes a stand-alone young adult fantasy mystery set in a seductive new world of glittering magic, shadowed secrets, and deadly intrigue.**

The Mesmerist
Copyright © 2022 by Claire Luana
Published by Live Edge Publishing

eBook ISBN: 978-1-948947-35-0
Paperback ISBN: 978-1-948947-34-3
Hardback ISBN: 978-1-948947-33-6

All rights reserved. Except as permitted under the U.S. Copyright Act of 1976, no part
of this publication may be reproduced, distributed, or transmitted in any form or by
any means, or stored in a database or retrieval system without the prior written
permission of the author.

All characters appearing in this work are fictitious. Any resemblance to real persons,
living or dead, is purely coincidental.

Cover Design: KDP Letters
Editing: Amy McNulty

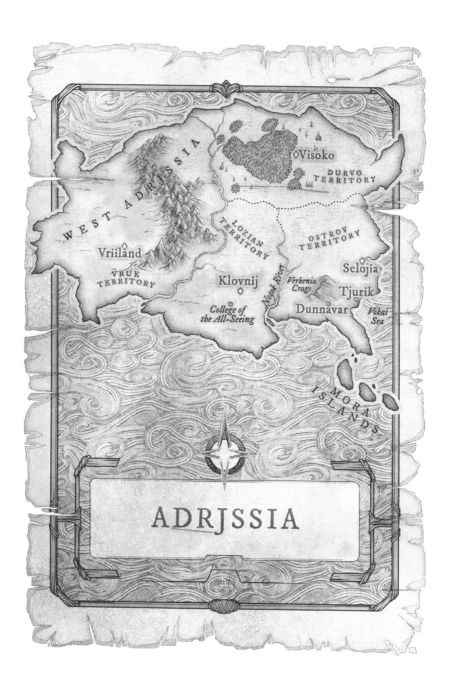

ADRJSSIA

# CHAPTER 1

*S*ome days paint the fabric of our souls with happy hues. Good fortune and breathless anticipation are both as bright as spring sunshine. Other days ink their woeful tales in dark lines and shadowed grayscale. This day would stain my soul with both—and something more besides. But I didn't know any of that. Not yet.

I didn't see much that day—a pastel slash across a man's neck as he trotted by on a handsome chestnut gelding, a glow of gold nestled beneath a woman's bosom as our cart trundled past. Nothing out of the ordinary. My focus was elsewhere, firmly fixed two hours ahead of us, when we would arrive at the palace in Selojia.

"Will you stop fidgeting?" Papa sat next to me, the reins clenched in his fists. Papa's nerves were keeping pace with my excitement, both blooming larger the closer we got to the capital. At this rate, we'd both burst before we made it through the gates.

"I don't know why you're so anxious about visiting." I smoothed the fabric of my finest dress over my knees. For the tenth time. Anything to keep my hands busy. "From the sound of Simeon's letters, Selojia is a place of wonders." It had been over six months since I'd seen my best friend, and I was eager to hear all about his adventures in person. I was certain there were juicy nuggets he couldn't risk sharing via letter.

"I'll be damned if I take the word of a starry-eyed eighteen-year old dumb enough to volunteer for the army."

"It's a noble profession and a good living. Plus, Simeon was invited to train for the royal guard. It's an honor."

"I'll be double damned if I sit here and receive a lecture from you on the benefits of military service. You forget I had the *honor* of serving as fodder for two years"—I mouthed the next part with him, for I knew it was coming—"and not all of me made it back." Papa had lost his right leg to just above the knee in the war against the Vruks of West Adrjssia, before I'd been born.

A burst of red swirled above his head. *Double damned indeed.* He'd seen my mouth moving. I hurried to head off whatever rebuke was coming. "I'm sorry, Papa. I'm just excited to see the city. I know you think it's dangerous, but it's been years since the war. You can't keep me cooped up forever."

"I'll do my damndest," Papa said under his breath, but I planted a kiss on his weathered` cheek and he pursed his lips to hide a smile. The red dispersed like a vapor in a breeze. Papa had my same walnut hair, though his was mostly gray now, and his disapproving frown buried itself beneath a furry moustache.

Guilt flashed through me as quick as lightning, and I was glad I couldn't see my own colors. In his last letter Simeon had said the princess was looking for another companion, and he'd put in a good word for me. I could hardly imagine the Simeon with whom I'd climbed trees and thrown snowballs having the ear of the princess, but I wouldn't miss this chance. Papa may have been happy to farm verbenia in the middle of nowhere, but I wanted more from my life.

Adventure and glamour and…something. Anything more than a one-room cabin and the monotony of pulling weeds day in, day out. Plus, the palace library was supposed to be the grandest on the continent; if there was an answer to the strange phenomenon coloring my vision, I'd find it there.

The cries of the weeping gulls were the first clue we were nearing the capital, and the Vokai Sea beyond. When the carriage trundled over a hillside, I surged to my feet, my hands flying to my mouth. A tapestry of green and gold stretched below us—fields ripe with fat grapes and furry with summer wheat. Beyond that, a sprawling city rendered in tan stone clustered around domes of teal copper and burnished bronze. All leaning down to the shimmering ribbon of the sea—stretching vast and endless.

"Sit down or you'll crack your head." Papa grabbed my wrist and forced me down. But he couldn't dim my delight.

"It's magnificent!" I'd been to the ocean before, when Papa and I had visited the little fishing village of Tjurik half a dozen leagues from our farm, but that view had been nothing like this.

"It's a nest of hornets and snakes. An honest man can't turn around without getting bit. Soon the winds will whip up, and you won't be able to walk the streets without Desenjia finding every seam and hole and grasping at them with her icy fingertips. Then winter will fall and the mist will blanket everything. Imagine months of not seeing the sun. That fog has hidden more foul deeds than a man could conceive of."

I rolled my eyes. "Simeon said everyone weaves tiny bells into their hair so the entire city is like a tinkling symphony."

"A cacophony, more like it. You try getting anything done with those infernal bells ringing nonstop. It's enough to drive a man mad."

As we drew nearer to the great oaken gates that funneled into the city, I contented myself to take it all in silently. Papa was a lost cause. Life had soured him beyond hope of rectification. I wouldn't let the same happen to me.

My excitement threatened to choke me as we trundled into the city. I fisted my hands in my dress to keep them from shaking. Two flags fluttered on a tall pole above the city wall: the purple flag of Adrjssia, with the spiny chiton rendered in gold thread in the center like a sunburst, and another beneath—black, with an unblinking purple eye embroidered in silver. That second flag meant the king's Mesmer was at court. A declaration, and a warning.

"Will we see the Royal Mesmer?" I asked, though I knew what Papa's reaction would be.

"Ovyato help us, I hope not." Papa drew a finger in a horizontal motion across his eyes, a ward against the power of the Mesmers. Supposedly, that was where the Mesmers discerned your truth—through your eyes, they could see all the bits of you—every fevered hope and dream, every buried secret and covetous thought, every lie or crime or wrong. Justice in Adrjssia was total and unyielding. Justice was the Mesmers.

The intoxicating scenery of the city quickly captured my attention. We passed glittering fountains and finely-wrought temples, bright market squares and dizzying staircases snaking up the city's steep hills. And then there were the people: copper-haired Durvo women and silk-clad Lozians and even a Vruk warrior, his wide shoulders swathed in fur and his thick neck wrapped with an iron torc. And swirling around all of them were colors: tangerine and cerulean blue and brown like loamy soil. As they assaulted my senses, I leaned back and let my eyes close.

Papa patted my leg. "It takes some getting used to."

Up and up we went toward the Ostrov Palace, which perched atop a hill at the height of the city. I could feel Simeon growing closer; I was even more eager to talk to him now, to hear everything about the city, the royal family, his training. How many stories he must have from a place like this.

At the palace gate, Papa was given directions by a guard in purple and silver livery. "You'll want to find Jaro, the royal steward. The queen has left special instructions that your cargo be delivered directly to him."

Papa thanked him and flicked the reins.

"The queen is expecting us?" I asked. The verbenia we carried was a medicinal herb; it struck me as odd that the queen would see to it personally. I supposed it *was* rare. It was the only thing that banished my headaches—I took it daily. Perhaps she had similar need of it.

"It's valuable," came Papa's only reply.

Our wagon rolled through a shadowed archway into a busy courtyard. Other wagons were being unloaded against the northern wall, and in another corner, lads of perhaps ten years old sparred in the packed dirt with wooden swords. Out from one open set of doors strode a handsome man in rich clothing with curly brown locks, accompanied by a tall, dark-skinned soldier in purple livery.

"Simeon!" I squealed. I launched myself off the side of the wagon while it was still moving and flew across the courtyard, throwing myself into his arms.

Simeon let out a surprised, "Oof!"

The other man laughed. "I see you've acquired a dervish."

Simeon placed me down and pulled back, his big hands resting lightly on my shoulders. His dark eyes looked me up and down with amazement, taking me in. "Jana, look at you—"

Butterflies stormed in my stomach as I did the same to him. It had been so long since we'd seen each other. Would it still be the same easy way between us? "Look at *you*!"

Simeon had always been handsome—as tall as a birch with a lean, muscled form and expressive, arching eyebrows. His mother, descended from the elusive Mora clan, had given him dark skin and shining ebony hair that made him stand out even more. But he had grown since I'd last seen him—his face had matured, scruff shadowed his angular jaw, and his muscles had filled out under his well-tailored uniform. The palace ladies must have been swooning.

"A-hem." A throat cleared and I startled like a deer, remembering the other man.

Simeon laughed and I wanted to melt into him as memories washed over me—a childhood filled with that laugh. "Sorry, Georgi. I forgot myself. It was like I'd seen a ghost."

"A very lovely ghost." Georgi regarded me appraisingly. I had filled out too this last year, my figure moving from girlish to something more. I'd worn my newest dress—a light green cotton cinched with a bodice of emerald embroidered with copper leaves. My long, brown hair curled loosely about my shoulders. I had wanted to look good for the princess.

"Adrijana, this is Lord Georgi Hristov, cousin to the Princess

Nevana. Georgi, this is Adrijana. We grew up together—she's like a sister to me."

Cousin to the princess? I fumbled my way into a curtsy. "It's a pleasure to meet you, my lord," I managed. Lord Georgi was handsome too. He had the nut-brown skin and bright green eyes of a Durvo clansman—he must have been related to the princess on the Queen's side. He also had a dimple in his chin and a smile as bright as a moonbeam.

"Please, call me Georgi." A smudge of pink twirled above each of his ears. I'd seen it often enough to be able to gauge its meaning. It meant he fancied someone. My stomach swooped like a swallow as I realized who. *Me. My cheeks flushed with pleasure.*

"Simeon!" My father had parked the wagon and crossed the courtyard to join us in slow, uneven steps. He transferred his cane and clapped hands with Simeon. "You've grown."

"Welcome, Iordan. It's good to see you. They feed me well here." Simeon patted his stomach before introducing Georgi.

"We need to get our cargo unloaded so we can get back on the road," Papa said. "You'll excuse us, of course?" My heart sank, but I knew better than to argue with Papa in front of a stranger.

"You mean to leave so soon?" Georgi asked. "Surely, you'll stay through the feast tonight?" Tomorrow would be the equinox festival, when summer officially turned to autumn. In our village, Dunnavar, we celebrated on the day, but perhaps here they reveled on the equinox's eve.

"We haven't secured lodging, and it'll be impossible to find during the festival." Papa shook his head. "It was always going to be a quick trip."

"Nonsense! You've come all this way," Georgi protested. "Surely, a day of rest is in order—plus, there will be fine food and dancing tonight. You could stay at the palace, as my guest. Wouldn't you like to attend?" he asked me.

Papa shot me a warning look.

I ignored it. This was my chance. I could never vie for the position

7

CLAIRE LUANA

of the princess's companion if we turned tail and left this very afternoon. Plus, I deserved more time to catch up with Simeon.

Papa could go straight to the Lord of Winter's hoary Frostlands.

So I said the words that would change everything. "Lord Georgi, we would love to attend."

# CHAPTER 2

$S$imeon and Georgi located the royal steward for Papa, who took delivery of our four crates of dried verbenia.

Georgi stood next to me as Papa negotiated his payment and Simeon directed some servants to help with unloading.

My skin prickled with awareness as Georgi eyed me sideways. "It's an unusual harvest. Only grows in a few places outside of West Adrjssia, from what I understand. How did your father get into farming verbenia?"

"He's been growing it for most of my life. Ever since we moved after—" I trailed off. No need for him to know that we'd moved after my little sister had drowned in the lake near our old house. "Well, since I was five. Our village borders an outcropping of exposed limestone, which is what the verbenia likes."

Georgi nodded. "And your father only grows for the queen?"

"Yes, she purchases our whole harvest each year." I turned to regard him. "Are you so curious about all medicinal herbs, my lord?

"Like I said, please call me Georgi." He reached over the side of the wagon and pulled loose a sprig that was poking out the side of one of the crates being unloaded. He twirled it in his fingers and then sniffed it. "And in my role, I find it wise to know as much as I can about anything as powerful as this little plant."

I cocked my head. "Powerful? What—"

Papa appeared at my side, his presence a wedge that drove me a step back from Georgi. "The steward has been kind enough to find chambers for us. Shall we go get cleaned up?"

Simeon joined our little circle. "I'm sure Nevena has a dress you can borrow for tonight. I'll ask her."

*Nevena? He was on a first-name basis with the princess?* And what was wrong with the dress I had on? I managed a smile. "I would be much obliged."

Papa put an arm around my shoulder and shepherded me away. "Come, my dear." When we were out of earshot, he added, "you've really done it now."

Papa's anger was like the windy season to come—all bluster and no substance. He explained his reticence in a series of growled mutterings. The only coherent thread I could draw from the lot of them was that I "wasn't to speak of our business to anyone."

I had never considered Papa a private man. He was friendly enough with our neighbors. But here among the finery of the Tsarian royal family, I couldn't help but think he was acting like a man with a secret. His colors confirmed it—the pear-green of anxiety clung about his shoulders like a cloak, while midnight blue smudged his temples. The color of lies.

I set aside my curiosity. I had the whole ride home to unravel that mystery, whereas I had only hours here to secure a place in court. That needed to be my focus.

The rooms the royal steward located for us were larger than our entire farmhouse. I craned my neck as we walked in, ogling the fresco that decorated the ceiling. It was a map of Adrjssia before the Vruk Rebellion—back when the country had been united. The territories of the five clans were rendered in startling detail: the mountain strongholds of the Vruks to the west, the lush forests of the Durvo clan, the fertile plains of the Lozians, when they had ruled all from their shining capital of Klovnij. For my people, the Ostrovs, the painting showed our craggy eastern coast, and finally, the outlying islands of the seafaring Mora clan—before they'd abandoned us all to sail into uncharted waters. "It's remarkable," I breathed.

"It's a relic." Papa stood at the floor-to-ceiling windows, leaning heavily on his crutch. I went to stand beside him and squinted into the bright of the sprawling city.

"Can you not just enjoy yourself tonight, Papa? For me?" One night without worrying or complaining about the base nature of mankind. Was that too much to ask?

When he finally looked at me, it was as if his dark eyes were searching for something. "I should have forced you to stay home."

My fists clenched the fabric of my dress. "Well, you didn't. So you might as well make the best of it." This was precisely why I hadn't mentioned Simeon's efforts to secure me a job at the palace. Papa was old-fashioned and seemed to distrust everyone outside of our village.

I was grateful for the knock on the door, which gave me an excuse to abandon his strange melancholy.

Two servants entered, one with a tray of food, the other with an armful of colorful cloth. The girl with the dresses had hair as bright as a copper kettle, which marked her as Lozian as clearly as her golden eyes. She smiled brightly at me. "Shall we find you a dress?"

The red-haired maid was named Hristina. Together, we selected a sleeveless gown of burgundy cinched with a fitted velvet bodice. The long apron panels that trailed from the bodice were trimmed with champagne embroidery depicting jaunty larkspur flowers. The fabric flowed like water, and I couldn't stop myself from stroking it with my calloused fingertips. Was this how the princess's companions dressed every day? If so, I was more resolved than ever to secure such a life for myself.

Hristina had served in the palace for most of her life and was filled with helpful information. She chattered away as she braided half my hair around the crown of my head, letting the remaining loose curls fall long down my back. The princess had been searching for a companion for some time and was quite picky. She was morose this time of year, as it marked the second anniversary of the crown prince's untimely death, and so I wasn't to take it personally. I was to keep an eye out for the Vruk ambassadors, who were rude and uncouth, especially when the royals weren't looking. They lived at the palace according to the terms of the peace treaty that had ended the Mesmer War—and fractured Adrjssia into two nations in the process.

When Hristina was done, I hardly recognized myself. I'd always thought myself pretty enough—with a heart-shaped face, strong eyebrows and a generous bosom—but she had transformed me into something beautiful.

"What do you think, Papa?"

Simeon or Georgi had procured Papa a change of clothes as well, and he stood tall in a neat pair of gray trousers, a crisp, white shirt, and a long, navy jacket with a high collar. He nodded and smiled, but the cloud of anxiety about his shoulders sparked and strengthened. *What reason does he have to be afraid?*

I shoved down my disquiet. I had worried about Papa my whole life. I could take one night off.

We made our way slowly through the lavish hallways of the palace, my stomach tied in a nervous knot. As we approached the din of the ballroom and walked through the open double doors, I blinked against the assault of color. Wall-to-wall windows boasted an ombre sunset that dyed the Vokai Sea pink, while a sea-glass chandelier, hung from the high ceiling above, refracted the fading light. And then there were the people—clad in dresses and coats of nearly every style and color, smudges of emotion clinging to them as they danced.

Lord Georgi appeared before me, sporting a finely-tailored suit of forest green trimmed with gold. "Adrijana, you look magnificent." His colors were honest—that flush of rose above his ears again. I couldn't help but grin in response. "I must introduce you to Nevena so she can see how splendid you look in that dress."

"I'd like to thank her." My stomach swooped nervously. I would have one shot to make a good impression with the princess. I could not ruin it.

"Come, both of you." Georgi took my hand and tucked it in the crook of his arm. He skirted the dance floor and wove us slowly around courtiers and partygoers while he engaged Papa in polite small talk. My heart squeezed in gratitude as I realized he was considerate enough to set his pace to match my father's.

We neared the front of the ballroom, where the Adrjssian king and queen sat in two ornate thrones. My mouth fell open at the sight.

"It does take some getting used to." Georgi leaned in and whispered conspiratorially.

There was no more tactful way to say it—the king and queen were purple. Not just the rich fabric they wore, but their skin itself, tinged lavender as if from a lovely dye. "The chiton has been the symbol of the Adrjssian royalty since the country was first united," Georgi said. "When Milov the First discovered the mollusk's extraordinary properties, we were but a scattered bunch of warring clans. With the superhuman strength, health, and longevity granted by the chiton, it took him less than twenty years to consolidate power to himself and turn us into a unified realm."

"Did the purple skin help?" I knew the tale, but I thought to play along.

Georgi chuckled. "The history books are silent on that point. Have you ever seen a chiton?"

I rolled my eyes. "What do you think?"

Georgi laughed. "Fair enough. They're tiny, the size of a gold coin, nestled right in your palm. It's hard to see what all the fuss is about." But much fuss had been made. Wars had been fought for control of the sea beds where they grew.

"Have you ever eaten one?" I asked.

"Only the royal family are allowed to eat them. And only they and their servants may wear purple in any form. It's said to be the color of the gods' favor."

I looked around at the revelers, realizing that he was right. Every color was represented, except that one.

My eyes snagged on a man standing as still as a statue near the king's throne. He was tall, though not as tall as Simeon, and had the golden hair of a Lozian, curled to one side in an unusual cut. His features were finely-rendered, as if an artist had endeavored to depict the face of a god disguised in human form. His stance was arrogant, the angle of his strong chin haughty.

As remarkable as the man was, it was none of those things that drew my gaze to him. It was his coloring. The vivid violet of his eyes, taking in the room with hawkish intelligence. And the blank white mist shrouding him. I couldn't see his emotions at all.

I knew at once who this man was.

"And what of the Mesmers?" My voice was small. The hairs on the back of my neck rose as the man's gaze swiveled and pinned me where I stood. As if he had heard my words.

Georgi's response echoed in the distance, but my attention was transfixed by the Mesmer. "Yes, their eyes are naturally purple. It's why they were thought to be divine, once upon a time. Eerie as hell, if you ask me. I give them a wide berth."

*Eerie as hell* didn't begin to describe it. The power in the Mesmer's amethyst eyes froze the breath in my lungs. I couldn't move under the weight of his evaluation. Mesmers could see into your emotions, your thoughts, your very soul. They delved into your secrets and dove in the waters of your deepest desires. What was he seeing in me now? Surely, I was no different than anyone else, no more wretched in my ambitions and secret crushes and petty jealousies than any other man or woman at this festival. I prayed it was so.

The Mesmer took a step toward me. Then another. And then he was across the room in a blink, standing only inches from me, peering down upon me with unveiled curiosity.

Yet—he was not. It was him, but not him. An ephemeral, phantom form. A ghost? A vision?

My breath came in quick bursts as my mind tried to reconcile the phenomenon before it. The Mesmer hadn't moved. He still stood beside the king, surveying the crowd with bored arrogance.

So how could he be standing beside me?

I squeezed my eyes shut and prayed that when I opened them, the apparition would be gone. That my temporary madness would have passed.

Georgi patted my hand, his words of concern faint in my ears.

I opened my eyes.

The apparition grinned. Then spoke. "And I thought today would be boring."

I opened my mouth and screamed.

# CHAPTER 3

*T*he din of the party fell silent as all eyes turned to regard me.

Papa was before me, his gnarled hands tight on my upper arms, his tired gaze searching my face. "What's wrong? Are you ill?"

I looked about wildly. The apparition was gone. "I thought..." I shook my head. "I thought I saw something." Heat snaked its way up my neck and blazed through my cheeks. If I could see my own colors, I would have found the crimson stain of humiliation.

"Carry on!" Georgi called cheerfully, turning in a circle. "A jest is all! A jest."

The musicians in the corner resumed their tune, and the buzz of chatter filled the soaring space once again.

"I'm so sorry." I pressed a shaking hand to my mouth. "I'm terribly sorry—"

"What did you see?" Georgi didn't look cross, only curious.

I pursed my lips. He'd think it mad. Perhaps I *was* mad.

But then I looked back at the Mesmer and saw that he was grinning. As if we'd shared some sort of private joke. Or more like *he* was enjoying a joke at *my* expense.

"A figment of my imagination, I'm sure." My hands balled into fists.

I didn't know why he had singled me out, but I wasn't going to stand for it. I would give him a piece of my mind. I would tell him off—

*He's coming over here.* The crowd of partygoers parted before him, moving instinctively out of his way, as if he were a magnet repelling them. He moved with feline grace, his hands clasped behind his back, his steps unhurried.

He closed the distance between us far too soon.

Up close, the Mesmer's beauty was even more striking. Threads of gold in his hair refracted the light, the angles of his cheekbones casting his curving mouth in shadow. But it all paled compared to his eyes—a vivid purple that scarcely seemed natural. *The color of the gods' favor*, Georgi had said. It certainly seemed this man was blessed.

For a moment, we were a tableau—my father stiff, my breath still, Georgi confused. The Mesmer relaxed as a feast-day eve.

Propriety demanded someone speak, but the Mesmer clearly had no concern for such things.

I broke first and dropped into a curtsy, even as I chided myself not to let the man win. "My lord."

"Not necessary," the Mesmer replied. His voice matched the apparition's—deep and indulgent. "I am but a humble servant."

I straightened and faced him.

Georgi spoke. His voice had gone cold. "Adrijana and Iordan Mironacht, meet Dragan Vulpe. He is the Para-Mesmer serving the Tsarian royal family, and Adrjssia. Second only to the Prime Mesmer."

The Mesmer—Dragan—gave a tight-lipped smile. Perhaps he didn't like being second best. A chink in his armor?

"I heard your outcry and wanted to assure myself you were well." Dragan hadn't stopped looking at me with that secret smile.

I wouldn't give him the satisfaction. "I am well. A misunderstanding is all."

He inclined his head and held out a hand. "Would you like to dance?"

"Dance?" I was taken aback.

"You're familiar with the concept?"

I looked from my father to Georgi and found their expressions a

17

matched set. Tight-lipped disapproval. I was already in deep with Papa, but Georgi had been kind, and he was my best chance to meet the princess.

But I'd *seen* something. The question was what. The Mesmer held the answers in his still-outstretched hand. Whatever his private joke was, I was desperate for the punchline.

So I murmured, "One dance," and placed my hand in his.

His thumb on the back of my hand was like a brand, claiming me. We reached the dance floor before I was ready, and he stepped in close, his arm circling my waist.

I stiffened. He smelled musky, like candle smoke and spice, and being this near him was utterly overwhelming.

"Whatever is the matter now?"

"I don't know how to dance," I admitted.

He laughed. "Leap first and look second? I can admire that. Never fear. I can dance well enough for us both. Follow my lead."

Dragan began to move around the floor and I found his haughty words to be true. He directed me expertly, swaying and turning me to and fro, before pulling my body back against his.

Soon I was comfortable enough with the steps to focus on the point of this whole mad operation. "I saw you."

He looked down at me, his eyes trailing from my brow to my cleavage. "I saw you too. You're quite lovely in that dress."

My heart tripped over its next beat. "That's not what I meant," I forced out. "I saw you. When I screamed. Standing…next to me. Don't try to deny it."

"Why would I deny it?"

"Because it's…madness."

"Or magic." His mouth curved in a smile. *Ovyato help me, why am I looking at his mouth?*

"Same thing," I muttered. I fixed my eyes on the detailing of his jacket—the buttons were molded like little eyes, watching, watching.

"Not the same thing at all, Adrijana."

"Everyone calls me 'Jana.'"

"I'm not everyone."

No, that much was clear. "Tell me what you did. Why...you did that to me." I forced myself to look into his eyes then, to demand the answer he owed me.

"I wanted a closer look at you. You caught my attention, and now I see why."

"Why?"

"No one else in that room saw what you did. Doesn't that strike you as odd?"

Of course it did. Why else was I dancing with one of the most feared men in the entire kingdom? I said nothing.

"Do you ever see other things? Colors or light?"

My breath hitched. How could he know that?

He chuckled. "I'll take that as a *yes*."

The song ended and he stepped back, his hands behind his back once again. "Thank you for the dance, Adrijana."

That was it? I had more questions than I'd started with.

He turned to go.

"Wait!" I blurted out. "Aren't you going to tell me what it is? Why..."

He inclined his head. "Come see me in my workshop tomorrow morning. We can have a more candid conversation."

Tomorrow? I couldn't wait until tomorrow. But he was already moving back through the crowd.

Georgi appeared at my side, his hand on my elbow. "The princess would like to meet you."

I struggled to compose myself as I fell into step beside him. My thoughts scattered like a startled flock of starlings. "I'm sorry I danced with him. I thought it would be rude to say *no*."

"It was the right thing to do. Just be careful with him. Dragan never does anything that doesn't serve his own interest."

"Doesn't he serve the king?"

"When he must. I'm just glad Valko's still around to rein him in."

"Valko?"

"The Prime Mesmer. He's been a close friend to the king since they were boys."

We came to a stop before the dais and I dropped into a deep curtsy. Princess Nevena Tsarian regarded me with open interest in her dark eyes. Her skin was a flawless lavender, her elaborately embroidered dress a deep purple of a matching hue. A silver circlet studded with amethysts was woven amongst the curls of her chocolate-brown tresses.

Simeon stood tall behind her in his tailored uniform, his dark eyes flicking to me before returning to scan the crowd. A sliver of jealousy snaked through me at the thought of them spending time together. Had they grown close? Simeon and I had been best friends since the age of six, when we'd found a clutch of abandoned baby rabbits and nursed them into adulthood. I didn't want to be replaced. But could I blame Simeon if he was drawn to her? Nevena was impossibly lovely, and powerful besides.

"Welcome," Nevena said warmly. "Simeon has told me so much about you, and now you've befriended my cousin as well. And Mesmer Dragan. You've made quite an impression."

Her words were friendly, but I couldn't tell if there was something else beneath. "I'm just glad to have the chance to see the splendor of your court. Thank you for lending me this beautiful dress."

She waved a hand. "It suits you. You'll take it when you go."

"Oh, I couldn't—"

"I insist. The coloring is off, for me." She held up a lavender hand and gave a rueful laugh. "I do get tired of wearing purple, but little else matches."

I gave a weak smile.

King Petar and Queen Ksenjia stood from their thrones. The king was a tall, broad man with thick curls of black hair and a neat beard. The queen was fairer, slender with long, auburn hair worn loosely over her shoulders. As with the Mesmer, I could not see their colors. Instead of the slashes and bursts of emotion I was used to, the space around the royal family was surrounded by wisps of inscrutable fog.

"You look like your mother," I observed before remembering myself. "If you don't mind me saying so."

"I don't." Nevena watched her parents descend and head across the ballroom, toward the wide, open doors that paralleled the distant seashore below. The crowd began to follow.

"Where's everyone going?"

"It's part of the festival tradition. Mother will climb the east tower and make an offering to Desenja for a calm and kind season."

"We just leave offerings outside our door in the village."

"Everything's a spectacle here." Nevena sighed. "I suppose someday, I'll have to do the same."

"It doesn't sound so bad," I offered.

"Nevena's no fan of heights," Georgi explained.

The princess shot him a look.

"What? It's no secret."

She shrugged. "True. I always hated visiting Mother's family."

"Except for the fact that you got to see me," Georgi teased.

"Of course." Nevena returned his grin and grasped his chin in her fingers, giving it a little wag. "Though now I'll fear never be rid of you."

"Do the Durvo really live in houses amongst the trees?" I asked. I'd heard the tales, but it always seemed too fantastical to be true.

"We do." Georgi nodded sagely. "An entire town in the treetops, with ladders and bridges connecting them. It's beautiful."

"It's terrifying," Nevena said.

"Does no one ever fall out?"

"Occasionally," Georgi said. "Drunks. Children."

My mouth dropped open and Georgi burst out laughing. "I'm kidding. We're raised in the heights. No Durvo could fall from a tree any more than a Mora could get lost at sea. Besides, our parents' karakals tend to keep us safe when we're just toddling about."

Karakals—the animal companions of the Durvo clan. Small, calico felines with two thrashing tails, as comfortable in the treetops as their masters.

"Do you both have karakals?"

Georgi and Nevena nodded.

"Where are they?"

"Sleeping probably," Georgi said.

21

"Terribly lazy beasts," Nevena added, though the wistful smile on her face told me it was a gentle jest.

A burst of applause and cheers sounded from the balcony across the ballroom, where the crowd had gathered to watch Adrjssia's queen make her offering.

"Would you like to watch?" Nevena asked.

The ballroom had mostly cleared out. "Sure."

Nevena threaded her arm through mine as we walked. "Before you leave, I must hear all the dirt you have on Simeon." She threw a look over her shoulder to where he shadowed us silently.

I looked back too. The corner of Simeon's mouth twitched. "Well, I doubt he's ever been silent for this long a stretch. Does he just stand here?"

"Yes, he's a great hulking brute." Nevena grinned.

"It's the job, Your Highness," Simeon said.

"It speaks?" I drew my hand to my chest in mock surprise.

"Dirt," Nevena added as we passed through the double doors and into the salty night air. The crowd parted around us, allowing the princess passage toward the front of the balcony. "Did he fall into the feeding trough head first or have all his baby teeth knocked out so he spoke with a whistling lisp for a year? He just seems far too perfect. He must have some vices."

Simeon chuckled behind us.

I thought on it. "He does hate beets…"

"Whatever did beets do to you?" Nevena asked Simeon as we came to stand at the balcony rail. "How could I trust a man who discriminates against honest vegetables?"

"I say you can't trust a man who likes them," Simeon shot back. "They taste like feet."

"Seconded," Georgi agreed.

"How do you know what feet taste like?" I turned and arched a brow at him and he rolled his eyes.

Nevena laughed. "Oh, I like her, Simeon. She can stay—"

A sharp scream rent the air.

Followed by a collective gasp.

Then a muffled thud.

Nevena and I surged forward and threw ourselves against the railing, desperate to see.

Before us, the eastern tower stretched impossibly tall—a bright beacon in the fading twilight. Nevena's wail pierced my heart.

On the stones far below lay a crumpled figure, clothed in purple.

# CHAPTER 4

$S$hocked silence hung over the windswept balcony like a pall.
And then someone started to weep. Wails and cries took
to the air like winged demons.

Nevena had already left our side, pushing back through the crowd
to make her way down to her mother.

I could only stand, stunned, my hands over my mouth.

The colors around me turned to mourning gray, dark shadows
smudged across the eyes and foreheads of the courtiers in the crowd.

"Could she be alive?" But I knew the answer. The awkward angle
of her limbs, the eerie stillness of her form...

Georgi's face was ashen. "No Durvo could fall..." he muttered to
himself.

My stomach clenched. The queen had been raised in the treetops
—heights were a Durvo's playground. How could she have fallen from
a tower?

I jumped as a hand closed around my elbow.

"Things are about to get very ugly. Time for us to go." Papa led me
back into the ballroom and across the inlaid floor. We hurried for the
exit—Papa strained against his crutch, nearly stumbling in his hurry.

"Slow down!"

Papa's grip only tightened. "We need to get out of here before they start the inquiry into who did this."

"What do you mean, who did this?"

Papa shot me a look of disbelief. "Do you have wool between those ears? Someone just murdered the queen."

"Surely not... " I trailed off. We couldn't leave. I'd never be welcomed back here. I'd never see Simeon, I'd never become Nevena's companion. *I'll never know what the Mesmer was going to tell me.*

I yanked my arm from his grip. "Papa, we have nothing to hide. If we just run off—"

"You understand nothing." His hiss drove me back a step.

"Then explain it to me."

"There isn't time." He made to grab me again and I shied out of his reach. He lost his balance and only just caught himself on his crutch, but I refused to feel bad.

"*Make* time."

His eyes darted from the balcony to the entrance. I'd never seen him anything other than calm. His colors flicked from one to another —anger to fear—fear to the mustard-yellow of guilt. What did he have to feel guilty for? "Who do you think they'll look to first? Strangers. Those who just arrived. Us. Please, Jana. Trust me on this. We need to go now."

The word *please* broke my resolve and I let him pull me forward. Papa never begged; he commanded with quiet resolve. Something was terribly wrong.

As we reached the double doors where we'd entered the ballroom, we were met by a striking gray-haired man flanked by a dozen royal guards. His weathered face was lined and his eyes were a brilliant violet. He wore a long, black robe affixed with toggles bearing the purple eye. This must be the other Mesmer. The Prime Mesmer.

His voice swallowed me whole. "I want everyone in the ballroom. No one in or out until I say."

A wave of brown fear rolled over Papa as one of the guards pointed us forward. "Move."

When Papa took my hand, his palm was slick with sweat.

The Mesmer's eyes slid over us and then snapped back. "You. Who are you?"

"Iordan and Adrijana Mironacht, my lord." Papa's voice was strong, though his hand shook in my own. I was filled with a terrible certainty.

*Oh, Papa. What have you done?*

But when the Mesmer stepped forward, it was me he inspected, with the scrutiny one might give to a strange beetle on the cobblestones.

The crowds of nobles and festival-goers were returning to the hall, filling the space with quiet sobs and murmured voices. I spotted the two West Adrjssian ambassadors, their white-blonde hair and dark, leather jerkins standing stark against the silks and satins of the rest. The Vruk king would have much to gain from destabilizing the Adrjssian monarchy. Could they have had a hand in this?

The Mesmer straightened. "You." He pointed to the guard lingering near us. "Guard them personally. They do not leave your sight."

The king strode to the dais, standing before his throne. His handsome face was grave, his purple skin sallow.

The crowd fell silent.

"A terrible crime was committed tonight. The life of my beloved wife, and your dear queen, was taken. I will not rest until justice has been served."

The two Mesmers, Dragan and the frightening gray-haired man—Valko, Georgi had called him—joined the king. They stared dispassionately into the crowd. If they were grieved by the death of their queen, they did not show it.

The king continued. "Each and every one of you will be questioned by my Mesmers. You cannot hide your truth from them. Do not even try. When they are content that they have sufficient information from you, you will be free to return to your quarters. No one leaves this palace tonight. I regret that I must treat you, my dear guests, in such a fashion, but I will not risk the queen's killer escaping this place. I'm sure you want the same."

The Prime Mesmer stepped forward, his voice carrying throughout the room. "I'm not sure questioning is necessary. There is one among us who is capable of such a deed. An undeclared Mesmer."

The crowd exploded with chatter and outright cries.

I looked at Papa with shock. An undeclared Mesmer? It was the unchecked power of the Mesmers that had driven Adrjssia to war two decades before, that had splintered our country into the fractured state it now rested in. For Mesmers had power not just to read the mind and emotions, but to manipulate them—planting thoughts, controlling a person completely. Such an awful power could not go unchecked; the treaty ending the war had required all Mesmers to declare themselves.

Though, from the history I'd read, when the war had been finished, most Mesmers had declared themselves, only to be slaughtered. Only the Ostrov clan, my people and the current Adrjssian rulers, had protected their Mesmers and kept them alive.

Papa was looking at me with a sadness in his eyes that I didn't understand. The yellow stain of guilt flashed before his heart. "What?" I whispered.

"Iordan and Adrijana Mironacht, step forward," the Mesmer commanded.

My mouth fell open.

"Move." The soldier who had been set to guarding us shoved me between my shoulder blades and I stumbled forward. Papa limped beside me until we both stood before the throne.

"What is this?" the king asked. "I need to go be with Nevena."

Valko pointed at me. "This girl is a Mesmer. And I caught her trying to leave the hall after the queen fell."

My mind went curiously blank and a startled laugh escaped me. This was a misunderstanding, that was all.

The king's thick brows drew together. "You find my wife's death amusing, do you?"

I cringed and fell into a curtsy. "Of course not, Your Majesty. But this must be a misunderstanding. I'm no Mesmer." I straightened to find the king looking at Dragan with a questioning look.

Dragan gave the king a sharp nod.

*What?* I goggled at him.

"I was at her side at the time the queen fell." A new voice rang out, and I turned to find Simeon fighting his way through the crowd. "Your Majesty." He bowed. "I was with her the whole time. She couldn't have had anything to do with the queen's death."

I looked at Simeon with gratitude, but he continued to stare forward, his chin high.

"But that is the power of a Mesmer. She could have used her power to twist the will of a thrall to do this dark deed on her behalf. And she knew we could not question her because a Mesmer cannot see the truth of another Mesmer," Valko said coldly.

"But," Dragan added, "we can detect her manipulation, if she created a thrall. The attendees must still be questioned."

"Very well." The king motioned the guards. "Take the girl into custody. Question the rest to find this thrall."

The guard's gloved hand closed around my upper arm.

"Wait!" Papa cried out beside me. He stumbled to his hands and knees. "Your Majesty, please. My girl did nothing. She could not manipulate anyone. She's taken verbenia every day since she was five. Please, her powers are suppressed."

The world tilted, as if dropping out from beneath my slippered feet. I whirled to face Papa, fighting against the guard's grip. "What? What are you saying?"

"Enough!" barked the king. "I don't care. Take them both to the dungeon to be questioned. Everyone else, you will speak to my Mesmers one at a time."

The king strode off the dais and exited through a door in the back that had been disguised between two paintings. As soon as the door shut behind him, voices swelled as everyone began talking at once. Guards prodded Papa and me forward.

"Simeon!" I cried, trying to reach out for him. For a moment, my hand closed around his.

"It'll be all right," he said. "We'll get to the bottom of this." His hand was wrenched away as the crowd closed around us.

Angry faces blurred together and someone spat a curse at me. The guard next to me shoved the crowd back and I found myself grateful for his presence.

When we spilled out into the empty hallway, I took a deep shuddering breath, my lungs filling with air. As if I were finally safe.

Papa stared vacantly ahead of him, his face pale from shock.

My chest constricted again; bands of iron gripped me tightly as I realized the truth. I wasn't safe. And perhaps I never would be again.

# CHAPTER 5

The dungeon at the Ostrov Palace lay deep beneath the palace. Its walls were made of dank, weeping stone that leeched away both heat and hope. Papa and I were shoved into neighboring cells; he protested, but I did not. I wanted nothing to do with him.

The door thudded shut behind me ominously, cloaking me in darkness, but for the torches that lined the hall and flickered through the barred opening atop the door.

I surveyed my new domain with dismay. A stone bench and a wooden pot were the only furnishings. I shivered and rubbed my arms. I wished I had worn my wool dress and leather boots—I would freeze in this place in this silken dress and thin slippers.

Perhaps that was what they'd intended.

"Jana," came Papa's muffled voice.

"Don't talk to me," I snapped back. It was his fault we were in this mess—his fault we'd been caught leaving the ballroom like a pair of criminals. Everything was his fault... *"She's taken verbenia every day since she was five."*

My knees gave way and I sat down hard on the bench. It couldn't be true. I couldn't be a Mesmer. Everyone knew that Mesmers were devious, calculating creatures. Unprincipled and dangerous. I was just...me.

There was no denying that I had a strange ability. I saw colors where others saw nothing. But my gift wasn't Mesmerism. It was a sweet thing, useful and gentle. I had no power to manipulate anyone's thoughts, to make them forget themselves or become a prisoner in their own mind. I had no power at all.

*"She's taken verbenia every day since she was five."*

What in Ovyato's holy name did verbenia have to do with anything? The plant was a simple herb—it helped my headaches.

But...Georgi's words returned to me. *I find it wise to know as much as I can about anything as powerful as this little plant.*

"Jana, please," Papa called again. "I'm so sorry."

"I have nothing to say to you!" I clenched my hands into fists, wishing he was in this cell with me so I could rage at him.

His voice echoed through the stone. "I'll tell them it was my fault. That I did it. I'll fix this."

"You've already done enough!" I screamed back. I dropped my head into my hands. My fingernails had left little crescent moons in my palms. "No more lies."

Papa fell silent.

A shiver wracked through me and I stood, pacing the pitiful length of the cell. I needed to stay warm. Anger would help with that. "I guess, without lies, you have nothing to say." I scoffed.

His response was a long time coming. So quiet, I barely heard it. "I did what I thought was best. And that's the truth."

I placed a hand on the wall separating us. I was beyond furious at him, but he had answers I needed. "What does the verbenia do?"

"It blocks a Mesmer's power."

My breath hitched.

"It turned your beautiful eyes green," he explained.

My eyes... "My eyes were purple?"

"As bright as a wisteria bloom."

I turned and sagged against the damp wall. How was any of this possible?

"Your mother was one too."

I whirled, my word cutting. *"What?"*

"You have to understand—it wasn't safe back then. The Vruk soldiers slaughtered hundreds of Mesmers. The only way to secure peace with the West was for the king to agree to close his borders to the refugees. The only way she could be safe was to hide what she was. When things calmed down, we made it here, into Ostrov territory, but then she died when your sister was born. And you were growing and then we lost your sister and…" Papa's voice choked off. "You were all I had left. I didn't want to give you to the king for training, but I didn't know how to control your power. You were young and willful. So I did what your mother had done during those uncertain years. I suppressed it. Hid it."

"You lied to me." My voice caught. "When were you going to tell me the truth? Ever?"

Silence. "You were happy."

"I was living a lie!" I slammed my palm against the stone.

"Shut up!" some deep voice down the hallway hollered—another prisoner, no doubt.

Weariness washed over me and I collapsed back onto the little bench. I finally understood why he hadn't wanted me to come on this trip, why he had tried to hurry us home. If he had just explained, I would have understood. The danger of lingering here—an undeclared Mesmer—hiding who she was.

With his lies, Papa had doomed me. Doomed us both.

Hot tears slid down my cheeks and I curled into myself, hugging my knees into my chest. The bench was too small to sleep on, really, and cold and hard besides, but I couldn't find the energy to care.

The fight drained out of me. Whatever happened now was out of my control. With that disquieting thought ringing in my mind, I drifted off into a shallow sleep.

\* \* \*

THE DOOR to my cell banged open.

I jerked out of sleep and tumbled to the floor in an ungraceful heap of dirty silk.

Brushing my hair out of my face, I found the two Mesmers looking down at me. Valko, dark and threatening, and Dragan, bright and thoughtful.

"Bring her." Valko stepped back as two guards collected me from the floor and set me on my feet, prodding me into the hallway.

They led me into a larger room furnished with a wooden table and chairs. I was shoved into one chair with a heavy hand before the guards went to stand on either side of the door.

Before me, Dragan shrugged out of his fine woolen coat and handed it across the table to me.

I took it. "What's this?"

"You look half-frozen."

I looked down and saw that goosebumps pebbled my skin; my fingers and toes were so numb, I could no longer feel them. "Thank you." I slipped into the coat, wrapping my arms tightly before me. It smelled of him—smoke and cardamom, a hint of vanilla.

I looked back to find Valko watching me as if he knew the thoughts in my head. I reddened before I remembered what he'd said in the ballroom. Mesmers couldn't read other Mesmers. Nor manipulate them. Besides the royal family, they were the only two individuals I'd ever encountered where I couldn't see snatches of color—the Mesmers were swathed in only swirls of pale mist, unreadable as a blank page. If I was truly a Mesmer, they must see the same around me.

Valko opened his mouth, but Dragan spoke first. "Are you well? Have you been mistreated?"

Besides the obvious? "No." My voice was hoarse.

"Get the girl some water." Dragan motioned to one of the guards, who disappeared out the door. He returned with a metal cup and I took it gratefully. The Mesmers watched me as I drank. It seemed like all they did. Watch.

"What?" I finally snapped, banging the empty cup down. "Am I a spectacle to you?"

"An enigma, more like," Dragan murmured.

Valko shot him a cross look. There was clearly no love lost between these two, though they presented a united front when the king was near. "We finished our questioning of the festival guests."

I waited. "And?" I finally broke.

"No guest showed sign of mental manipulation."

"And several guests, including Simeon, Lord Georgi, and the princess herself, spoke to your whereabouts at the time the queen...passed on."

My thoughts clicked into place. "So you believe me that I had nothing to do with the queen's death."

Dragan inclined his head. "We do. But there is one more step we must take to verify your innocence."

"What?" I hugged myself tighter.

"We must test your blood for verbenia. It's the only way we can be certain you had nothing to do it."

I had to prove my innocence to them. A little blood wasn't too much to ask to get out of this mess with my life and freedom.

"Okay."

Dragan strode around the table and leaned over me, reaching into the pocket of his jacket. I fixed my eyes on the wood grains of the table rather than the closeness and the heat of the Mesmer. The table's surface was marred by grooves and divots. How many poor souls had sat at this table? What had caused those marks? Fingernails? Knives?

"Your arm, please, Adrijana." Dragan's voice was soothing. He had placed a needle and a glass vial on the table.

I shrugged off one of the arms of his coat and laid my elbow on the table.

"I've done this many times," he said as he wiped my inner arm with a cool cloth that smelled faintly of alcohol. I looked away.

Valko paced the room, his arms crossed before his narrow chest, his thin lips twisted in a frown.

A sharp pain bit into my arm and I hissed.

"Almost done..." Dragan's fingers were warm and sure on my arm, and soon the pain subsided to a dull ache.

34

He handed the vial to Valko and pressed a piece of soft gauze to my arm, which he secured in place with a longer gauze wrap. When he was done, Dragan smiled at me, his fingers lingering for a moment. "All done."

I pulled his coat back on and regarded Valko, who was pouring a drop of thick, purple liquid into the vial. As the drop joined my red blood, it transformed until it was indistinguishable from the rest.

Valko and Dragan exchanged a look and Valko stoppered the vials, dropping them both into the pocket of his thick robe.

"Well?" I asked.

"Your father's story appears true," Valko said gruffly.

My shoulders slumped in relief. Praise Ovyato. I wasn't going to be executed. Or rot in prison. I pushed to stand on shaky legs. "So I can go."

Valko flicked his finger for me to sit back down. "Not so fast."

I locked my knees and braced my hands on the table. They knew I was innocent. They had no grounds for holding me any longer—

"Please, Adrijana," Dragan said gently. "Sit down. There is much for us to discuss." He settled into the chair across from me, crossing one booted ankle over his knee.

I grudgingly sat too.

Valko stayed standing, his arms crossed before him. "There is still the matter of your being an undeclared Mesmer. Which is a crime in Adrjssia."

"It was—" I cut myself off. As furious as I was at Papa, I didn't know what they'd do to him. I didn't want to blame him.

"Your father already confessed to the crime, with the entire court as witness," Dragan said. "It's time to think of yourself. Did you know what you are?"

There was nothing I could do to help Papa. I swallowed back tears. "No."

Dragan nodded.

"Mesmers are valuable, and there are fewer than a dozen of us left in Adrjssia. You will train here and serve the royal family. As we have," Valko said.

I bristled. As desperate as I was to learn what these strange abilities meant, I didn't want these men running my life. I didn't want to be a captive in my own story. "Slavery is outlawed in Adrjssia. I am a free person. If I choose *not* to serve the king—"

Valko cut me off. "Then your father will suffer for your selfishness. The sentences for crimes pertaining to Mesmerism can be draconian. It would be a shame for him to be made an example of."

I glared at Valko, at his eyes glittering like uncut gems. Hatred reared within me, cold and deep. He had me trapped, and we both knew it. The irony was not lost on me. I'd wanted to come to the palace, I'd wanted adventure and change and excitement. And now I had it, with a generous helping of terror and fear besides. And a duty as thick as iron bars to hem it all in.

Resolve hardened within me. I would agree to his deal. I would let him train me and teach me to be strong. Then somehow, someday, I would find a way to take back my freedom.

I was glad in that moment that these men couldn't see my colors. I supposed being unreadable had its advantages. I looked to Dragan. "If I train with you and serve, you will let my father go? Pardon him for his crime?"

"A man who flouts the law must be punished—" Valko began.

"But the punishment will be mild," Dragan cut in with a glance at the older Mesmer. "A fine. A tithe from his harvest. It would be a shame to lose such a talented verbenia farmer."

I searched Dragan's handsome features for signs of deception. He met my gaze with his own violet stare, his striking eyes ringed with fringes of golden lashes. Without the swirl of color and emotion, I couldn't read him. I didn't know if he could be trusted.

I felt poised on a cliff's edge, a blade at my back, empty air at my front. Armed with only a reed-thin hope that this stranger would catch me if I fell.

Dragan gave me a tiny nod.

So I jumped.

# CHAPTER 6

*I* woke from a troubled sleep filled with unblinking, purple eyes. After the Mesmers had left, the guards had taken me to a room in one of the eastern towers. It was larger than the guest room Papa and I had been staying in—with warm, sandstone walls, a downy, white bed, and a set of bay windows facing the sea. It was finer than anything I'd ever enjoyed, but it brought me no joy.

Everything felt raw and wrong. I couldn't stop thinking about the sound of the queen's body hitting the ground. The tenor of Nevena's wail. I didn't remember my mother—she died when I was just three years old, lost while birthing my little sister, Arabel. I didn't know what was worse: to never know one's mother, or to know her and then lose her tragically.

My few hazy memories of my mother were like shifting sand in the light of Papa's revelation. She'd been a Mesmer. Had she loved her ability or hated it? Had it been a gift or a burden? How much might have been different, if my mother had lived. She could have taught me. Perhaps then I would have known how to feel about it. I would have grown up understanding how to use my powers, to not be corrupted by them. And I wouldn't be sitting here like a pampered prisoner, desperately afraid of who I truly was.

A knock on my door brought me to my feet on the cold tile floor. Someone had been thoughtful enough to leave a cotton sleeping shift and sky-blue woven robe in the empty wardrobe, so I wrapped it around myself as I crossed to the door.

A trill of nervousness wended through me. *What if it's Dragan?* "Who's there?"

"Hristina," came the muffled reply. Right. The red-haired maid who had assisted me yesterday. I shook off my foolishness. I was sure the Royal Mesmer didn't make unannounced, personal visits to women's quarters.

I opened the door to let Hristina in. Her lovely face was bright with excitement, her arms full to bursting with a pile of cloth. Her hair was braided tightly in a lovely pattern that wove and wound together.

"Oh, I forgot," I said. Another servant followed Hristina inside, bearing a tray with a teapot and covered plate.

"What?" Hristina dumped her burdens on the unmade bed. The other maid set down the tray on a small table by the window and scurried out.

I rubbed my face. "That the Windy Season began today." It was tradition for the citizens of Selojia to braid their hair into tight and elaborate coifs, to keep the wind from tangling and snarling it in the months to come. I'd only seen such plaiting a few times, on visitors passing through our village. I'd always braided my hair into two thick ropes and called it good.

"Yes, that." Hristina faced me and lifted one of my wavy, brown locks. "I'm here to do your hair. And get you set up with the wardrobe you need." Her golden eyes sparkled. "I asked to be your maid, and the steward agreed!"

"My maid?"

Hristina's bright smile faltered. "I assumed you would approve—if you wish for someone else—"

"No, no." I hurried to cut her off. "I just... I've never had a maid." I'd come here expecting my best prospects to be serving the princess as a maid or a companion. And now, I was being waited on? It was too much.

"So you approve?"

I forced a smile. "Very much."

"Excellent! Why don't you sit and eat, and I'll get started on your braids? It's quite time-consuming."

I did as instructed, munching on a fine meal of thick honey bread smeared with fig jam, and a whole ripe peach. The tea was minty and brisk and tasted quite decadent topped with the real cream they'd set out in a little carafe.

When I offered Hristina my last slice of peach, she surprised me by taking it right out of my fingers with nimble teeth, as her fingers were twined in a complicated pattern near my right ear. I laughed, beginning to relax in her presence. She didn't seem afraid of me, not in the least.

"You are Lozian, are you not?" I asked her.

She pursed her lips, her smile falling.

"I'm sorry, was that rude? Please forget I asked."

She shook her head. "It's all right. My coloring gives it away. Yes, I grew up in Klovnij for my first few years."

"Did your family come here during the war?" For hundreds of years, a united Adrjssia had been ruled from the fertile capital of Klovnij, governed by the Lozian clan and their Mesmers. Towns like Selojia had been just territories, sending tribute and taxes to the central capital. Then the Vruk clan had invaded, and everything had changed.

Hristina's eyes stayed fixed on her fingers, deftly weaving the strands of my hair. "My parents worked in the Mesmer College."

"The College of the All-Seeing?" I asked.

She snorted softly. "Everyone just called it 'the College of Eyes.' We fled when the city fell. My father was killed in the fighting, my mother died soon after we made it here. I lived on the streets for two years. It was Dragan, actually, who got me the job here. The Para-Mesmer, I should say."

"Really?" I was eager for any new piece of information I could get to fill in my vague picture of the man.

She shrugged. "Maybe it was for love of our clan, I'm not sure. I was always too cowardly to ask. I'm grateful, and that's enough."

"Did he come from Klovnij too? I thought the Ostrovs closed the border to all refugee Mesmers." It was a dark mark on the history of our clan: the Slaughter at the Crossing. Mesmers fleeing the destruction of Klovnij had been turned away at the Notok River, the crossing into Ostrov territory. It was the price the current King Petar had paid for peace with the Vruks and the allegiance of the other three clans, and it was sadly a price many had been willing to pay.

"I don't know how he made it here, but he did. Perhaps you can get the whole story someday. It never seemed my place."

I suppose I would get to know both Mesmers better, as I was going to be training with them.

"What can you tell me of Valko?"

A gust of wind rattled the windows as Hristina spoke. "Just to watch your step."

\* \* \*

AN HOUR LATER, Hristina finished. The time had passed quickly; chatting with her had been a welcome distraction from my dark thoughts. She stretched her spine with a relieved groan while I went to examine her handiwork in the mirror.

My mouth dropped open at the sight of the complicated crown of braids she'd woven into my hair, gathering and swooping into a swirl at the nape of my neck "It's amazing!" My scalp itched something fierce, but I supposed I'd get used to it.

Hristina handed me a white gown, a lime green burst of pride haloing her red hair like a crown. "The queen's funeral will be held this evening. Everyone will wear mourning white for three days."

I pulled the gown on. It was a formal style, with apron panels hanging down from the front and back of the bodice, embroidered with silhouetted weeping gulls. But I found I already trusted Hristina to guide me in the unfamiliar ways of this place. If this was what she thought I should wear, then wear it I would.

Apparently, the afternoon was mine and so I asked her to take me to the Mesmers. Questions swirled within me, and I figured it was as good a time as any to get some answers.

It was a short walk. "The Mesmer workshop, library, and quarters are all in this tower," Hristina explained. "It's why you were given the quarters you were. So you can be close to them."

*Close to them.* My skin pebbled with goosebumps as a memory surfaced—Dragan's hand pressed to the small of my back as we danced.

We reached a set of double doors carved with a pair of eyes and I knocked, my heart suddenly racing.

Hristina lingered and I smiled at her. "Thank you very much for showing me the way."

She gave a little curtsy and turned with a flash of blue disappointment. It seemed I wasn't the only one who had noticed Dragan's good looks. I filed the observation away for later.

I knocked again, more soundly this time, and the door flew open to reveal Valko, his hawkish eyes flashing, his silver-gray hair wild. He wore his black robes unbuttoned, revealing a rumpled shirt beneath.

I resisted taking a step back and opened my mouth to ask where Dragan was. And then paused. *Idiot!* Why should I be asking for one Mesmer and not the other? I couldn't be seen to favor Dragan.

"What?" Valko barked.

I tilted my chin up. "I would like to speak with you about my training."

He grunted and opened the door to let me inside. "Dragan!" he hollered before slamming the door behind me, nearly catching my skirt.

My eyes widened as I surveyed the Mesmers' workshop. It was a long, rectangular space with tall, vaulted ceilings. To my left, leading to a set of wide windows, were two rows of shelves flanking three huge marble worktables. To my right lay a yawning stone fireplace, holding court before two worn armchairs and a massive velvet sofa.

The room was filled with books and scrolls, drawings and models hanging from the ceiling with twine. It was like entering the dizzy mind of a madman and wondering if there was perhaps a touch of genius there too.

Dragan emerged from a door at the end of the room to my right, clad in black trousers, knee-high boots, and a loose, white shirt rolled up at the sleeves and hastily buttoned to reveal a stretch of tanned chest. His golden hair was unbound and curled haphazardly around his ears.

My mouth went dry.

"What do you want, you crusty old cretin—" Dragan fell silent at the sight of me. He straightened. "Ah. Adrijana. The newest member of our peculiar little club."

Valko scowled. "I've work to do. You deal with her."

Dragan motioned me to follow him. "Come. Let's leave Valko to his unpleasantness."

I followed Dragan through the door from which he'd come with a glance over my shoulder. Valko had already returned to one of the worktables and was muttering to himself over some piece of parchment. When the door closed behind us I couldn't help myself. "Are you always so rude to each other?"

"Oh, yes." Dragan waved a hand. "It's how we show our esteem."

I craned my head. We'd entered a library replete with shelves twice as tall as a man. Filled with more volumes than I'd ever seen.

"Esteem?" I asked, confused. "I sensed none between you."

"Precisely." Dragan pointed at a worn leather armchair before a fireplace that was twin to the one we'd passed.

I sank into the chair, confused.

"Your father has asked to see you before he leaves."

I blinked at the change of subject. "What?"

Dragan spoke more slowly. "He was released from his cell, per the terms of our agreement. He is readying to return to your village and entreated me to tell you that he has more to explain. Would you like to see him before he goes?"

I looked down at my hands in my lap, emotion warring within me. I knew I shouldn't let Papa leave without saying goodbye. Who knew how long until he returned? A year, perhaps—next equinox. But as I considered the false pleasantries I'd have to give, the awkward good-bye, I found I didn't want to see him. I was still furious at what he'd done. Let him suffer for his lies. Just for a time. "No." I shook my head.

Dragan raised one golden eyebrow but said nothing.

My cheeks heated. "You think I should."

"I think I am not one to lecture anyone on forgiveness."

"Thank you."

"No gratitude necessary."

I fell silent, examining my fingernails, self-conscious under the weight of his penetrating stare. My questions had fled me, my mind curiously blank.

"I suppose you'd like to know what happens now."

I looked up. "Yes. Very much."

Dragan stood and strode to the fireplace, throwing on another log. "They suit you, you know."

"What?"

"The braids. As lovely as the queen's. Well, the late queen."

I traced the swirl of my braids to hide my pleasure at the compliment. "Do you have any idea who did it? I mean, who killed her?"

Dragan sank back into his chair. "Theories, nothing more. Not yet, anyway."

"And they're so certain she was murdered?"

"Those raised in the treetops do not fall over tower edges for no reason. The mortar between some of the stones of the railing had been tampered with. Weakened. When she pressed against them, they gave way."

"How awful." So it truly had been murder.

"It is my hope that you will be able to assist us with our investigation. Once you have undergone your training."

My stomach flipped uneasily at his words. "Does it change you? Our powers? The training? Will I still be...me?"

He cocked his head at me, the firelight playing across the contours of his face. "How long have you been taking the verbenia daily?"

"Since I was five."

"I never experienced what you will—your powers turning on

suddenly. Mine were always with me. Always a part of me. But I suspect you will realize you have been living as a pale imitation of yourself. That finally, you have become your true self."

I closed my eyes, embarrassed to even ask my question. But I knew the fear wouldn't leave me, either, not until I voiced it out loud. "People say Mesmers are evil. They make the mark against us. I won't become ..."

"A monster?" Dragan let out a small laugh. "Valko's bedside manner could be improved, certainly, but the Mesmerism isn't to blame for that. He's just insufferable."

I offered a weak smile. "I'm serious. Everyone in our village said the Mesmers were fiends and deviants. They said the Mesmer War was divine justice."

Dragan's lips thinned to a narrow line. "It was once thought that Mesmers were gifted their powers by the gods. As blessed as the royals with their chitons, if not more so."

I cocked my head. I couldn't tell if he was purposely being obtuse, or if it was just his way. "What does that have to do with it?"

"In two days, the verbenia in your system will wear off and you will experience the fullness of your power for the first time in your adult life. And then you will see the truth of this power we have. As Mesmers, we are equals only to the gods. And since there can be no new gods, then we must be devils."

"You're saying that they demonize us because our power is too great for them to understand?"

"It's easier to be afraid than to understand. Don't make that same mistake." Dragan flashed me a grin. "Besides, it's not so bad being a devil. You'll see."

# CHAPTER 7

*I* had no memory of ever attending a funeral before, and certainly not a royal one. But I found myself being herded by servants into the great hall that had been filled just last night with feasting and dancing.

The thrones had been removed from the dais, and in their place rested a large, wooden platform covered in a white shroud. The outline of a profile was visible beneath—nose, chin, breasts, crossed hands, but no details. I was grateful for it.

Garlands of jasmine blooms had been wrapped around the tall, stone pillars and hung from rafters, cloaking the entire space in a potent perfume that made me woozy. I looked around for a familiar face—Simeon, Georgi, Hristina, Dragan, or even gruff Valko—but they were nowhere to be found.

In the thronging crowd, I was utterly alone.

Smoky gray was smudged across the crowd of faces like a bruise, true sadness at the loss of their queen. She was loved. There was anger too—red smoke simmering over the crown of some heads, a desire for vengeance, no doubt. Or at the very least, answers.

Two men moved through the crowd, their colors incongruous against the rest. Milky white and unreadable, like the Mesmers themselves. But they were the farthest thing from. They were the Vruk ambassadors.

I'd heard Georgi and Simeon speak of them yesterday, but the sight of them sent a prickle of fear up my spine. They were both big, muscular men, with the white-blond hair and icy-blue eyes of their clan. The stockier, bearded one had hair to his shoulders on one side, with the other half shaved, which I recalled marked him as nobility. The other was tall and lean, with shorter hair shaved in a patch over one ear, which was reserved for the warrior class. Intricate lines of green-inked tattoos sprawled across half of his forehead and the shorn patch of his scalp. Both men wore the woven leathers and furs of their mountain home, despite the lingering warmth of the Sunny Season in Selojia.

They could not have looked more out of place here—their very presence seemed profane. Yet I was sure they couldn't be turned away, as they were the official ambassadors from West Adrjssia.

I hadn't realized I was staring with open curiosity until the short-haired man fixed his glacial gaze on me. He was handsome in a rugged way, all sharp angles and lines. But the expression on his tattooed face was ugly. He murmured something to the other and they began wending their way through the crowd. Toward me.

I whipped my head forward and glued my eyes to the platform. I was infinitely aware as they grew closer...as they shouldered their way to a stop...one directly on either side of me.

The short-haired Vruk grabbed my elbow and leaned over to hiss in my ear. He smelled of leather and tobacco and dread. "We heard a new witch had come to court. The Lord of Winter has set to me the holy task of wiping the abomination of Mesmerism from these shores. Perhaps I should start with you."

My breath hitched and I stiffened my spine. So at least this man was part of the Sons of Zamo Idvo, the Vruk holy organization that had slaughtered hundreds of Mesmers during the war. How had King Petar allowed them to be here?

I pulled my elbow from the man's grip and fisted my hands in my skirt to hide their shaking. "I am under the king's protection," I hissed back.

The other man let out a low chuckle. "So was the queen."

My mouth dropped open and I whirled to look at him, but the ambassadors were already fading back into the crowd.

In their place Dragan moved toward me, dressed in a trim cream coat with gold buttons over a white shirt and tan pants. His curls had been twisted into a row of loose braids, and I found I missed the wildness of his golden locks.

"Come with me." He ushered me forward with a broad hand on my back. The throng parted for him as it had that first time I'd seen him. Would this be my future? To always be apart from the people around me?

"I saw you met our Vruk friends." His breath tickled my ear as we came to stand in the front row next to Valko. To my left stood Georgi, his face blotchy with sorrow. A calico karakal sat by his feet, its tails lashing. I'd never seen one before in real life. It was bigger than I'd expected, about the height of a medium-sized dog.

"Adrijana?" A hand settled on my shoulder and I startled, turning back to find myself gazing into Dragan's penetrating purple eyes. He'd asked me a question.

"Yes. The Vruks." I lowered my voice and leaned in. "They threatened me."

He nodded. "The noble is Spiridon, with the half-shaven head. The tattooed man is Matija. He is a Zamo through and through. Be on your guard around them both, but especially Matija."

"Why are they allowed to stay here if they're a threat?"

"The treaty calls for an exchange of ambassadors at all times. These two are unpleasant, but their threats have been idle thus far, so they're allowed to stay. But I fear your presence will inflame their hatred more."

"Why?"

"The Vruks always had a particularly virulent hatred toward female Mesmers—especially the beautiful ones. Sometimes, desire stokes hatred even hotter."

My mouth went dry as my stomach turned. I cleared my throat. "He said something about the queen. Could they be...?" I trailed off in a whisper.

Dragan leaned in until his mouth was just inches from my ear. This close, I could see the faint lines crinkling the corner of his eyes, the beginnings of golden stubble on his square jaw. "Could they have killed her?" He straightened calmly and gave me an infinitesimal nod. "We will speak of it later."

My mind whirled to life with thoughts of assassination plots and religious killings. Luckily, I was distracted by the royal family filing in through the door at the back of the dais. King Petar first. Nevena next, her face covered by a thin mourning veil. Another man followed, handsome, dark-haired and bearded, his skin faintly purple as well. He had a thin scar running through one of his thick eyebrows. This must be the king's brother, Prince Aleksi. I knew little of the lineage of the Tsarian royal family except that the king had one younger brother, and the queen had two younger sisters—one who was the Dynast of the Durvo clan. Georgi's mother.

A priest of Ovyato, the god of summer and patron of the Ostrov clan, presided over the funeral. I found myself numb to the words. I watched the queen's karakal, a handsome chocolate-brown feline that lay still on the pallet by the dead queen's feet, punctuating the priest's eulogy with heart-rending yowls. I couldn't imagine the sorrow it must have been feeling—to lose its lifetime companion.

I thought of Papa and guilt washed over me. He was the one person I had in the world, and in my anger, I hadn't even said good-bye. Perhaps I would write to him, when I was ready. Try to mend some of the damage between us.

Before I knew it, the funeral was over and they were carrying the queen out of the room. The procession would lead down to the sea, where her body would be burned. Normally, the ashes would be scattered in the ocean, but I wondered if the Durvos had another tradition.

I caught sight of Simeon at the far side of the room and lingered as the crowd began following the queen's bier.

"I'm on duty," he said as I came to a stop before him.

I tried to hide my flinch. "Okay. Sorry." I turned.

"Wait." He sighed. "I'm sorry. It's just strange, seeing you like this. You're one of them."

I looked down. "One of who?"

"A Mesmer."

I searched his face. There was hurt there. Did he think I'd lied to him all this time? "Papa kept it from me. I didn't know." Well, that wasn't entirely true. I'd known there was something different about me. "Can we talk about it another time? I think...I could use a friend here."

He nodded. "You'll always have me, Jana."

"Thanks. And thank you for what you said yesterday to the king. That you'd been standing with me."

"It was the truth."

I nodded. The throne room was mostly empty now.

"I need to catch up with the procession. Promise me you'll be careful, all right?"

My brow furrowed. "What do you mean?"

"The Mesmers...they're not like other people. They have their own agendas. Especially Dragan. Just keep your eyes open." With that, Simeon hurried off, leaving me even more confused.

A wave of weariness washed over me. I'd never had to worry about schemes or deception—I'd always had the means to discern the truth at my fingertips. But the list of people I couldn't read was growing. The royals, the Mesmers, and now these ambassadors. Why?

I found I didn't want to go down to the river to watch the queen's body burn. No one would miss me there. And that fluffy bed was calling.

\* \* \*

SOMETIME IN THE NIGHT, my stomach woke me. I'd skipped dinner and was now ravenous. I lay for a while, looking at the ceiling, willing myself back to sleep, before I threw off the covers in a huff. There had

49

to be something I could scrounge in the kitchen—a loaf of bread or some stew. Though finding the kitchen was going to be no small feat.

I pulled on my robe and slippers and poked my head out. The sconces in the hallway were lit, so I didn't need to bring a candle with me. I headed down out of the Mesmers' tower toward the main part of the palace, my senses singing with awareness.

The kitchen must be near the dining hall, so if I found that, I would know I was close. I would start my search at the great hall. I reached a junction in a quiet hallway where I had to go left or right. I looked one way, then the other, biting my lip. I didn't recall coming this way before.

I saw movement out of the corner of my eye to the right and blinked to clear my vision. It was a wisp of something that looked like fog. Moving.

My body stilled as I regarded it, unsure if I was imagining it. But it swelled and grew, undulating in the air. It was a bit like the haze I saw around the royal family or the Mesmers, but there was no one nearby. I'd never seen fog like this on its own.

It was moving away, spilling around the corner. On a whim, I followed. I'd never been one to resist a mystery.

The fog led me through the maze of empty hallways—one turn and then another. I tried to memorize them, but I feared I was becoming hopelessly lost. The mist was moving faster now, and I needed to jog to keep up. And then, at the junction of two stone hallways, it vanished.

I stood, breathing heavily, annoyed at myself for being led on a wild goose chase by what was probably a figment of my imagination.

But then the sound of whispered voices reached me and I froze. The voices sounded angry, or at the least, upset. A man. And a woman.

I pressed myself against one wall and crept forward until I was inches from the corner. I risked a peek around the corner and my eyes widened. A man and a woman were arguing in hushed tones. Prince Aleksi was unmistakable in his mourning clothes, the low candlelight staining his lavender skin maroon. I didn't recognize the woman, but I did my best to memorize her features. She was older, a bit plump, also in mourning white, though her clothes were not so fine and her brown hair was threaded in only half a dozen braids. So a servant, perhaps? The king's brother paced before her while she cowered, her back pressed against the wall. As he moved, I saw that she had a streak of white hair flowing back from one of her temples.

I pulled back, not wanting them to see me. But listening all the while.

"I'll say nothing, Your Highness, you know I won't," the woman said. "If I haven't all these years, why would I now?"

"Because she's gone. And it looks…Well, you know how it would look."

"I swear on Ovyato's holy name, I'll say nothing."

"I know you won't say anything, but your emotions will tell a different story. Those cursed Mesmers see too much."

I let out a little gasp and the conversation fell silent.

"Did you hear that?" Aleksi said.

"Yes," the woman whispered.

I gathered the skirt of my nightgown and ran.

# CHAPTER 8

The next two days passed quickly and quietly, but for the vicious, biting wind that rattled my windowpanes. The Windy Season was truly upon us.

I gained my bearings in the palace, taking care to avoid any shadowed halls. I did not see the Mesmers, and they did not seek me out. The princess had closeted herself in her room in her grief, and Simeon was busy about his duties. Georgi had returned home to the forests of Visoko, in order to mourn the queen's passing with his family.

Hristina was my only company, when her tasks brought her to my room, and so I spent my days staring out the window, watching the whitecaps on the sea below, and feeling a growing certainty that I'd been forgotten entirely.

My guilt was rising about the way I'd left things with Papa, and I even sat down to write him a letter. But I still didn't know what to say. I hadn't forgiven him yet. So the paper sat blank on the little desk by the window.

With the third day dawned a strange and frightening ailment that I was ill-equipped to handle. Hristina made her way into my room as she did in the morning, pulling back the curtains to let in the buttery light of morning.

I squinted at her, standing haloed by the sun, and gasped. I threw an arm over my face. "Close them!" I croaked, motioning frantically.

"What's wrong?" She did as I instructed, but it did nothing to dim the vision.

I hazarded another look. Hristina glowed before me like a spring egg, the space around her filled with shimmering and dancing colors. I held up a hand to block the vibrancy.

What's wrong?" she repeated as she hurried to my side.

I shied away from her, squeezing my eyes shut against the visual onslaught.

She shook my shoulder gently. "My lady? Adrijana? Shall I fetch the doctor?"

"No. Fetch the Mesmer." I amended that with, "Dragan if you can find him." Valko if he was my only option.

The door shut behind her and I sagged in relief, opening my eyes. I flopped back in bed, attempting to massage the afterglow from my vision. Dragan had said it would take two days for the verbenia to wear off. I suspected that it had. But if this was what it was like to be at the height of my power, I didn't know how I would bear it.

I forced myself to my feet and hurried to make myself presentable. I splashed water on my face from the ewer and pulled on a simple dress of cornflower blue wool trimmed with creamy embroidery. I was lacing my last boot when a knock came on the door.

"Come in!"

Dragan looked as if he hadn't slept—his shirt and trousers were rumpled and his black vest was unbuttoned. There were no blinding colors surrounding him, only a cool, white fog shrouding his form. Hristina followed him inside and I held up a hand against her luminosity.

"Thank you, Hristina. You may go," Dragan said. When the door closed I turned with relief, my eyes still half-closed against the afterglow.

Dragan stepped in close and took my head in firm but gentle fingers, his thumbs resting on my cheekbones. "Show me."

I allowed him to tip my head up so he could look into my eyes.

As I blinked blearily at him, he grinned. It transformed his face like the sun spilling over the horizon at dawn, bathing me in warmth. "So, the truth is revealed."

"What?" I was having a hard time focusing. My common sense seemed to flee at his nearness.

"No one can doubt you are a Mesmer now." He released me. "Do you have a mirror?"

I pointed to the dressing table and he retrieved the little silver thing and handed it to me.

My heart raced to life as I looked into the glass. I gasped. My eyes were vibrant purple, shining like two amethyst gems.

A wave of confusing emotions swamped me as I handed back the mirror. With that change, the door of my cell clanged shut. I was truly a Mesmer now, with everything it meant. Power, yes, but danger too. Hatred and fear. And servitude. I belonged to Adrjssia now, well and truly.

"You're displeased?"

"Of course not," I forced out. "They'll just take some getting used to."

"They're the real you. Your green eyes were a lie."

True. But lies can be comfortable. "And the brightness—the colors? I could hardly look at Hristina."

"That's where your training comes in. You will be able to block it out, in time. Come with me, and we'll begin." Dragan gave me his arm and led me through the palace. It was still early morning, and so the hallways were fairly empty, but when we did pass servants or nobles, I was forced to squint and trust him to lead me.

As a woman approached, my eyes widened in recognition before I quickly shut them. When she passed, I hazarded a glance back. Her colors were the gray of sadness, dimmer than others I'd seen.

"Who is that woman?" I whispered.

Dragan looked over his shoulder. "The late queen's companion."

54

Ah. That explained her oppressive sorrow. But not her late-night conversation with Prince Aleksi.

We reached the Mesmer's workshop and I was relieved to find it free of the dark cloud of Valko's presence. Dragan showed me to a chair at a little table by the far window. A tray with cooling tea and a plate with hard-boiled eggs, thick, flaky rolls, and a slice of pickled fish sat before me. "Help yourself." Dragan motioned to the food.

I was starving, so I did.

Dragan leaned against the end of the high worktable, crossing one booted ankle over the other as I tried to ignore his scrutiny.

When the sound of my munching threatened to overwhelm the space, he finally spoke. "Why did you ask about Teodora? The queen's companion?"

I paused in my chewing before washing my mouthful down with a swallow of strong tea. I briefly considered lying, but I didn't know why I should. I was a Mesmer now. I needed to trust them. "I saw her and Prince Aleksi arguing late one night."

"Tell me what you saw."

I quickly recounted my nocturnal adventure, doing my best to remember the exact words spoken.

*"I'll say nothing, Your Highness, you know I won't. If I haven't all these years, why would I now?"*

*"Because she's gone. And it looks... Well, you know how it would look."*

"Do you think he had something to do with the queen's death?" I asked.

Dragan frowned, rubbing his sternum absentmindedly. "I have always found him trustworthy, but he *is* one of few we cannot question." He gave a little nod, as if considering to himself. "And he knows it."

"Why can't we question him?"

"The ink of the chiton nullifies our power. It is part of the reason the substance is prized and taken by the royal family. It acts as a safeguard to guarantee the rulers are not corrupted by the powers of Mesmerism."

"Like the verbenia," I said.

"Yes, though verbenia inhibits our power, while the chiton ampli-fies it. But taken by a non-Mesmer, the effects are essentially the same. We cannot read or manipulate a person under the influence of either."

"Is the effect permanent? There will never be a way to question the prince?"

"It must be taken monthly, from what I understand. Perhaps, if sufficient evidence was brought before the king, he would order his brother to undergo questioning. But it could not be an idle accusa-tion. What you saw is not enough."

"So we'll find more."

Dragan chuckled. "*You* will do nothing but learn and train. There are currents of power in this palace that would sweep away the igno-rant. Do not risk yourself by playing at detective."

I bristled. "You were the one who said I could help find the queen's killer."

He took the seat across from me. "When your training is complete. For now, Adrijana, you help by your very presence."

He must have seen my confused look. "The appearance of a third Mesmer here strengthens our king's position in a time when he would otherwise look weak. Though Valko is too grumpy to admit it, I believe your presence here reflects divine timing."

Oh. I thought on it. "Adrjssian strength will make the Vruks nervous, won't it?"

Dragan inclined his head. "You begin to see the currents already. It is why you should give the Vruk ambassadors a wide berth."

"I will." That was one command I would have no problem follow-ing. "Are there truly no Royal Mesmers other than the three of us?"

"The Mesmer War decimated our numbers. It was genocide. Hundreds of Mesmers were slaughtered. From what we know, only nine of us remain. Well, now ten, with you. The remaining declared Mesmers live quiet lives away from prying eyes."

That sounded nice. I suppose those Mesmers hadn't been coerced into service like I had. But maybe I could win my freedom, if I served well. And for the time being, this was the only place I could learn how to manage my abilities.

"Now, let us not speak of the past all day. Shall we train?"

I nodded eagerly and took my last swallow of tea before standing. "I'm ready."

He laughed and took my hand, pulling me back into my chair. "Easy there, karakal. We will speak of theory first. What do you know about Mesmerism?"

I twined my hands under the table, rubbing one thumb along my palm, where the memory of his touch still lingered. My nerves sang in his presence, my body jittery and alive. *Focus.* I catalogued my knowledge quickly. The list was pitifully short. "I know that emotions are reflected in different colors. And appear connected to different parts of the body. I know that Mesmers cannot see each other's emotions." I thought of his ghostly-white form standing next to me in the throne room. "And I know that somehow you...separated yourself from your body."

A frown curved Dragan's mouth.

My cheeks heated. It wasn't my fault Papa had kept me in the dark all these years.

"Well, that means there's little for you to unlearn. The living have an energy field around their physical bodies. We call it the *ora*. Mesmers can see that ora, read the information it contains, and if the situation calls for it, change what we find there. Now, there are three information centers contained in a human body called 'nodes.' The sacral, the heart, and the cranial." Dragan pointed to his stomach, his heart, and a point between his brows in turn. "Mesmers have a fourth center, at the top of our heads. The crown. It acts as a shield, protecting our oras, and connects to our other nodes, giving us our ability to read the oras of others. Or even leave our bodies, as you saw me do."

"What do the other three nodes do?"

"The sacral node is a primitive place of desire—those things that pertain to our survival. Shelter, sustenance, reproduction. Humans, animals, and even plant life have this node. The heart node pertains to emotions. Humans and animals both have this node. It seems to be the one you are most adept at reading, though we will train you to read all three. The cranial node projects our thoughts and is exclusive to humans. Like I said, only Mesmers have the crown node. Leading to the conclusion that we are a more advanced form of life than the rest of humankind."

I let out a little laugh at his arrogance, but then fell silent as I saw he was serious. I fumbled for a topic. "How do plants have desires?"

"They have basic needs as well. Sunlight. Soil. Water. Here, let me show you. It's a good place to start."

I followed him across the room to stand before a messy bookcase. On a shelf at eye-level sat a potted plant with glossy, green leaves. I saw nothing around it, no blur of white or color.

"It just looks like a plant." I risked an uncertain glance at Dragan.

He stepped behind me and rested his hands lightly on my shoulders. The warmth of his fingers seeped through the fabric of my dress. "That is because you have been looking with your heart node. And plants have no emotions. You must go deeper. Look from here." One of his hands splayed across my lower abdomen, pressing me back against the muscled length of him.

My breath stilled even as my heart swooped and dipped. Warmth pooled deep within me where his hand rested, my skin prickling with awareness. I could focus on nothing but him—the heat of his breath on my neck, his hand across my belly.

"Use the sensation," he murmured. "It is a map to where your sight lies."

I stopped trying to fight it and dove into the feeling, the exquisite, unabashed desire kindling within me. Clumsily, I tried to settle my awareness there and focus on the plant. Did it want water as badly as I wanted to turn in Dragan's arms and kiss him?

I let my eyes unfocus and go hazy, questing out with my senses. *Show me something—please.*

Shimmering gold appeared around the little plant, gilding each delicate leaf. I gasped. "I see something."

"What?"

"Gold." I turned and Dragan stepped back, opening the space between us. I shoved down my disappointment. "What does it mean?"

"It wants sunlight." He picked up the plant and carried it to the table where I'd eaten by the big windows. "Emotions change on the breeze and thoughts, well... Humans are remarkably adept at lying, even to themselves." He turned and met my stare with his own, and I thought perhaps I might drown in those endless purple eyes. "But desires, Adrijana, desires never lie."

And so that was the beginning of my education. About Mesmerism, and something more.

# CHAPTER 9

*W*hen our lesson was done, Dragan escorted me back to my chamber. Once before the door, he handed me a thick book titled *Principles of Mesmerism*, and a slim leather-bound volume without a title. I frowned at it and flipped through a few pages of its hand-written script. It looked like a journal, with dates on the top of the entries. "What is this?"

"This is the truth," he replied. "Not the lies you've been taught. It is up to us to remember our history, and the many wrongs perpetrated against our people."

I realized the first date was a little over twenty years ago. I looked up sharply. "The Mesmer War."

He nodded. "Valko does not like to speak of it, and he would keep this knowledge from you. But these dangers are not gone; they are only more cleverly disguised. You must be ready." With that, he turned on his heel and strode away.

I slipped back into my room and sagged against the door, clutching the books to my chest.

I couldn't banish the feel of him pinning me in place with a touch, as surely as a butterfly stretched on the board of a scientist. Though I thought the butterfly did not enjoy it so much.

I settled into the bright window seat and flipped through the journal. It took me a moment to orient myself, as the journal bore no name or signature that might have explained the identity of its owner. But it soon became clear that the pages belonged to a Mesmer who had worked at the College of Eyes in Klovnij. A teacher of some sort, because the writer spoke of their students and trouble with a particular class.

And the scribe was a woman, I soon learned, as I happened upon an entry from a little less than a year before the war had begun.

*Mesmerism may not give us foresight, but I knew that Andrej Yostaar would be trouble. Two months after his father died of a mysterious ailment, leaving him Dynast of the Vruk tribe, he was already flouting the law prohibiting any clan from keeping a standing army. Four months in, he and his barbarous band were raiding Lozian farms along the border. It's been six months now, and he's claimed enough territory to put him in spitting distance of the verbenia crags. And finally, the stagnant old men who run this College have roused from their slumber. Oh, would it be a most devastating blow if he seized those farms and learned of the plant's true potency? Would it perhaps upset the delicate balance of power in Adrjssia, as the threat of the Mesmers is all that's kept the hungry Vruks in check these last hundred years? If only someone had pointed that out six months ago, when we'd first received word of his ascension. Oh wait, I did. But the power to see does not keep the Council from being blind fools, particularly when it comes to listening to a woman. I fear we'll all pay for their prejudices.*

I found myself smiling, despite the seriousness of the topic. I think I would have liked this Mesmer. I flipped forward a few entries and read on.

*They invited him here, to Klovnij. Does no one see they've welcomed the wolf to dine in the henhouse? They arrived in the city today, parading through the gates a hundred strong—hardened warriors all, bristling with weapons. He calls them his guards, but they're so clearly an army. Does no one remember such a thing is forbidden? What good are laws when no one has the backbone to enforce them? If not for the Mesmers, I fear he would seize the city from the inside this very night.*

*I, together with several of my colleagues, was forced to attend the feast in*

*Andrej's honor. The Vruk Dynast is a handsome man, in a hard-bitten way, with flaxen hair and bright, blue eyes striking against his rugged face. But that is all that commends him. His attitude is superior, and his muscled form reminds one not of a champion, but a bully. He presented to the king a gift of one of their strange giant rodents—a "fossorial," they call it—which sniffs for gems and gold in the mines deep in Vruk territory. The poor thing was as blind as a bat and clearly terrified... What use do we have for such a creature, removed from its home? What a casual cruelty.*

*As the night progressed, I couldn't shake the feeling that his glacial eyes followed me wherever I went, though I assured myself I was imagining it. I realized how wrong I'd been when I'd tried to make a subtle, early exit, and he cornered me in the hallway. I did not like his leering smile, or the way that his hand lingered on mine after we shook, but I tried to ignore it for the sake of diplomacy. But I could not ignore his servant, who walked slowly by, tapping with his cane. It was the second such servant I had seen, remarkable for the purple strip of fabric covering the man's eyes. Though a sense of foreboding hung over me, I could not help but ask. "What happened to your servants' eyes?" And I do not exaggerate his glee when he replied, "That is how we deal with Mesmers in my country."*

A knock sounded on my door and I found myself filled with a similar sense of foreboding. But it was just Hristina leaving me my dinner, as I wasn't yet able to block out the oras of others at will. I let out a nervous laugh and gave myself a little shake to banish the strange nervous spell the journal had cast over me. Despite my trepidation, I couldn't stop reading.

I filled myself with stew of roast quail and a salad of bitter greens and kumquat while balancing the open book on my lap. The Vruk Dynast she spoke of, who was now King Andrej of West Adrjssia, had continued to harass the poor Mesmer woman, his advances becoming increasingly aggressive. The Mesmer College had urged Adrjssian King Njavo to take a position of strength—making clear that further aggression, particularly in the southeast region, containing these verbenia crags, would be met with the full might of the Adrjssian military.

But Andrej was a savvy negotiator, and his time in Klovnij had shifted his priorities.

*Andrej knows of the verbenia. I'm certain of it. For very suddenly, he has become exceedingly smug (even more so than his natural countenance), and has begun agreeing to all of the king's demands. In fact, he has agreed to return to his territory and obey all of the dictates of king and council. He has only asked for one thing in return. An ambassador from the College of the All-Seeing, to "help dispel his people's natural dislike of Mesmers." And of course he has made a special request for a particular Mesmer to fill that role. Me.*

*I could not take it anymore. The College's strictures forbid us from reading, or especially influencing, a foreign dignitary, except in time of war. Yet I would not be traded like a piece of livestock to so vile a man. I would not let rules of decorum or propriety hamstring me while our nation was stolen in the night. We are already at war; the king is just too foolish to see it.*

*And so I opened my crown, and I quested to find the truth of Andrej. I found his ora strangely blank—white and as empty as the Misty Season. He has learned of the verbenia's true potency, and now he's taking it. We are already too late. Yet when I brought this to the Council, they had the audacity to discipline me for breaking our strictures. As if handing me over to a predatory madman isn't enough of a punishment. How am I the only one who sees the truth of this? The king and Council will take him at his word and then he will steal everything from us. He will gain access to the verbenia crags, and with them, the power to shield his entire army from Mesmer influence. And then they will come for us.*

*But I won't let that happen. Not if I can prevent it.*

I flipped to the next page, my tea gone cold. And I found it blank. I flipped more pages. Nothing. That was the last entry. I closed the journal, my mind reeling.

All the history books said that the Mesmer College Council had started the Mesmer War when they'd used the power of Mesmerism to seize the Adrjssian military, overthrow King Njavo, and attack the Vruk territories. But clearly, that was only half the story. Those actions hadn't reflected unchecked Mesmer aggression but a desperate last stand—once the College of Eyes had realized the true intent of the Vruk Dynast.

This realization did not answer my most burning question, however: What had become of the author of this journal? I would ask Dragan tomorrow, though I suspected I knew the answer. It had not ended well for her.

# CHAPTER 10

*W*hen morning came I bounced out of bed, eager and breathless. I dressed quickly and grabbed a scone smeared with jam and fresh sheep's cheese before heading to the workshop.

I was licking my fingers clean and pushing back the wisps of hair escaping my braids when I slipped through the doors and stopped short.

Valko.

He didn't hide his displeasure at my sudden appearance, and I'm sure my expression held similar regard.

"You."

"Is Dragan about? I thought we could continue my lessons." In truth, I was dying to ask Dragan about the woman from the journal.

"He's with the king today." Valko pointed to a stool by the nearest workbench and I perched gingerly on it, half-hidden behind a scattered pile of open books.

"He said he gave you reading. What have you learned?"

I recoiled slightly, my mind scrambling for an answer. Dragan had said that Valko might not approve of me learning the truth behind the war. But Dragan had given me a second book, too. *The Principles of*

*Mesmerism.* "I...I just got started. I was memorizing the colors of the emotional spectrum—gray for sadness, red for anger..." I trailed off.

"You already knew this, did you not? Have you learned nothing new?"

"I didn't realize..." I didn't realize I was going to be tested on day one. But somehow I didn't think Valko was interested in excuses.

He took a pair of spectacles off his nose and threw them onto the table in disgust. "Perhaps Dragan treats Mesmerism as an amusing parlor game, but what we do here shifts the fate of nations. You must work harder than you ever have before to master this material and make yourself ready to serve."

I pursed my lips. "I'm no stranger to hard work." Did he think me a pampered housepet? I had grown up at my father's side, working the verbenia crags, come rain or shine. I had the callouses on my palms to prove it.

"Good. Now we will work on the cranial node and accessing thoughts. The cranial node is the most complex of the energy centers—"

I was loathe to interrupt him, but there was something more pressing. "Sir, perhaps there is something more fundamental I can learn."

He pursed his lips and motioned for me to continue.

"It's only that, the brightness of the oras around me makes it painful to be around other people. I've had to take my meals in my room and sequester myself. Dragan said there's a way to...stop seeing?"

"You didn't cover this yesterday?"

I shook my head.

"It's considered the ultimate rudeness for a Mesmer to walk about with their crown node open, taking in at will the thoughts and emotions of those around us. It is only our ability to turn off our power that makes us tolerable to polite society."

"I'd like to learn. It's very distracting."

Valko stood and crossed to the messy bookshelves and retrieved a strange silver object. "Did he speak of the frequency of energy yesterday?"

I shook my head, and Valko clucked his tongue in displeasure. "Each of our nodes responds to a different tone of energy. The best way to recreate this, to isolate each center, is through sound. This tuning fork is tuned to the wavelength of the crown node. It will help you feel precisely where the center is so you can more easily flex the mental muscles to close it. It may be difficult at first." He sat on a stool across from me. "Are you ready?"

I nodded, though I didn't really think I was.

Valko whacked the fork against the table and then pressed its end down. A pure, clean tone rang out, filling the room and my senses. Overwhelming me.

Pain split through my head, as if a bolt of lightning had sizzled down from above. With a gasp, I clapped my hands over my ears, but it made little difference. The sound wasn't coming in that way.

I squeezed my eyes shut and hunched over on my stool. "Stop! Make it stop!"

The sound was trailing away and my shoulders slumped in relief.

Until Valko clanged the fork again and the sound and its piercing pain smothered me once more. "The only way to make it stop is to close your crown node," he said in a loud voice.

I took a desperate, shuddering breath, fighting against the sound. My stomach somersaulted and my vision swam. I toppled sideways off the stool, hitting my palms and knees hard on the stone floor. I panted and curled forward, pressing my forehead to the cool stone. I was going to be sick ...

Valko's voice reverberated close by, swimming through the haze of the sound. "Let the pain direct you to the site of your node. You have the ability to close it—the pathway exists. You only need to do it once and you will be able to do it always."

A sob escaped me. The pain was blinding—throbbing. I could feel it stealing my consciousness. I was going to pass out. "Stop. I can't."

Valko clanged the fork again and the tone rang out even brighter.

A raking scream ripped from my throat as starbursts of pain shot through my thoughts like a meteor shower.

"Are you even trying? A child can do this. Stop wallowing in self-pity and do something about it."

Anger bloomed to life in me, beating back the edge of the pain. *Curse Valko to hell.* I wouldn't be cowed by him. I wouldn't let him see me writhing on the floor like a worm.

I seized the spot of the pain—the point at the top of my head where it felt like a nail was being hammered in. I shoved the pain away. The noise, the frequency and vibration. I didn't know what I was doing except that I was done listening. I was done letting him hurt me.

And it was like a door slammed shut. The sound still existed, in some distant place. But it was quiet. Blessedly, peacefully, quiet.

I pushed up to my knees with shaky arms, wiping my eyes, and then my nose. The back of my hand came away bloody.

Valko was crouched over me, his purple eyes shrewd. Calculating.

I eyed him warily.

He handed me a handkerchief, as well as a spartan bit of praise. "Good."

* * *

VALKO FED me a cup of bitter tea and dismissed me to my room, with a barked order to rest and eat heartily. As I walked back, my limbs felt like jelly, my head like it had been pounded by a drum. But the colors around those I passed were gone; bright oras blinded me no longer.

Valko seemed a cruel and petty tyrant, but at least his methods were effective. I was glad to have gained something for my ordeal.

As the tea kicked in, I found myself starving. I went first to the kitchen for more breakfast and then found my way out into the gardens. I longed for fresh air to banish the cloying scent of the workshop and the lingering fog in my brain.

It had been three days since I'd been outside.

The Windy Season was in full force now, and gusts snapped the purple pennants flying high above the courtyard. The walls around this garden had been built high, though, and I was sheltered from most of the wind. The sun was out, and I settled heavily on a bench, closing my eyes and letting the golden light warm my face and gild the inside of my eyelids.

"Enjoying the day, Adrijana?" A lilting female voice startled me from my reverie.

It was the princess, with a uniformed Simeon following a respectful distance behind her. The sight of him made my heart ache. How I longed to share a meal with him, to laugh and run together like we once had. I'd wanted to come to the palace in part to be near him, but I was beginning to wonder if being here with him was in fact harder. The formality between us felt artificial and wrong.

"I was warming up," I admitted to the princess as I stood and gave her a curtsy.

"May I join you?"

"Of course." I gestured to the bench.

She settled beside me, the burnished copper thread of her fine skirts glittering in the sunlight. Her karakal jumped into her lap and she scratched it behind its ears.

"It's so beautiful," I murmured. I'd never seen one so close. Its thick fur was fine and glossy, its dark eyes intelligent, its pricked ears tufted like thistle down.

"She knows it," the princess said.

The karakal padded from Nevena's lap to mine and performed a circular dance before settling down directly on top of me. I let out a little laugh of delight.

The princess gave me a wistful smile. "She likes you. Good. Karakals are excellent judges of character."

"May I pet her?"

"She'll be most offended if you don't."

I ran my hands over the animal's fur, wondering in the silky softness of it. "What's her name?"

"Roja."

"Hello, Roja," I crooned.

"She doesn't normally like Mesmers."

"I'm not sure I do, either," I muttered.

"What do you mean?" Nevena cocked her head at me. Her lavender skin was sallow, with deep bags under her eyes. She wore her grief plainly.

"Nothing," I said hastily. "I had a particularly difficult lesson with Valko this morning, that's all."

Nevena looked out over the garden. "I wonder, sometimes, what the Mesmers' true agenda is."

I frowned. "They serve the king. The country."

Nevena said nothing, the little puff of air from her nostrils was her only response. Did she disagree? "I think we could be friends, you and I. Would you like that?"

"Of course."

"Perhaps..." She hesitated and then looked at me. "Do you know why my mother's companion has been summoned for questioning?"

I licked my lips. "I didn't know she had." Dragan must have taken my report seriously. Aleksi was immune to Mesmerism, thanks to the ink of the chiton, but Teodora would have to speak the truth.

"Yes, she is to appear before the Mesmers tomorrow. She loved my mother dearly and they were together for two decades. I can't imagine what they think she knows."

"Maybe it's just a formality," I offered weakly.

"Do you think you could be my eyes, in that workshop?"

I worked my way through her words. It took me a moment before I understood the import. "You wish me to spy on them for you?"

"Nothing so dramatic." She waved a hand. "But if you observe anything alarming, or at odds with the best interest of Adrjssia, you could bring it to me."

What a position that would put me in. I chose my next words carefully. "Would a friend truly ask such a thing of me?"

Nevena looked at me sharply. She was very lovely, with delicate features and dark, swooping eyebrows. She seemed almost too breakable to be Queen. But there was nothing soft about her reply. "A friend might not, but a princess would."

So now I was supposed to choose between loyalty to the Mesmers and the princess? Weren't we all supposed to be on the same side? I couldn't keep the thread of frustration from my voice as I responded. "Rest assured, Your Highness, my loyalty is to Adrjssia. If I see anything at odds with our best interest, I will bring it to you." I picked up Roja the karakal and deposited her in Nevena's lap and then stood, giving the princess a stiff curtsy. "I think I will take my leave."

Disquiet dogged me as I strode across the courtyard back toward the interior of the palace. I desperately needed a friend here. But maybe such a thing wasn't possible. Simeon jogged after me. "What's wrong? Did you say something to upset her?"

I shook my head. "She asked me to be her spy! To report the Mesmers' actions."

"You should consider it. Everyone knows the Mesmers can't be trusted."

I put my hands on my hips. "Based on what?"

"Look at what happened before the war. The Mesmers of the College overthrew King Njavo, seizing power."

Was I allowed to talk with Simeon about the journal? I wasn't sure how closely guarded a secret it was. "Maybe they had a good reason, Simeon. Maybe they were doing it for the good of the realm."

"Overthrowing the king only served their own interests."

"How could starting a war with the Vruks that ended with their slaughter and destruction possibly be in their own interest?"

"They couldn't have known how it would all end. Jana, mesmerism...it's unnatural. That power is too great. It corrupts."

I looked at him in disbelief. In that uniform, he looked like a different man. Indifferent and distant. "Is that really what you think of me?"

"Of course not—"

"I share their power, and I am the same person I've always been. Dragan and Valko have done nothing but express concern for the crown, for the country. They are loyal and committed to Adrjssia." I thought of Prince Aleksi, whispering in the dark. "If the princess wants to find disloyalty, maybe she should look to her own family."

"What does that mean?"

I instantly regretted my comment. I'd said too much. Dragan had asked me to keep what I'd seen quiet until we knew more.

"Nothing." I shoved past him. "What do I know? I'm only a lying, untrustworthy Mesmer." I broke into a run, fleeing back to my room before my tears broke free. Simeon was well and truly wrapped around the princess's finger if he couldn't see past her prejudices when it came to his oldest friend. I'd thought we could pick up our friendship where it had left off, but it was clear that he was farther away than ever.

I flew into my chamber and slammed the door, sagging against it. Only to see chaos come into focus. My chamber was in shambles—my ripped pillows spewing feathers, dresses strewn about, drawers hanging askew.

I pressed a shaking hand to my mouth. Someone had ransacked my room.

# CHAPTER 11

*I* hurried through the hallways toward the workshop. Such mischief should have concerned the royal guards, but Simeon had made clear what type of reception I'd get from them. I was dangerous—other. My problems were my own.

The workshop was empty, and so I went into the library. "Dragan? Valko?" My voice echoed in this lonely place. I continued through the library into another hallway. Just as empty. A wave of hopelessness washed over me.

I leaned against the wall and let myself scoot down to the floor, giving myself over to the feeling. I missed Papa. It had always been him and I. From scraped knees to squabbles with friends to worries over the health of our verbenia, Papa had always been there. We'd been a team. Though now even those memories were tarnished by the weight of his lies.

A servant hurried by and I scrambled up. "Miss, excuse me. Can you point me to either of the Mesmers' chambers?" I paused. "The Para-Mesmer?"

"Second on the right 'round the corner," the woman replied.

I made my way before Dragan's chamber door and found myself hesitating, though my heart raced onward like a wild thing. I scolded it. The man was far too attractive for his own good, it was true. And I found him fascinating. Magnetic. But that was surely just the pull of his magic I felt, singing to my own. My purpose here was genuine. I needed his help. He would understand that. I wiped my eyes and knocked.

The door opened to reveal Dragan, tousled and relaxed. His feet were bare, his shirt half buttoned, the braids in his hair undone. My breath stilled for a moment.

"Adrijana?" It was a question.

"Someone ransacked my room," I blurted out. "I got back, and it had been torn apart."

Dragan's expression darkened and he gestured me inside. My body shivered as the door closed behind me, so very aware that we were alone. In his chamber.

"Tea?" he asked, pulling out a chair for me to sit in. His room was similar to mine, though larger and more lived in. The decor was a tribute to his Lozian heritage. A richly-colored woven rug covered the cold stone beneath my feet, and the large bed was covered with pillows in the bright colors and geometric patterns of hexagons and triangles. On one wall was a tapestry depicting the silhouetted forms of a veruja butterfly swarm at dusk.

"Did you ever see it?" I stood before the tapestry, marveling in the intricate weaving.

"The migration?" Dragan paused before the fire. "Yes, one year, when I was very young. It was beautiful—and then heartbreaking."

"They die, right? After they lay their eggs?"

He nodded. "Fertilizing the soil for the next generation. And for us. It's why Lozian crops are the healthiest in Adrjssia. Or were, anyway, before the war."

I drifted by a bookshelf filled with neat volumes and returned to the chair he'd pulled out for me. Dragan's chambers were orderly and disciplined, like he was. But these touches of personality..... or history... I wondered if I would get to see it in the man himself someday.

Dragan made our tea, a black leaf blend flavored with orange blossoms, and sat beside me. I quickly recounted my tale.

"Was anything missing?"

I frowned. "I'm not sure. I didn't stay to look through things. I don't have many possessions, anyway."

"Go through it in your mind's eye. Mesmers have excellent memory for visual details."

Curious, I let my eyelids flutter closed. I was surprised to find I could visualize my room in remarkable clarity. I looked around the room, trying to remember what might have been missing. I'd left the Mesmer's journal on the window seat. And now it was gone. "I think the journal you gave me is gone. They took it." I opened my eyes and found Dragan staring at me unabashedly. My cheeks heated. "Is it lost forever?" I found it a remarkably distressing thought. All that the Mesmer woman had been through could have been wiped out in a moment. What if the thief had burned it?

"We have other copies."

I let out a relieved sigh. "Who was she?"

"Iskra Juric. She was a teacher of diplomacy and foreign studies at the College of Eyes."

"Was she sent west to be the Vruk ambassador?"

Dragan nodded. "I believe she was much mistreated. But still, she managed to get word to the Mesmers of an imminent attack from Vruk forces. When King Njavo would not send Adrjssian forces to face them, the Mesmers seized the military and used Mesmerism to direct the troops to fight. In retrospect, it was precisely the type of move Andrej was hoping for. Proof that the Mesmers could not be trusted. The College signed its own death warrant."

"Why would King Njavo not oppose the Vruks?" I didn't have much education in the way of military theory, but it seemed fairly straightforward that a ruler would want to oppose a force of hostile invaders.

"He had learned of the existence of verbenia, and what it could do, a truth that the Mesmer college had closely guarded for generations. It had caused a fissure between the crown and the College, and according to the other primary sources, the king didn't believe Iskra's report was real."

"So he played into Andrej's hands as well."

"Without a doubt. I'm certain it was Andrej who told him of the verbenia and drove the final wedge between his enemies."

"It sounds like a miracle Andrej didn't take the whole country."

Dragan stood, pacing before the fireplace. "Not yet, anyway."

I looked up sharply at that, but he waved a hand. "Do not fret about such things. Valko does plenty of that for all of us. Let us focus on your mystery."

Right. My room. Talking with Dragan had almost made me forget. "Who would want Iskra's journal?"

"The journal's existence is not common knowledge, but it's not the most closely guarded secret, either. It's been in our library for many years. I wonder why someone would take it from your room. Why now?"

I looked into my teacup. This puzzle was bigger than I. I could feel it.

"Shall we do some digging ourselves? See what we can find?"

"How?"

He grinned. "Projection."

"What's that?"

"The first night we met, when you saw me standing at your side, I was Projecting."

My eyes widened. "You can teach me how to do that?"

"Of course." He stood and held out a hand. "Come."

Overcome by curiosity, I placed my hand in his and let him lead me across the room to stand beside the bed.

"Lie down."

My mouth went dry. I glanced at the downy white bed nervously. "In your bed?" His fingers were firm on my hand.

"Unless you want to lie on the floor, which I assure you is not as comfortable."

I met his eyes and saw amusement there. But, for a moment, my mind flitted away to a vision where he took my face in his hands, walked me back against the bed until my knees buckled—

"I assure you, Adrijana, your virtue is perfectly safe."

I pulled my hand from his—embarrassment banishing the fantasy. Ovyato help me, what was I thinking? "Of course," I mumbled as I sat down on the bed. I went to untie my boots, but Dragan knelt down and took one of my feet in his firm hands, beginning to loosen my laces. "I will give you the theory of it, and once you have Projected from your body, I will join you so I can help you travel about the palace. We shouldn't go far at first; it can be a strain. In time, you'll be able to Project over great distances."

He finished unlacing my other boot and stood. I pulled them off and lay down on the bed. My skin was alive with his nearness and the intimate nature of this lesson. Heat pooled deep within me, a sensation that was unfamiliar but not entirely unpleasant. I didn't know how I'd be able to focus on Projecting, but I'd try.

Dragan pulled a chair over to the side of the bed and sat in it. "Close your eyes. Even your breathing. Deep breath in, deep breath out."

I did as he instructed, and my heart rate began to slow.

"We have two bodies. Our physical body and our energetic body, the ora. Some might consider it a soul, but it doesn't really matter. Mesmers are concerned less with spirituality and more with practicality. We read the oras of others through use of our crown node, but it also acts as a tether point. With practice, a Mesmer can split his own ora from his body. And travel about at will."

I opened my eyes. "What happens to the body?"

"Even breathing," he replied.

I closed my eyes again, trying to do as he said.

"The body waits for the ora to return. It is a vessel for the ora and our consciousness. When you first learn to Project, you must be lying down. It takes years of training to be able to keep the body upright without the soul to direct it. Some can never manage it."

I recalled Dragan standing in the front of the great hall, while his silvered spirit form hovered inches from me.

"It's what you did at the festival."

He nodded his assent. "I never meant to scare you. The last thing I was expecting was an undeclared Mesmer who could see my ora. Now, the first time is the most difficult. But I want you to imagine you are floating above your body, looking down at it. Picture the details. The room, me sitting here. All of it."

I formed a mental picture and filled in the details I'd taken in earlier. It quickly took on a life of its own, adding more images of things I hadn't consciously considered. I could imagine myself lying with my eyes closed. My dark hair braided, my full lips pressed together, forming the shadow of my two dimples. I looked like a sleeping princess. "I can see it," I said, and in my mind's image, my mouth moved. Disbelief coursed through me. I hadn't intended that.

I looked at Dragan and found he was looking back at me. "You're almost there. Now is the hard part. You must pull yourself out of your body so you are floating above. Imagine that there is a rope above you and use it to pull yourself up, to peel yourself out of physical form. Your ora will resist at first—it will try to protect you. Right now, your ora is connected to your physical body at each of the nodes. But once three of those connections are broken, your ora will be able to leave your body, connected only by a long tether tied to the crown node."

His words chilled me. "Could I accidentally break all four?" And float into the ether, leaving only an empty shell behind?

"No. The last connection cannot be broken, except by death. This is another way Mesmers are unique. Now try."

I did as he said and pulled myself upward, straining against the tugging sensation at my belly, my heart, my brow. I felt the tethers snap and my eyes flew open. But the eyes of the body resting on the bed stayed closed.

I was looking at Dragan while floating above the bed.

He grinned. "Welcome to the ethereal realm. You're a quick study."

I smiled back. It was strange, to feel the pleasure of the compliment, but there were no bodily sensations. No heated embarrassment or pesky desire.

"Practice moving about. It will take some getting used to." Dragan came around the other side of the bed and lay down next to me. No sooner had his eyes close than his ora was floating out of his body, joining mine.

He offered me his hand again. "Shall we?"

Dragan led me out of his chamber into the hallway. Passing through the door was strange—it added a slight resistance, like walking through water rather than air. I could feel an echo of his hand in mine, and I began to get used to the sensation of walking.

We turned a corner and came face to face with two guards. I slowed, but Dragan pulled me forward. Past them. *Through them.*

I looked over my shoulder with amazement at their retreating forms.

"They can't see us. In the palace, only Valko could see us." Dragan pulled me through a wall and I found myself back in my chamber. "It's usually best to start with the scene of the crime. Look for anything else out of place, anything that might indicate who did this."

He strode forward, but I stayed glued to the spot by my sudden unease. "You could just spy on me? In my chamber?"

He turned and let out a laugh. "You would most certainly see me if I did."

Oh. Right. I could see him too. "But others. You could spy on anyone. The king...the princess..." I thought of Simeon, or Georgi. Wouldn't it be tempting to pay one of them a visit...?

"Adrijana, the power of the Mesmers is great. It is why we are feared and disliked. Why the Vruks tried to wipe us out during the war. I use this power sparingly. Valko nearly never. And only to spy on our own people when the king has commanded it."

"I'm sorry. I didn't mean to imply you did anything wrong. It's just...I can't believe anyone can do this."

He stepped in close. "*Anyone* can't, Adrijana. You are unique. Precious." The way he looked at me then, I wasn't sure if he meant precious to the kingdom, or to him. I found myself desperately wanting it to be the latter.

"All right," was all I could think to say.

"There is one chamber you should feel free to spy upon, at your leisure."

"What?" A surprised laugh escaped me.

"Come." He seized my hand and *pulled*. The world sped by in a blur and I stumbled to a stop, surprised to find myself in a new room. The view from the window revealed a northern view of the city and the green cliffs beyond. We were in a completely different part of the palace.

My stomach was reeling. Strange, as I had no stomach.

"How'd you—" But I froze, my voice cutting off in a squeak.

Lounging by the fire, polishing a rippling sword, sat one of the Vruk ambassadors. The short-haired, tattooed man who had threatened me. Matija.

My lip curled in distaste as my vision blurred for a moment, then sharpened again.

Dragan glared at the man with open hostility, his ghostly arms crossed over his chest. "The Vruks take verbenia daily, so we Mesmers cannot read their oras. The fools don't realize that we have other tricks. I don't have the proof yet, but it's my bet that we'll find the queen's killer in this room."

The room spun around me and I shot out a hand and caught myself on Dragan's shoulder. I doubled over. "I don't feel very good."

Dragan's concerned face was the last thing I saw before the world went black.

# CHAPTER 12

*I* awoke in Dragan's chamber with a gasp. I was as cold as ice. "What happened?" I asked through numb lips. A shiver wracked me.

Dragan went to quick work, wrapping me in a blanket and scooping me out of the bed as easily as if I were a doll. He set me down gently in a chair before the fire. "I'm sorry. I shouldn't have pushed you so far on your first Projection. Your body is in shock."

He threw another log on the fire and hung the kettle on its hook above the flames. He turned back to me and knelt down, taking my icy fingers between his own. Dragan rubbed them vigorously and then brought them to his mouth, warming them with the heat from his breath. Another tremor took hold of me, but I wasn't sure if it was only from the cold.

"Forgive me." Dragan's hair was mused, his composure gone. "I never should have been so careless."

"Is it ver-ry dan-g-er-rous?" My teeth chattered as I tried to speak.

"It can be. If you push your ora too far from your body. You will get better with practice, and there are ways to amplify your power. Copper rods to ground you while you Project. And ways to strengthen your body. Certain mushrooms especially. You should drink a tea blend daily, while you are building up your endurance."

He released my hands and crossed to a bookshelf, retrieving a bottle of amber liquid and a delicate little glass. "Lozian port. It'll warm you."

He passed me the glass and I took a sip, nearly gagging. Dragan took a swig from the bottle. "It's best if you swallow it all at once."

I braced myself and threw back the draught with a cough. It burned the length of my throat and I shuddered. But then a peculiar warming sensation did begin.

Slowly but surely, my body began to thaw. Sitting in the other chair, Dragan stared into the fire, as if he'd forgotten me.

When I was warm enough, I slipped from the blanket, grabbed my boots, and let myself out.

* * *

IT DIDN'T TAKE me too long, upon returning to my chamber, to set things right. I didn't have many possessions, after all. When all was neat again, the journal was nowhere to be found. It appeared to be the only thing the guilty party had taken.

I soaked in a warm bath and then slept like the dead that night, my body achy and sore. I awoke to Hristina throwing back the curtains in my room, letting the light in.

I groaned and slunk further beneath the covers.

"Sleep away the day if you please," she said cheerfully. "But there are plots afoot."

I cracked open an eye. "What do you mean?"

"The Vruk ambassadors returned to their chambers after dinner last night to find it in a state. Like the Windy Season itself had been unleashed inside. They're furious and on the king about solving the crime."

I sat straight up. "Someone ransacked their rooms? When I came home yesterday afternoon the same had happened to mine."

Hristina recoiled. "Truly? I wondered what your pillows had done to offend you. You should tell it to the Mesmers then, for when they put the staff to the question. Perhaps the incidents are connected."

My mind was whirling. I was certain they *were* connected, but I had no idea why. Who would want something from my room, and the rooms of the Vruk ambassadors? Perhaps Mesmerism was the connection, though I didn't understand what a thief might have wanted from a Mesmer's chamber, and from the rooms of two men who hated Mesmerism with a passion.

I threw off the covers. "Help me get dressed."

\* \* \*

NEITHER DRAGAN or Valko were anywhere to be found in the workshop or library. I headed back toward the dining hall, where I cornered a man in the king's guard.

Grudgingly, he led me to an audience chamber. "They said they weren't to be disturbed. Your funeral."

I chewed on my lip, poised at the door. I let out a huff. Surely, they didn't mean me. I should be learning from whatever they were doing in there. As I went to push through the door, a handsome man with blond braids threaded with silver beads peeked his head around the corner of the hallway. He quickly disappeared when our eyes met. I frowned. Where had I seen him before? I searched through my memories and found them quite vivid, like Dragan had said. I seized upon one where he had appeared, though his hair had been pulled back in a ponytail then. He'd stood near Prince Aleksi during the queen's funeral. Prince Aleksi's companion or servant, perhaps?

I waited for another moment, but the man did not reappear. So I slipped through the door, closing it quietly behind me. The room was empty but for three ornate chairs. Teodora, the late queen's companion, sat in one, a tear-stained handkerchief twisted in her hands. Valko and Dragan sat in the others. Suddenly, the appearance of Aleksi's man came into sharp relief. Was he spying in an attempt to discern what was going on with Teodora's questioning?

The heels of my boots echoed on the polished wooden floor, and all three turned to regard me. I didn't hesitate, even under the weight of their stares. I belonged here as much as they did.

Valko scowled at me, but I marched past them, grabbed a vacant chair, and set it next to Dragan. Settled into it. Glared at Valko. Dared him to say I didn't belong.

His purple eyes held mine until finally, he sighed and turned back to Teodora. I allowed myself a shuddering breath.

"We were just getting started," Dragan said. He quickly tapped the top of his head. It took me a moment to realize what he meant: Open my sight once again.

Trying not to think of Valko's cruel lesson, I willed my crown node open again. A shimmering oval of energy appeared around Teodora, smeared by bright colors like a canvas. Gray grief. Fiery anger. But mostly, the brown of fear.

Valko addressed Teodora. "You were not questioned because you were not in the great hall during the queen's unfortunate passing. But it became known to us that you have been taking verbenia, which was peculiar enough to warrant this discussion."

"I took it at the queen's orders," Teodora protested, twisting the fabric of her skirt in her nervous fingers.

"Nevertheless, the king has insisted that we follow every lead, which is why your dose was allowed to wear off," Valko explained. "So now I ask, did you have anything to do with Queen Ksenjia's death?"

"No." Teodora shook her head wildly. I wasn't sure exactly how to read thoughts yet, but her emotions didn't change.

"Do you know anything that could help us find her killer?"

Another shake of her head.

Valko cocked his head, regarding her like a bird of prey. "But you know something. Something about her that we do not."

She shook her head again, but the brown fear smeared across her ora, obliterating the other emotions. I was certain she was lying.

Dragan spoke next. "Why were you talking with Prince Aleksi in the corridor late several nights ago?"

Teodora began to shake. "What?" She gasped.

"Did Prince Aleksi have something to do with the queen's death?"

Valko leaned in. And then hissed. He and Dragan exchanged a look of shock.

*What? What had they seen?* Damn it, the next lesson they taught me would be how to read thoughts. But...I knew the concept, didn't I? Dragan had said that the cranial node governed thought, so perhaps focusing on my brow would allow me to access that part of her ora, like focusing on my belly had led me to see the plant's desire.

Dragan stood and strode back toward the door where I'd entered. I heard him speaking in low tones to a guard. I did my best to ignore it, focusing instead on the space between my eyebrows. The swirl of energy there.

I willed it to open—willed my consciousness to look through that lens. Something shifted. It was subtle, but there was an echoing force there, a sensation I hadn't felt before.

I opened my eyes and found that Teodora had changed. Rather, her ora had. Gone were the colors and in their place was a swirling mess of black and white words.

My mouth dropped open in awe. The words flickered and changed so rapidly, I could hardly catch them. Her mind was racing. I leaned forward and squinted, focusing on one phrase at a time.

*Memory dishonored...*

*Tried to resist...*

*They loved each other.*

It was my turn to gasp.

Teodora's bloodshot eyes flicked to me, and I clacked my mouth shut. Sweet Ovyato, we'd just unearthed what might have been the biggest secret in the kingdom. Queen Ksenjia and Prince Aleksi had been having an affair.

Mental pieces slid into place as I recalled his words in the dark of the hallway. *"Those cursed Mesmers see too much."* Aleksi had feared Teodora would be questioned and reveal the truth of his affair with the queen. An affair that would make him look, if not immediately guilty of her murder, at least subject to unwanted scrutiny. No wonder the queen was dosing her closest companion with verbenia. Was that why she'd ordered so much of the plant from Papa every year? She couldn't risk the Mesmers accidentally discovering her secret.

A thought tickled the back of my mind, as slippery as an eel. There was something else there, but what?

Dragan returned to his seat. "Prince Aleksi will be joining us for questioning. But in the meantime, how long was this going on?"

Misery streaked Teodora's face. Her thoughts said it all. *From the beginning.*

Valko cursed under his breath.

For decades? For decades, Aleksi had been going behind his brother's back... Another thought dawned on me. "The princess," I murmured in horror, and Dragan and Valko both shot me a look.

I pressed my lips together. Was the princess, or the late crown prince before her, truly the child of King Petar? Or Aleksi?

Teodora shook her head wildly. "Nevena is a legitimate heir. The queen was certain of it."

Even still... No wonder Prince Aleksi had wanted to keep Teodora quiet.

"Aleksi had nothing to do with the queen's death," Teodora went on. "He loved her. He still does."

"But they were at odds," Valko said. "You cannot hide their quarrels from us."

I squinted, trying to catch the thread of her thoughts. They moved so quickly. I would need much more practice to be as good as Valko apparently was.

"Queen Ksenjia once promised Aleksi they would go live in Visoko, with her clan, as soon as Nevena was grown. So they could truly be together. But she had been delaying. She didn't want to leave, couldn't bear to break Nevena's and Petar's hearts with the truth of things. Aleksi was pressuring her to honor her word. But he would never have killed her for it!"

Perhaps, but it was looking worse and worse for Prince Aleksi.

"Please, you can't tell anyone. It will break Nevena's heart. And the queen's legacy will be ruined."

"We cannot keep this from the king," Valko said. "What he does with the information is his choice alone."

Teodora buried her face in her hands as her shoulders shook.

My heart ached for her, churned at the wretched thoughts burning through her mind. "It's not your fault," I said. "She shouldn't have asked you to keep a secret like that."

Valko thundered at me. "You can observe or you can leave."

My hackles rose. "It's true—"

Dragan interrupted, his tone unconcerned, unhurried. "What of the break-ins around the palace? Do you have any knowledge regarding those?"

Teodora spoke through her handkerchief. "He told me nothing." Truth. Her thoughts mirrored her words.

Realization sparked in me. I'd been trying to make a connection between my chamber and the ambassadors, and I had it. "The verbenia. What happened to the queen's supply after she died?"

"The king had it locked away so no one could avoid our questioning," Valko said gruffly.

"The ambassadors take it, right? They must have access."

Dragan nodded. "Matija's tattoos have verbenia in the ink, so he is forever immune. But Spirodon takes it. We don't have authority to force him to stop."

"If Aleksi needed some for Teodora and no longer had access to the queen's supply, perhaps he tried to steal the ambassadors'?" I posited. "He could be behind the break-ins."

"But why your chamber?" Dragan asked.

"My father is one of the primary suppliers of the herb. Perhaps he thought I might have a personal supply somewhere."

Dragan and I exchanged a look. But if Aleksi was the culprit, it didn't explain why he would have taken Iskra's journal.

Valko looked to Teodora. "Could this be true? Do you think Aleksi would try to secure verbenia for you, to keep you quiet?"

She didn't need to answer. The affirmation was as plain as day.

The far doors burst open to reveal two guards. "Prime Mesmer, we went to retrieve Prince Aleksi. He's gone."

# CHAPTER 13

*J*jogged after Valko and Dragan through an unknown hallway. They seemed to have forgotten me, but I wasn't about to be left behind. Whatever happened next was part of my education, if I was to be a Royal Mesmer someday.

Plus, I was damn curious. Had Prince Aleksi murdered his lover the queen and then fled when the light of suspicion had turned upon him? Or was he being set up?

Valko gave two quick knocks on a set of gilt-encrusted double doors before charging inside. These were the king's chambers, I realized, with a trill of alarm.

Dragan turned to me and hissed, "Stay silent."

So they *had* remembered I was there.

The king's sitting room was resplendent with carved furniture inlaid with abalone, rich brocade curtains in vibrant shades of purple, and a plush rug underfoot that I longed to curl my toes into.

King Petar himself sat at a desk near the window, dressed in navy trousers, a fine white linen shirt, and an unbuttoned amethyst jacket. His dark curls were bare, without the heavy weight of his crown. He could have been any one of a number of wealthy merchants or noblemen, heavy-ladened under the weight of bad business or hard times. But for the lavender tint to his skin.

The king threw down his quill with a long-suffering sigh. "What dire news have you brought me now?"

"I fear it is more dire than I can even express." Valko sat down in the chair opposite the king, his expression softer than I'd ever seen it.

The king sat back, his eyes searching the face of his Prime Mesmer. "Out with it."

Valko's words were as sharp as a surgeon's knife. "Queen Ksenjia and your brother had been having an affair for many years. And now Aleksi has fled."

The king sat perfectly still for a moment, unblinking. "You are certain?"

"Quite," Valko replied.

With a great roar, King Petar swept the contents of his desk onto the floor with a crash. I flinched.

He brought a fist down on the wood. "What are you waiting for? Find him!"

"May we use your study?" Valko asked.

"Use whatever you gods-damn need," the king thundered.

Valko led us across the room and through a discreet door. My heart hammered a staccato beat. I didn't envy the family reunion Aleksi would face if we caught him.

The door opened to another ornate room lined with bookshelves. Two plush, velvet couches faced off before the empty fireplace, and the Mesmers wasted no time lying down upon them. They were going to Project?

"Wait! What should I do?" I asked.

"Stay silent and don't bother us," came Valko's brusque reply.

"I can Project. I can help search."

Valko sat straight up and stared down Dragan, who had the where-withal to look apologetic. "She's very talented," Dragan said.

"She's not ready for such advanced magic."

"Well, it's done," Dragan countered. "And it'll be easier to search with three."

Valko ran a hand through his gray hair. "Fine." He pointed to the rug between the couches and I didn't hesitate to lie down. I would prove my usefulness, my right to be one of them.

"Keep her close," Dragan said. "The docks."

"I'm not fool enough to kill her." Valko growled back and then looked at me. "Search the harbor and the docks. He might be trying to leave by ship. If you find him, return here immediately and wake one of us." He tossed me a vial with what looked like salt within. "Smelling salts. It can be hard to rouse a Projecting Mesmer otherwise."

I settled onto the carpet, my sweaty hand wrapped around the vial. I walked through the steps Dragan had taught me—struggled with them. It was more difficult when I was agitated and excited, as I was. But finally, I pulled myself out of my body, righting myself until I stood on the floor in my phantom form. The Mesmers were nowhere to be found. They must have already gone.

Cognizant of the ending of my last Projecting experience, I started slowly, jogging back through the king's chamber into the hallway.

King Petar was slumped at his desk, his fingers threaded through his dark hair, his head in his hands. It was a posture of such unexpected vulnerability, I found myself wanting to comfort him. But even being here was a gross invasion of privacy, and I had a stray royal to find. I hurried on.

As I broke into a run in the hallway, I began moving more swiftly than I ever could have in my own body. I seemed to skate over the ground, the scenery speeding by in a blur.

I couldn't help it, I broke into a grin as I vaulted over the balcony and landed on light feet ten steps below. I was starting to get the hang of this. I would be down to the harbor in no time.

I'd only been in Selojia a few days and hadn't yet had the opportunity to leave the palace. I longed for more time to take in the overwhelming sights and sounds of the city—merchants selling colorful wares, bawdy patrons spilling out of tavern doorways, minstrels standing on boxes on street-corners. It blurred as I navigated it all, not bothering to dodge out of the way in the busy streets, but moving right through people.

It was strange, though, for though I could see and hear, I lacked my senses of smell and touch, and I suspected, taste. It turned the winding streets into a vignette, a dream city rendered in half-light. I promised myself I would come back and take it all in, the good and the bad, in exquisite tactile detail.

The city was a maze of streets, but it all sloped down toward the water, where the city spilled itself onto a long stretch of weatherworn docks, and beyond that, the sea. I knew if I kept moving downhill, I'd find my way eventually, and before long, I did.

My elation dimmed. Over three dozen ships sat in port, and a thousand people swarmed the docks. How was I supposed to find one man among all of this?

I tried to think sensibly. Aleksi would be seeking a vessel big enough to take him far from Selojia. That ruled out the smaller skiffs and fishing vessels. He'd need one that was leaving port imminently. And likely a fast boat as well.

I ran parallel along the docks, examining the vessels, keeping my eyes trained for any clues of Aleksi's presence. I reached a handsome three-masted vessel with a wide hull and swooped up onto the deck. Sailors swarmed the wooden planks like ants, readying the ship to sail.

I hurried below deck, poking my head through closed doors, witnessing all manner of private acts—a sailor shaving, another sitting atop a wooden pot, a couple pressed against the wall in a tiny cabin, silk pooling about the woman's feet.

I finished my search of the vessel and hurried back out, grateful I couldn't blush in this form. I was struck, yet again, by what an invasion of privacy this power could be. Especially in the wrong hands.

I ran down the docks and searched two more ships, dismissing half a dozen others as not fitting the profile. I let out a huff of frustration —habit only, as I had no breath in this form.

And then I saw the horse. It was a fine bay beast, with an arching neck, glossy coat, and long, delicate legs. A sailor was leading it up off the docks. It could be Aleksi's horse! It still wore its saddle and bridle.

I ran up to it, and the horse shied away from me, fighting against its handler, dancing on its back legs.

"Whoa! Whoa." The grizzled sailor struggled to get the horse back under control.

I took two big steps back and the horse settled. I had gotten close enough to see a chiton tooled along the leather of the saddle. The royal symbol.

"Cursed beast," the sailor muttered, yanking it along.

For a moment, I stood, stunned. The horse had detected me. I supposed animals were more sensitive in certain ways.

I shook off my fascination. I would ask the Mesmers about it later. I had to focus on my task. Aleksi was definitely here.

I chewed my lip. Should I summon the other Mesmers? No, best I set eyes on the stray prince first. Which of the vessels was he on?

Two slips down bobbed a sleek double-masted ship with a cherry-red hull that looked fast and light. Its sails were up and it was leaving port. Aleksi must be on that ship, but I needed to see him with my own eyes. I couldn't risk a mistake.

I glided down the dock and came to a screeching halt at the end. The vessel had slipped from its berth, out into the water of the harbor. *Curses!*

I looked down at the water. Could I skate across the water, like I did the land? Or jump? There was only one way to find out. I wished Dragan had gone over some of this in our lesson, but it was no matter. I was here now, and I wouldn't let him go.

I scooted up on the dock, giving myself some distance. And then I ran for it. I leaped, soaring into the air, sailing toward the ship...

My trajectory was off. I realized it too late. *No, no, no....*

I plunged into the water.

I splashed and spluttered for a moment before remembering I didn't breathe in this form. I couldn't drown.

A delighted laugh escaped me as I looked around the water. A school of silver fish as bright as coins darted by—*through* me.

The water was fairly clear, turquoise and lovely, and I could see chains and anchors, the shadowed hull of Aleksi's ship. The barnacled columns holding up the docks. Swimming was as easy as willing myself forward. There was no need to move my arms or legs. It made me wonder whether or not I could move on land without actually moving my feet.

But I needed to see Aleksi. I couldn't delay any longer.

I shot up, out of the water. Hovered along the railing like an avenging angel, looking directly into the face of Prince Aleksi.

He was peering numbly into the water, his face a mask of regret.

I needed to tell the others. I looked back at the palace, perched high above the city. It would take me far too long to get back the way I'd come. Aleksi would be gone. But could I fly?

I pointed my ethereal body in the direction of the palace and willed myself forward. Faster. Faster.

The ground whirled by beneath me, nothing more than a blur, and I whooped with delight as I zoomed through the open window and barreled back into my body. I sat up with a gasping breath. Pain exploded in my head, and I felt warmth beneath my nose. I wiped away the blood. I'd pushed myself, but I'd had to. This was bigger than I.

Crawling to Dragan's couch, I waved the smelling salts under his nose. It was a moment before he sat up, gasping a breath. He shook his head as if to clear it. "You found him?"

"The harbor. He's on a boat, already leaving."

"What did it look like?"

"The boat?"

Dragan nodded impatiently.

"It looked fast. Two masts. Red hull."

"Damn. That's the Firebird. The king's racing schooner. It's the fastest in the city. If we don't stop it, he'll be long gone." Dragan lay back down. "Wake Valko. Tell him what you told me."

"What are you going to do?" I asked. But he'd already closed his eyes again.

I did as Dragan had requested. Valko absorbed the information quickly and lay back down without a word, his eyes closing.

I wiped another drip of blood from beneath my nose, hesitating a moment. Then I lay back down as well. To hell with caution. I wasn't going to miss whatever was about to happen.

I slipped from my body more quickly and launched myself out the window, soaring down toward the bustling harbor. The Firebird was nearing the crescent moon of the breakwater.

I landed on the deck to find Dragan and Valko arguing.

"It must be done!" Dragan cried.

"You could kill yourself," Valko shot back.

"Then you will finally be rid of me, old man," Dragan bit back, and he soared across the deck.

"Fool boy," Valko muttered. "You're just as reckless as Silviya."

"What? What's he doing?" I asked.

Valko seemed surprised to see me for a moment, then turned back. "Something foolish. And forbidden."

My question died on my lips as I watched Dragan pull a cudgel from a sailor's belt. He held it in his spectral hand and sliced through the nearest rope in one powerful blow.

"How...?" I whispered, my eyes wide with shock. Dragan's spirit form was interacting with a physical object. I hadn't known that was possible.

Cries of fear rose up around the deck as the sailors caught sight of the floating cudgel soaring about the deck, slicing though the lines holding the sails up.

"Get him!" Aleksi appeared from below deck, the blond-haired man I'd seen outside Teodora's questioning at his side. "It's not a ghost, it's a man!"

But it was too late. The last sail flew free from the mast and fluttered to the deck. The Firebird was dead in the water.

# CHAPTER 14

$\mathcal{F}$or a moment, everything was still on the deck. The sailors' shock had rendered them mute. Then the cudgel slipped from Dragan's hand and clanged to the wooden boards, and all nature of cacophony erupted. Most distinct were the shouts of fear and prayers to the gods for deliverance from demons.

A man in an Adrjssian uniform, who appeared to be the captain, started shouting order at the sailors to get below and put the oars out. Oars? I looked to where Dragan had been standing, but he was gone. Valko still surveyed the scene from near the rail, a scowl on his face.

"Will they be able to escape?"

"No. Any ship in the harbor will be able to catch them. He's just ensuring the boat doesn't drift onto the shore." Valko pointed at me. "Stay here. Watch him. I need to inform the royal guards."

I opened my mouth to ask where Dragan was, but Valko was already gone. "Goodbye to you, too," I muttered. "'Good job finding the prince, Adrijana.'"

But Valko's rudeness was the least of my worries. I strode over to where the prince stood at the back of the ship, his vacant stare fixed on the aquamarine bay. From this angle, the expanse of the city was magnificent, crowned by the dome-topped spires of Ovyato's temples.

The palace itself sat above it all, as aloof and indifferent as a beautiful queen on her throne.

Aleksi himself looked stricken, his hands gripping the rail tightly. I wished I could detect his thoughts, but the chiton the royal family ingested kept me from reading him.

The ponytailed man came up beside him, almost to where I was standing, and I drew back, out of the way. It was an uncomfortable sensation to share the same space as another person, even if I was only here in my spectral form.

"It's all gone terribly wrong, Ioseph." Aleksi didn't look at the other man. He seemed mesmerized by the sight of the city. "I never should have fled. Guilty men run."

"You're not guilty, sir." This man, Ioseph, must be Prince Aleksi's companion. But what part did he have to play in all of this? Had Aleksi himself ordered him to loiter outside the room where we had questioned Teodora, or had this man done so of his own accord?

"But I am. Just not of the crime they will accuse me of."

"Falling in love is not a crime."

"Then why do I feel so ashamed?" Aleksi did look at his companion then. His eyes were full of tears.

"Because you are a good man. It's not fair what they will say of you. What they will do." Ioseph smashed a fist on the rail, and I jumped. "I shouldn't have suggested you flee. This is all my fault."

"It's not." Aleksi shook his head. The wind had tugged free dark curls from his many braids, making him look half-feral. "I am my own man. You forced nothing on me. I thought giving my brother time to see things clearly would aid the situation. Give me time to reach out to my own contacts in Vrilaand to look into Ksenjia's murder."

I raised my eyebrows. Vrilaand was the West Adrjssian capital. So Aleksi thought that the Vruks had killed the queen?

Aleksi continued. "Besides, how could we have known that those Mesmers would find us so quickly?"

"You are certain it was them? How could a Mesmer move an object with his mind? I've never heard of such a thing," Ioseph said.

"They keep their powers closely guarded, even from the king. I have learned the hard way that when a strange or suspicious happening occurs in Selojia, it is always the Mesmers."

The captain of the vessel hurried over, red-faced and sweating. "Prince Aleksi, I cannot explain what happened. But we must return to shore to reequip the Firebird. We don't have lines for the sails. We can't continue."

Aleksi nodded. "Thank you, Captain. You may return to port."

As the captain withdrew, shouting orders at his sailors, Ioseph rounded on Aleksi. "They will be rallying the guard as we speak. You cannot mean to return?"

Aleksi swept a hand out the sea. "What do you suggest I do? Take a rowboat? The game is up."

"They'll torture you, sir." Iordan paused and lowered his voice. "They won't be gentle."

"I'm not sure I deserve gentle."

"Don't give yourself up." Iordan hesitated and reached around beneath his coat. I bent over to get a look at what he was retrieving. A dagger! He offered it to Aleksi. "End things on your own terms, Aleksi. That is the alternative."

Aleksi looked at the knife, blinking. "You would have me take my own life? My brother and his Mesmers would see it as a sure sign of guilt."

"If you give yourself over, they might torture a false confession out of you anyway. I've heard the Para-Mesmer's tactics are barbaric."

I frowned. Dragan? A torturer?

Aleksi leaned down, his forearms on the rail, his head hanging. "I wish Ksenjia were here. She always knew what to do."

"I know you don't want to live without her."

Aleksi paused. "No. No, I don't. But I do want to find who murdered her." He sighed.

"Will you be able to do that from a jail cell? From beneath the executioner's axe?"

Ioseph was mincing no words. Even Aleksi looked at him sharply at that. "You think I have no hope of proving myself innocent?"

"Of the murder, perhaps, but the punishment for adultery..." Ioseph trailed off.

I looked from the dagger to Ioseph's face, which was an unreadable mask. His arguments seemed sound, but the more he continued to press it, the more I wondered why he was so eager for his friend and companion to die.

Aleksi pushed the dagger away with a gentle hand. "No, Ioseph. I will face my brother. I will tell him how sorry I am. I will explain myself, even if he doesn't have the ears to listen right now. I have been hiding for so many years. I will not hide at the end."

Ioseph turned to look out at the sea, his fingers tightly gripping the knife hilt. Was he angry?

I couldn't help myself, I opened up my crown node. I'd never read a person's ora while Projecting, but I thought it should be possible. And yes! Colors swirled around Ioseph—red like a cloud above his head, and the mustard of guilt. But there was something else. I leaned forward. Circling his head was a mass of purple, swirling and undulating. What did it mean? I realized in that moment that I had never seen purple in an ora before. What emotion showed purple?

I focused on my cranial node, forcing it open so I could read the thoughts flashing and disappearing around him like winking stars. They were coming so fast—his thoughts were racing.

*Won't let it happen—*

*Get him to say anything—*

*It must be done—*

*My last gift—*

The thoughts were shot through with purple as well, and as I puzzled over its meaning, one thought darted by, quick as a silver fish.

*Forgive me, my friend.*

"No!" I cried, but of course, no one could hear my warning. I lunged at Ioseph, my hands moving uselessly through his outstretched arm as he stabbed Aleksi in the side.

My mouth was open in shock. It happened so fast. Ioseph stabbed again, a second time, higher. A third. Puncturing lungs and vital organs.

No one on the Firebird was paying any attention to the two men standing at the back rail—no one except me. And I wasn't really here. "Stop it!" I shouted again, into the air.

Though it wasn't in response to me, Ioseph fell back then, his chest heaving.

Aleksi's lavender face had gone white with shock, one hand pressed to his side. "Why?" He gasped.

"You deserve a clean death, my friend."

"But they'll…hang you—" Aleksi's legs went weak, and he staggered against the rail. Inadvertently, I moved forward to catch him, once again realizing there was nothing I could do. I didn't know how to grab the knife the way Dragan had. And besides, the damage had already been done.

I looked back at Ioseph, who was standing tall, his eyes shining with tears.

"No they won't, sir. It's been an honor." Then he took the knife and slit his own throat. His body tipped forward over the rail, but I couldn't hear the splash over the sound of my own screams.

But the nightmare was not over. Because from below the rail, where Ioseph's body had fallen, came a white, ethereal spirit. It looked like a Mesmer's Projecting ora, but I knew at once what it was. This was Ioseph's essence, severed from his body, drifting higher, like a misty smudge in the sky. Expanding in ever larger circles.

Searching.

I could make out the spectral form of Ioseph's face, twisted in grief. He let out a thin, reedy cry, keening in loss and sorrow.

My eyes rounded in horror. I could not look away. Was this what happened after you died? This awful loneliness and confusion? I would never forget that terrible sight—that banshee wail—as long as I lived.

Ioseph's lost spirit spiraled closer. His gaze slid over me and then snapped back. His eyes locked on mine. Sweet Ovyato, he *saw* me.

Had I been in my body, my blood would have frozen in that moment.

Ioseph affixed me with his hungry gaze and barreled straight toward me.

All semblance of pride shattered beneath the weight of my terror. For whatever reason, I knew deep in my bones that I couldn't let him touch me. So with Ioseph's scream still grating against my eardrums, burrowing into my soul—I fled.

# CHAPTER 15

*I* woke in my chamber a day later. I was groggy and bleary-eyed, and my head felt like a plow had run furrows through it.

Hristina was at my side as soon as my eyes opened. "Thank Ovyato. We were so worried." She helped me sit up and offered me some water. I drank greedily. "What happened?"

"I know only that Simeon carried you here himself. The Mesmers said you overextended yourself with your magic and needed to rest."

It all came rushing back. My swooping flights to and from the harbor, my bloody nose, Aleksi's desperate escape. *Dragan wielding the cudgel.* Aleksi's murder and his companion's suicide. That horrible specter, screaming at me...

The sight of the blood pouring from Ioseph's gaping throat flashed in my mind's eye. My stomach somersaulted. "I think I might be sick." I threw back the covers and shoved out of bed, only to find my legs treacherously weak. Hristina caught me under my armpits and maneuvered me back onto the bed before quickly retrieving the clean chamber pot and offering it to me.

Just in time, too, as I soon emptied the meager contents of my stomach into it. I couldn't stop the images flashing. The quick jerk of the knife into Aleksi's side. The waterfall of blood pouring from the gruesome slash on Ioseph's neck. His body tipping over the side of the rail and splashing into the ocean. The menace of his spirit, coming for me. I didn't remember anything after that. I must have returned to my body.

I wiped my mouth with the back of a shaky hand.

Hristina took the pot from me and set it by the door and then handed me the glass of water and a handkerchief. She seemed unfazed by my sudden illness, and I was grateful. "You need to rest."

"I need to see the Mesmers." I blew my nose. Did they know what had happened? "Prince Aleksi?" I asked Hristina.

It was then that I realized she was wearing a dress of white. Mourning colors. She shook her head. "He killed himself."

I opened my mouth to correct her, but then swallowed my comment. I needed to speak to Dragan and Valko first. I didn't know what I was supposed to share and what might be secret.

A knock sounded on the door. Hristina went to answer it, and I quickly smoothed my hair and wiped my eyes. I was wearing only my shift.

Hristina turned to me. "It's Simeon. Are you well enough to receive him?"

The thought of seeing Simeon's familiar face brought unexpected tears to my eyes. "Yes, please."

Hristina opened the door and Simeon stepped in, wearing a white version of his uniform, trimmed in gold. He stood by the door while Hristina retrieved me a robe and I pulled it on. "Are you well?" he asked as he eyed the pot by his feet.

"I will be. Hristina, would you give us some time to talk? I'd love some food, too. My stomach is feeling much better."

Hristina curtseyed and retrieved the pot before slipping out the door.

The minute the door was closed, I flew across the room into Simeon's arms. I had missed him. I had missed our friendship. He was solid and dependable and *familiar*. As he rocked me and stroked my hair, I realized how much I needed a friend.

"It's all right," he murmured. "Whatever they've done to you, we'll make it right."

I furrowed my brow and pulled back. "Who?"

"The Mesmers." Simeon took my hand to lead me to the table by the window, and we both sat. "I found you sprawled in the hallway outside the king's chambers, unconscious. I don't know what they did to you, but anyone could have found you like that. Taken advantage..." Simeon's fingers tightened into a fist on the little table, and the expression on his handsome face was grave. "I was ready to kill them, before Nevena talked me down."

I sat back, more confused than ever. "You found me in the hallway? But I was in the king's sitting room with Valko and Dragan." Perhaps I had woken, tried to stagger to my room, and passed out again? I had been quite weak after Dragan and I had first Projected, and I had surely worked myself much harder yesterday.

"Those purple-eyed bastards were nowhere to be found." His voice was so cold when he spoke of them. Foreign.

The last thing I needed was to stoke Simeon's prejudices against Mesmers. "I'm sure the Mesmers had no idea I was ill. There was a lot going on, with Aleksi trying to flee."

Simeon slouched back in his chair with a sigh, and for a moment, he looked like himself again. The boy I'd grown up with, whose only care had been sneaking an extra berry tart after supper. "Do you know why you were sick, Jana? Are they making you hurt yourself somehow?"

"They're not making me do anything," I said. "I wanted to help find Aleksi. I *asked* to help."

"And how could you do that when he had already fled the palace?"

How to explain? "Mesmers have the ability to detach their minds from their bodies and visit other places. We were searching for him."

"It's called Projecting, right? Nevena has spoken of it."

"I found him. Aleksi. In the harbor. But then..." I squeezed my eyes shut.

"You saw it, didn't you?"

I nodded, and the darkness behind my eyelids started playing the macabre scene again. "I don't know how I'll get that image out of my mind."

"Nevena is devastated. Her own uncle killing her mother? I wouldn't know how to reconcile it, either."

My eyes flew open. "Nevena thinks Aleksi killed her mother?"

Simeon was running a finger along the grain of wood in the table. "He did. The Mesmers searched his room and found damning evidence."

I sat up. After overhearing Aleksi and Ioseph's candid conversation, I wasn't so sure. "What evidence?"

"I guess he used a chemical compound to weaken the mortar of the stones where she would stand to perform the candle-lighting ceremony. The stuff is called muriatic acid. They found a jar of it hidden in his chamber."

But that...made no sense. Unless Aleksi was hiding his guilt even from his own closest companion. And if so...why the remorse? Why be willing to return and face his brother? I shook my head. "I'm not sure. He didn't seem guilty."

"You always see the best in people, Jana. But some people don't deserve the benefit of the doubt. Nevena admitted Aleksi was always secretive."

"Because of the affair, certainly. But does that mean he killed her?" I pursed my lips. It seemed that every other word out of Simeon's mouth was about Nevena. "There's something I don't understand."

"What's that?"

"How did you become Nevena's personal guard so quickly? And you two seem so close. Surely, her father has something to say about her spending her every waking hour with..." I trailed off, not sure how to frame it in a way that wouldn't come off wildly offensive.

Simeon's dark eyes flashed. "Say it. With a peasant?"

I sighed. "I'm a peasant too, Simeon, no judgment from me. It just strikes me as odd that he allows it, when you so clearly care for her."

Simeon bolted to his feet, the chair legs scraping harshly against the floor. "Nevena is a grown woman and the king trusts her to make her own staffing decisions. I admire her as a person and a monarch, but there is nothing inappropriate going on between us, and I don't appreciate the suggestion that there is."

"Simeon—" I tried to take his hand, but he pulled his back, out of my grip. "Simeon, I'm sorry. I'm not accusing you or Nevena of anything." Not outright. But his reaction raised my curiosity. I was fairly certain he was in love with her, even if nothing had happened between them. I couldn't help myself, I opened my crown node, just to take a quick peek at his colors.

I blinked in surprise. His ora was blank—milky white. Like the Mesmers. Or the Vruk ambassadors. "You're taking verbenia." I realized my mistake as soon as I said the words.

Simeon shied back a step, his thick brows drawing down in anger. "Are you trying to read me? Spy on me? Nevena said it's not permitted. I might expect that snake Dragan to flout the rules, but not you, Jana. Their corruption of you is progressing faster than even I feared."

I stood then too, leveling a finger at him. "That's not fair. I didn't ask for this. And I was only curious. You're the only person I know and trust here and you've barely said two words to me since I arrived. It seems you're too busy with your own secrets to bother with me."

"I have a *job*, Jana. And how would I spend a moment with you when those...*charlatans* are always draped about you?!" He turned and stalked toward the door, pulling it open. I followed and slammed it shut before he could walk through.

"At least those *charlatans* tell me the truth. What are you hiding, Simeon?" I looked into the storm-cloud of his face.

"Everyone has the right to their secrets, even mere peasants." Simeon practically spit down at me. "The Adrijana I used to know would have respected that." Simeon yanked the doorknob from my grip and stalked through, leaving me with nothing but the ringing of his cruel words.

# CHAPTER 16

I munched on a scone smeared with thick cheese and smoked fish after Hristina dressed me in a simple green dress and tucked in the wisps of my braids. The food, though fine, tasted like sawdust in my mouth. How could Simeon be so harsh? I shouldn't have looked at his colors, but I had spent my entire life privy to his every emotion before I'd learned what the power was and how to suppress it. It was habit—second nature to me. How could he see it as such a betrayal? I wasn't a different person just because of my violet eyes.

If anything, *Simeon* had changed. His devotion to Nevena was all-encompassing, a blackberry thicket crowding out all else. It must be *her* secret he was keeping—he wouldn't have access to the verbenia without her. What could it be?

I didn't understand why he hated the Mesmers so much. Valko was unpleasant, and I was sure to a third party, Dragan could come off as mysterious, even calculating, but they both served the king without question. All they had done since I'd arrived was try to unravel the mystery of the queen's death. They didn't deserve such scorn for it.

Was that the future I had to look forward to? Do my best to help and yet be hated and feared for it?

At least Valko and Dragan understood what it was like.

"Are you all right, my lady?" Hristina refilled my empty water glass.

"I need to see the Mesmers." As I stood, my head swam, and I had to brace myself on the table to stay upright.

Hristina clucked her tongue. "At least let me escort you. I don't want your legs to give out again."

I nodded, acknowledging the wisdom in the suggestion.

We moved much more slowly than I would have liked, but Hristina filled me in on the palace gossip on the way. The king had tried to keep secret the evidence revealed by the search of Aleksi's chamber, which meant, naturally, that the entire palace knew.

The king had closeted himself.

The princess was beside herself.

The Vruk ambassadors were gloating over the corruption of the Adrjssian royal house.

The Para-Mesmer was looking pale and wan, while the Prime Mesmer was slamming doors and scaring the servants away.

Wild rumors flew through the city like startled hares.

Things were not good in Selojia.

I parted ways with Hristina and let myself into the Mesmer Work-shop. Valko looked up from his desk with a scowl. "You. Not dead, I see."

"Disappointed?" I shot back before I could stop myself.

"I'm busy."

"I think you'll want to hear what I have to say."

"And what's that?"

"I saw how Aleksi died."

"He killed himself." Valko pinched the bridge of his impressive nose, not convinced.

"No, he didn't."

Valko examined me for a moment and then pointed at a stool by the huge worktable, where he'd tortured me with the tuning fork the day of our first lesson. "Sit. Dragan!" he hollered. "If you're not too busy moping before the mirror, come grace us with your presence."

Dragan appeared in the doorway that led to the library. "What do you want, you useless old—" He cut himself off when he saw me.

My eyes widened as I took him in. His normally tawny skin was gray, and thick bags shadowed his purple eyes, turning them into two bruised plums.

"You look…" I trailed off.

"It'll take a few days for me to get my strength back." His movements were slow and deliberate, as if each movement pained him, but he managed to pull up a chair at the table next to me and settle into it.

"What you did on that ship…" I paused. "It did this?"

"He's lucky to be alive," Valko barked. "And where would his foolish actions have left us?"

"Without your better half, certainly," Dragan murmured. "Now, Adrijana. Are *you* well? I'm sorry I could not attend to you right away after the Firebird, but as I myself was unconscious, it would have been difficult."

"I'm fine," I said. "But some things happened after you both left that I think you should know about."

Dragan ran a hand through his hair. It even seemed to lack its shimmer of gold. Valko sat on his desk. "Tell your tale."

So I did, doing my best to recount every detail and every bit of the conversation between Aleksi and Ioseph. When I finished, I announced, "I don't think Aleksi did it."

"But they found the muriatic acid in his room," Dragan mused.

Valko was stroking the unruly stubble on his chin. "It could have been planted to make Aleksi look guilty. And he could have been killed to keep the truth from coming out when the chiton wore off."

"But we questioned Ioseph," Dragan pointed out. "He knew nothing. There were no hidden plots there. It seems more likely that Aleksi was the killer, and Ioseph, who didn't know, took his extreme action out of misguided loyalty."

"I must inform the king," Valko said, and without another word, he left us.

Dragan stood up slowly and crossed to Valko's desk. "The acid wasn't the only thing that was discovered in Aleksi's chamber." He retrieved a familiar bound leather book.

"Iskra's journal!" My eyes widened as I took it. "So he truly did ransack my room?"

"Or perhaps he had Ioseph do it. I believe you were correct. They were looking for verbenia to keep Teodora from revealing the truth."

"But why take this journal?"

"Perhaps they thought it was your writings, and that it might hold some clue to procuring the herb. I'm not certain," he admitted.

I put it back on the far shelf. "I read the whole thing already. I think it's safer here."

"Very well."

Dragan came to stand at the bookshelf next to me, idly running his fingers along the spines. "There is one other part of your tale that I feel I must address. We haven't had time for all your lessons, with everything that's been going on. But here is one you must heed. Mesmers must avoid the dead and dying. We are far too attractive."

I cocked my head. "What do you mean?"

He looked at me coolly, letting his hand drop. "When the human spirit is loosed from the body at the time of death, there is a moment, before it passes on to the afterlife, when it is lost. Bereft—floating in an unfamiliar sea. Freed from the limitations of the body, the spirit can see Mesmers for what we are. Different. Powerful. In that lonely sea, we are a lifeline."

I stilled. "I knew somehow that I mustn't let him near me. What happens?"

"According to the books, they beseech our help, clinging to us. It is a decidedly unpleasant experience, as you learned firsthand. Some of the oldest records tell legends of a spirit latching on to a Mesmer. Permanently."

Bad enough to have Ioseph's dead spirit grasping and pleading at me. But to be permanently yoked to it? To have that attached to me for all of my days, hooked on to me like a leech—I shuddered. "I'm glad I fled."

"You were wise to follow your instincts. Though you cannot always do so."

I blinked at his words. "Why?"

"You think Aleksi is innocent, don't you?" It wasn't really a question.

I shrugged. "He was so distraught when he spoke of her. He *loved* her. Teodora was speaking the truth when she said so, and what reason would Aleksi have to fool his companion?"

An amused smile twisted Dragan's fine mouth. "Perhaps he was fooling himself. It is often those who love us who present the greatest danger."

I put my hands on my hips. "You think me naive."

He didn't deny it. "It is not a condemnation."

"It feels like it."

Dragan stepped closer, looking down at me, peering into my face as if he could see straight to my soul. His proximity sent a tendril of excitement through me, and I stamped it down like the last embers of a fire. Why did being alone with the man curl my insides with delicious warmth? "You saw Aleksi run. You know he invaded your space to cover his lies. The means of the murder were discovered in his room. *And* you know he lied to his brother for years. Yet you doubt his guilt? Why?"

I struggled to articulate it. "He doesn't seem guilty."

"Is it because he was handsome?" Dragan's amused smile widened until I wanted to smack it off his face. "Handsome men can be villains too."

I looked at my feet. His nearness was addling my thoughts. "Because we can't be sure! With Mesmerism, we know. We see the truth ourselves. But we can't be sure with Aleksi."

"Our abilities are a gift, Adrijana, but they should not supplant the other resources given to us. Men speak lies not just with their oras, but with their words, their deeds, their mannerisms and tells. One does not need to be a Mesmer to spot a liar. It is simply easier. The evidence does not lie. I tell you plainly now—Aleksi is the killer."

My shoulders slumped. "I'd hoped it was one of the Vruks."

Dragan let out a dark laugh. "That would have been easier to bear, but would have meant war."

I thought of the man described in Iskra's journal. "Would the Vruk king not welcome war?"

"Yes," he admitted. "Which is why we must work twice as hard to prevent it." Dragan returned to the chair and settled into it. "Now, Adrijana, I think you should be resting."

I could tell I was being dismissed. "Don't you mean that *you* should be resting?" I raised an eyebrow.

"Yes, I think that too." He chuckled.

I was loath to return to my chamber all alone. Simeon's words still haunted me. His criticism wasn't fair. I hadn't changed, *he* had. He was pulling away just because I was a Mesmer. "Dragan," I began. "Do you... Do you think Mesmers are destined to always be alone?"

His violet eyes fixed on me, as if caressing every feature of my face. And then he held out a hand to me, in invitation.

I placed my hand in his.

"Yes, we are," he said plainly, looking up at me. "But sometimes we have the fortune of being alone... *together.*"

Maybe it was sight of his weakness that made me speak my truth. As if his honesty demanded my own. "I don't think I could do this without you."

He ran his calloused thumb over the back of my hand. "I swear that you won't have to."

# CHAPTER 17

$\mathcal{I}$ stood in the hallway outside the workshop for longer than I cared to admit, loneliness curling my insides. Without Dragan—or even gruff Valko—I was alone in this place. Finally, the hunger in my stomach led me to the dining hall, where I prayed lunch was still happening. I had taxed myself dearly yesterday, and I needed to eat to regain my strength.

When I walked into the hall, every head swiveled toward me. The drone of conversation dimmed, as if my very presence made them want to hold their tongues and swallow their secrets. One soldier even swiped his finger before his eyes, drawing the symbol that supposedly warded off the Mesmers' gaze. How little people actually understood Mesmerism. I had closed my crown node before I'd left my room; I could see nothing more than any ordinary person.

I dropped onto an empty bench, doing my best to ignore the scrutiny. I wouldn't let prejudice drive me into my rooms like a hermit. I had every right to be here. Eventually, conversation resumed, and a servant came with a bowl of porridge sprinkled with nuts and honey, a steaming cup of tea, and a plate of bread and cheese. I attacked the bread and cheese with a vengeance while the porridge cooled.

For the first time here, I felt profoundly alone. I glanced at the front of the room, where Nevena sat by herself at a long table, staring into her tea. As always, Simeon stood behind her and to her right; another guard flanked her left. Was it possible she felt as lonely as I did?

My chewing slowed. Perhaps I should go make amends. I had been dismissive to her during our last encounter. I still understood little of how things worked here, but I was beginning to see. As a Mesmer, I was set apart. As a princess, she was too. Perhaps that would be enough of a common ground.

A shadow fell across the table and I stiffened. The Vruk ambassador, Matija, towered over me. He was without his heavy fur this morning, but beneath his linen tunic, he was built of roping muscle and malice. "Sitting all alone, are you, Mesmer? Where are your Mesmer friends now?"

I did my best to glower at him, squashing my unease. "They're busy with their official duties."

He placed his palms flat on the table before me and leaned in. When he whispered, his breath was hot in my ear. "No one to care for you. No one to come for you. I'd take care, witch. There are many shadowed corners in a place like this."

I drew in a sharp breath. "Are you threatening me?"

"Just concerned for your safety. Their evil eyes can't see you everywhere."

Fury boiled in me. "You'd be surprised. You think your precious verbenia protects you, but—"

"Adrijana!" a welcome voice sounded behind me and I whirled, barely daring to hope. But I wasn't imagining it. It was Georgi, returned from Visoko. His dun-colored karakal stalked at his side, its tails lashing. He drew to a stop beside me, putting a friendly hand on my shoulder. "Are you well?"

The ambassador's blue eyes had narrowed, as sharp as two spears of ice.

"Fine," I bit out, turning back to Matija, buoyed by the presence of a welcome ally. "Matija was just sharing a little Vruk wisdom. Isn't that right?"

Matija spun on his heel and stalked back across the dining hall, taking all my fire with him. Once gone, I felt shaky and weak.

"Are you sure you're all right?" Georgi asked. I found him more handsome in his mud-stained traveling clothes, his cheeks flushed from the cool air, than I had in his royal finery. A few blond strands had escaped from his braids and curled about his temples. "Adrijana?" Ovyato, I'd missed the way he put me at ease. I embraced him. "I'm glad you're back."

When I pulled away, Georgi's emerald eyes were resting on me with a warmth that set my cheeks flaming. "I came as soon as I heard about Aleksi. I rode day and night. I doubt my horse will ever forgive me. But I couldn't let Nevena go through this alone."

"You're a good cousin." I glanced to the head table. Nevena was watching us.

"Come on." Georgi put a hand between my shoulder blades. "Come join us."

"Nevena and I—" I began, but he shook his head.

"I insist." Georgi picked up my tray of food and carried it to the head table, setting it down next to Nevena. She stood and embraced him, burying her face in his chest. A muffled sob reached my ears, and Georgi rocked her gently. "Hush, cousin. All will be well again."

My eyes flicked to Simeon, but he was watching Nevena, his brow wrinkled with worry. Guilt turned my stomach. I should not have spoken so plainly to him, and I should not have given in to the temptation to read his colors. He was right, people were entitled to their secrets. But it unsettled me to think that my best friend had secrets from *me*.

Nevena released Georgi and turned to me, gesturing to the chair next to her. Nevena's hair had been braided anew and she wore a mourning dress of white and silver. Nothing was out of place about her appearance except the haunted expression in her tear-filled eyes. "Please, Adrijana, sit. I've been wanting to speak to you."

I settled into the chair, my tray of half-eaten breakfast growing cold before me.

Georgi pecked a kiss on Nevena's cheek. "I'm going to find Uncle.

I'll see you both later." His easy presence abandoned us, leaving a tense awkwardness.

I cleared my throat. "Your Highness—"

"I fear—"

We started at the same time and then fell silent with nervous laughter.

"You first. Please." I nodded.

"I owe you an apology. For what I asked of you last time."

"Please think nothing of it. I overreacted."

"It's only that, I think I didn't articulate what I meant quite right. It's not that I wanted you to spy for me—"

"Princess, please, it's forgotten—" I insisted, but she held up a hand.

"My father and Valko grew up together. He trusts the Mesmer implicitly. And Dragan..." She let out a little laugh. "Well, Dragan keeps his own counsel. But someday, I will be Queen, and Valko and Dragan will be gone. You might be Prime Mesmer someday, and I only hoped that we could develop the type of relationship my father and Valko have." She looked at me then, her eyes shining betwixt dark lashes, two jewels set against her creamy, lavender skin. "Allies."

I let her words sink in, finding myself slightly awed. I could hardly decide whether I should take my next meal in my room or the dining hall, and Nevena was planning years—decades—into the future.

My gaze flicked to the far side of the room, where Matija and Spirodon sat talking in hushed tones, their shoulders hunched. If Valko and Dragan were gone someday, I would need allies in this place. The princess would make a powerful one.

"I'd like that," I admitted.

"Then it's settled." Nevena took another sip of tea.

I ate a spoonful of porridge. How did one go about becoming allies? Friends? It had been so long since I'd had to make a friend. What did one talk about?

"This is her seat, you know." Nevena patted the chair.

"Your mother?"

She inclined her head against the hard back. "Just days ago, we were all here. Mother, Father, Uncle. Now it's just me."

A ripple of unease undulated through me. How much did she know about her uncle? About what had happened on the deck of the Firebird? I had to assume the Mesmers and the king had told her everything. "I lost my mother too." Thoughts of Papa welled to the surface. At least I still had him, if I could find a way to see past his lies.

She turned to regard me. "Yes, when you were young, Simeon said."

"I know it's not the same...but I understand a bit of what you're going through."

"Thank you." She turned back to her breakfast. She took a bite of the egg dish before her. "My father is closing the investigation into my mother's death. He says we need to put the ugliness behind us."

"So he is certain Prince Aleksi is responsible?" I asked.

She looked sidelong at me. "The Mesmers assure him that Aleksi is the culprit."

"The evidence does point to him."

"But you are not convinced. I can hear it in your voice. Why?"

I hesitated. Dragan's logic was sound; my doubt was no more than a lingering feeling. "I'm not sure I can articulate it. He did not seem guilty to me, at the end. I'm not sure you should put much stock in my gut feeling."

"Even when my gut tells me the same thing?"

I eyed the Vruk ambassadors. Matija was glaring our way. "I can think of others with far more to gain from taking out one of Adrjssia's monarchs. But what I do not understand, if you don't mind me saying, is why your mother? She is not in line for the throne, correct? If the Vruks sought the throne..." I trailed off.

"Why not assassinate me?" Nevena finished.

I winced. "I'm sorry. I didn't mean to suggest such an ugly thing."

"It is an ugly truth I've lived with ever since I was four years old and realized that other children's tutors don't carry swords." Nevena pursed her lips. "Ever since my brother died, King Andrej has been writing to my father, suggesting a strategic alliance between his son, Prince Elian, and myself."

"A marriage? Would your father agree to that?"

Nevena put her fork down and pushed her plate away. "He never has. But I think I have begun to see the outline of their plot. With my mother's death, supposedly at Aleksi's hand, I have lost two protectors, and my Durvo relatives are outraged on my mother's behalf. They were our closest allies for the last twenty years, and now a wedge has been driven between us. It was very cleverly done, really."

I was beginning to make sense of it as well. "King Andrej might hope that by rendering you and your father vulnerable, your father would assent to a strategic alliance with the Vruks."

"Thankfully, my father is not yet convinced. He remembers Andrej's cruelty from the war. By all accounts, his son is not so bad, but Father swears he will never yolk me to that family while Andrej lives. When a wolf is hounding your flock, you do not invite him in for supper, unless you yourself want to be on the menu."

I chuckled. "So if it is a Vruk plot, it has failed."

Nevena sighed. "Not in all respects. I do feel that I am more alone than I've ever been."

"Not alone. You have Georgi. And Simeon. And me. Your father and his Mesmers may have given up the search for your mother's killer, but we will not."

To my surprise, Nevena took my hand under the table and gave it a squeeze. "The idea lifts my spirits. We may be an unlikely company, much underestimated. But I think, perhaps, that is exactly what it will take to outmaneuver the Vruks."

We both turned to Spirodon and Matija and found them looking back at us, open hostility in their eyes. I smiled grimly. "Then that's exactly what we'll do."

# CHAPTER 18

The days shortened as the Windy Season began to yield its domain. Zamo Idvo, the god of winter, brought the season's smothering mist sweeping over the city of Selojia, blinding us all. I couldn't even see the sea from my window. It was like living inside a cloud.

As was custom in the palace, Hristina undid the cascade of braids from my hair and threaded tiny bells into my curls, so the soft chime of gentle melody accompanied my every movement.

I spent my days in the Mesmer workshop, reading history or training with Dragan and Valko. Not a morning went by in which Valko didn't seem surprised and put off that I was still there, but my time with Dragan more than made up for it. He was a patient teacher and brilliant Mesmer, though it was becoming increasingly clear to me that the two of them disagreed on nearly everything. Valko thought Dragan's focus on Projection was too risky; Dragan thought Valko's preoccupation with theoretical learning was too pedantic. I learned to make myself scarce when they really butted heads.

The only thing they agreed on was that I should not yet be taught Compulsion. It was what the Mesmers called it when they manipulated a person's thoughts or emotions, and they deemed it too dangerous, too prone to misuse. Naturally, their proscription only made me more determined to seek out the knowledge myself. I had no desire to rob anyone of their free will, but if Iskra's journal and the continued hatred of the Vruk ambassadors had taught me anything, it was that the world was not a safe place for a Mesmer. I needed every arrow in my magical quiver.

To teach myself to Compel, I needed instruction on the method and a willing victim. The first I found in the Mesmers' massive library, buried inside a weighty tome. The second I found in Georgi.

While my days were spent in the Mesmer workshop, I spent most of my evenings with Nevena, Georgi, and sometimes Simeon, when he was off duty. It seemed my old friend had mostly forgiven me for my earlier overreach, and I accepted it gratefully. Nevena had been heavy with grief for weeks, but Georgi was a balm for all of us—his ever-present good spirits were impossible to resist. We drank sweet Lozian wine in Nevena's sitting room, cuddled her and Georgi's karakals, and played heated games of Royals with Nevena's illuminated card deck. Occasionally, we talked politics, speculating on the news out of West Adrjssia, but relations had been strangely quiet since Prince Aleksi's death, other than unsubstantiated rumors about the Vruk para-dynasts calling their warriors together. Sometimes, we ventured out of the palace into Selojia, strolling along the docks beneath the wings of the weeping gulls or exploring the tangled market streets in the center of town.

I didn't need the aid of my crown node to tell that Georgi was still sweet on me, and admittedly, I found his attentions quite flattering. He was handsome and funny and kind, but something held me back from encouraging anything more than a friendship between us. I had no doubt that that something was Dragan Vulpe.

But nevertheless, I suspected that Georgi's affections would make him a particularly amenable subject for my experiments, and I was not above such a mild exploitation. Georgi was walking me back to my room when I blurted out my proposition out to him. "Do you think I might practice on you?"

He halted, a curiously hopeful expression on his face. His karakal,

Brisko, lashed his tails at the delay. "Whatever would you need to practice, Jana?"

My face heated as I realized how it had sounded. "My Mesmerism, of course."

He caught up with me, fighting a smile, the bells in his hair seeming to laugh at me. "Of course."

I whacked his arm with the back of my hand. "My lord, I cannot believe you thought me so bold."

He laughed. "A man can dream."

I shook my head. "So is that a *yes*?"

"Whatever you need, Adrijana, I am your humble servant."

"I was hoping you'd say that."

"What *do* you need?" We had arrived at my room, and he stood a few respectful feet away.

I chewed my lip. I couldn't practice in the workshop, where Dragan or Valko might see, and there were few truly private spots in the palace. I opened my door and motioned my head inside. "Come on."

Georgi put a hand to his heart as he followed, though a devious smile spread wide across his face. "Already, this task seems onerous. I'm having second thoughts."

I rolled my eyes as I shut the door behind him and his karakal. "Don't get any ideas."

"I will get only the ideas you put in my head." Georgi settled into one of the chairs by the fireplace without invitation. "That is what we are practicing, is it not?"

I put another log on the fire and poked at it to stoke it a bit higher. "How did you know?"

"You've mentioned your displeasure at the Mesmers' incomplete education a time or two, and you don't seem the type to let sleeping karakals lie."

I dropped into the other chair. Brisko had already curled up in a ball before the fire. "Are my thoughts so plain?"

"Only to someone paying attention." His eyes seemed to reflect the intensity of the firelight for a moment, but then he went on. "Besides, we mere mortals are not completely hopeless at understanding human motivations."

"True." I laughed.

Georgi straightened in his chair. "All right. What do I do?"

I pulled my chair in closer, facing his. "Based on my reading, we will need to make eye contact. And then, whatever node I wish to Compel, I connect to my own. And sort of conform your thoughts, or emotions, or desires, to my own. It's all a little vague in the book. That's why I want to practice." I cleared my throat and locked on to Georgi's emerald eyes. They were quite lovely, with flecks of gold around his irises and crinkles at the corners from his ever-present smile.

"So, I just have to sit here and look at you? Sounds like I got the better end of this lesson."

I shook my head to hide my pleasure at his words. Georgi was a far more suitable candidate for my affections than Dragan. If only I could get my own yearnings to cooperate.

"Let's start with emotion. It's what I've always been most comfortable with."

"All right. How will you make me feel?"

"Happy?"

"I'm not sure that will help your practice much."

"Why?"

"Because I'm already happy."

"You're incorrigible. All right. Fearful, then."

"Your eyes really are mesmerizing, Adrijana," Georgi said lightly.

A pleasant warmth nestled itself in my chest. "Shh. I have to concentrate."

I opened my crown node and took in Georgi's colors. The pink around his ears had grown stronger and was mirrored by a swirling rose-colored mass in the center of his chest. My own heart skipped a beat. He truly cared for me.

But the realization made me I hesitate, my stomach clenching. This felt too intimate, too raw. I was taking advantage of Georgi's feelings for me to force him to bare his soul even more. This was the type of manipulation Mesmers were hated for. "Maybe this was a bad idea." I looked away, breaking the eye contact between us.

"Adrijana." Georgi reached out and gently took my chin, turning my head to meet his gaze once again. "I have no secrets from you. I'm here of my own free will."

"You're sure?"

"I'm sure."

"Okay." I turned my attention back to his heart node and the emotions being emitted there. I was working on fear. How to make him fear?

It was challenging, to hold his gaze and fix my efforts on the area of his heart, but I pushed my own ora out so it grew larger and enveloped his own, as the book said.

"I feel something..." Georgi said. "Nervous. You're nervous. And...excited."

I frowned, my cheeks growing hot. This *was* too intimate. "I think I'm doing it wrong. You're not supposed to feel what I'm feeling."

"Well, now *I'm* feeling nervous."

I scrutinized his colors. There was a subtle purple smear over his stomach—the place where I usually saw the green of nervousness. Did that mean something? The only other time I'd ever seen purple in someone's ora had been with Aleksi's companion Ioseph, right before he'd stabbed the prince.

"Do you think I'm making you nervous? Am I doing it?"

"Try another."

I imagined the dark brown of fear heavy about my own brows. Pressing, sucking.

And the color appeared in his ora as well. Except again—streaked with purple.

"Oh, yes, you're definitely doing it." Georgi let out a shaky laugh. "I have goosebumps all over, and a chill is running up my spine. I'd like it to stop now, please."

I thought of the golden glow of happiness, nestled below my bosom. And his colors reacted, much faster this time.

Georgi exhaled a sigh of relief. "That's better. Wow, I feel like it's a feast-day morn and I'm coming down to piles of gifts."

I let out a delighted laugh. "I can't believe it's working!"

"Are you surprised? You're a natural." Georgi smiled at me with such plain adoration that my own heart fluttered. He was good to me. I was infinitely comfortable in his presence. Would it be so bad to explore where things went with him? Give him a chance? A curl of desire wended through me as an image of him kissing me flitted through my mind's eye. I bet he would be an excellent kisser.

But no, it wasn't a good idea, I knew that. Not until I found a way to truly eliminate my feelings for Dragan. I blinked to banish the thought, but too late. For Georgi was surging forward, his body between my knees, his hands on my cheeks, his lips to mine.

My shock and good sense yielded quickly. Georgi tasted sweet, like the rose cardamom tea we'd been drinking, and his lips were as soft as silk yet moved with steadfast determination. I found my own hands curling in his hair with a soft ring of bells. The sensation of kissing him was objectively pleasant, but it did not further stir the desire within me. I knew then, with a tinge of disappointment, that Georgi was not for me.

I put my hands on his shoulders and gently pushed him back. But he would not move. If anything, he surged forward, his mouth hard against mine, one hand twisting into my hair.

Surprise grew to alarm as I pushed harder against him, to no avail. His tongue invaded my mouth, and I struggled to make sense of what was happening. This wasn't Georgi! Something was wrong.

My heart roared into a staccato panic, and I opened my eyes as I struggled to focus amongst the onslaught. His hand was roving roughly over my breast, down to my waist. Our oras were tangled, and I could see little beyond flaming red of his passion—so I went deeper. I delved into my sacral node and saw the problem at once— his desire was a twisted mass of violet appetite. Somehow, I had twisted him, perverted his desires. I needed to re-Compel him.

With all my might, I seized his face in one hand, pressed his chest with the other, and shoved him away. I held his chin in a vise grip, my fingernails digging into his flesh, and locked eyes with him. Frantically, I quenched his desire, pulling it out at the roots.

Georgi fell back on the floor, his green eyes dazed, his chest heaving. His karakal yowled, jumping into Georgi's lap and snarling at me, its hackles raised.

Tears blurred my vision as I wiped my mouth with a shaking hand. What had I done? Somehow, I had broken the kindest, most decent man in Selojia. "Georgi? Can you hear me? Are you all right?"

Georgi shook his head slowly as he lay a comforting hand on Brisko's back. "What—What happened?" He squeezed his eyes shut and blinked rapidly. He looked up, and when he saw my tears, the color drained from his face. "Ovyato help me, did I—Adrijana, did I hurt you?" He set Brisko aside, kneeling before me. He reached out, but then drew his hands back. Afraid to touch me.

I shook my head, my chest too tight to take a full breath. "No. I fear I hurt you. I never should have toyed with my magic. You're not a test subject, you're a person, and you've been the kindest person—" My voice cracked. I still didn't understand what had happened. Our oras had been joined, and my own fleeting desire had what, ignited his? By proximity to just a flash of impulse, he'd been driven near mad? No wonder Dragan and Valko hadn't trusted this method to me. I was a walking disaster.

"Do you think you will be all right?" I asked.

Georgi used the arm of the chair to maneuver himself to his feet. "In body, yes. But I have wronged you grievously, Adrijana. How can I ever forgive myself for touching you with such force?" He turned away, his face in his hands.

"It wasn't you. It was my Mesmerism gone wrong." I tugged on his arm, trying to turn him. "Please, don't blame yourself."

"I think I should turn myself in."

"For what? You did nothing wrong."

Georgi still wouldn't look at me. "Forcing oneself on a woman is a crime in Adrjssia. I'm a danger."

"You're not listening." I wiped my eyes with exasperation. This was beyond me to fix. I wouldn't risk Compelling him further, in case something went even more awry. I needed help. Help that I really did not want to ask for. I took his hand. "Please, Georgi. Tell no one. Let us sleep, and we will speak of this in the morning. Please? Promise me? You won't tell anyone until we talk tomorrow? Don't anything drastic."

Georgi let out a sigh and pulled his hand from mine. "Very well." Without another look, Georgi left my chamber, leaving me alone with the certainty that I had wronged him deeply and irrevocably.

# CHAPTER 19

*S*leep eluded me that night. I perched in the window seat, looking out through my tears into the emptiness of the cold, misty night. I was overcome by the urge to Project to Georgi's room to check on him, but I resisted. I had invaded his privacy enough.

Tomorrow, I would tell Dragan everything. He would help me set it right—fix whatever I had damaged in Georgi's ora. I couldn't expel the heavy weight that had nestled in my chest. What if I'd done something to permanently damage Georgi? He was a dear friend, and this was how I'd repaid him? The prejudices against Mesmers took on new meaning for me. How terrifying, to know that you were vulnerable to such an invasion, that your mind and body could be taken over by another's whims. I hadn't had any ill intent, yet I'd still caused harm. And I would have to live with that.

I thought of Papa, and a different kind of guilt overwhelmed me. I had been in Selojia three months, and I hadn't written him one letter. He had been doing what he thought was right, too. If it was so easy for my Mesmerism to go astray now, how much wilder would it have been as a child? I had faint memories of being willful or petulant, and the thought of combining a child's tantrums with the power to Compel was chilling. Was it something innate? It hadn't taken much training for me to manage it, however horribly I'd botched it. Perhaps if Mama had lived, she would have known how to control a Mesmer child. But verbenia must have seemed like the only option for Papa, other than turning me in to the Royal Mesmers for training. And he'd already lost Mama, and my little sister, Arabel.

I rifled through the little desk and found paper, ink, and a quill. I stared at the blank page for a long while before penning a simple note.

*Dear Papa-*

*I am well. My training is progressing, and I am feeling more at home here in Selojia. Simeon is very busy with his duties, but we enjoy some time together. I think I am beginning to understand why you did what you did. I think I will forgive you, in time. Perhaps you could come for the Spring Equinox Festival. I would like to see you.*

*Love, Jana*

* * *

THE WEAK LIGHT of dawn washed out the colors in my room, rendering it in faded grayscale. I splashed water on my face and changed into a fresh dress, then went to the workshop to wait for Dragan.

To my surprise, I found him asleep on the leather sofa by the fire-place, a leather-bound book tented over his chest. I paused for a moment before waking him, breathing in the serenity of the scene. He looked younger when sleeping, his golden curls falling over his fore-head. A flock of butterflies swooped and dipped through my stomach, and I knew I had been right to keep Georgi at bay. For better or worse, I had feelings for Dragan. I thought, maybe even, that I was in love with him.

I couldn't identify what exactly drew me to him—if it was his magic or his enigmatic confidence, the lightning spark of his mind or the rugged contours of his face that I longed to run my fingertips across—but I was well and surely caught.

"Are you going to stand there all day, or are you going to speak?"

Dragan stretched languidly, revealing a band of lean flesh beneath the hem of his shirt.

My cheeks heated. "I was debating whether or not to wake you." *Fool girl.*

"Well, I am awake, so you may put your great debate to rest." He sat up on the sofa, rubbing his face. "Put some tea on?"

Grateful for something to do to delay the humiliating admission I was dreading, I busied myself in lighting the fire in the little stove and putting the kettle on top. Dragan disappeared and when he returned, he had changed his shirt, tucked it in, and combed his hair. He once again looked the role of my aloof mentor. "You're up early, Adrijana. Are you well?"

I sat on the opposite couch and tucked my hands under my thighs to keep them from shaking. "Not really. I've done something, and I need your help to undo it."

Dragan raised an eyebrow. "This sounds good."

I squeezed my eyes shut. "It's not." I sucked in a deep breath. "I practiced my Compulsion on Georgi and something went wrong and I fear I've broken him."

When I looked at Dragan, his other eyebrow had raised to join the first.

"You and Valko said it was too dangerous and prone to misuse and I value your counsel, but I felt I needed to know how. For defensive purposes."

"Do you feel unsafe here?"

"The Vruk ambassadors leer and threaten, but they aren't the only ones who hate Mesmers. Everyone does. The servants mark across their eyes to ward against me, and I hear their whispers, calling me a witch."

"They are right to be afraid of Mesmerism misused, Adrijana," Dragan said severely. "I thought we impressed upon you the importance of ethical limits on the use of our powers."

"You did. You have. And I will take whatever punishment I deserve for disobeying. But please, just help me fix Georgi."

"Of course. What is his condition?"

I swallowed, my mortification stealing the words from me. How could I explain what had happened? I would sound like the most foolish of girls, playing with hearts and things she couldn't understand.

"I cannot help if you won't tell me."

I put my hands over my eyes and quickly recounted what had happened, wishing beyond wish that the ground would swallow me up for eternity.

When I had finished, I peeked through my fingers at Dragan. His lips were pressed together, as if he were holding back a smile.

"What? Say something. I beg you."

"It does not sound as if Georgi is broken, as you say. Did you work with his thoughts at all? His cranial node?"

"No."

"It is not uncommon for the desires of men to grow out of control, especially young men. They are easily influenced. It sounds like you did exactly what you needed to by pulling the swelled desire from him. Stopping it in its tracks."

"But he was beside himself! He wanted to turn himself in. He thought it was his fault."

Dragan rolled his eyes. "I suppose that will not do. We do not want word of this mishap to spread as the residents of the palace are just growing comfortable with your presence among us."

"What can be done?"

"I can take the memories from him, so it's like it never happened."

I frowned. "That doesn't seem right."

"Leave it alone or make him forget. Those are your choices as I see them."

My shoulders slumped. I didn't want misplaced guilt plaguing Georgi, or awkwardness between us. "Very well."

Dragan stood and offered me his hand. "Let us go then."

"Now?"

"Unless you fancy him telling a few people first?"

I huffed and placed my hand in his. His fingers lingered on mine for a few seconds longer than I thought necessary. As I followed him, I couldn't help but overanalyze it. Surely, he saw me only as a pupil, an ally. Though sometimes, I caught him looking at me when he probably thought I couldn't see. Or he touched me when it wasn't strictly necessary. But it could all have been my imagination. It likely was. Wishful thinking.

When I caught myself too far down the road of such a daydream, I had only to imagine what Valko would say if he learned of my foolish crush—his disgust, his dismissal. I'd worked hard to gain a shred of respect from him—the thought of losing it was all I needed to douse my pesky emotions with a cold bucket of reality.

Dragan rapped on Georgi's door, and it was a moment before he opened it. The sight of Georgi's bleary-eyed face sent another wave of wretchedness through me. How I wished I could undo the events of last night and return to the easy friendship between us. I feared things would never be the same. Dragan could make Georgi forget, but not me. I'd always know what I'd done.

"Adrijana asked me to check on you, after what happened last night. Can we come inside?"

Georgi stepped aside, but his karakal stood inside the room hissing, with its back arched like a bow.

Dragan ignored the creature, sidestepping around it and closing the door.

"Brisko—" I knelt and reached out, but the karakal swatted at me, and I drew my hand back.

"He's a little shaken this morning," Georgi said. "As am I."

I stood with my arms crossed as Dragan sat down across from Georgi. "I'm just going to check your nodes, to make sure you are well. Would you mind meeting my eyes?"

Georgi obliged.

Dragan leaned forward slightly. "Hmm. Very good." He clapped Georgi on the shoulder and then stood. "You are quite well, my friend. All is how it should be."

Georgi looked from Dragan to me with a bit of a dazed expression. "What—What are you doing here?"

"Adrijana asked me to check on you; you were suffering from a headache. You're right as rain, though. Eat a hearty breakfast today."

My mouth dropped open and I quickly closed it. Had Dragan already done it? I opened my crown node and found the thoughts swirling around Georgi's head smeared with purple. What I had come to recognize as the telltale sign of a Mesmer's influence.

Georgi blinked several times and stood. "Adrijana, are we still going to the market with Nevena today?"

I pasted on a smile. "Absolutely."

"I'll see you soon then."

Dragan ushered me outside and closed the door. I stood, stunned. "You did that so quickly. How—"

"Years of practice."

"It was such a simple thing, for you to steal his memory." I shook my head, unnerved.

"Don't forget you asked it of me, Adrijana." Dragan began walking away.

I jogged after him. "So he is well? Everything else? His sacral node? I didn't damage it?"

"He is well, though I fear his infatuation with you has been ripped out at the root. You'll find him a suitor no longer."

Oh. An unexpected pang of loss struck me. It had felt nice to be admired. "It's for the best. I didn't feel the same." My voice was quiet.

Dragan shot me a sidelong glance. "The only thing harder than being a Mesmer is being a Mesmer in love. Love is built on trust, and with Mesmers and those who cannot see...there can be no trust. They will always doubt us."

"Can a Mesmer not love another Mesmer?" The words were out of my mouth before I could stop them.

He looked straight ahead. "Yes. If you are lucky enough to find it. But our people have been short on luck these past decades."

I said nothing, trying to digest any hidden meaning to the words.

Dragan went on. "And as much as Valko and I tried to make it work, we just weren't compatible."

My head swiveled his way with amazement, and I found a hint of a smile on his face. "You jest!"

Dragan laughed, a low rumble that made my insides quiver. "Yes, Adrijana, I jest."

"I think that's the first joke you've ever told me."

"Someone needed to lighten the mood."

We had reached the doors of the Mesmer workshop. I needed to head back to my room to get my cloak for my outing with Nevena and Georgi today. "Thank you for your help. Truly."

He inclined his head. "I'm always on your side. You can trust me with anything." He turned to go and I grabbed his sleeve. "Wait. I have one more question. When I see purple in a person's ora—it means they've been Compelled, doesn't it?"

"Yes."

"Then you should know: Ioseph's thoughts were smeared with purple, right before he plunged the knife into Prince Aleksi."

Dragan stood frozen, looking at me. A minute passed before he finally blinked. "You are certain?" The question was quiet. "You left it out of your report to us."

"I didn't know the import. Dragan, I'm certain. Does that mean—"

"Yes," he said, interrupting me. "It means a Mesmer wanted to silence Prince Aleksi. And unless there is an unknown Mesmer working in the palace…then there are only three suspects."

Dragan. Valko. Or me.

# CHAPTER 20

*M*y trip into town with Nevena, Georgi, and Simeon was a balm to my guilt. Georgi was as bright and cheerful as ever, though not quite as attentive to me, and it was easy to pretend that the events of last night had never occurred. It made me wonder, though, how many other things the Mesmers had erased.

I mailed my letter to Papa and we strolled through the market, haggling over silks and Durvo chestnuts and drinking spiced plum wine.

No amount of pleasant conversation and shopping, however, could calm my unease over the revelation of my conversation with Dragan. Could one of my two mentors have truly influenced the prince's companion—forced him unwittingly to kill? For what purpose? Aleksi's death only served to further weaken the Tsarian royal family in the eyes of the country, especially our enemies, the Vruks. There had to be another explanation for the Compulsion I'd seen in Ioseph's ora. I had only to find it.

I was so lost in thought on my way back to my room that I missed it at first. The mist. I drew in a shocked breath when it finally registered what I was seeing. I'd almost forgotten about it. Mist shrouded everything now. It hung on the trees and swirled at the windows. But this mist was different. It was inside the palace. And it was moving—as if it had a purpose. A mind. Perhaps, an answer?

Excitement and dread blazed to life inside of me. One of my first nights in this place, the mist had led me to Aleksi and Teodora arguing. It had given me the initial clue that had helped us piece together some of the mystery surrounding the queen's death.

I frowned, even as I followed the mist down the quiet corridors. It had been so long. Why now? Where could the mist possibly have been leading me?

The path it floated was a familiar one. We were heading toward the Mesmer's workshop, the nearby wing where Valko and Dragan kept their quarters. A thrill vibrated through me at the thought of knocking on Dragan's door. I shoved the fantasy down ruthlessly as a chill came over me. Dragan's words rose in my mind, unbidden. *"Unless there is an unknown Mesmer working in the palace...there are only three suspects..."*

The murmur of voices had me flattening myself against the wall before I turned the corner. I crouched down and risked a glance. My eyes flew open in shock.

One of the Vruk ambassadors—Spirodon—was standing before the door the workshop. Talking to Valko.

What could that man possibly want with a Mesmer? They hated our kind.

I longed to Project down the hall to hear better, but Valko could see me. I did my best to still my breath and listen.

I couldn't make out anything more than snatches of conversation.

"Told you—"

"—said the king..."

I ground my teeth in frustration. I needed to get closer. The mist had brought me here for a reason. There was a servants' hallway at the end of this hall. Perhaps I could hide in there and Project—

My thoughts were interrupted by the sound of heavy boots approaching from behind me.

I scrambled to my feet and darted down the hallway, toward the servants' door. I just glimpsed the figure coming my way as I slipped into the servants' hallway. Matija. Come to join Spirodon.

Fear curdled my stomach as I paused on the landing above the stairs. The cursed bells in my hair jangled softly with the movement of my ragged breath, the sound deafening in the quiet corridor. Even if Matija hadn't seem me, he must have heard me. I struggled to hold perfectly still so no stray chime would give me away.

I sent up a prayer to Ovyato that Matija had missed my presence. That Spiridon had finished his conversation with Valko, and the both of them were returning to their quarters. They'd pass by and I'd be able to let myself out and get back to my room unnoticed. There was clearly more going on here, but I wasn't going to be able to find out tonight—

The door swung open. Spirodon's bulk filled the doorway.

I froze, pressed into the corner.

His blue eyes fixed on mine. For a moment, he was frozen too. Surprised.

It was the only chance I'd get. I ran for the stairs.

His hand closed around my wrist like a shackle and I was jerked backward, my shoulder groaning in protest. He slammed me against the wall, his forearm like an iron bar across my throat. "Not so fast," he growled.

Matija filed in behind Spirodon and the door swung closed, darkening the alcove. They filled the space—muscles and steel and menace.

"I thought I saw a little Mesmer mouse trying to scurry away." Matija sneered. His features looked jagged in the dark, but his eyes glowed, as if lit by some unearthly hatred. "We've been watching you, witch. Waiting for our chance. Now Zamo Idvo has blessed us."

"What did you hear?" Spirodon asked.

"Nothing." I gasped. "I was coming to the workshop, and I didn't want to cross paths with you." I fought through the terror that threatened to sweep me under. All that Valko and Dragan had taught me, all I'd learned about my power, and yet I was still helpless against men like these. I couldn't use any of my tricks—calm their emotions or plant a stray thought in their heads. Not against men who drank verbenia with their morning tea so it filled their veins. Or tattooed the stuff into their very skin. Matija's markings looked ghoulish in the dark of this corner. "Release me at once," I spit at them, my voice gravely beneath the pressure of Spirodon's forearm.

They exchanged a gleeful look.

"Do you know, little mouse," Matija said, "what is the source of your power?"

I stilled. What was he talking about? The crown node?

Matija leaned in close and ran his thumb over one of my eyelids. I tried to jerk away, but he caught my chin in his other hand. "These eyes." His thumb dug in harder. "During the war, there was a price on Mesmer eyes. One violet eye was worth ten gold pieces."

"Stop it!" I cried as panic overtook me. I thrashed against him.

A dark chuckle. The pressure loosened and my knees went weak. For a moment, I was grateful for Spirodon's arm holding me up.

Matija continued. "All the Mesmers in West Adrjssia have already lost their eyes. It's been so long since our king has enjoyed such a prize. His dagger is known as the Shadow-Bringer, for the number of purple eyes it has cut out. So many that it's absorbed their power. Anyone who wields it can see just as you can."

His twisted threat rang of truth—the truth I'd read in the pages of Iskra's journal. Through she'd never mentioned anything about a dagger absorbing the power of Mesmer eyes. Yet how could she have? She'd left the journal behind when she'd traveled into Vruk territory.

"We could take her." Matija turned to Spirodon, who had remained mostly silent. "We could ride tonight. The king would be pleased."

"You can't take me anywhere," I managed through my stifling panic. "I'm a Royal Mesmer."

"Put a little verbenia in you and you're no one." Matija pulled a leather pouch off his belt and reached inside.

I recognized the scent of verbenia. Once, that smell had meant safety. Weeding with Papa in the field. Hanging boughs to dry from the rafters in the shed. Sprinkling it on a warm meal, to keep the headaches at bay. Now I knew that if they got that herb in me, I'd be finished. At their mercy.

So I did the only thing I could think of. I Projected.

My body went slack as my spirit lifted free. The absence of my body's physical panic was a blessed relief—my mind cleared.

"What the hell?" Spirodon caught me, letting my body slump against the wall.

They both stood back for a moment. "Is it a trick?" Spirodon asked.

I weighed my options and found them greatly lacking. When Aleksi had been trying to escape, Dragan had managed to grasp a sword and use it to cut the lines on the Firebird. It was the only thing I could think of—I needed that power now. I knew it was dangerous— Dragan had been ill afterward. But if I didn't do something, over-taxing myself would be the very least of my concerns.

Matija had a knife in his belt, and I focused on it. I closed my hand around it, but it went right through. I growled in frustration. I didn't have much time.

"What should we do?" Spirodon asked.

"I can think of one something," Matija replied. The tone in his voice made me look up sharply.

His eyes were fixed on me. His hands went to his belt and he started to unbuckle it.

Horror coursed through me, followed by a roar of righteous fury. I seized the knife and my fingers closed around the leather handle. I slashed at Matija, just catching him across his cheek.

"By Zamo!" Spirodon and Matija both backed away from the floating knife. The steep staircase descended behind them. I surged forward, and with every ounce of focus I could muster, I shoved.

They both tumbled down the stairs, head over heels. I might have just killed them, but I didn't care. I'd bought myself a moment.

I dove back into my body, the knife clattering to the floor next to me. My head exploded in pain as I retook my physical form. My stomach churned and I tasted bile. I scrabbled for the knife hilt and then staggered to my feet.

The Vruks were groaning from the bottom of the stairs. They were alive. And no doubt furious.

I lurched out through the door back into the hallway.

My vision swam as I felt my way along the corridor, using the wall for support. I moved as fast as I could, but I could hear them behind me. The door to the servants' hallway crashed open.

A whimper escaped me and I stumbled into a run. Dragan's door stood at the end of the hallway like a beacon. I threw myself against it, pounding with my fist. I tried the knob, but it was locked. "Dragan!" I screamed, glancing over my shoulder.

"You bitch!" Matija howled as he staggered toward me. Spirodon was limping behind him, a sword in his hand.

"Dragan!" I pounded again with all my might and then turned back to face the Vruks. My back was to the door, Matija's knife tight in my fist. If this was my time, I wasn't going to go down without a fight.

I raised the knife in my hand—

The door opened behind me, and I tumbled inside.

# CHAPTER 21

*T*he Vruk warriors came to a skidding halt.

Dragan stood between me and the ambassadors, barring the doorway with his presence. His tone was biting. "I suggest you move along."

Matija gave him a shark-like grin. A line of blood ran down the sharp angle of his cheek. "Just having a bit of fun."

"Find your fun elsewhere. And do not forget that this young woman is under the protection of the king."

"The king can't even keep his brother from plowing his wife. Not sure his protection is worth much," Matija shot back.

"Be gone, or I will remove you forcefully." Dragan's voice was calm.

Spirodon put a hand on Matija's shoulder and tugged him back.

Matija's ice-chip irises turned to me. "Goodbye, little mouse. Watch where you scurry."

Dragan stood in the doorway until they disappeared around the corner. Then he slammed the door with such force that I jumped.

"Wretched men," he muttered, taking a long breath in through his nose. He turned to me, crouching down. "Are you all right?"

I shook my head and the infernal bells in my hair tinkled. My throat was thick with tears and I knew if I spoke, the dam would burst. He took my shaking hands in his and pulled me to my feet. My legs buckled, as my head spun again.

I let him help me to a chair by the fireplace, let him place a glass of liquor in my numb hands. I took a sip. It was bitter and tasted of anise. The heat of the alcohol burned some of the shock off, but still I felt hot and cold, woozy and weak.

Dragan sat down in the other chair with a glass of his own. He didn't rush me. As if he knew that I would tell him in my own time.

Perhaps five minutes passed before I was ready to speak. "I saw it again," I croaked. I tipped my head back in the chair, fighting exhaustion. Seizing the dagger in Projected form had sapped more of my energy than I could understand.

Dragan cocked his head.

"The white mist. The mist I saw the night Teodora and…Aleksi were arguing." I wasn't sure why it was hard to say the dead prince's name. The image of Ioseph's haunted spectral face flashed through my mind and I squeezed my eyes shut.

"Did it show you something again?"

I found myself hesitating. Valko and Dragan disagreed on many things, but there was still an implicit alliance between them. Between them and me. We were three set apart here. Necessity bade us to trust each other. But I couldn't deny what I'd seen. Valko had been having a clandestine conversation with Spirodon. If Valko was up to something, if he'd been the Mesmer who had a hand in the queen's death… it changed everything. I had to tell Dragan what I'd seen. "Spirodon was at Valko's door. Speaking in hushed tones."

Dragan sat very still, but for one index finger tapping the side of his glass. "Curious."

"Do you know why he was there?"

The crackle of the fire filled the silence between us, together with the gentle sound of the bells in my hair as I slowly adjusted in my chair.

It appeared it was Dragan's turn for reticence. Finally, he spoke. "No. Did you hear their conversation?"

"It was too quiet. Do you think…?" I couldn't voice my treasonous thought. I didn't particularly like Valko, but I had come to respect him. I didn't want him to be working with the Vruks. Betraying the king he'd walked alongside since boyhood. Perhaps the Vruks were manipulating him somehow. Though, Valko didn't seem like a man easily manipulated. Blackmail perhaps?

"I'm sure there's an explanation. I'll get to the bottom of it. I would ask you to not investigate on your own."

I was too shaken to protest, so I gave a weak nod. "Why does the king let them stay here?"

Dragan's handsome features softened in sympathy. "You know the treaty required the exchange of ambassadors. In the hope that open communication would prevent further bloodshed. But they're just bullies, Adrijana. They have no real power here…so they do what they can to intimidate."

I looked into the swirl of liquid in my glass, trying to keep the memories at bay. Spirodon's arm at my throat, Matija's thumb pressing into my eye. The man unbuckling his belt. "It felt like more than that."

"Of course." He shook his head. "Of course. I wasn't there. My wishful thinking doesn't help keep you safe."

"Wishful thinking?"

"I don't want to believe they would really have hurt you, because of what it would mean."

"What would it mean?"

"That the peace between us is little more than an echo."

"They said…they were going to take my eyes." I raised the glass to my lips and drained it all in a shaky swallow. "I thought—I didn't know it was done anymore."

Dragan retrieved the bottle from the mantel and refilled his glass. I held out mine and he refilled that, too.

He stood at the mantel for a moment, one hand braced, his head hanging low. The firelight silhouetted the long, lean lines of him. My breath caught. As much time as I spent around him, I was still sometimes struck mute by his presence.

"The treatment of Mesmers in West Adrjssia is inhumane. Andrej was merciless then, and rumors say that time has only twisted him more. King Petar never should have agreed to the Treaty. He never should have handed us over like that. We all paid for the crimes of a few."

Curiosity overcame me. I had never heard Dragan criticize the king outright. But he would have been a child when the war broke out. I knew he was Lozian, and that he'd made it here somehow despite the Ostrov clan closing its borders. Hristina had given me that much of the tale, at least.

"Will you tell me your story? How you came to be here? Also, are you going to eat that?" My stomach was rumbling like a thunderstorm, and there was a plate of uneaten bread, cheese, and meat on his desk.

He retrieved it and placed it on my lap, then pressed a hand to my temple. "Are you well? You're still as pale as a ghost."

I didn't know if Dragan would be angry at me when I admitted what I'd done, and I didn't want to lose this chance to learn more about him. "Your story first."

He turned and sank back into his chair. "I was four," Dragan said finally.

I was already attacking the plate of food.

"My mother was a teacher at the College of Eyes. She saw the ugliness brewing between the Vruks and the Lozians and was smart enough to know when to leave. Valko had trained for a time at the school, and they'd grown close. I think maybe even they were lovers."

My eyes bulged. "Your mother and Valko?"

He let out a bark of laughter. "Not something I enjoy dwelling upon, believe me. We hid with friends of my mother near Klovnij for most of the war, but when the tide of the war turned and the Vruk army was drawing near, she knew we had to go. She thought she could find safety here in Selojia. We were a day from the border when Petar gave his order that no Mesmers would be given safe harbor in Adrjssia. By that time, the school had fallen, King Njavo was dead, and Klovnij was a ruin. Word of the atrocities the Vruks were perpetrating on any Mesmer they found had spread like wildfire. The taking of eyes was the least of it."

"I've never been able to understand how King Petar turned his back on all those innocent Mesmers."

"You have to understand, in the eyes of some, no Mesmer is innocent. And Petar was just the Dynast of the Ostrov tribe then. With Klovnij fallen, Petar knew that he had the best chance of consolidating Adrjssian power to himself and ending the war. To make Selojia the new capital. But he needed to convince the Durvo and what was left of the Lozians to join with him. Turning his back on those Mesmers, like my mother, was his only chance to secure the loyalty of the other clans and oppose the Vruks with a united force."

"So he did."

Dragan nodded. "So he did. The Vruks flooded through the plains, killing and maiming as they went. The Mesmers they captured were not given easy deaths. Including my mother."

A soft gasp slipped through my lips. "They caught her?"

"We got to the border. She knew she'd never be able to make it across, but she Projected and found Valko. Convinced him to take us, if we made it to him. She thought we could sneak through, beneath notice."

"We?"

Dragan swirled his glass and the silvery liquid caught the firelight like flames. "Me and my sister."

I straightened, pausing my chewing. "You have a sister?"

"*Had* a sister. A twin."

*Oh.*

"Mother was captured at the border, but we made it across in the middle of the night. We were two four-year-olds traveling by foot in a foreign land. We moved slowly. We had to be cautious, hide rather than come across people. We were hungry, dirty, tired. Valko had promised to send a rider to get us, but he hadn't found us yet. Silviya, my sister..." He cleared his throat.

That name... The memory came flooding back. Valko and Dragan shouting on the deck of the Firebird, before Dragan's spirit sliced through physical matter. A terrible certainty flooded over me. I knew how Silviya had died.

"She Projected. To see our mother. We'd been doing it every night. They were feeding her verbenia, so she couldn't see us, but it helped us to know she was still alive. The third night, what we saw…" Dragan ran his hands through his golden hair.

"They were torturing her?" My voice was hoarse.

"It was…" Dragan shook his head. His violet eyes flicked to the fire, to his glass, to the corner of the room. Anywhere but at me. "It was inhuman. Silviya had always been stronger than me. We didn't even know it was possible, but somehow she knew. Even in her spirit form, she seized a knife from the table and killed the Vruk torturing our mother. Stabbed him right in the throat. And then…when Mother begged her to end her suffering…she did."

A tear slid down my cheek unbidden. The horror of a child having to kill her own mother—to see the truth of all the cruelties of men at such a young age—it was unthinkable. "I can't imagine," I whispered.

"It was too much for Silviya. We couldn't have known, but Projecting into physical form takes tremendous energy. It drains the ora quickly. She was so small, and we were weak with hunger and fatigue." Dragan met my eyes then. "It killed her."

My mouth went dry. It was a long moment before I spoke. "It's why Valko didn't want you to do it on the Firebird."

"It shouldn't even be possible. Only the strongest Mesmers are capable of it, and even then, it takes too much."

"I did it tonight," I admitted, setting the empty plate on the floor beside my chair. I was feeling slightly better.

Dragan's eyes shot up. "What?"

I pointed to the Vruk dagger that lay abandoned on the floorboards where I'd collapsed over the entryway. "I thought they were going to kill me."

Before I knew it Dragan was on his knees before me, his strong hands cradling my face, tilting my head so he could see me in the light. "Are you feeling any weakness? Heart racing? Sudden cold or heat?"

With his hands on me, his face so close to mine…yes, yes, and yes. "I'm fine," I managed.

He sighed and tipped his forehead against mine. "Promise me to never do that again. You are far too precious to risk like that."

I was alive with awareness, every nerve ending on fire with his nearness. His mouth was inches from mine, those finely wrought lips I'd wasted countless hours daydreaming about. My body screamed at me to kiss him. My mind wasn't so sure. What if he didn't kiss me back? What if he *did*? "Too precious?" I managed.

He leaned back on his heels, dropping his hands from where they'd rested on my cheeks, branding me with the fire of his touch. "Precious…to the kingdom."

Disappointment flooded me. Followed by relief. Thank Ovyato I hadn't kissed him and made a complete fool of myself. "Of course."

"You need rest, lots of rest. Come. Let's get you back to your room." Dragan offered me his hands, and I took them, leveraging his strength to pull myself up. A wave of nausea and dizziness overtook me as I straightened, and I tipped against Dragan's strong form.

The world tilted and I found that he had swept me up in his arms. "You're too weak to go back to your chamber. I don't want you to be alone if the sickness gets worse."

Wait, what?

Dragan settled me onto his downy comforter and started unlacing my boots. "I'll sleep on the floor."

The splitting pain in my head had returned when I'd attempted to stand, and my mind was too addled to protest or worry or overthink what it meant to sleep in his room. In his bed.

"Do you need help getting undressed?"

My cheeks blazed with heat. "Just help me sit up. I can manage."

Dragan levered me up into a seated position. "I'll step outside while you get into bed. Is there anything else you need?"

*You.* "No. Thank you."

The door closed, leaving me alone in his room. I undressed with slow movements, hoping not to jostle my aching head. When I was clad only in my shift, I slipped my legs under the covers and settled back with a groan of relief. The pillow smelled of him—ink and candle smoke and a spice that I thought might be cardamom, though I couldn't be sure. I buried my nose in the soft fabric, drinking him in.

As I waited for him to return, I took in my surroundings through different eyes after hearing the story of his tragic childhood. The sketch of the little girl on his bookshelf—it must have been his sister. Silviya. The Lozian furnishings—trappings of a life that had been stolen from him. A family he'd never have again. A soft knock sounded on the door. "Okay!" I croaked.

To my surprise, Dragan came and sat gingerly on the edge of the bed next to me.

He reached out a hand and took hold of one of the bells in my hair, pulling it gently until it unthreaded from my curl. "I always thought these were a fool tradition."

I didn't disagree. They'd given me away in the servants' stairwell earlier. But words were lost to me. All I could do was stare at Dragan, close enough to touch yet impossibly distant. Was he leaning in?

My breath caught.

His kiss landed softly on my cheek. "Sleep well, Adrijana."

And then he was gone—across the room lying a blanket on a rug before the fire, fluffing a pillow, taking off his jacket.

I let out a soft sigh, certain that despite my exhaustion, I'd be getting very little sleep that night.

# CHAPTER 22

hen I woke, Dragan was gone, and Hristina was quietly dusting the books on the shelf.

"Hristina?" I croaked. I tried to sit up but was overcome by a wave of vertigo and flopped back against the pillow. "What are you doing here?"

"Dragan asked me to watch over you and help you back to your room when you woke. I thought I might as well tidy while I was here. He always scares the maids out."

My lips tugged in a smile. That sounded about right. "Help me up."

"Are you sure you should be out of bed?" Hristina asked, but she did as I asked, taking my arm and helping maneuver me into a seat on the bed. "Dragan said you need lots of rest and lots of food."

My stomach chose that moment to yowl in protest. "I'd like to go back to my room. I feel too strange lingering here." Too nervous, more like. I didn't think I'd be able to sleep more if I thought Dragan might return at any moment.

Hristina helped me into my shoes, and with my arm around her, we slowly exited Dragan's room and headed down the hallway to mine. I was embarrassed to admit how weak my legs were—how much I had to lean on her. "Are you all right?" I asked as we made it about halfway. Her face was as red as her hair. "Do you need a break?"

"Maybe," she puffed. "Can I sit you down against the wall for a few?"

"Yes, let's." I braced myself against the wall, but as Hristina tried to shift my weight down to the floor, we both started to lean.

"Whoa, whoa!" A pair of strong arms caught me and I looked up to find Simeon had us both. He was out of his uniform and wore brown trousers and a sky-blue tunic that brought out the lovely ebony of his skin. "Are you all right?"

"Lady Adrijana is ill," Hristina said. "I was trying to get her back to her room, but…" She trailed off, embarrassed.

Before I knew it, Simeon had swung me up in his arms and was carrying me toward my room.

"Lucky we happened upon you," Hristina said as she jogged behind us.

"Not luck at all, actually," Simeon replied. "I was looking for Jana."

My eyebrows flew up. Simeon had been looking for me? Since I had come here, I could count the times he'd come to find me on one hand, and most of those had been errands for Nevena.

He settled me gently onto the fluffy coverlet of my bed and pulled up a chair next to me. Hristina hovered in the doorway.

"Maybe some food?" I asked her. "I am hungry."

"Of course." She curtseyed and was gone, shutting the door behind her.

"What happened to you?" Simeon looked me over. "You look awful."

I pursed my lips. "You sure know how to make a girl feel special."

Simeon rolled his eyes. "You know what I mean."

I took a breath, willing my voice to remain calm while recounting the events of last night. "Matija and Spirodon cornered me in the hallway and threatened me. I had to use my magic to get away, and I overexerted myself."

"What?" Simeon's voice dipped an octave. "What did they say to you?"

I squeezed my eyes shut. "It's done, I really don't want to talk about it."

"Jana, I need to know what goes on in the palace. Especially with the Vruks."

My eyes snapped open and I glared at him. "It's always about your job, isn't it? You couldn't just be concerned for your friend. Well, you can put in your official report that Matija threatened to cut my eyes out like the Vruks do to the Mesmers in West Adjssia."

A storm of emotions crossed over Simeon's face: fury, disgust, and regret. He ran a hand through his hair. "Jana, I'm so sorry they threatened you. We'll assign you a guard to keep them at bay."

Did I want a guard, following my every move? How would I ever get to the bottom of the purple in Ioseph's ora with someone shadowing me? I finally replied, "I don't know if that's necessary."

"It's not so bad. There are some nice fellows. Krystoff seems taken with you. He'd jump at the chance."

My cheeks warmed. "Is he the brown-haired one with the silly little mustache?"

Simeon hissed, as if wounded. "If he heard you say that, he would be devastated. That mustache is his pride and joy."

I chuckled. "I'll think about it. So, why were you looking for me?"

Simeon gestured to his clothes. "Nevena gave me the day off, and I thought you and I could go into town. If you wanted. The mist has actually broken today."

I craned my head to look out the window and saw that he was speaking truth. There were slashes of blue sky showing through the ever-present white. "I would love to, but I don't think I'll be walking anywhere today. My body is too tired."

"That's all right. We could stay in, play Royals? Or I could read to you like you did for me when I broke my leg."

I smiled wistfully. We'd spent that entire summer sitting under the willow tree by Simeon's farm, reading every book in the village. "I don't want you to have to spend such a pretty day stuck inside with me."

"It's all right." Simeon looked down, smoothing a wrinkle in his trousers. "Jana, I haven't been fair to you. In truth, you being a Mesmer shook me more than I care to admit. And it was wrong of you to try to read me." He looked up.

"I know."

His eyes met mine. "But I've really missed my friend."

A lump grew in my throat. "Me too." I leaned forward and seized him in a hug, burying my nose in the lemon-fresh scent of his shirt. "I don't want to fight anymore."

"Let's not then." He pulled back and then his eyes lit up. He jumped to his feet. "I have the perfect idea how to get you outside. Wait right here?"

I motioned to my legs helplessly. "It's not like I can go anywhere."

"Great. I'll be right back!" Simeon bounded out of the room, almost knocking into Hristina on the way out the door.

She looked over her shoulder at him with a surprised laugh, righting the tray of food that had almost fallen. "Where is he going, all wound up?"

"I'm not sure. But I suspect I'll need a full stomach for when he returns."

I inhaled a breakfast of warm honey muffins and roast chicken sausage and was just washing down the last of my tea when Simeon returned—wheeling a chair.

"What is that?" I leaned forward. I'd never seen anything like it.

"When the queen had the prince, she was ill for a few months. She had it made so she could go outside." Simeon parked it by my bedside and removed the tray before leaning down and helping me into the chair.

"Are you sure the king won't mind? If it's something of hers..."

"It's been living in the hospital ward for the last decade. Various patients use it. It's not considered hers anymore."

"How did you even know about this?" I asked as Simeon took the two handles behind my shoulders and began to roll me out into the hallway.

"Nevena sprained her ankle when I first arrived. She used it for a week or so."

I pursed my lips. Of course, it had something to do with Nevena. I shoved down my jealousy. Though Simeon had long been my best friend, times changed. I would much rather have him in my life in some capacity than cling to a past that was long gone and miss my chance to know the man he was becoming. "Where are you taking me?" I asked lightly.

"There's only one garden that you can reach without stairs," he explained. "The royal rose garden. The king and Nevena are meeting with the ministers all day, so it should be empty."

Simeon took the back hallways, so we didn't attract too much attention. When he wheeled me into the fresh air and sunshine, I could swear my soul sighed inside me. The garden was designed in a spiral, and Simeon began wheeling me between rows of fragrant purple blossoms, toward the center. I reached out to feel the soft petals of a blossom.

"Careful," Simeon warned. "The thorns have a toxin that will make you itch like crazy for a few days."

I drew my hand back in. That didn't sound like fun. We arrived at the center of the garden—a large circle of benches surrounding a tinkling fountain. From the waters emerged a marble statue of a well-formed man leaning down to pluck something out of the water.

"Ovyato discovering the chiton." Simeon nodded toward the fountain.

"But the lore says the spring goddess Lruzina discovered the chiton."

Simeon shrugged as he parked my chair and settled onto a bench. "Revisionist history, I suppose. Nevena said her father put it in soon after he became king. Or that's what her mother told her."

I frowned as I thought about how little I really knew about the royal family. "Does Nevena have a better idea of who killed her mother yet?" I hadn't spoken about it with Nevena for some time. I had new information now, though. Aleksi's companion had murdered him under the Compulsion of a Mesmer. I had promised to share with her any information I had. But I found myself hesitating. I didn't want to believe Dragan had had anything to do with the queen's death, or even Valko, really. Might it be an undeclared Mesmer, then? We were already so mistrusted, I didn't want to cast suspicion on the Mesmers until I knew more. I needed something more concrete before I shared the information.

Simeon shook his head. "It weighs on her, the not knowing. I can see it. She's suffered so much tragedy. More than one person should have to endure."

That's right. Her older brother had died, too. "How did the crown prince die?"

"A hunting accident. He was out with his father, the Royal Mesmers, and a dozen royal guards. They party got separated going after a stag. A boar came out of nowhere and attacked the prince's horse. It unseated him and then mauled him. I know one of the guards who was there. He said the boar seemed mad—it wouldn't stop going for the prince. The guards brought the animal down, but it was too late. The damage had already been done. The prince bled out."

My heart was hammering in my throat. Mesmers could cause an animal to act strangely. How easy would it have been for a Mesmer to Compel the boar to attack the prince, knowing the animal would be killed—and any evidence of Mesmerism would die with it...

"Were both of the Royal Mesmers present?"

Simeon turned to me. "In the hunting party, but not where the prince died. Why?"

I feigned nonchalance. "Just curious."

Simeon's eyes wouldn't leave me. "Have you seen Dragan do anything suspicious?"

I straightened. "Dragan? Why Dragan? Why don't you ask about Valko?"

"Valko is the king's man through and through. I don't believe he'd go against the king's wishes. But Dragan is a wild card—"

Something Simeon said struck a spark of an idea within me. Valko would act only at the king's direction...but what if King Petar had told Valko to Compel Ioseph? To end his brother? Or even...to end his wife?

My eyes grew round and I hissed in a breath.

"What?" Simeon cocked his head.

"Are you certain King Petar didn't know about the affair between Ksenjia and Aleksi?" My mind was whirling. If the king had known of his wife and his brothers' long-term dalliance…would he have been furious enough to want revenge? To ask his old friend to help him end the two people who had betrayed him? Though that didn't explain the crown prince's death. Unless that truly had been an accident…

"I'm fairly certain. I think Petar would have shared the information with Nevena."

"Unless he wanted revenge." I looked up at Simeon. My voice was hushed. "Has anyone considered that King Petar could be the killer?"

Simeon hissed in a breath. "That's treason to even speak of."

"But he had a clear motive to end both of them," I pointed out.

"Motive doesn't make someone a killer—"

A shrieking caw sounded in the air above us, cutting off Simeon's next comment. He stood abruptly. "We need to go." He started wheeling me back up the circular path.

I craned my neck. What had made that sound? I hadn't heard anything like it before. Against the clouds above us, I thought I caught sight of a massive, silvery stretch of wings. I blinked rapidly, putting a hand up to block the sun. "I think I saw a bird. It was huge."

"I'm sure you're just tired."

I searched for it again but could see nothing against the misty sky. I was about to turn away when I saw it clearly—a huge, silver bird, soaring past a patch of blue. "Right there!" I pointed, though I'd lost it again. There was only one bird I'd ever heard of in Adrjssia that fit this creature's description. A Mora star-bird. But star-birds hadn't been seen on the continent since the Mora had sailed away over twenty years ago. "Simeon, I swear I saw a—"

"Your Majesty." Simeon put a warning hand on my shoulder, and I turned, my eyes widening as I saw that we faced the lavender countenance of King Petar himself. I did my best to incline a bow from my seated position. "We were just leaving."

King Petar smiled. "I'm just hiding from my ministers for a few moments. You'll keep my secret?"

"Of course," Simeon and I both replied.

With an incline of his head, the king strode past us, and Simeon started jogging down the path, out of the garden. But I couldn't get the vision out of my head. I turned back to him. "Simeon, I swear I saw a star-bird. Did you see it?"

Simeon looked straight ahead, his words clipped. "I didn't see anything, and you know star-birds haven't been seen for years. I think you're probably just overtired. I'll get you back to your room."

I settled back into my chair, disappointment warring with another strange sensation. A certainty that Simeon was lying to me. But I hadn't the least idea why.

# CHAPTER 23

*W*hen I woke the next day, I found my body recovered enough to head to the Mesmers' workshop without the aid of the chair. Questions were burning in my mind, and I suspected it was the only place I would find answers.

But when I stepped inside, I was rocked back on my heels by the storm cloud that was Valko. He was pacing across the length of the floor with a piece of paper and a quill, muttering angrily to himself, pausing periodically to stop and scribble something on the paper.

Dragan lounged on the couch in the corner, and when he saw me, he jerked his head toward the library. I hastily followed him through the door and into the quiet, cavernous space. "What's going on?"

Dragan ran a hand through his hair. He looked as tired as I felt. The walk, short as it was, had winded me. I still hadn't recovered completely. "We received reports that a large Vruk military force was approaching the border. Our inquiries were finally answered this morning. Andrej says it's a training exercise." He scoffed.

"That's ridiculous. Can't they see we'd take it as an aggressive action? It could start a war."

"I'm afraid that's exactly what Andrej wants. I just can't figure out why *now*. What's changed?"

155

"Maybe we should do some more spying on the ambassadors? Perhaps they will let something slip."

"Perhaps. They are hunting today. Tonight, though…" Dragan looked at me. "I do not think you should be Projecting yet, Adrijana. You are still weak. I can take care of it."

"Absolutely not." I shook my head resolutely. "I'm feeling much better. If you're making any moves against those horrible men, I want in."

"It will just be observing them."

"Still. At least I'll be doing something other than waiting around for them to corner me and cut my eyes out." I shuddered involuntarily.

Dragan inclined his head. "Meet me at ten o' clock in the corridor between our rooms. We will go together."

"Thank you!" I clasped my hands together. Spying on those bastards would make me feel better.

"Now, I think it's best if you continue to rest today, rather than working on your studies."

I frowned, but I *was* feeling tired already. "Does the library have any books on the Adrjssian clan animals? Like karakals?" I wasn't sure why I didn't mention star-birds.

"Foul beasts. Always spitting and scratching," Dragan said. "But yes, I think there's a book somewhere." He disappeared down one of the rows.

"You don't like the karakals?" I asked, amused. "They can see us, can't they? When we Project."

"Most animals can. It's quite fascinating, actually." Dragan returned and handed me a thin, blue, leather-bound book with gold foil lettering: *An Adrjssian Bestiary*. "I suspect they can detect our psychic mental projections, but perhaps it's some sort of distortion in the air? If I had more time, I would love to design an experiment around it."

I clutched the book to my chest. "I'm sure someday you will."

I walked back to my room, reading the book as I went. The sketched depiction of the star-bird was just like what I'd seen in the sky. The birds were silvery-white, with a wingspan as tall as a man. The name came from their affinity with the stars, and how they helped Mora sailors use the stars to navigate the open sea. They were said to fly ahead of the boat, holding the right course, as surely as if the sailor had calculated the way himself using his complicated nautical instruments. And up against the night sky, the birds were said to shimmer like living constellations. The star-birds bonded with those of the Mora clan whom they deemed worthy when the clan youths reached the age of maturity.

It was all fascinating, but it did little to answer my question. Why was such a creature hovering over a garden in Selojia? Especially as the Mora clan hadn't been spotted on our shores since the Mesmer War.

Unless it was connected to Simeon somehow? But he was only half Mora. And if it was his creature, then why did he claim not to see it?

* * *

AFTER EATING a gourmet lunch brought by Hristina, I undressed and got into bed for a nap. Just the action of walking to the Mesmers' workshop and back had tired me, and I knew I would get less sleep that night. It was only seconds before I drifted off.

I woke to a firm hand on my shoulder and jerked up to sitting position. It was Dragan.

I pressed my hand to my chest as if to keep my heart from galloping away. "What are you doing?"

"You were supposed to meet me."

"Is it 10 o'clock already?" I'd slept all afternoon? "I'm so sorry."

"It's all right. You're still recovering from the other night. It takes days to regain your strength. Maybe I should go alone—"

I threw off the covers and surged to my feet before I had the wherewithal to remember I was clad in only my thin shift, with nothing beneath. "I'm coming too."

He looked me up and down, from toe to crown—a leisurely sweep that made my nipples pebble in an entirely inconvenient way. "In *that?*"

I jutted my chin out. "No one will see me but you."

"But *I* can see you," he purred. "It's hardly decent."

"Surely, you've seen women in far less." As soon as the words were out of my mouth, heat flooded my cheeks. Dear gods, what was I saying? I was well and truly addled.

A smile curved the corner of his mouth. "Boldness suits you." His amethyst eyes shined like gemstones in the dark. My pulse roared in my veins, filling my ears. He was so near. In my chamber. In the middle of the night.

But he shouldered off the long, velvet jacket he wore, its lapels studded with shiny silver epaulets. He draped it about my shoulders. Pulling the collar into position, his hands tugged on the fabric before resting lightly above my collarbones. "You don't have to be involved in this," he said quietly, almost as much to himself as to me. He let his hands drop.

"If you're involved, I'm involved."

He pursed his lips. I couldn't understand the shadow of melancholy that flashed across his face. "I worried you'd say that."

"Dragan—" I began, but he was already rounding to the other side of my bed, his mask of aloofness firmly affixed in place. "Let's get to it. Vruk plots to discover and all that." He toed off his knee-high boots and settled atop the covers.

I lay down next to him. It only took me seconds to slip from my body and go stand beside Dragan's spectral form, which was already at the door.

"Ready?"

"As I'll ever be."

It was a peaceful way to travel about the palace. The torches burned low, and most of the inhabitants were asleep. Dragan and I could speak freely without fearing anyone would hear—pass through doors or walls to take the most direct route.

We strode boldly into the Vruk ambassadors' sitting room, where the two of them sat before a low-burning fire. Matija slouched in his chair, peering morosely into a mostly-empty glass of whisky.

Spirodon was reading a book, a pair of eyeglasses perched on his nose.

Had I been in my body, the sight of them would have sent a surge of terror through me. But in this form, my emotions remained at a convenient distance. So I only glared.

"You bested them." Dragan looked sideways at me. "They'll know not to cross you now."

"Or maybe they'll look for a rematch."

"Let's make sure that doesn't happen."

We perused the room, eying a pile of letters on the desk beneath a half-eaten bowl of stew, books stacked on a set of shelves. We couldn't move anything, so we could only see what was exposed.

"I don't see anything out of the ordinary," I whispered.

"You know they can't hear you." Dragan spoke normally, standing and reading over Spirodon's shoulder. It was eerie.

"It's hard to get used to." I spoke louder.

Matija surged to his feet and I jumped back. He strode to the desk, passing through me, and refilled his drink, slopping some over the side. "The bitch needs to be taught a lesson." I froze. No mistaking which *bitch* he was talking about.

Spirodon closed his book and took his glasses off, folding them neatly and tucking them into his shirt pocket. "Are you still on about that?"

"She shoved us down the stairs." Matija's face twisted.

"You did threaten to cut her eyes out," Spirodon said. "Which we have no authority to do here. You could have started a war."

"I would have done him a favor. Who cares if the war starts a few weeks early?"

I looked at Dragan with alarm, but his gaze was fixed on the men. They spoke of war as if it were inevitable. Planned.

Spirodon shook his head. "You Zamos never think of strategy, only of killing. The conflict cannot start until our troops are in position.

Besides, I'm far more interested in *how* she did what she did. Until we know more, you are not to cross her."

"Mesmers can't move objects. It's not natural."

"Nothing about their power is natural. It's possible the Mesmers here have developed a new ability. I've written to the king. He will ask Iskra about this power."

My mouth dropped open, and my shock was mirrored on Dragan's face. The woman from the journal—the Mesmer Iskra who had served as ambassador from the College of Eyes. She was still alive? She was *still* held by the Vruk king? My stomach churned at the thought of what horrors she must have undergone in the past two decades.

"Andrej should give me Shadow-bringer, and I'd end the three abominations here in a heartbeat."

"You know the king never lets that dagger out of his sight. I think he believes it lends him strength."

"He needs all he can get. He looked as if Zamo Idvo himself were dogging his steps the last time I saw him. Can't believe the old bastard has held on this long."

"Andrej is as tough as nails. But I fear you're right. If we don't secure the chiton for him soon, he won't make it to the Planting Season."

"We can't let that happen. Prince Elian is short-sighted and weak."

"You just say that because he doesn't fawn all over the Sons of Zamo like Andrej did. But he'll be a good king. He might actually spend more time caring for his people than slaughtering Mesmers."

"Slaughtering Mesmers is *how* you take care of the Vruk clan."

"Spoken like a true Zamo." Spirodon stood. "Now, you can stay up and drink yourself into a stupor, but I'm going to bed."

Dragan and I remained for a few more minutes, watching Matija nurse his whisky. I held in my questions. It didn't feel right to discuss it in this man's presence, even if he couldn't hear us. "Let's go," Dragan finally said.

Questions bubbled through me like a creek swollen by spring rain as I hurried beside Dragan back to my chambers. Finally, I led with the only one I could articulate. "Dragan, did I just hear what I thought I did?"

His violet eyes darted back and forth, racing with connections. "We knew the Vruks were preparing for war. Positioning their troops. But we didn't know why. Until now."

"King Andrej is dying."

"Yes. He wants the chiton, and the long life it provides. There's nothing we can do to stop this war. Diplomacy will fail. The king is desperate."

So there would be war. I didn't know what role I would be expected to play in a coming conflict, but I suspected my leisurely evenings with Georgi and Nevena and Simeon were at an end.

We floated back into my room, and I got out of bed, shaking out the numbness in my fingertips.

"Dragan, did I make a mistake? With the knife? They didn't know we could move objects with our oras, and now they do."

He met me halfway, and to my surprise, took my face in his hands. "Adrijana, you fought for your life. You did nothing wrong. We will deal with whatever comes of it."

"All right," I said softly.

He didn't let go. Didn't look away. His gaze rested on my lips.

My body thrummed in answer to his closeness. The air between us was thick. Charged. His prior words came forth in my mind, unbidden. *Boldness suits you.*

I surged onto my toes and kissed him.

I'd thought only to press my lips to his—a test that could be waved off as a midnight madness. But the hunger in his answer shocked and thrilled me. Stole my breath.

One arm locked around my waist, pulling me flush against him. The other hand tangled in my curls. His mouth was hot on mine, his tongue insistent. I yielded to him eagerly. *Finally.* The thought blazed like a comet through me.

Finally, I could touch him in all the places I'd longed to. I ran my fingers through his golden locks, reveling in the silky softness. My other hand angled up the hard planes of his stomach, his chest.

Finally, I knew I wasn't alone in this feeling—that I wasn't imagining it all. Finally, finally. *Finally.*

For so long he had filled my thoughts, and now he filled my senses, surrounding me until all I knew was him. The hint of sweetness on his lips, the heat of his hands on me, the hardness of his arousal insistent against my hip.

I trailed one hand down to his belt, tugging free the tails of his shirt. And then I froze.

He dragged in a ragged breath, leaning his forehead against mine. "Adrijana..."

"Look..." I whispered.

He slid a hand up my neck, tilting my face. "I see you, Jana. Sometimes I think you're all I see."

Any other moment, I would have reveled in his praise. But I had to show him. "No, look!" I pointed behind him, to where the white mist floated just inside my door.

He turned, his muscles tensing beneath my hands.

"You see it too."

He turned back to me and affixed his lips to mine. "No, I don't see anything," he murmured between kisses.

I gave him a little shove. "Dragan, yes, you do. You see it. It's the mist that led me to Aleksi in the hallway, Valko talking to the ambassadors. What if it's trying to show us something?"

"That mist almost got you killed in a stairwell. I'm inclined to tell it to go to hell." His eyes gleamed in the darkness and he reached inside his jacket to cup my rear and pull me hard against him. I gasped and my eyes fluttered shut. The mist *had* led me to the Vruks, who'd attacked me. But that hadn't necessarily been its fault.

His mouth branded a trail of kisses around the shell of my ear and down the column of my neck. Dear god, the man was good at that. Through a flutter of my eyelids, I caught sight of the mist again.

"Dragan!" I screeched. It was closer, hovering right behind him. As badly as I wanted to be swept up in the fire of Dragan's kisses, there was no way I was going to be able to focus on anything with some strange mist hovering inches from us.

"Fine!" he roared, rounding on the strange phenomenon. He put his hands on his hips, breathing heavily through his nose, his head hanging for a moment. "Fine." When he turned back to me, there was no sign of anger. "I believe the mist wants us to follow."

"I believe you're right." My skin felt like it was on fire, my body thrumming. It took a great deal of willpower to focus my attention on practical matters. Like shoes. I went to slip into my silken slippers and frowned, looking about. I'd put them by the bed beneath my dress—

"By the door." Dragan pointed. He was sitting in the armchair putting his own boots on.

He was right. They sat neatly by the door. Had he moved them? Maybe I'd put them there after all. I shrugged and slipped them on, noticing another oddity. I had a long, thin scratch on the back of my hand. I didn't remember getting that. Perhaps I'd scraped it on a rough stone coming back from the workshop?

I put aside the strangeness and followed Dragan out the open door. The mist was already in the hallway, pulsing softly, as if it were gesturing impatiently for us to follow.

"Have you ever seen it before?" I asked as I buttoned Dragan's jacket up tightly, aware of my strange attire. But it was late, and it was unlikely we'd encounter anyone else about.

"It only seems to appear to you."

"Lucky me." I grimaced. The mist's timing certainly could have been improved upon. I couldn't quite shake my giddy disbelief about the night's events. I'd kissed Dragan. Dragan *had kissed me*. What did it mean? Could we do it again? Ovyato help me, I hoped we'd do it again. The man knew how to make my body sing like a master bard strumming a lute, and I had the distinct impression that we'd hardly scratched the surface of his skills.

The mist was leading us into the royal garden where Simeon had taken me just yesterday. It mingled with the fog that hung over the courtyard like a held breath, until it was nearly invisible.

"This garden is attached to the royal wing." Dragan spoke softly.

A gust of wind caught my hair, tangling it about my face. I caught it with a hand, corralling it as best I could.

"There should be a guard on patrol out here." Dragan frowned.

I stumbled, my foot snagging over a root of one of the rosebushes. I looked down and a scream escaped me.

It was a booted foot. Attached to a body.

# CHAPTER 24

*I* barely caught my scream as I saw the guard's royal livery. Simeon! No, it couldn't be...

The man's torso lay beneath one of the many violet rose bushes, and it was difficult to make out his face in the dark. I fell to my hands and knees, peering beneath the bush.

"It's not your friend," Dragan said. "Look at his hand. The skin is too light."

Thank the gods. As soon as the thought surfaced, I felt wretched. The man was clearly dead, and this was someone else's son or friend. Perhaps husband or father. And then I caught the angle of his face and saw this thin mustache. Krystoff—the guard Simeon had recommended for me.

It felt like someone had punched me straight in the gut. I stumbled back, one hand to my stomach, the other over my mouth.

"Do you know him?" Dragan asked.

"Krystoff. A friend of Simeon's. He was going to..." I trailed off. It didn't matter now.

"How did he die?"

"We need to bring him to the workshop to be examined. But first..." Dragan pointed toward the arched set of doors that led into the royal apartments. The mist was hovering before them. "This might not be over."

Dragan seized my hand and we hurried into the palace. "This door should be locked. And there should be a guard. This is wrong."

Across the large sitting room where we'd Projected to find Prince Aleksi, a door was cracked, letting out a sliver of light.

"That's the king's chambers. There should be a guard there, too." Dragan sprinted into a run and burst through the door. "Your Majesty!"

I followed close on his heels and gasped as I took in the scene. Two guards were lying prone on the ground, both dead. Their skin was purpled and swollen, their lips flecked with foam. Who had done this? *What* had done this?

"Your Majesty!" Dragan flew to the king's huge, four-poster bed, laying a gentle hand on his neck to feel for his pulse. The king lay tangled in his sheets, his lavender skin darkened to an unnatural hue.

"Is he dead?" I asked in horror, coming around the other side, climbing onto the monstrous bed.

The king's eyes flew open.

I nearly tumbled off the bed in fright.

"Your Majesty!" Dragan cried. "What did this? Who?"

He took a rasping breath. "Zviya…"

Zviya? Who was that?

Amongst the silken covers of the bed, something brushed against the bare skin of my calf. Something cool. Sinuous.

"Jana." Dragan was staring at me, his eyes gone round with horror. "Don't. Move."

Ever so carefully, I looked down.

There was a huge black snake sliding by me. Headed for Dragan.

I screamed.

It lunged at Dragan with a hiss, launching its muscular body across the bed. He moved faster than I would've thought possible and it sailed past him, landing on the tiled floor.

The snake turned on him with a wild hiss, ready to attack again.

166

But then, as if tamed by its master, it settled back down, coiling into a neat spiral, laying its head down.

"What—What did you—" My voice was faint.

"We control emotions, remember?" Dragan strode across the room and seized a sword from the scabbard of one of the dead guards. The snake looked at him placidly, its tongue flicking. I felt a fool. In the heat of the moment, all my training had fled.

With one powerful stroke, Dragan took the snake's head right off. I couldn't help but flinch as he did the deed.

"The king needs anti-venom. Find a guard to fetch the doctor."

I darted into the hallway. "Guards!" I cried. "The king need help! Guards!"

Of course it was Simeon who appeared, coming out of Nevena's suite of rooms. I tried not to think of what that meant. I skidded to a stop before him. "The king's been attacked. We need a doctor. And anti-venom."

"Anti-venom?" His dark eyes were wide with larm.

"A big black snake. Zviya, he called it."

Simeon sucked in a breath and then turned and ran.

I hurried back inside the king's chambers. Dragan was lying on the couch. He must have Projected. I didn't know where.

There was nowhere safe to look. The guards dead on the ground stared up with vacant gazes, their faces puffed and twisted in unnatural horror. Near the king's bed, the snake lay in a pool of black blood.

Tears blurred my vision. How had this happened?

The king's rasping breaths reached my ears—towed me toward him.

I didn't know what the protocol was for this. Did he want to be left alone? Should I try to help? I suddenly felt awful ever suspecting that he could have been responsible for his brother's and his wife's deaths. Clearly, the same person who had killed Queen Ksenjia was back to take down another member of the royal family.

"Water," he rasped.

That, I could do. I poured a glass from the pitcher across the room and climbed on the bed to help him drink. I did my best to help prop him up as he drank, but still water dribbled down his beard and over the front of his white shift.

He'd drank half the glass before he collapsed back against the pillows. He looked at me.

"Does it hurt?" I whispered.

"Like Zamo Idvo's own spear," he croaked. "If it weren't for the chiton, I'd be dead. Might be anyway."

"No." I shook my head. "The doctor is coming with an anti-venom. You'll be right as rain soon enough."

"Can you…make it stop?"

A tear strayed down my cheek. "You know I can't. The chiton blocks our power. I'm sorry."

His eyes fluttered shut. "Never should have…closed the border. So many lives. Glad you…made it."

What? Was he talking nonsense? No—he was speaking of the Mesmer War, nearly twenty years ago. The decision he'd made to turn the Mesmers away, deny them asylum. "You did what you thought was right," I said gently.

His swollen lips moved, the words so quiet, I could barely make them out. "Knew…it was wrong."

He fell silent for a long moment. So long I wondered if he'd slipped from life. Fear lanced through me. He couldn't die like this. I took his hand and squeezed, shaking him.

"Tell Nevena—"

"You tell her yourself. You fight."

The doors crashed open and people flooded into the room. The doctor, accompanied by Simeon. Nevena, who threw herself onto the bed, across her father's chest. "Papa!"

"He's weak," I said. "He was asking for you."

"Back, back." The doctor shooed us, pulling out a vial and a syringe.

I retreated, going to stand next to the couch where Dragan lay. It seemed too vulnerable, leaving his body unguarded with all these people around.

A hand reached out and grabbed my knee and I jumped with a squeak. I thought my heart might not last through the series of frights it had had tonight.

Dragan sat up. "Valko's on his way. He didn't have any anti-venom."

"Sounds like the doctor does."

"Let's hope it's enough." Dragan stood. "The venom was in his blood for a long while. Despite the life-giving properties of the chiton, it might not be enough."

"Let's hope it is." Simeon turned and came to stand before us, his eyes narrowed at Dragan. "Let me ask you, how did you and Adrijana come to be here?"

I glanced sidelong at Dragan. Would he speak of the mist? That would make us sound crazy.

"Isn't this an inquiry for the head of the king's guard?" Dragan asked coolly.

Simeon pointed to one of the men on the ground. "You'd rather speak to him?"

Dragan sighed. "We found a guard's body in the royal garden. We grew concerned about foul play. We came inside."

Simeon crossed his arms, looking back at the scene. "You killed that snake? Quite a feat of bravery."

"Hardly. Mesmers can control animal emotions, the same as they control humans."

"We are just animals, after all, aren't we?" Simeon said.

Dragan inclined his head.

Simeon continued, "so a Mesmer could have controlled the snake, instructed it to make its way into the royal suites, killing everyone it encountered?"

"It's possible."

My mouth dropped open. "Simeon, what are you suggesting?"

"Where were you this evening, Dragan?"

"He was with me," I shot back. "We were together the entire time."

Simeon leveled his gaze on me, taking in my strange attire. Shift, slippers, men's coat. My face heated.

"I admire your enthusiasm," Dragan said, unperturbed. "But perhaps you should direct your suspicion where it is better suited."

"Where's that?"

"If I were you, I'd arrest the Vruk ambassadors."

"Why?"

Valko breezed into the room. "Because the Zviya asp is native of West Adrjssia. It's how the Vruks end their lives, if they've dishonored the clan. They train the snakes in their spare time."

*Ovyato help us.* I sat down heavily on the sofa as Valko took control of the situation, directing the guard's bodies to be taken to the workshop for examination, the snake's body to be disposed of, the king to be given space. Now that the adrenaline of the moment was over, I was exhausted and cold.

Something about what Simeon had said bothered me.

Both the Vruk ambassadors had been in their room, and they certainly hadn't seemed to be overseeing some clandestine assassination plot. Perhaps there was a third Vruk in the palace, trained to manage the snake, to make it heel.

But there was another potential explanation. A Mesmer could easily manipulate an animal to make it attack. Dragan and I had been together, but Valko's whereabouts were unknown. The mist had led me to his door—where he'd been speaking in low tones with the ambassadors. Could this have been the subject of their conversation? Confirming the details of their plan?

I watched Valko out of the corner of my eye. It was said that he and the king had grown up together, that they were as close as brothers. But was that enough to rule him out?

Dragan appeared in front of me. "I think it's best if you head back to your chambers and try to get some sleep. The king is stabilized for now."

Standing, I asked quietly, "Will he live?"

Dragan shrugged helplessly. "We don't know. He's strong, but...the venom was in his system a long time."

"And Matija and Spirodon?"

"Should be on their way to the dungeon as we speak. You'll be safe, in your chamber."

I nodded, my eyes flicking from the king's prone form, to Valko, to the pool of black blood. I wasn't sure I was safe anywhere in this palace anymore. Maybe I never had been.

# CHAPTER 25

*I* fell into an exhausted sleep—my nerves raw from the events of the evening. I slept late into the morning, when Hristina finally woke me.

"My lady." She shook my shoulder.

"Mmm?" I cracked an eye.

"The princess is asking for you."

That woke me up.

I washed quickly and let Hristina help me into a navy dress with an embroidered sea of ocean waves along the cuffs and hem. My stomach yowled at me, but I bypassed the dining hall to head for the princess's rooms.

I found her sitting by the window, Georgi in the chair beside her. Her face was haggard, but her hair and dress were perfect and pressed.

Simeon stood by the door, as silent a sentinel as ever. He nodded slightly to me as I entered.

Nevena rose and embraced me. I squeezed her tightly. "I'm so, so sorry, Nevena."

She held me for another moment before letting me go, hastily wiping a tear away. "I feel like my family is vanishing before my very eyes."

"Is he...?" I trailed off.

"Hanging on by a thread." She sank into a chair.

Not dead. Thank Ovyato.

"I spent the morning with my father's ministers. Gods, *my* ministers? I've been granted provisional authority while Father is ill. This all feels like a bad dream."

Georgi pulled over another chair for me and refilled Nevena's tea. "We're not going anywhere, cousin. Whatever you need."

"What I need—" Nevena cut off as a maid appeared with a tray of pastries, cheese, and fruit. "Thank you." She waited until the maid retreated out the door.

Georgi was helping himself to the food, and my stomach gurgled audibly.

"Go ahead." Nevena waved.

I wasted no time. The tray was ladened with a flaky pastry twist I'd never seen before, braided around a filling of cinnamon and covered with powdered sugar. "These are lovely."

Nevena stared at them morosely. "They're called 'plitkas.' They're my favorite."

"I asked the kitchen to make them," Georgi said.

She pressed a hand to her heart. "At least I have you. You're all the family I have left now."

"Your father is a fighter," Georgi protested. "He could still make it."

She shook her head. "The doctors patronize me. The venom was in his bloodstream for far too long. It's only a matter of time."

I let the tray of food fall to my lap, suddenly ill. "Have the Vruks confessed?"

"They protest their innocence. Claim they were in their rooms the whole time. That they had nothing to do with the snake."

"They're telling the truth, at least about being in their rooms. They must have someone aiding them."

"How do you know this?" Nevena cocked her head.

"Dragan and I were...spying on them last night."

She looked at me shrewdly. "You and the Para-Mesmer have grown quite close."

I blushed. The memory of his lips crushed to mine flashed before me. "I value his mentorship."

Georgi gave a grunt of displeasure but said nothing, looking into his tea. A flash of guilt struck me over my and Dragan's manipulation of his mind and memories. It was for the best, I reminded myself.

"So if the Vruks were in their room, it means we have a third collaborator loose about the palace." She grabbed a plitka and tore into it. "Someone no one saw hide nor hair of. It's the same as with my mother. It appears our murderer is a ghost."

A ghost... or a Mesmer. "Dragan and I discovered something else last night. The Vruk king is dying. He wants the chiton to save himself. I would imagine that these assassinations have been to destabilize Adrjssia so the invasion goes more quickly."

Nevena let out a hollow laugh. "They press on every front."

"What do you mean?"

"Just recently, King Andrej renewed his overture to my father regarding a marriage alliance. As if I would ever marry those who murdered my kin." Nevena spit.

"If Andrej truly wants the chiton, is he doing this all to secure it?" Georgi said. "Eliminate your parents and leave you vulnerable. Move his troops to the border so you feel threatened. And then extend the ultimate solution: a way to save everything. A marriage to his son."

"Effectively giving him control over Adrjssia and the chiton supply," Nevena agreed. "Smart bastards. But they can't force me if I'm already married. If I make myself a far more advantageous match."

I couldn't help my curiosity. "Who? A Lozian? You're already closely tied with the Durvo." The Lozian clan had little power since Klovnij had fallen in the Mesmer War.

"There's another clan." Nevena flashed a shrewd smile.

I wrinkled my brow. "The Mora? They've left Adrjssia. Sailed away and didn't look back." Though the star-bird said otherwise ...

"That's what they wanted us to believe. But the younger generation is tired of wandering the seas. They want a berth in which to lay their heads. I've promised them that, in exchange for their support. And their ships."

"How did you even find them to negotiate such a deal?"

"Imagine my surprise when I learned I had an heir to the Mora clan serving as a guard in my own palace."

What? It couldn't have been. I looked at Simeon, standing against the door. Dark skin, lithe, and tall. He was the only man I knew with Mora heritage... "Simeon?" I asked incredulously.

"It's true." Simeon crossed to stand beside Nevena. He laid a gentle hand on her shoulder. "My mother is sister to our Dynast." Suddenly, so much fell into place. Nevena and Simeon's closeness. I'd always wondered why King Petar allowed them to spend time together when there'd been an obvious connection between them. It hadn't seemed like something the king would approve of. Clearly, there'd been more to the story.

I shook my head in disbelief. "You always said your mother didn't get along with the Mora chief, and that's why you didn't sail away with the rest of your people. Was that a lie?"

"A half-truth. There were several challengers for my aunt's position of Dynast, and my mother feared they'd try to eliminate me, as her heir. My aunt was unable to bear children of her own. So we hid on the mainland. I didn't even know myself until Queen Ksenjia came to my mother two years ago."

"The *queen* came to our village?" I goggled at him.

He nodded. "In secret, of course. She was well-informed about Mora politics before the clan left Adrjssia, and she learned where my mother and I had settled. She offered me a position here so we could all get to know each other better, without cluing in the Vruks. She hoped we could make an alliance."

Nevena threaded her fingers through Simeon's. "We will never be free while the Vruks hold West Adrjssia. This way, while they're focused on massing at our western border, we'll sail around, take their city, and force their surrender."

It was astonishing. Simeon—a Mora royal. Simeon, to marry the Princess of Adrjssia. "So Simeon...will be the king."

"King consort." Nevena kissed the back of Simeon's hand. Even with my crown node closed, it was plain to see that love shone between them, as bright as a beacon. My heart spasmed. I was happy for Simeon, I was. But still. For so many years, Simeon had been mine, and I'd been his. Now he and Nevena would belong to each other alone.

I cleared my throat. "I am honored that you'd share your plan with me. But I'm curious. Why?"

"Because we need your help," Simeon said. "We need you to marry us."

I let out a bark of laughter. Then looked from Nevena to Simeon to Georgi. None of them were smiling. Or laughing. "You're serious."

Nevena leveled her gaze at me. "The Vruks have an ally in the palace. Until we know who it is, the people I trust are in this room. Simeon has vouched for you—he says we can trust you with our lives. Our future."

Simeon nodded at me once, and warmth nestled in my chest. At least there could always be trust and esteem between us.

"Of course, I will help however I can. But I can't marry you. I'm not a priest."

"Actually, by Adrjssian law, a Mesmer can perform the marriage rites."

This was madness. "But I'm not even a full Mesmer. I'm still in training."

"The law says nothing about training. Your power is enough. Will you do it?"

"Surely, we could ask Valko—" Even as I said it, my doubts from last night surfaced.

"No." Nevena shook her head. "My father trusted him, but I don't. Not with this. If the Vruks learn that the Mora are our allies, the plan falls apart. We'll have no chance of gaining the upper hand. You must do this. You alone. You cannot speak a word of this to Valko or Dragan."

"Dragan can be trusted, I swear—"

"Adrijana, your princess commands you to mention it to no one,"

Simeon said firmly, giving me a glimpse of the power he might one day wield. "Will you obey?"

I glared at him for a moment, then turned to Nevena. "Yes. Of course."

"Let us proceed then." Nevena stood.

"What, now?"

"No time like the present." Simeon grinned and wrapped his arm around Nevena's narrow shoulders. "We have all we need to bind us by law. A Mesmer and a witness."

She gazed up at him with a reverence I recognized. For I felt that for another. A pang of longing for Dragan filled me. A desire to pick up where we'd left off.

"Should we go to the window?" Georgi suggested. The large bay window revealed only a white wall of mist, but it did make for a comelier altar than the table filled with empty tea cups and plitka crumbs.

As I stood, I realized something. I turned to Simeon. "Was this the secret you were keeping? Why you've been taking verbenia?"

He nodded. "We couldn't risk one of the Mesmers picking it out of my head."

"And the star-bird? Yours as well?"

"Yes. Xaranti likes to stay close, but we can't risk her being seen just yet."

I shook my head, amazed at it all, but grateful to be let in on the secret. "How did you keep her secret when we were children?"

"She just came to me a year ago. When I was of age."

Nevena's karakal, Roja, was curled on the window seat, and when I approached, she leaped to her feet with a hiss, her two tails thrashing.

I shied back.

"Roja, mind your manners," Nevena *tsked*, waving her off the seat with a hand.

Roja darted off through our legs.

"I wonder what's gotten into her." Nevena shook her head.

This day was getting stranger by the minute. Georgi handed me a book.

"What's this?"

"Adrjssian legal code. It has the marriage rites," he said. "Unless you want to wing it?"

"Ovyato no." I positioned myself before Nevena and Simeon, my back to the window. Georgi stood across from me with a smile, his eyes fixed upon me. I fumbled with the bookmark, burying myself in the pages.

The words were all there, the explanation. The Mesmer would say the rites and then bind the emotions of the couple together at the end. Neither Valko nor Dragan had taught me that. "There's some magic I've never tried before," I admitted. "I'm not sure exactly how to do it."

Simeon's and Nevena's gazes were fixed on each other, their hands clasped. "I'm sure you'll figure it out." Nevena was unperturbed.

This was madness. I opened my crown node, taking in the dancing rainbow of the oras around me. Nevena's ora was streaked with gray sorrow, but her and Simeon's love for each other pulsed and shone in dancing shades of blush and rose, overpowering any other emotion. I softened. However sudden this felt, it would bond together two dear friends who loved each other—and potentially save the kingdom in the process. I was proud to play a part in it.

Georgi's ora no longer showed any smears of pink as he watched me, which I was grateful for. My heart belonged to a golden-haired man with violet eyes.

I cleared my throat. "Are you sure you're ready?"

"Read the book, Jana," Simeon said with a smile.

So I did.

# CHAPTER 26

*J* walked back to my room slowly, my mind twisted in knots. I couldn't make sense of all that had happened. The Vruk, the Mora, the Mesmers—it all made my head spin. Why didn't people just say what they thought—do what they say? I supposed a Mesmer of all people should know better.

Then there was the strange mist and Valko—two more mysteries that didn't sit well with me. Had Valko had a hand in his oldest friend's assassination attempt? And if not, how had the Vruks manipulated the asp and made it do their bidding?

Valko had said the Vruks trained the asps—but that sounded like the power of a Mesmer. Was it possible there was some Mesmerism in West Adrjssia after all? But they hated our power.

I needed to talk these things out. Research. I was certain the strange mist had some connection to what was going on—it seemed to be the only entity who was two steps ahead in this whole sordid mess. If I found a way to summon it, or even communicate with it, perhaps it could tell us where disaster would strike next.

My feet carried me toward the Mesmer workshop—the most likely source of answers. I was steadfast in ignoring the other puzzle knocking persistently at the door of my mind. Me and Dragan. Our kiss. The dizzying feel of his hands across my skin.

I pressed a hand to the stone wall, pausing for a moment to steady myself. Gods, I couldn't even think of what had happened between us without my body quivering. I wanted him badly. And the thought that maybe I could have him scared me more than anything. If I appeared at his chamber door tonight, would he take me to his bed?

I'd kissed boys before—Simeon when I'd been nine, Bostam Rusk last year after the harvest fest, Jamye the blacksmith's apprentice once I'd noticed how nicely his form had responded to months of hammering metal. Georgi. Poor, sweet Georgi. But all of those had been eclipsed by Dragan's kiss. It was all I could do to ignore the way my body ached for him—in places I hadn't even known existed.

But if we were together…it would change everything. For me, for us, for my life here. I should think on it rationally and with a cool head, understand the meaning of my choice. But damn it if I didn't want to throw caution to the wind and leap. Freefall had never looked so enticing.

I let myself into the workshop and began browsing the shelved titles for something that might give me insight into what was unfolding in Selojia.

The door opened behind me and Valko stormed inside. He crossed to the messy desk and pulled out a stack of folded parchment. He didn't seem to even know I was there.

I schooled my features to look neutral. "Valko."

He startled, his hands scrambling with the parchment. As if to hide something. "You."

*What was on that desk?* "I want to help."

"You can help by staying out of the way." He looked like he had aged a decade. "I don't want you getting pulled into this mess."

I softened. I had learned that it was best to ignore Valko's snips and keep asking questions. He liked knowledge and would share it, when pushed. "The Vruks. Do you think Matija or Spirodon controlled the asp?"

He shook his head. "Those two—no. There's something else afoot here."

I couldn't help but agree with that. "The power to manipulate an animal sounds like Mesmerism. Could the Vruks have Mesmers of their own?"

"They despise Mesmerists. Have their eyes plucked out. You know that, Adrijana."

I approached his desk and pulled up a stool. "But don't the Vruks dose their whole population with verbenia?"

"It's mixed in their morning tea."

"When I was being dosed, my eyes were green. I looked normal. But still, I could see colors around people—emotions. My powers were still there. Wouldn't it be possible that these snake charmers are Mesmerists who don't even know what they are? Like I was?"

Valko leaned against his desk for a moment, considering. "It's a novel theory. But I do not think so. The verbenia nullifies our powers. You could see emotions, but you couldn't manipulate them. They wouldn't be able to affect the snakes."

I frowned. So much for that theory. I thought of the only other clue I had. The mist. If I spoke of it, would he give away some clue, some tell that he was connected?

"Out with it," he said.

"What?"

"Your other question." He sighed. "Ask and then leave me in peace. I have a country to hold together while my friend lies dying."

"Have you ever heard of a Mesmer seeing—mist?"

"Mist?" He gestured out the window, to the wall of white outside. "It's the misty season. There's mist all around us."

"Inside. Moving. Almost as if—it had consciousness."

He frowned. "Did you see such a thing?"

I hesitated. Did I want to share the secret of the mist with him? I wasn't sure. I didn't know if he could be trusted anymore. "No, just wondering if it's possible. What it could mean."

He gave me an exasperated look. I'd never been a good liar. "In this hypothetical scenario, did this mist have colors or shape like an ora?"

"No. White. Formless."

He shrugged. "I'd say the person was imagining things. Jumping at ghosts when they should be focused on their training."

I narrowed my eyes. "It's a little hard to focus on training when people keep dying."

"It's none of your concern, Adrijana."

"None of my…?" I spluttered. "I live in this country too. I'll fare just as poorly as you if the Vruks defeat us."

Valko just blinked at me with a weary expression on his lined face. "Anything else?"

"No. Thank you for your help." I stood and marched toward the door. "Or lack thereof," I muttered under my breath.

I slammed the door behind me, letting out a growl of frustration in the hallway.

Dragan turned round the corner, striding toward me like a blond angel. "That door must be guilty of a grave injustice."

"Valko. He's just so—so—argh!"

"Yes, that is one of his defining characteristics." A smile curved on Dragan's striking face.

I shook my head. "I amuse you."

"To the contrary. You enchant me."

My breath caught. Here, in the hallway, in the daylight, I wasn't nearly as bold as I had been. But I was just as desperately drawn to him. I reached out and took his hand. "Dragan… What happened last night—"

His thumb drew slow circles on the back of my hand, addling my thoughts. Stoking the fire inside me. "It was a mistake," he said.

Disappointment pierced me through as surely as an arrow. But something strange happened inside of me. Instead of withdrawing as I should have, his words fueled the fire hotter. What I'd felt last night had been beyond anything I'd ever known. It had been like taking verbenia all my life and then suddenly seeing the blinding light of true colors. I wouldn't let it go without a fight. At least not before I drank from that forbidden cup. Fully. So I met his eyes in a challenge. "Was it?"

"You're young—"

"So are you, Dragan. Besides, I'm of age," I said. He tried to pull his hand back, but I held on. Took a step closer. He couldn't kiss me like *that* and expect me to walk away.

"But I'm in a position of authority over you. I don't want you to feel...obligated."

"I'm not dazzled by your power or your position. I'm as powerful a Mesmer as you."

"Of course. That's not what I mean—"

"I want *you*, Dragan." Dear Ovyato, what was I saying? Was I really confessing my feelings for him?

Dragan stilled, his eyes tracing my features with such diligence, I swore I could feel the feather-light touch. "It complicates everything," he whispered.

"Everything is already complicated. This is simple." *Please, let it be simple.* I stepped in close again, chasing his eyes when he tried to avoid my gaze. "Do you have feelings for me?"

"I think you know the answer to that question." He growled. "It's not enough."

He felt the same. I dropped his hand so he couldn't feel how badly I was shaking. I grabbed the lapels of his jacket instead. Pulled him closer. I had to convince him to give us a chance. "Maybe this time, it's enough."

He shook his head. "I'm not the man you think I am—"

I pressed a finger to his lips and his eyes hooded, fixed on my mouth. "I know who you are. You don't scare me." I traced my fingers along his bottom lip, as soft as silk. I was a woman possessed, a seductress drunk on her own power. "Just once." I just wanted to taste him one time—

That surge of force overtook me once again as Dragan crushed his lips to mine, as we crashed back against the wall, his body pinning me. Hard. Insistent.

His hands cradled my face as he devoured me with his kisses—soft and hard, gentle and unyielding all at once.

I couldn't think, I couldn't breathe, I was no longer thought or emotion, just pure animal desire—golden and warm and all-consuming. The words he had once spoken flashed bright in my mind. *"Desire never lies."* I longed for Dragan the way that plant had longed for sunlight. I'd been trapped in the dark too long, and now, suddenly, I could see.

My body took over. My hands roamed over his back and into his hair like possessed things. My blood boiled like a kettle left on too long.

He pulled back, leaving empty air between us, and I let out a little animal mew of disappointment. But he grabbed my hand and tugged me down the hall. "Not here."

We were going to his room. Yes, finally—and then we were inside, the door slammed, alone, alone, blessedly alone.

Dragan rounded on me; my back hit the door with a thump. He pressed his forearms to the wood beside my ears, framing me, capturing me as surely as a fox in a snare. He was breathing heavily, a flush on his cheeks. "Are you certain? If we go much further, I won't want to stop."

I grabbed his belt and pulled his hips against mine. "I'm certain."

"I was praying you'd say that." He seized me by my thighs and pulled me up so I straddled his narrow hips. I gave a squeak of surprise, wrapping my arms around his shoulders. We crossed the room in a blink and flopped onto the bed, me beneath him.

He ran his fingers down the curve of my chin, my neck, up and over the top of my breasts. "Let's get this off, shall we?"

A tidal wave of heat roared through me, leaving a delicious low ache in its wake. "You first." I pulled his coat over his shoulders, and he shrugged out of it, letting it fall. I wanted to see him—the stretch of muscles I could feel beneath the soft cotton of his shirt. He pulled his shirt over his head and I let my hands drift over his strong chest, the rippled expanse of his stomach. He knelt above me, watching me revel in him.

"You like what you see?" he said with that arrogant smirk that was so Dragan.

"Passable." I pressed my lips together to keep from smiling.

184

His jaw dropped in mock outrage. "Passable?" He tipped on top of me, catching himself with strong arms, and dipped down to claim a kiss. "I'll show you just how delicious *passable* can be," he whispered before flicking his tongue up the sensitive shell of my ear.

"We'll see." My words trembled and with a throaty laugh, Dragan set to proving his point.

* * *

THE AFTERNOON BLED INTO EVENING. Dragan and I only came up for air when my stomach growled so loud that I cringed in embarrassment.

I'd never known such giddy abandon. Dragan and I explored every inch of each other with silken touches and warm lips. I couldn't seem to get enough of him—I was like a starving woman at a feast, gorging myself and then pausing, only to see something far too delectable to deny myself.

"We need food," Dragan finally announced, his lips lingering on the curve of my shoulder.

I pouted. "Don't go."

He brushed a curl off my forehead. "I'll be back, Adrijana. Trust me."

I sighed. "I worry that everything will change when one of us walks out of this room."

"It won't change how I feel about you." The words were soft. "I'll bring wine."

I considered.

"And cheese."

I relented. "Fine, for the cheese, I'll release you."

He laughed and grabbed for his trousers. "Never met a woman who could say *no* to cheese."

My heart tugged at the thought of all the other women he might have wooed with promises of fine dairy, but I shoved the thought aside. What was it to me that he had been with women before? I didn't expect him to be a priest. Especially with a form like that.

185

I watched him get dressed, my cheeks heating at the memory of how brazenly I'd run my hands over the planes of his body.

When the door clicked shut behind him, I flopped back into the bed. Try as I might, I couldn't keep the grin off my face. I pressed my lip together, but it kept resurfacing. Surely, I had never felt this blissful in my entire life.

* * *

I SLEPT in Dragan's massive bed that night, tucked tight in the crook of his arm.

My dreams were strange.

In the dream I slipped from the bed, from my body, leaving him lying like an angel, one arm thrown up above his head as if to ward off the night.

But then he floated from his body as well, a spectral smile breaking across his face.

"I want to show you the world, Adrijana. Come with me?"

"Is this a dream, or is it real?" I examined our bodies, twined together, my head resting on his chest.

"Who says it can't be both?"

"Typical opaque Mesmer answer."

He took my spectral hand. "Let's go."

The silver cords connecting to our bodies unspooled into the night as we flew above the palace and over the sea. As we flew away from land, the mist eventually thinned, revealing a fingernail crescent moon and the night sky studded with stars.

"What do you know of the Mora?" I asked him, thinking of Simeon and Nevena's new alliance.

"That they refused to get involved in the squabbles between the other clans. That when the Ostrovs tried to force them to join our alliance, they sailed away for more fruitful shores. Taking the entirety of our naval might with them."

The sea stretched endlessly beyond us. "It's hard to imagine there's land to find out there."

"But there is. The Thracian invasion from the west many centuries ago showed us that. Our little continent isn't all there is."

"Do you think they'll return?"

"Yes. They are tied to us. The four gods, the four land clans, we represent the seasons. The Vruks are winter, the Ostrovs are summer, Durvos for fall, and Lozians spring. The turning of our world, our cycle. But the Mora—they are something more. The path our world treads through the stars. Their cycle is longer and stranger, but it is a cycle nonetheless. They will return."

A shooting star dashed across the sky, hurling itself from the heavens. We floated above the ocean for a time longer, watching the stars.

"Come," Dragan finally said. "There's something else I want to see."

We zipped through the night sky to the west, inland over Selojia, over the Lozian plains. In the distance, a different kind of light marred the horizon. "What is that?"

"That is the Vruk army."

The glow was from their campfires.

We landed amongst a legion of hide-and-fur tents. Flags of blue and white with the Vruk sigil—a single mountain peak over a row of jagged icicles—flew over tents painted an ochre red that looked suspiciously like dried blood.

I looked about in dismay. "There have to be hundreds of them."

"Thousands."

We walked through the tents, past fires surrounded by grizzled warriors drinking and dicing. It was strange, feeling so exposed to the enemy around me. *They can't see you,* I reminded myself. But I couldn't help but imagine these men pouring through the streets of Selojia, axes and hatchets spraying blood. The Adrjssian people wouldn't stand a chance.

Dragan led us to a tent that was larger and more ornate than the rest, its walls hung with panels decorated with twisting knots and symbols. "Who's in there?"

"That is the tent of King Andrej, leader of West Adrjssia and the Vruk clan."

I was curious to get a look at him. I started forward, but Dragan caught my hand. "Don't."

"Why not?"

"Shadow-Bringer. King Andrej is in possession of a dagger imbued with the power of a Mesmer. According to the legends, when he wears it, he's able to see us."

I gaped. "So it's not just a myth?"

"I don't think so. We can't risk it, anyway. The power of every Mesmer eye he cut out was funneled into that metal. It's a dark magic."

I looked back at the tent. If I could have shivered in this form, I would have. My sense of invulnerability crumpled around me, leaving me exposed, here among our enemies. "Let's go."

As I turned to leave, I caught sight of a smaller tent set next to the king's. An eye with a slash was scrawled above the front flap in crude, white paint. The sign for warding against Mesmers. "Dragan, look. What do you think—"

My words caught in my throat as a woman emerged from the tent. She was short and slim, but her shoulders were thrown back, her posture almost regal in her velvet dress. Around her silver hair, and across her eyes, a purple strip of cloth was tied. A blindfold.

An awful certainty flooded me. That blindfold hid vacant sockets where violet eyes had once been. "She's a Mesmer, isn't she? A former Mesmer."

"Yes," Dragan admitted. "Come. Let us leave. You shouldn't have to think about such awful things." He took my hand and jerked me up into the sky. I looked back, drinking in the sight of the woman. Her dress and tent were fine. It seemed she was taken care of, despite the cruelty evident on her face. Who was she to the Vruks?

She'd stopped walking, and I swore she was looking at me. And then she lifted a single hand and waved.

My mouth dropped open. I pulled free from Dragan, floating in the sky. "Dragan, she waved at me."

He turned back. "The Wretched cannot see any longer. It's not possible."

"The Wretched?"

"The Mesmers who have had their eyes taken. It's what the Vruks call them."

"Dragan, I'm certain—" Looking back down at the dot-like tents below, I couldn't find her. She'd vanished. "I swear she looked right at us and waved."

"If that's true, then it's even more imperative that we don't tarry here. Come." Dragan retook my hand and we flew back to Selojia, to his chamber, to our bodies.

I woke with a gasp, shoving up to one elbow.

His eyes were gleaming dully in the night.

"That wasn't a dream, was it?"

"I thought it would be good for you to see what we face. To understand. I'm sorry if I upset you."

I settled back down, my cheek on his warm chest. "You didn't," I lied. "But that woman. Dragan, I'm not imagining what I saw."

"I believe you think you saw her wave. But it's not possible, Ardijana. Maybe she was just raising a hand to block out the light of the moon. Or wave away a fly."

"Maybe," I admitted. But she'd been looking right at me.

He pulled me in close, and it wasn't long before his breathing evened.

As for me, it took me a long while to get to sleep.

# CHAPTER 27

*J* woke to a kiss from Dragan laid gently on my cheek. I
smiled and pulled him back down for more.

He was already dressed, his hair combed. "Day awaits."

"I knew this would come." I pouted.

"I'm going to oversee the search of the ambassador's chambers.
Would you like to come?"

I perked up at that. "Yes." It would feel good to do something
useful. "I need to change and bathe, though." My hair was a tangle
after an afternoon and evening spent with Dragan.

"Of course. Meet at their chambers in an hour?"

"Perfect." I sat up, the covers pulled up over my chest. "Hand me
my dress?"

Dragan picked it up off the floor, regarding it with a look of
contemplation. "You mean this dress?" I reached for it, and he tugged
it out of the way playfully. "I think you might have to come get it."

I rolled my eyes. "Dragan..." Though we had explored every inch
of each other, there was something far more exposing about standing
before him in the daylight, with no more than a thin shift.

His eyes softened as he handed it to me. "You're beautiful, Jana.
Never doubt it." He pressed a kiss to my cheek and let himself out.

After dressing, I walked back to my chamber on legs made of jelly. My body was deliciously sore, aware of new sensations and secrets.

I found Hristina inside, tidying. She turned in surprise, her hands on her hips. "And just where have you been?"

I blushed. "I fell asleep in the workshop. Studying late."

"Uh-huh." She clearly didn't believe me. "You look a fright." She came and picked up a tangled curl. "Where have all your bells gone? You don't have one left. And look at these—" She grabbed my hand, examining my fingernails. "You look like a common ruffian."

I frowned. My fingernails were packed with some sort of white dirt or powder. How had that gotten there? But I hardly remembered all the places Dragan and I had been tangled yesterday. My bells must have fallen out, and the dirt under my nails, well, there had to be some explanation.

"I think a bath is in order," I said sheepishly.

Hristina clucked her tongue. "I think you're right."

WHEN I MET Dragan in the ambassadors' chambers an hour later, Hristina had scrubbed me down, threaded my hair with fresh bells, and wrapped me in a dress of cerulean silk. The cut on the back of my hand was still angry and red, and the skin around it itched fiercely. Perhaps if I had time later, I'd go to the medical ward and see about obtaining some soothing cream.

Dragan was sitting behind the ambassadors' desk when I entered, reading a letter. He looked up, taking me in with a languid sweep of his violet eyes.

I couldn't help the wave of heat that overcame me, the memories that flooded to the surface.

"You look well this morning," Dragan said.

It was then that I noticed Simeon, pawing through some books on the shelf in the corner of the room.

"As do you. Simeon, are you here to help us look?"

"The king's condition is grave." Simeon leaned against the bookshelf. "Neven—the princess—is distraught. We have to find some answers."

"We will," Dragan said.

We better. Or Nevena would be next.

"Where should I look?"

"That bookshelf." Dragan pointed, while Simeon said, "The fireplace."

They looked at each other, nonplussed. Dragan inclined his head. "The fireplace is a fine place to start."

The mantel above the fireplace was crowded with books and scrolls. I grabbed a stack and went to sit in one of the leather armchairs, when I noticed something. A little pile of white dust had collected on the ground to the left of the fireplace.

I frowned.

My eyes traced the bricks. There was something familiar about this place—something right on the tip of my brain. It was like a mote of light hanging in the air, but when I tried to fix my thoughts upon it, it darted away.

The mortar around one of the bricks was cracked. It was subtle. So subtle, I almost didn't notice it, though I somehow knew it was worth further examination.

I set the books down and went to crouch before it, my fingers questing around the brick. Brushing more of the white dust free. The brick was loose!

I worked at it, puling with my fingernails, inching it out.

The brick came out in my hand. I looked inside the hollow left by it. Empty. I frowned. I'd been sure there was something inside.

Then I looked at the brick in my hand and gasped. It was hollowed out. I pulled out three letters, all addressed to Spirodon. No other address. They'd come from somewhere in the palace.

My heart racing, I went back to the chair and unfolded the first letter with shaking hands.

"Have you found something?" Simeon asked.

He and Dragan both came to stand behind me, reading over my

shoulder. The first letter wasn't addressed to anyone, and no one had signed it.

*Your proposition is an interesting one, but forgive me for wondering why you'd take such a risk. How can I trust this offer is genuine, and not a feint to ensnare us in a treasonous plot against the king? And are you so certain you can consolidate power after he is dead? Even a bad king is worse than a civil war. I need proof of both before we even consider your offer.*

"Is it just me, or does this sound like a conspiracy against the king's life?" My voice was faint.

"It's not just you," Simeon said. "Is there anything else? Any name or signature? Anything to show who these are from?"

Simeon took one letter and Dragan took the other, scanning the contents.

I looked at the hole in the fireplace facade. *How had I known it was there?* Was it luck? Some Mesmer intuition? I thought of the white dirt under my fingernails. It looked identical to the ground mortar from the fireplace. But I'd been with Dragan all night. There was no way I'd come here and discovered the letters.

Simeon read his.

"*I thank you for the assurances you provided. They are sufficient. Princess Nevena may be an issue. She is headstrong and suspects West Adrjssia had a hand in her mother's death.*"

Simeon's face was growing dark, and he choked over the next words, the letter shaking in his hand.

"*She would fight against such a match. Is her hand the only prize you are willing to take? For it will not be easy doing. Nevena has several cousins in the Durvo clan who might be good matches and would tighten your ties with Selojia. And we have plenty of fertile farmland in the West that would provide ample sustenance for the Vruk people. Consider it as an alternative.*"

Dragan sat down heavily in the other chair, his face gone pale, one hand before his mouth.

My mind was spinning like a top. Someone in the palace had plotted with the Vruks to end King Petar's life. To sell Nevena or some poor other defenseless Durvo girl to the Vruks like cattle.

"Read yours," Simeon said.

Dragan cleared his throat.

"*We are in agreement. Make your move before the next full moon. We will be ready.*"

"That's it?" Simeon asked, snatching the letter from him and turning it over to look at the back.

"You need more?" Dragan let out a choked laugh, his eyes still unfixed, staring at the floor before him. "It's clear as day."

Dread prickled up my spine. The handwriting on my letter looked familiar to me. I thought I knew who they were from as well. But there was only one person who would shake Dragan so. "You know who they're from."

He cleared his throat. "I think...Why don't you both come with me?"

For once, Simeon didn't ask questions. We followed Dragan out of the ambassadors' chambers, through the palace hallways.

I knew where we were going. The Mesmer workshop.

It was empty when we entered, but for the mess of years of scholarship and living.

Simeon took it all in with obvious interest. It seemed he'd never been here.

Dragan crossed to Valko's desk, rummaging through the papers there. He looked at me. "You said you saw him here? Saw him hide something from your view?"

I nodded woodenly.

Dragan returned with a large journal, laying it out on the table in the center of the room. He smoothed one of the letters on top of the left page so the two sat side by side.

Despair clawed at me as I took in the undeniable.

"This is the Prime Mesmer's journal?" Simeon asked. His voice was low. Dangerous.

Dragan dragged a hand through his hair. "I'm afraid so."

I let my eyes close, suddenly feeling very tired. Valko. I'd never liked the man—he was a brusque, unfeeling taskmaster, but he was one of us. A Mesmer. The list of those I could trust was so short. I hadn't wanted to believe that he was what they said we all were. Devious, untrustworthy, traitorous. I hadn't wanted those prejudices to be proven right.

"At least we know." Simeon put both hands on the table, as if he needed its strength to hold him. "Valko was working with the Vruks to plot the king's death." He brought down his fist on the table with a crash, making me jump. "Nevena will be devastated."

"What's happened?"

We all looked up with a start.

Valko was standing in the doorway that led to the library, a scowl on his hawkish face.

Simeon slowly pulled his sword out of its scabbard. "Prime Mesmer, you are under arrest for the attempted murder of King Petar."

Valko let out a harsh laugh, crossing his arms before him. "What nonsense is this?"

Dragan held up a letter. "We found these in the Vruk ambassadors' chambers. They're in your handwriting. Planning treason. The murder of a king."

Valko shook his head. "You understand nothing. These letters are not about our king. It was King Petar who gave me the mission to work with Spirodon in the first place!"

My brow furrowed. Could he be speaking truth?

"If that's true, why wasn't I told?" Dragan asked.

"Because the king doesn't trust his Para-Mesmer with every piece of intelligence. Not the way he trusts me."

"Unfortunately for you, the only person who can confirm your story lays dying," Simeon said.

"That's not true," Valko said. "Spirodon can speak the truth of it. The verbenia is almost out of his system. Question him tomorrow."

Simeon shook his head. "Regardless of what you say, I need to take you into custody in the meantime. We'll sort it out. If you are innocent, then you'll be released in no time."

Valko's face darkened. "I will not be arrested in my own home! I have given everything to this country—this monarchy—and I will not allow my loyalty to be questioned."

"You do your cause no aid by resisting arrest." Dragan stepped forward. "Go with Simeon." He met my eyes and motioned with his head toward the door. He wanted me to go. Get backup?

I inched out of the way as Simeon and Valko faced off.

"Leave my workshop," Valko thundered.

"Not without you in irons," Simeon said.

Valko's amethyst eyes narrowed, but then he blinked in surprise. Had he been trying to Compel Simeon?

"Valko, stop this," Dragan said, his hands out as if he were dealing with a wild beast.

A frenzied rap on the door stunned all of us.

Another knock came and the door opened. "Prime Mesmer?" It was an older servant, with graying hair at his temples. As he took in the scene—Valko and Dragan facing off against each other, Simeon with naked blade in his hand—he let out a little yelp.

"What is it?" Valko asked.

"Prime Mesmer, I bear grievous tidings. The king—" He stumbled over his words, pausing.

"Out with it!" Valko barked.

"The king has died."

All the fight left the room.

Valko sank into a chair as if his legs couldn't hold him.

Simeon sheathed his sword. "I must check on the princess." He looked at Valko with indecision but seemed to see a broken man. Would he send guards to arrest Valko? I didn't know. My shock was too great to think of what came next.

Simeon murmured to the servant and strode from the room.

I found my legs weak as well and dropped heavily into the chair across from him. The cut on my hand was throbbing.

"I couldn't protect him," Valko murmured to himself.

The queen dead, now the king. West Adrjssia on the verge of invasion. I thought of Papa's leg, the invisible wounds the last war had carved in him. Another war seemed inevitable. How many more would suffer?

A longing for Papa, for home, rushed through me. I had yearned to come to Selojia, desperate for adventure. Now, I only wished for a day without plots and danger and death. Maybe it had been a mistake to come here. My eyes traced Dragan's features and I softened. No. How could it have been a mistake when I'd found something so precious?

The door opened and half a dozen soldiers filed into the room.

Valko just stood and gathered his robes around him. He looked at Dragan, dark violet eyes sharp and penetrating. Then he looked at me. "I would like to speak to the princess alone. Would you carry my request?"

"Of course," I whispered.

With a nod, he followed the soldiers out. Dragan followed too, leaving me alone in the workshop.

My eyes filled with tears. Everything was dreadfully wrong. Valko couldn't have done this.

Somehow, this was all the Vruks' fault. It had to be. They were the ones who were cruel and intolerant. They were the ones with the vested interest in tearing Adrjssia apart with suspicion and doubt. They were the ones who benefited if the royal family was murdered.

My fingers curled into fists. I needed to be with Dragan when he questioned the ambassadors tomorrow. To see for myself what they said about Valko. I owed him that much, at least—to ensure that admissions they made about his complicity were genuine.

Dragan reentered the workshop and closed the door, leaning back against it for a moment.

"I want to question the ambassadors with you tomorrow."

His eyes widened with surprise. "Why?"

"Something doesn't add up. I need to hear what they say for myself."

Dragan crossed the room and looked down at me. He reached out and swiped a thumb across my cheek, wiping a stray tear. "Such things are not pretty. Are you sure you can handle it?"

"Of course."

"And you will not think less of me, to see the things I must do?"

I took his hand and kissed his palm, praying I spoke true. "Never. I understand these are hard times."

197

He hesitated. "I think it's a bad idea. I could relay everything said—"

"I *have* to be there, Dragan. I have to see for myself."

His shoulders slumped. "Very well."

I wiped the remnants of my tears from the corners of my eyes.

Dragan leaned in, taking my chin in a gentle hand. "He does not deserve your tears. He is a traitor."

"How can you say that? He dedicated his life to this kingdom. There has to be another explanation."

"Did you not read the letters yourself? Did you not see him lingering outside the ambassadors' door? Did you not yourself see the sign of Compulsion in Ioseph before he killed Aleksi?"

"Those letters…" I shook my head. Something else was stoking the unease within me. "How did I know they were there? I went right to them."

"With Mesmerism comes a powerful intuition. We cannot always explain it. But clearly, something's been guiding you, Adrijana. Showing you the clues to unravel this mess."

"The mist. But it didn't show me the location of the letters." And then there was the matter of the white powder under my fingernails, which I had no explanation for.

"Do not doubt yourself, Adrijana. And do not doubt what we have found. Sometimes the simplest explanation is the true one, even if we do not wish it to be so." Dragan took my hands in his and rubbed his thumb across my knuckles. I hissed as his thumb swiped across my cut.

Dragan frowned. "This looks bad. What happened?"

"I think I caught myself on a thorn in the rose garden."

"It must itch like crazy. There's a salve that will help. I'll have Hristina bring you some."

My heart squeezed at his concern. But my thoughts quickly returned to the horrible event before us. "What I don't understand is why. Why would Valko conspire to kill the king? After standing by him all these years?"

"For money or for power, men will betray it all."

"But he is strongest at the king's side. What power could he gain from killing him?"

"By law, the Prime Mesmer is next in the line of succession after the royal family."

My eyes widened as Dragan pulled me into an embrace, burying his face in my curls. I couldn't banish a sudden bolt of realization. If that was true, then no one stood to gain more from the king's death than Valko. Except perhaps Dragan.

# CHAPTER 28

*A* chill permeated me as I walked from the Mesmers' workshop toward my chamber, except for the cut on my hand, which throbbed even hotter. I ignored it.

I needed to talk to Nevena about what I'd learned. I'd promised to be her eyes and ears. But what had I learned? Nothing concrete. Simeon would fill her in on everything regarding the letters and Valko's arrest. Simeon—her husband. I still hadn't gotten used to that, not by a long shot.

So what more did I have to add? Did I truly think Dragan could have had something to do with the king's death? I gave myself a little shake, as if I could dislodge the horrible thought once and for all. No. I'd been with Dragan the night the king was poisoned. He couldn't have controlled the snake. Our oras had been together.

Relief welled in me. It couldn't have been him. I let out a shaky laugh as guilt needled me. After all Dragan had done for me, after all we'd shared, my suspicion had flared at a moment's notice. How could I ever think such a thing of him? Dragan was one of the few people I *knew* I could trust here. These plots and intrigues were twisting me in knots.

Back in my room, I flopped onto the bed. I was overcome by the desperate urge to talk to someone, but whom? Nevena's father had just died, and Simeon was busy comforting her and dealing with his duties. I couldn't talk to Georgi without feeling guilty over what I'd done to him. Valko had been arrested and Dragan—I didn't want to appear too eager. Needy.

Whom I really wanted to talk to was Papa.

A knock came at the door. Hristina let herself in before I could answer. "I brought you some lunch and some salve from the Para-Mesmer." She put the tray down on the desk and brought me a little pewter pot. "Why didn't you tell me you'd injured yourself?"

"I thought it would go away. But it won't stop itching."

"The roses do that. This should help."

I opened the little pot and rubbed some of the herbaceous-smelling salve on my cut. It was deliciously cool and tingly on my skin. "Thank you."

"Do you need anything else?"

"No. You're a dream. I'm feeling tired. I think I'll take a nap."

Hristina gave a little curtsy, the bells in her copper hair jingling softly.

After she let herself out, I lay back down on the bed. I hadn't been completely honest with her. There was something else I needed to do.

I slipped out of my body and headed out my window to the west. I couldn't talk to Papa, but I could at least see him. Papa had warned me when we'd come that Selojia was a nest of snakes. I'd laughed him off, thought him a bitter old man.

But I was starting to see how right he was.

Our cottage looked the same as the day I'd left—packed stone walls and a dull, tiled roof. He'd let the flowers in the window-boxed shrivel, and the backyard garden was looking bedraggled. I shook my head. Papa never took care of himself. Always the verbenia.

I found the interior quiet. I was pleased to see that while things weren't nearly as tidy as I'd kept them, Papa wasn't living in total disarray. A piece of paper was open on the rough-hewn dining table, and my eyes widened as I took in the text. It was my letter, so worn that it threatened to fall apart at the folds. My heart squeezed. Next to it, beside a pot of ink and a dirty quill, was an envelope scrawled in Papa's messy handwriting. Addressed to Adrijana Mironacht, at the Ostrov Palace, Selojia. I longed to pick up the letter and tear into it, to hold it against my chest. Why had it taken him so long to write back? Never mind. I'd read it in a few days when it arrived at the palace.

I emerged from the cottage and headed down the lane toward the rock cliffside where we grew our verbenia. I found Papa right where I'd expected him to be, his cane leaned against the rock, his gnarled hands retying the lattice-work that supported the tendrils and vines of the herb. Even with my emotions dimmed in my Projected form, I could swear a lump was forming in my throat. Gods, I had missed him. How had I not realized just how much?

I sat down against the rock, leaning back so I could take in his face as he worked. He looked older and thinner, but he still whistled softly, an Ostrov folk tune that I recognized. I closed my eyes and let the familiar refrain wash over me. For a moment, it was like nothing had changed.

Except I was a ghost who wasn't really here.

I didn't regret going to Selojia. If I hadn't, I never would have discovered who I truly was. And I never would have found Dragan. But I regretted that I'd left Papa behind. That I'd rejected him. "I'm sorry, Papa," I said softly. "I'll come visit in person as soon as I can."

I stood and a wave of dizziness overtook me. I shot out a hand, holding myself up against the stone wall. My vision blurred and tilted.

What was happening? I shouldn't have been able to get dizzy in this form, right? Was something going on with my physical body? I needed to get back. I made to dart into the sky, but the world went dark as consciousness slipped away.

* * *

I woke in my bed, the nearby window bathing me in the weak, gray light of the Misty Season. My head pounded and my body ached as if I'd been tossed about in a butter churn.

I blinked at the window. The light was wrong. It was pouring in, as it did in the morning. But it couldn't be morning. Tenderly, I scooted up to sitting position and put my feet on the floor. A wave of nausea and vertigo washed over me. The cut on my hand was still red and tender. It itched terribly.

On shaky legs, I walked to my desk and settled heavily into the chair. The soup Hristina had brought me was cold and congealed, the roll rock hard. How long had I been asleep? More importantly, where was that salve she'd given me?

I poured myself some water and drank it greedily. Everything hurt. Right down to my teeth and my eyeballs. Something was very wrong. I needed to find out what was going on. I forced myself to stand and slowly walked into the hallway. Hopefully, Dragan would be in the workshop.

Just steps from the door, Hristina slipped out of the workshop. She let out a peep of surprise when she turned and found me there. "My lady! You're awake."

"Awake? How long was I asleep?"

"Over a day has passed. You were sleeping like the dead."

"A day!" I yelped. What the hell had happened that had taken me out for a day? "I need to get to the dungeon. Dragan was going to question Spirodon, and I need to be there."

"I saw the Para-Mesmer coming from that direction over an hour ago. You might have missed it."

*No, no!* That couldn't be. I needed to see the truth of Spirodon's answers myself. I needed to get down there now.

My body protested any movement, and I was forced to lean heavily on the stone walls for support. I hadn't felt this weak since the time I'd contracted yellow flu when I'd been nine and had been abed for two weeks.

I made my way into the bowels of the palace, remembering that only months ago, I'd been trapped behind bars. Falsely connected with the queen's death. And now—there were so many more dead. The threads were a tangle. I located the first guard I could find, a squat man with a thick, ruddy beard. I did my best to straighten my spine and rally my imperious Mesmer calm. "I need to speak to Spirodon. The Vruk ambassador."

"The king's killer? The Para-Mesmer ordered no one in or out of his cell." The guard picked at one of his teeth with the fingernail of his little finger.

"I'm sure he didn't mean me." So Spirodon had confessed?

The guard smirked at me. "Pretty sure you count as no one."

I pressed my lips together. I didn't have time for his rudeness, or to rely on traditional means of convincing him. I opened my crown node and seized his emotions, twisting his tan boredom into brown fear. "Let me in the cell. Now," I barked.

The man's face paled, and his eyes darted back and forth wildly. "Right away."

My stomach clenched and unclenched as I followed him. I shouldn't have done that. Manipulate someone in my anger. It broke the rules and was unethical too. But the man had been infuriating! "So he confessed?" I asked.

"Squealed like a stuck pig." The guard unlocked the thick, wooden cell door and opened it wide, standing aside so I could step inside.

"Spirodon—" My knees almost buckled as I saw what was inside. Spirodon's body swung gently from the ceiling crossbeam, his limbs unmoving. The purpled, bulging condition of his face left me no doubt. The ambassador was dead.

# CHAPTER 29

$\mathcal{I}$ closed the cell door slowly behind me, the shock of what I had just seen dousing me like a bucket of ice water.

"He's dead." The words were faint.

"Whatcha talking about?" The guard peeked through the small, barred opening near the top of the door. "Ovyato's balls!" He fumbled with his keys as he tried get the door back open. He dropped them, swore, and swiped them up off the cold stone floor.

I pressed myself against the weeping stone wall, my breath coming in and out in small, panting spurts. I had no love for Spirodon, but I hadn't wished the man dead. Quite the opposite. Now I'd never be able to confirm the truth about Valko's letters.

"Guard," I said.

The man was emerging from the cell, his eyes haunted.

I clapped. "Guard!"

He looked at me.

"Did Dragan question the ambassador already this morning?"

He nodded. "An hour ago. I need to go tell my captain. The Para-Mesmer will be furious—" He was rambling.

"Go." I shooed him away, then thought better. "Wait. What about the other one? Matija?"

"He's two cells down."

"I will see him." With Matija's tattoos infused with verbenia, the drug would never completely wear off. I wouldn't ever be able to read his ora, but as Dragan said, there were other ways to tell if a man was lying.

The guard unlocked a wooden cell and pushed the door open. I poked my head inside. Matija was chained to the far wall, his head hanging, his blond hair grimy. But when he looked up at me, his glacial-blue eyes still gleamed. Matija was not cowed.

"I need to report what's happened…" The guard was clearly antsy to leave.

"Go. I'll be fine. Just leave me your keys." The guard dropped the heavy ring into my hand and hurried away.

"Tell me of Spirodon and Valko," I asked the ambassador. Everything ached and I wished there were a place for me to sit down. But I held myself tall and still.

His lip curled. "From Spirodon's screams, I think the princess's pet already got all he needed. Why the hell should I tell you anything?"

"I'm trying to verify what was said. I was supposed to take part in that questioning and I was…indisposed."

"Why don't you just ask him yourself?"

I licked my lips. He couldn't know yet that his friend was dead. *Should I tell him?* I didn't see why not. "I'm afraid Spirodon is dead."

Matija went still at that, his ice-blue eyes unblinking. "You lie," he growled.

"I'm sorry. He hung himself."

His lip curled back. "Now I *know* you lie."

I shook my head. "I saw his body myself."

Matija straightened—lithe and predatory. I stood my ground. I would not be intimidated by this man. Not again.

"Then you saw what they wanted you to see. Vruks don't commit suicide. Zamo Idvo forbids it."

"But—who's 'they'?" Why would someone kill Spirodon and make it look like suicide?

He let out a dark burst of laughter. "You truly are a sheep among wolves, aren't you?"

Anger kindled in me. "Perhaps Spirodon was simply a coward, ashamed of what he'd done."

Matija exploded across the room, his chains stopping him just inches from me. I took a step back involuntarily

He sneered at me. "Mark my words: Your Mesmer friend did this. He may have bested Spirodon and he may get me, but there are a whole lot more of us, and we're coming for you. For you purple-eyed freaks and your whole damn country."

"I'll see you at your execution," I said coldly. The moment I stepped out of his cell and slammed the door, I sagged against the dirty stone wall. My heart was racing. The man was awful, but I didn't detect any lies. He didn't believe Spirodon committed suicide. He believed someone had killed him.

But if Spirodon had confessed to working with Valko, why kill him? He would have been executed shortly, anyway.

A chilling thought overtook me. Unless he hadn't confessed, and someone had wanted to cover that up. To make sure he wasn't questioned by another Mesmer. Namely, me. But how could Dragan have known that I would fall ill and be out of commission the day of the questioning? Surely, that was a coincidence. It had to be.

"Adrijana?" A voice called out from a few cells down. A voice I recognized. "Is that you?"

I found Valko in a large cell, comfortably appointed with a narrow bed, desk, and armchair. He was sitting at the desk behind a stack of books.

"Glad to see they've made you comfortable." Down the hall, guards were milling around Spirodon's cell, arguing and gesturing. I showed myself into Valko's cell and closed the door behind me.

"A benefit of fifty years of service." Valko placed a bookmark in the volume on his lap and moved his foot out from behind the desk, revealing to me that he was chained to it. "But they still take precautions."

Valko looked different. As if the last twenty-four hours had aged him. But then I recognized the true difference. "Your eyes." They were green, not the deep purple I was used to.

"Yes, they're dosing me with verbenia so as not to allow me to enchant the guards and traipse out of here. It's a strange feeling, to be cut off. I haven't felt so isolated in years."

"I remember."

Valko cocked his head at me, that gesture that always made him look so much like a bird of prey. "You look unwell, child."

"I'm not sure what happened. I passed out and slept for over a day."

He furrowed his brows. "You have no guesses why?"

I ran a finger lightly over the tender skin on the back of my hand. "I took a cut from one of the roses in the king's garden."

He shook his head. "A scratch from one of those roses would cause a minor skin irritation, nothing more. It would not make a person truly ill."

"Maybe I have a strange constitution?"

"I think there is perhaps a darker answer."

"What do you mean?" I feared I already knew what he was going to say. For I'd been thinking it myself.

"Someone wanted you out from underfoot."

"Someone... Someone like—"

"Dragan." Valko's focus shifted behind me, and my skin prickled to awareness.

A possessive hand settled on my shoulder. "Come to visit your old mentor?" Dragan's words were untroubled, but there was tension in his hard body as he pulled me against his side.

I struggled to stay neutral as I turned to regard him. "I came down here to talk to Spirodon. But—"

"An unfortunate turn of events, indeed."

Valko sat up. "What happened to Spirodon? Has he confirmed that we were in fact plotting to kill the Vruk king, not King Petar?"

I recoiled slightly. Why would a Vruk ambassador plot to kill the Vruk king?

"I'm afraid he did not. He confirmed just the opposite. That you and King Andrej plotted to take down the Adrjssian monarchy. First poor Queen Ksenjia and then Petar."

Valko snorted. "Lies. If he said that, it's only because you tortured a false confession from him. I would like him questioned again, with Adrijana present. I trust her judgment to discern the truth. You've done your best, but I don't think you've corrupted her yet."

My stomach clenched. I think that was the first time Valko had ever expressed faith in me.

Dragan smiled tightly. "I'm afraid that won't be possible. Spirodon is dead. After his confession, he took his own life."

Valko's mouth dropped open, frozen for a moment. Then he started to clap. "Bravo, Dragan, bravo. Even I didn't see that coming. You've tied everything up neatly, haven't you?" He stood and stalked forward. The chain around his ankle halted him just feet from us. He turned to me. "Adrijana, you must know these are lies. King Petar was my best friend. I would never kill him. I need to speak to the princess. Tell her." He reached for my hand, but Dragan pulled me back by my shoulders.

Dragan shook his head. "You'd like that, wouldn't you? To try to turn her back to your side. No, I think your reign of lies has ended. The princess has learned all she needs to from you. Besides, she'll be busy with the coronation tonight."

"Do this thing for me." Valko's evergreen eyes entreated me.

Dragan put his arm around me, but my body didn't respond with tingles as it once had. Not when I was so desperately confused. Dragan's voice drew my attention, soft as velvet. "Come. Hristina told me you were unwell. I would not want you to overtax yourself. Not with the coronation tonight."

My mind was whirling. This was happening all too fast. This was wrong—pieces were out of place, jammed together to make a picture that felt false.

"Come, Adrijana." Dragan pulled me toward the exit, and I had no choice but to let him tow me.

"Wait. Adrijana." Valko retrieved a book from the little table and held it out to me. "Continue your studies. You are the future of

Mesmerism in Adrjssia. It's important you continue your studies." Valko waggled the book at me, his eyes intent.

I reached for the book and Dragan took it first, turning me toward the door. I looked over my shoulder at Valko. *The book*, he mouthed.

Dragan flipped through the book as we left the cell and walked back out of the dungeon. Apparently content the tome contained no hidden messages, he handed it over to me. I tucked it carefully against my breast, praying that it contained the piece of the puzzle that would bring the rest into focus.

# CHAPTER 30

My mind spun as we walked from the dungeon.

"Should you be up and around?" Dragan asked. "I came to get you this morning to question Spirodon, but I couldn't wake you."

Valko's words echoed through my mind. Was it possible that my illness wasn't from the scratch on my hand? I had been rendered indisposed at a convenient time. I'd missed Dragan's questioning of Spirodon, and the ambassador's apparent confession. Now he was dead, and I'd never be able to verify what was said.

"I am feeling better," I said, realizing I had paused far too long after Dragan's question. "But I'm tired. I think I'll go back to my room and rest before the coronation." I needed to be clear from him, to give myself space to think.

"I think that's wise." Dragan wrapped an arm around me and I leaned against him for strength, ignoring the feeling of unease that rippled through me.

We were back to my room quickly, and he turned to me, taking my hands in his. "I need you well, Adrijana. I can't do this without you." He leaned forward and kissed me softly. I stiffened involuntarily, and he drew back with a look of confusion on his face.

211

"I'm just not feeling well still," I fumbled for an excuse. "Everything will be better once I rest." What if Dragan had nothing to do with anything and I was ruining what was between us with wild suspicions?

He traced a finger down the side of my face, sending an involuntary shiver through me. "Sleep well. I will see you this evening."

With a nod, I slipped inside my room.

I flopped back onto my bed as weariness overtook me. I hadn't been lying, not completely anyway. I did feel terrible still. The trip to the dungeon and back had left me weak and achy. But what was worse was the fog of my confusion, as thick as the mist outside. I had the sense that I was missing something, but I couldn't tell what.

I cracked the book Valko had given me: *The Adrjssian Era*. There had to be some clue here, something he was trying to communicate. But as I turned through the pages, nothing stuck out to me. I flipped back to the first page. Well, I would just have to look more carefully then.

* * *

I WOKE to Hristina shaking me, the book tented on my chest.

"My lady," Hristina said. "It's time to get ready for the coronation."

"Hmm?" I looked out the window. It was dark already. I sat up and regretted it immediately. "I fell asleep!"

"It's good you were resting. You were so ill."

I got to my feet and wobbled.

Hristina reached out a hand to steady me. "I brought you some food. Why don't you sit and eat something while I do your hair?"

Hristina dressed me in a gown of white trimmed with silver leaves and did up my hair with pearl-studded pins.

"Hristina, that salve you gave me. Do you have more of it? My hand still itches." The salve was the only thing that I couldn't account for. Maybe I'd had a bad reaction to some ingredient in it.

"Of course, my lady." She opened a drawer in the desk and pulled out the little pot.

I turned it over in my fingers. It had no label. "And where did you get it? The medical ward?"

"The Para-Mesmer gave it to me. He said it would help you."

I licked my lips. Dragan. Of course. It seemed everywhere I turned, there he was. "Thank you." I shoved the little pot into the deep pocket of my dress. I would stop by the hospital ward after the coronation and see what I could find out about this salve.

I shoved down my unease as I made my way to the throne room, where the palace's occupants had gathered to watch their newest monarch be crowned.

The mood was somber, with the crowd in mourning white. King Petar had been much loved, and his death was a blow to the people of Selojia.

The gathered courtiers parted for me and I took a spot near the front. I'd grown used to it—the nervous glances, the wide berth the people gave me, the whispers that followed in my wake. But tonight, for some reason, it bothered me. Maybe because Valko wasn't here with us. His presence had been like a shield—unflappable and unimpeachable. Now, did they wonder if all Mesmers were traitors?

Georgi leaned forward and smiled at me, a few nobles down, and I gave him a warm smile back. At least I still had Georgi.

Simeon stood with three other royal guards on the dais, as handsome as I'd ever seen him in his uniform. When would Nevena announce the truth of their marriage? He deserved to stand at her side before all the world.

The horns struck up and Nevena made her way down the aisle. She looked resplendent in a dress of the deepest purple damask satin, trimmed with white fur. Her brunette curls were threaded with tiny silver bells that chimed as she walked. Huge, amethyst teardrops hung from her earlobes, and another even larger stone was nestled in her bosom. She looked breathtaking. A true queen.

It was Dragan who stood on the dais to put the crown on her head. He looked so handsome, it made my heart hurt, but the sight of him filled me with something other than enchantment this time. A spiderweb of disquiet shrouded me. Perhaps he truly was only trying

213

to help. To shield me from the worst of the court's ugliness. Or perhaps he had secrets of his own.

What I needed was more time to put the pieces together. More time for Valko.

The room erupted into applause and I looked up with a start. Dragan had placed the golden circlet on Nevena's brow. It was done. She was queen.

It didn't take long after Nevena descended the steps for the crowd to break apart. Nevena was surrounded by well-wishers and syco-phants. So I headed for the next best thing.

"Simeon." I sidled up next to him. "Can I have a word?"

Simeon murmured to one of the other guards and took my arm, navigating me through the crowd to a quiet corner. "What is it?"

"I need to talk to Nevena about Valko. I'm not sure he's guilty."

"Why do you say that?"

"So far...just a feeling. But I was supposed to question Spirodon with Dragan, I expressly asked to, and then I fell mysteriously ill. Dragan was the only one who heard Spirodon's confession and who could vouch for its veracity."

"I was there, Jana. He confessed."

"You were?" I blinked in surprise.

"Yes. Dragan didn't do anything to force the confession. Spirodon was transporting letters from King Andrej to Valko, arranging to kill King Petar and marry Nevena to Prince Elian. Effectively allowing Andrej to take over all of Adrjssia without a drop of blood spilled."

"But you wouldn't be able to tell if Spirodon had been Compelled to say that. And then he died, so I couldn't question him myself. Matija said Vruks don't commit suicide."

"Matija is a snake who can't be trusted. I never wanted that man here. And if you think Spirodon was Compelled, then what...?" Simeon lowered his voice. "Are you telling me you think Dragan did this? I thought you two were as thick as thieves."

I bit my lip. Did I think Dragan had done it? The man that I'd bared myself to just two nights prior, body and soul? No. I trusted him. He wouldn't do something like this. "I don't think he did it, but I just feel like there is more going on here than we understand. And before Valko is sentenced…we should take more time. Valko's asked to see Nevena. I think she should see him. Give him a chance to explain. There are other Mesmers in the kingdom. Maybe one is hiding in the palace somewhere."

Georgi walked over and joined us. I patted his arm as Simeon continued. "The queen has considered the evidence and plans to sentence the Prime Mesmer tomorrow. His execution will follow immediately after."

"What do you mean, 'immediately after'?"

"Exactly what I said."

Panic lanced through me like a bolt of lightning. "So Valko could be executed tomorrow? Simeon, Nevena needs to talk to him."

"What's this?" Georgi asked.

"Jana thinks Nevena should let Valko explain himself." Simeon lowered his voice. "But between us, Nevena is furious at Valko for trying to sell her off to the Vruks. I'm not sure she'd be in a frame of mind to listen to anything coming out of his mouth. She said his continued existence grieves her."

Georgi nodded. "Besides, she's been through enough, Adrijana. She lost her brother, then her uncle and both her parents. We shouldn't burden her with any unsupported suspicions."

"If you truly think Valko is innocent, we need proof." Simeon's words were firm, but his eyes were kind.

"You're both right." I heaved a sigh. "It's nothing more than a feeling."

"Feelings are important. But facts matter more. Find something before tomorrow if you want to save Valko." Simeon put a gentle hand on my shoulder.

My mind spun as he walked away. Where to find proof? And before tomorrow? I might as well set out to steal the moon from the sky.

"Are you all right?" Georgi asked. "I didn't see you at dinner last night, or breakfast."

"I was sick." I shoved my hands into the pockets of my dress. My fingertips brushed the little jar of salve. "Actually, Georgi, do you know anything about medicine or herbs?"

"Some. I used to help my cousin at our hospital back in Visoko."

I pulled out the jar and handed it to him. "What does this smell like? Can you tell what it is? Dragan gave it to me."

Georgi took the lid off and sniffed. He drew back, blinking. "It's familiar, but I'm not sure. I can try to figure it out, if you want?"

"That would be wonderful. But be careful. I think I had an odd reaction."

"Adrijana?"

I spun to find myself face to face with Dragan, clad in a coat of heather gray trimmed with silver eye buttons. I summoned a half-hearted smile. "Hello."

"I must speak with you in the hallway for a moment."

My heart thundered to life in my chest. He wanted to talk to me alone? Why? "Of course," I managed. "Georgi, will you excuse me?"

Luckily, Georgi had pocketed the little jar. "Of course."

We walked out of the busy great hall into the quiet corridor. I looked at Dragan with anticipation, willing my heart to slow. I prayed he couldn't hear it racing from where he stood.

"You've drawn away from me," he finally said, catching me straight on in the eyes.

I opened my mouth to protest, but my excuses fell flat. He was right. I *had* been avoiding him. "I just needed a little time."

"If it was because of what happened...between us, it would grieve me deeply. I hope I did not push you too far, too fast."

My mouth dropped open. He thought it was because we'd been together? Certainly, that was part of what made this all so much more confusing, but that wasn't the reason. "I'm sorry if I gave you that impression. You didn't push me. If anything, *I* pushed *you*." I gave an awkward laugh.

He let out a sigh of relief. "So you don't regret our time together?"

"No, of course not."

"Then what is it? Are you still feeling unwell?"

"No, I'm better."

"Then what? Please tell me. We're all each other has now, Adrijana. We need to be honest with each other."

Honest? But was he being honest with me? "It doesn't sit well that you questioned Spirodon without me. I wanted to be there. I needed to be there. To put my own questions to rest."

He blinked. "But you were ill. Unconscious. The princess—the queen wouldn't wait."

"I know, but I just wish...I don't know."

"It's unfortunate Spirodon committed suicide. Otherwise, you would have been able to put your mind at ease. I see why you're upset, but please understand, none of it was my doing."

I frowned. Was I being unfair to Dragan, taking out my frustration over an untenable situation on him? And if Valko was guilty, he would have a solid interest in turning me against Dragan.

I threw up my hands. "I don't know. The whole thing feels fishy. I can't believe we're executing him without knowing more."

"What more is there to know?"

My mind was spinning. "The only concrete evidence we have is from the Vruks. What if they're framing him? To take out one of Nevena's most valuable assets and knowledgeable advisors?"

It was Dragan's turn to frown. "The Vruks have sent an emissary announcing that the death of their ambassador will be declared an act of war. They are moving their troops into Adrjssia as we speak."

"See! If they wanted war, they could have manufactured it through this hoax."

Dragan shook his head. "I don't know. Spirodon wasn't lying. I would have been able to tell. And King Andrej didn't appear to need any excuse to declare war. He was already on our borders."

"True." Further words slipped from me as Dragan stepped in. He was so beautiful this close. Breathtaking. He took my face in tender hands and kissed me. Chaste and sweet.

My body responded, rebelling against my better judgment. I'd wanted this for months. Why was I ruining it with irrational suspicions? Valko had never been kind to me, had never gone out of his way to make me feel at home here. Not like Dragan had. My fingers tangled in Dragan's hair and I pulled him closer, deepening the kiss. How had I gone without this? I'd been a fool, a conspiracy theorist. Dragan had been there for me, from the moment I had walked into the great hall that first night. How could I distrust him after all we'd been through?

Dragan broke off the kiss with a heavy breath.

I let my hands fall. "I'm sorry. For acting distant." *For doubting you.*

Dragan took my hand and kissed my knuckles. "There is nothing to be sorry for. Your worries are always safe with me. Please don't keep them to yourself."

"I won't."

"Promise me something?"

"Of course," came my knee-jerk reaction. After a kiss like that, I'd promise him anything. The sun, the moon, the stars, my heart. "Stay away from the sentencing? If the queen does order Valko's death, I don't want you near. I don't want his soul attracted to you."

It was a sensible precaution. I wasn't sure I wanted to witness Valko's death, anyway. "Consider it done."

"Thank you." He kissed the knuckles of my other hand. "I should get back inside. I will see you soon."

I let him leave and lingered in the hallway, considering. Perhaps I had been too unfair. Dragan had never given me cause to doubt him. I wouldn't start now.

# CHAPTER 31

*I* spent the evening with the book Valko had given me. I was
convinced that there was something there to find—something that would explain the confusion that roiled within me. Something that would help me save him. Or at least delay things until I was
sure he was guilty.

But page after page was filled with information I'd already learned
—history, theory, method. Even the sections he'd underlined failed to
reveal their secrets to me. The book did explain how the Royal
Mesmers had come to be in line for the Adrjssian throne—the Lozians
had instituted that particular rule to discourage civil war or chal-
lenges from the other clans back when they'd ruled from their capital
in Klovnij. Apparently, King Petar hadn't changed the law, even after
the war. Probably to keep the same disincentive in place.

But that particular legal tidbit, though interesting, did nothing to
illuminate my present dilemma, certainly nothing that would be
enough to save Valko. I had hoped the book would divulge a critical
piece of the puzzle, and I was sorely disappointed.

The weak light of dawn seeped through my window, another day
of gray mist and fog. It matched my morose mood and seemed a
fitting day for a sentencing. And an execution.

I made my way to the dining hall and swallowed down a breakfast of porridge and raisins. When people started to file out, I lingered, as if by my absence, I could prevent what would come next. But I couldn't.

I had promised Dragan I wouldn't attend the sentencing, but I couldn't stay away. I was a part of this. Half of me hoped some desperate, last-minute realization would strike me like lightning. Something that would change everything.

The crowd was gathering in the main courtyard, but I didn't want Dragan to see me. I made my way to a covered breezeway between two of the palace towers, one level up. A mass of white-clad bodies milled below. It seemed the whole palace had gathered to witness Valko's sentencing.

Nevena walked out into the yard, her shoulders thrown back and her face impassive. But I wondered, did she feel the vulnerability of her position? Did she feel alone? I was glad to see Simeon behind her, standing tall and still. His obvious devotion to her had needled at me when I'd first arrived, but now I was glad for it. She needed an ally she could trust no matter what. And Simeon was just such a man.

Two guards walked Valko out of a far door, flanking him as he made his way to the space before the crowd. He looked rumpled and unshaven, wearing a simple shirt and trousers rather than his intimidating black robes, but he too held his shoulders back, his head high. Proud and infuriating, as always.

Anxious murmurs filled the square, punctuated by a few hisses and boos. It did not sit well with people, the power Mesmers held over them. They were quick to turn.

Nevena held up her hands and the throng quieted. "We are here to address the issue of the guilt or innocence of Valko Dafovski, Prime Mesmer of Adrjssia. Valko, you are accused of the crime of treason, conspiring with our enemies to kill the king. How do you plead?"

"Which king?" Valko responded.

Nevena pursed her lips together. "Do you have another king? My father, the late king Petar Tsarian."

"Ah. Then I plead not guilty." Valko fixed the crowd with his sharp gaze, seeming to search the faces there.

"I have considered the physical evidence against you as well as the testimony of Spirodon Martiv, Ambassador of West Adrjssia. I am compelled by the evidence. I find that as to the crime of treason, you are guilty. Your punishment is death."

A cry of delight went up from the crowd at the prospect of seeing blood. I pressed my hand to my mouth, unsure if my breakfast would stay down.

Valko's face darkened at the queen's decree. But he did not shout or plead his innocence. Instead, his eyes kept searching—searching— until he looked up. And his gaze fixed on me.

I took an involuntary step back. He did not seem angry, just relieved, to find me watching.

And watch I did, as a guardsman in dark leather strolled out, holding a massive broadsword. I watched as Valko was forced to his knees, his neck to the block. I watched as the sword flashed in the early morning light.

And then I could watch no more. I squeezed my eyes closed. Heard the thunk as the stroke fell. The collective gasp of the crowd.

I willed my eyes open. I couldn't afford to be squeamish in this place. Dark blood was pooling next to Valko's prone body.

His spirit rose from his body, freed from its prison of flesh. It did not float or twist as Ioseph's had done. It had a purpose.

Me.

My fingers gripped the wood of the railing, my teeth clenched as Valko's spirit soared toward me. Though Dragan had warned me that freed spirits hungered to affix themselves to living Mesmers, I didn't fear that from Valko. He had a message for me. Somehow, I knew it.

As the spirit approached, I faced Valko's spectral form, with his large nose and furry brows. His spirit hovered until it was mere inches from my own.

"Adrijana!" I heard Dragan's panicked cry from below.

"Page 142," Valko's spirit whispered. Just before he vanished.

I HURRIED BACK INSIDE, my heart in my throat. The book, I needed to get to the book. I knew it was important, but I must have missed his hidden message. My stomach roiled—a whirling mass of confusion and anxiety. What would it say? What would I find?

I rounded a corner and someone stepped into my path. I drew up with a little shriek of surprise. It was Dragan. His hands hovered over my face, searching as if he might find something out of place. "Are you all right? When I saw him go for you..."

"I'm fine," I said. "He gave me a fright, that was all."

"I told you not to come! You promised. I knew he'd be attracted to your ora."

"I'm sorry." His intensity made me recoil. "I had to see. It's okay. I'm all right."

Dragan breathed out deeply and then tipped his forehead against mine. "If anything had happened to you, I never would have forgiven myself."

"Well, nothing did. Think of it no further."

A cleared throat drew us back from each other with a startled motion. It was Simeon. A blush colored my cheeks.

"The queen has requested your presence," he said. "Both of you."

"Now?" I asked. I wanted nothing more than to get back to my room and frantically flip to page 142.

"Yes, now." Simeon's words were exasperated.

"Lead the way," Dragan said.

Nevena was pacing her sitting room when we arrived. Her clothes and hair were perfectly put together, but there were bags beneath her eyes that spoke of restless nights. I hadn't been able to see them from my perch above. A pang of sympathy fluttered through me. She carried a heavy weight on her shoulders now.

Georgi was sitting at the window seat, Nevena's karakal on his lap.

"How can we serve you, my queen?" Dragan gave a half-bow.

"You can assure me that no one else is going to be murdered in my palace," Nevena snapped.

Dragan nodded. "You did the right thing. Valko's betrayal shook all of us, but the plot has been dealt with. You're safe."

I bit back my own doubts. The time for voicing them had passed. I hadn't been able to find proof of his innocence, and now it was too late. I needed to move forward. Focus on what was before us. War.

Nevena pinched the bridge of her nose. "Yes, you're right."

Dragan said nothing.

"I need details about the Vruk forces that are headed our way. Numbers. Weapons. Location. They are marching to war and we need to be ready. Can you find that for me?"

"Consider it done. I'll Project and—"

"Both of you," Nevena said. "I want both of you to go. I think it would do me good to get both of your perspectives on our enemy's strength." Her violet eyes bored into mine, and I took her meaning. She still didn't trust Dragan completely. I was to be her eyes and ears in the Vruk camp.

"Of course, Your Majesty." I gave a curtsy. "We'll retire now and see what we can find."

"Can we use the other sitting room?" Dragan asked.

The queen waved us off with a nod.

We showed ourselves out and made our way to the sitting room. We lay down on the two sofas without a word, slipping quickly out of our bodies. I'd become much better at this since my first day at the palace and kept up quickly as we soared out over the palace walls and over the tops of the tiled roofs of Selojia.

"Reports have the Vruk camp at three days' ride," Dragan said.

The landscape of Adrjssia was quiet and brown, the once-lush trees skeletal without their leaves. Wood smoke puffing from chimneys and herds of sheep munching on scrubby grass were the only signs of life. Trepidation filled me as we flew over my village of Dunnavar. Soon this valley would be overrun with Vruks. Did Papa know that the Vruks were coming? Simeon's mother? We needed to warn them.

I saw the first signs of the Vruk camp far too soon. A smudge on the horizon, smoky and gray.

We came to a stop, hovering over their tents. "Are there more of them than last time?" The tents were haphazardly placed, so I struggled with my count. "Over four hundred tents, I think."

"Each tent should hold four warriors," Dragan said. "That makes at least sixteen hundred."

"Sixteen hundred. That's not so bad. We have more soldiers, right?"

"But we're not better warriors," Dragan said. "Come on. Let's find where the horses are tied. See how many mounted warriors they have."

I followed him through the camp, trying to take everything in. Types of weapons. Numbers. Doubt dogged my steps. What did I know of war? I probably didn't even realize what I should be paying attention to.

Dragan stopped and I drew up next to him. His gaze was fixed on the king's tent. Mine was fixed on the little tent next to it, where I'd seen the blindfolded woman. *The Wretched*, Dragan had called her. There was no sign of her today. I looked around, and my eyes fixed upon a man carrying two full water buckets, balanced on a wooden yoke over his back. His eyes were blindfolded, like the woman's had been. He was headed right for us.

"Dragan, look."

He turned and regarded the man. "Poor bastard. They have him reduced to performing menial tasks. Like a slave. This is our future if the Vruks take Selojia. We cannot allow it to pass."

Dragan was fixed on the man's condition, but I was watching his path. It was subtle, but he snaked to the left as he walked. He should have walked right through us, but he didn't.

"He avoided us." I turned to watch him pass us by. "Look. He went around us. Why?"

"Some subtle intuition, perhaps. Some lingering remnant of his power. It's the least of our concern, Adrijana. We need to finish evaluating this camp."

And then I saw the man look back over his shoulder, just for an instant. And I knew, without a shred of doubt, that he had seen us.

But how in Ovyato's holy name was that possible?

* * *

THE TENSION DIDN'T LEAVE me until I was back in my body in the palace.

"What the hell was that?" I sat up. "He saw us, I'm certain."

"I still think it's your imagination," Dragan said. "But we'll include it with our report."

"Dragan, if the Wretched can still see, maybe we could use them as allies. Spies! They can't love being enslaved to the men who cut their eyes out."

"I don't see how it's possible. But if it makes you feel better, when I get a chance, I'll consult the Mesmer library and see what I can find."

"Thank you." I felt a pang as I realized that Valko might have known something that could have helped us. Already, I was feeling his loss. Why hadn't I asked him about the Wretched when I'd first encountered the old woman?

I put my hands on my knees and pressed to my feet and realized I had left white fingerprints on the fine fabric of my dress.

I looked at my hands. My fingertips were covered with a fine coating of something that looked like...I sniffed at it. Sugar? Powdered sugar?

I frowned. How had that gotten there? From breakfast, perhaps? I brushed off my fingers as best I could and tried to clean the worst of it from my dress.

Dragan was standing at the doorway. "Coming?"

"Yes."

We made our way back into the queen's chamber. "Took you long enough," she grumbled.

I looked at the clock on the wall. It had been over an hour. Not too long, by my account. She must be desperate indeed for the information.

"Well?" Nevena looked at us expectantly.

"It's not good, Your Majesty." Dragan filled Nevena in on what we'd seen, and the numbers we'd counted.

I found my thoughts wandering to the book back in my chamber. Page 142. I excused myself and headed into the hallway, closing the door quietly behind me.

A maid was coming up the hallway, heavy-ladened with a tray.

"Here, let me get the door," I offered.

She started as she saw me. "Thank you. You seem to be everywhere today."

I forced a laugh. "I guess so." I gave a little shake of my head as I walked away. I didn't recall seeing her at all. Perhaps she was mistaken.

# CHAPTER 32

*I* hurried through the door to my chamber and slammed it behind me. I flew to the book on my nightstand, sitting on my bed and flipping through it with shaking fingers. A paragraph was underlined in a thick, black ink. I could almost see Valko over-aggressively wielding his pen.

As I began to read, I frowned. It was a passage on the history of Mesmerism.

*In the reign of King Wajan of the Ryaiv Lozian dynasty, the queen was caught with her Mesmer lover mid-act. In begging for her life, the queen claimed she had not known of what she'd done, but that the Mesmer had not only corrupted her mind, but had occupied her body and forced her to commit the illicit acts. While such a thing is of course, impossible—a Mesmer cannot inhabit a body with an ora—the queen's accusations were enough to set off a wave of anti-Mesmer sentiment and distrust.*

I set the book down on my lap. What did that have to do with the murders? With what was going on now? I read the passage again, more slowly. Turning over every sentence and word. There was something here. There had to be.

Was Valko saying that the queen had somehow been forced to have her affair with Aleksi? Though that wouldn't illuminate who had killed her.

A thought flashed through my mind. Had a Mesmer occupied the queen's body? Forced her off the tower—onto the weakened stones?

If a Mesmer could truly inhabit a person and make them dance like a puppet master... I shuddered at the thought. No wonder we were feared and mistrusted. But no, the book said that occupying another person's body was impossible. "*A Mesmer cannot inhabit a body with an ora.*"

But the converse of that—

I went stiff with shock as the import rolled over me. The book slipped from my grasp, hitting the floor with a thud.

A Mesmer could not inhabit a body with an ora, but what about a body *without one*? Could a Mesmer inhabit another Mesmer, while that Mesmer was Projecting?

My heart strained in my chest and I swooped the book back up, scanning the rest of the page, and the next. Nothing. Nothing about the possibility of a Mesmer inhabiting another Mesmer. But if the passage was speaking truth ...

I shoved to my feet, my mind moving too fast for my legs to remain still. I paced the bedroom, my thoughts flying over events in my head.

I knew I had touched on the key, but I still didn't understand. Who had been doing this? And who had they been inhabiting? Had it been a Vruk Mesmer hiding in the shadows? A Wretched? "Okay," I said out loud, giving my hands a shake to dispel the energy pinging throughout me. "Let's go through this rationally. The queen fell from a tower. She wasn't a Mesmer, so she couldn't have been inhabited."

But she could have been pushed. No one had seen anyone on the tower with her...but a Projecting Mesmer could have been there— could have used his or her ability to manipulate the physical. Like Dragan had with the knife on the boat. Like I had when facing Spirodon and Matija in the stairwell. Another Mesmer would have seen the Projecting ora, but if none of us had happened to be looking, the murder could have happened in plain view of the entire Court, and none of them would have seen.

"It was made to look like Aleksi killed Ksenjia, but his Mesmer-Compelled companion killed him before he could speak in his own defense. Anyone could have planted the muriatic acid in his room to make it look like he had weakened the bricks. The next murder was the king's. A Mesmer controlled the snake that poisoned the king." I drew in a sharp breath. When that had happened, Dragan and I had been Projecting to the Vruk camp. Both of our bodies had been lying there, unprotected. Vulnerable. A Mesmer could have inhabited either of us.

I looked down at the healing scratch on the back of my hand. I'd thought it odd how I'd gotten it before Dragan and I had run to the garden to save the king and told myself I must have gotten it when Simeon and I had been in the garden the prior day. But Simeon had told me to be careful, and I didn't remember getting scratched when I'd been with him.

What if I had been in the garden a third time? Or at least my body had? Maybe it wasn't Dragan whose body was being used, but mine.

Clues began to fly to me now, little inconsistencies I had dismissed. I thought I'd set my shoes by the bed. Then they'd been by the door. All my bells falling from my hair. Of course. I couldn't be heard as the culprit had moved my body through the palace.

Bile rose in my throat at the realization of what had been done. The violation. Someone had been inside my body. *Wearing* my body. My knees hit the hard floorboards and I scrambled forward, just managing to grab the chamber pot in time to empty my stomach into it. Even as my stomach heaved again, the pieces kept clicking into place. The white dirt under my fingernails, matching the fireplace in Spiridon's room. My strange dream, where I'd seen it the bricks before me.

I'd been there. My ora must have slipped from my body in sleep, and the killer had pounced again. Had I planted those letters? Had *I* framed Valko?

But no, it hadn't really been me. It had been the Mesmer who'd

229

CLAIRE LUANA

been Projecting and using my body. Who had committed these acts? Another realization pierced me, and my stomach heaved again. Every time my body had been used, I'd been near Dragan. We'd been Projecting together, or sleeping next to each other. Could he have something to do with this? But then...he'd been with me. Projecting. When the king had been murdered. The night before the letters had been discovered. He couldn't have inhabited my body and poisoned the king. He'd been right there with me. So who? Valko? But then why would Valko have led me to where the letters were—making himself look guilty? If anything, he would have framed Dragan. And why would he have given me the truth in page 142? Out of guilt?

No, it didn't add up. There had to be someone else. An unknown element I wasn't aware of—that I couldn't account for. Another Mesmer.

I wiped a shaky hand over my mouth and shoved to weak legs. I made my way to the washbasin on the table and poured water from the pitcher into the basin. I froze before shoving my hands into the water. My fingers were coated with the remnants of sugar, when I hadn't eaten anything remotely sweet.

And the maid—hadn't the maid said she'd seen me? Seen me where? What had I been doing?

A swell of foreboding washed over me. Dragan and I had been Projecting into the Vruk camp. Which meant that just an hour ago, my body had been vulnerable. And clearly, if I'd been seen where I didn't remember being, then my body had been used. But for what?

I washed and dried my hands and face quickly and rinsed out my mouth, trying to rid myself of the taste of my vomit. I needed to find that maid. I needed to know what I'd been doing. Because there was only one monarch left. If the murderer was moving again, Nevena wasn't safe.

I flung the door open and sprinted through the hallways toward the kitchens. Surprised servants jumped out of my way, flattening themselves against the walls. By the time I burst through the door into the huge kitchen, I was panting.

I was about to ask for the whereabouts of the kitchen maid when the cook looked at me in surprise. "Twice in one day?"

I put out a hand to steady myself on the counter. "I was here already?"

The cook looked at me like I was daft. "Less than two hours ago."

"What was I doing?"

"Why, fretting over the queen's pastries, of course. You were acting a bit strange, if you ask me."

The queen's pastries...the powdered sugar. The plitkas, her favorite pastry.

My eyes grew round with knowing. "Where are they now?"

"Sent them up to her half an hour ago. Why?" The cook looked up from the dough she was kneading.

Horror overcame me. I had poisoned the queen's plitkas. Or *someone* had. Using my body. And I might already be too late.

# CHAPTER 33

*I*f I thought I'd been running quickly before, it was nothing compared to how I careened through the corridors now. *Nevena! Not Nevena.*

I prayed to Ovyato with what little breath I had left. Please, let her be all right. Please, let me not be too late.

I burst into the room and searched the scene in a panic. The queen was sitting at her side table, a cup of tea in her hand. Dragan was sitting in the other chair.

A little plate with a pastry was sitting beside the queen, the large tray in the middle of the table.

"Adrijana?" Simeon stepped forward from his post by the door. "Are you all right?"

"Don't…" I huffed. "Eat the plitkas." I put my hands on my hips, trying to suck in air.

"What?" Nevena snapped, looking to the pastry and back to me. "Why?"

"Have you had one?"

"No. Why?"

Tension drained through me, and my knees went weak. Simeon

caught me and helped me into another chair. I pressed my hand to my chest, trying to calm my roaring heart. "I think they're poisoned."

Simeon was before me in a blink, his hands on my shoulders, looking into my eyes. "By whom? How do you know this?"

My relief over finding Nevena safe gave way to panic. How to explain what I didn't even understand myself?

I looked at Dragan, who was staring at me with an unreadable expression. I needed help unraveling this. Stopping whoever did this. And he was the only person here who could help me do that. I needed to tell them everything. And trust that we would figure it out together. I did trust the people in this room. Dragan. Simeon. Nevena. I trusted them perhaps more than anyone.

"Valko gave me a book before he died. I found a passage that explained—"

"Valko is a traitor," Dragan said.

"No, he wasn't. He was framed."

"By whom?" Nevena asked, standing.

"The same person who murdered your parents."

"And who is that?"

"I don't know yet," I said. "But I know how they've been doing it. They're a Mesmer. It's possible for a Mesmer to inhabit the body of another Mesmer, when the Mesmer is projecting. When they've left their body. They were using another body to sneak around the palace, undetected."

"Is this possible?" Nevena asked Dragan.

"I've never heard of it." He shook his head.

"It's true. It was in the history book I found."

"Whose body has this mystery Mesmer been using for their dark deeds?"

I licked my lips. "Mine."

The room was silent for a moment. "I started noticing strange things. The scratch on my hand from the king's roses—I got it before we went into the garden. My things were moved to different places. People seeing me in places I didn't remember being. Someone has been using my body when I've been Projecting."

Simeon looked at the pastries. "The maid who brought these said she'd seen you. You—You poisoned the plitkas?"

"Not me," I pleaded. "I didn't do it. I was with Dragan, investigating the Vruk camp. Tell them." I looked at Dragan, but he was shaking his head.

"The queen died the day you arrived," Dragan said, slowly.

I blinked, recoiling in surprise. "What?"

"It all started with you." His amethyst eyes were unfocused, as if his mind was working feverishly. "The evidence grows too high. *You* were the one who saw some mystery fog in the corridor that led you to overhear Aleksi and Teodora. *You* were the only one who saw that Ioseph had been Compelled to kill Aleksi."

The hammering of my heart took on a different tempo. "But . . . if I'd been the one to Compel Ioseph, why would I ever admit it to you?"

Dragan continued. "You were the only one who saw Valko and Spirodon talking in the hallway."

Simeon shook his head. "Adrijana would never—"

"She found the letters in the fireplace, Simeon," Dragan pointed out. "You were there. We'd been looking for hours, and within five minutes of being there, she found them."

"Yes, because I discovered mortar under my fingernails that matched the fireplace. I didn't know how it got there."

"You saw the fog again, drawing us to the king's chamber. The snake didn't react to you. It didn't attack you," Dragan said.

"Roja distrusts you," Nevena added quietly. Her lavender face had paled. "She won't go anywhere near you."

This wasn't going how it was supposed to. "Right, but that's what I'm trying to tell you. The killer has been using me. Using my body. Don't you see?"

Dragan shook his head. "Who is this killer, then?"

"I don't know. A Vruk Mesmer perhaps."

"There are no Vruk Mesmers," Nevena said. "They all have their eyes cut out."

"I don't think that destroys their powers, though. Dragan and I were seen by one today. Perhaps the Vruks just led us to believe that they had no Mesmers so they could further a plot like this."

Nevena chewed on her lip, before turning to Dragan. "What do you make of this? You say it's not possible."

"It's not. I fear...I fear Adrijana has fooled all of us. Perhaps even herself."

"Dragan," I breathed. "How could you... What are you saying?"

"That there is no other killer. *You* are the killer."

My mouth went dry. "If I was the killer, then why in Ovyato's name did I warn the queen about the plitkas?"

"Right," Simeon said. Thank Ovyato *someone* was backing me up. "If she's the killer, she wouldn't have foiled her own plot."

"Perhaps you warned her so you could spin this wild story and throw the suspicion onto another."

"Who?"

"The only other Mesmer in this palace."

"You?" I was swimming in a sea of disbelief, the thick of it choking me, drowning me. How could he say these things?

Dragan turned to the queen. "There are only a few people who stand between Adrijana and the throne. As a Royal Mesmer, she is in line. And you, my queen, have no other family who could take the throne. Georgi is not in the line of succession. Perhaps by casting suspicion on me, she could kill two of the remaining birds with one stone."

The throne? I gaped. "I don't want the throne. I never asked for this. I never even knew I was a Mesmer until I came here! Simeon, tell them!"

He shifted uncomfortably. "I don't buy that Adrijana is grasping for power, Your Majesty. There has to be something else going on."

I flailed my hands. "Yes. Thank you. I'm being framed. I'm being used. I came here so you could help me figure out who's doing this."

"Perhaps there is another explanation then," Dragan pondered. He'd hardly looked at me while spinning his wild conjecture. As if I weren't even here. "Perhaps Adrijana doesn't know what she's doing.

235

Perhaps there is a part of her that is perpetrating these acts, while another part of her, the conscious part, was truly Projecting with me."

"Like a split personality?" Nevena's brows drew together.

"It is said that severe childhood trauma can create schisms in the personality."

"I didn't have severe childhood trauma," I said. "My mother died, but—"

"But you did." Dragan finally turned to me. "Weren't you ever curious why your father began dosing you with verbenia?"

I frowned. "Because I was causing trouble—"

"Not trouble, Adrijana. Because you were causing harm. He began dosing you because you killed your sister. Even at the age of five, you were a killer."

My mouth dropped open. No. Arabel drowned. I hadn't had anything to do with her death. I shook my head wildly. "You're lying. Why are you saying this?"

"I have a letter from your father saying as much. I can retrieve it, Your Majesty, if you need to see it."

"You have a letter from my father? Why?" What the hell was happening? Why would Papa write to Dragan? Or had Papa been writing me, and Dragan had been keeping the letters from me?

"Simeon? You grew up with Adrijana. Haven't you heard stories?" Dragan looked at my friend.

Simeon's face was grave. After a long while, he spoke. "Didn't your sister drown under mysterious circumstances? My mother said your father blamed himself for leaving you two alone together."

My hands flew to my mouth as tears burst free, unbidden. That couldn't be true. I couldn't have killed Arabel. I remembered playing with her—running through the meadow behind the house and hiding in the garden beneath the beanstalks. "Arabel's death was an accident. It doesn't mean I had anything to do with it."

"I'm sorry," Dragan said. His golden brows were drawn together, his perfect lips twisted in sorrow. Or a perfect imitation of sorrow. "Maybe you didn't mean to do these things here, but I think it's clear you're the key to it all."

Simeon came to stand beside me and laid a gentle hand on my shoulder. "Come on."

I looked at him through refracted tears. "What? Where are we going?"

Tears shimmered in his eyes too. "Adrijana, I have to arrest you."

Arrest me? Panic lanced through me. "But I didn't do it." Didn't I? Dragan's words had filled me with uncertainty. If I'd truly killed my sister and hadn't even known or remembered, perhaps it was possible that I'd killed the queen and king. But why? I wasn't a temperamental child anymore. What possible reason did I have to kill people I'd never even met? I'd only come here to be the princess's companion.

I looked at Dragan and found him watching me, his violet gaze sharp. It was just a flash before his face morphed back to an expression of worry. But it was a flash of something real. "Wait." I put up a hand, shaking off the fog of my shock. "If it's possible for a personality to split based on childhood trauma, what about yours? Every time my body was used, I was with you. I thought it couldn't have been you because you Projected beside me. But if it's possible to split a person—then you could have just as easily done so."

"What possible reason would I have to harm the people who took me in when I was young?"

"The reason you just thrust on me," I spat. Simeon was trying to capture my arm, but I pulled it free. "Only Nevena stands between you and the crown. If I hadn't foiled the plot today, she'd be gone, and you'd be king."

Dragan's eyes were sorrowful. "See, Your Majesty? Attempting to point the finger at me, exactly as I said she would."

My mouth dropped open.

Nevena was massaging her temples. "Enough. Adrijana, do you deny that you poisoned these plitkas?"

I wetted my dry lips. "I deny that I did it of my own volition."

"And all the rest. The snake? The letters in Valko's chamber? Ovyato help me, does that just mean I executed an innocent man?"

"None of it was me. Someone is doing this. Using me as a pawn. If you arrest me, they'll still be out there."

"Even if I believe your mad tale, at least if I arrest you, their pawn will be off the board." Nevena flicked her fingers to Simeon. "Simeon, take her to the dungeon."

# CHAPTER 34

Simeon was gentle as he led me down to the dungeon and put me into a cell. I didn't fight him. I was too stunned.

When he closed the door behind me, I pressed my palms to the rough wood. "Do you think it's really true?" I whispered.

"What?" He turned, his eyes pained.

"That I killed Arabel?" Tears slipped free, as soft as silk over my cheeks.

He shook his head. "We can't know for certain. It's all secondhand. Thirdhand. We have to talk to your father and find out more."

"Do you really think I could be a killer?"

Simeon's pause was far too long. Far too telling. "I don't want you to be. Dragan is right about the timing, though. It all started when you arrived."

"Not the crown prince's death," I pointed out.

"No one's sure that wasn't an accident. Until we know more, your place is here. We can't risk Nevena. She's all the kingdom has left."

Simeon vanished and I sagged against the door. He returned a moment later with a glass of water, offering it through the bars at the top of the door. "I thought you might be thirsty."

I pressed my lips together to keep a sob from escaping. I didn't deserve friends like this. Not if I was truly what they said I was.

I took it from him gratefully and put it to my lips. The herbaceous smell hit me like a ton of bricks. Verbenia. He'd laced the water. "What are you doing?" My hand dropped. How could he?

"It's policy, Adrijana. We can't leave a Mesmer in here with their powers intact. You could just Mesmerize the guards and walk out."

I looked down at the water. At the true cage that would bind me. Something flared inside me. A streak of rebellion. Perhaps it was the wickedness inside me that had led me as a child to end my sister out of selfish spite. Or perhaps simple self-preservation. I knew if I drank from that cup, I'd be done for. I'd never get to the truth of who had killed the king and queen.

Despite what Dragan had said, even if I'd killed my sister as a child, I didn't think I had committed the murders of the royal family. I didn't think my personality was split. He was so quick to point the finger at me. Didn't that make him the most likely suspect? The only other Mesmer here. The only one left standing.

If he had known about the possibility of splitting one's ora, wasn't it possible it was because *he* could do it? A flash of memory nearly bowled me over.

The very first time I'd seen him, in the ballroom of this very palace. He'd been standing on the dais. And then, a moment later, standing beside me. Peering into my eyes with curiosity. He had said it required years of training to be able to stand while Projecting, but what if that wasn't it at all? I'd never seen Valko do anything like that.

I sagged against the door as my knees threatened to buckle. Why hadn't I thought of it? Why had I never thought back, never questioned that first encounter? Why had I just taken his word as gospel?

Because I'd been enamored with him, that was why. Even then. He was powerful and handsome and exciting and I'd been a *fool*. A complete and utter fool.

"Adrijana, please. Drink it. Don't make me force you," Simeon said. "You can't Mesmerize me."

I looked at him. I couldn't drink this. But if I didn't, he'd make me. Tears pricked my eyes. "Promise me you'll help me find the truth."

"I promise," Simeon replied.

So I drank it down.

As soon as I heard Simeon's footfalls fade, I thrust my index finger down my throat until my stomach heaved. I vomited into the wooden bucket they'd left for a chamber pot, one hand braced against the cold stone. Whatever Simeon had promised, I needed to look out for myself. I prayed that no one would come close enough to notice my eyes were still purple.

When my stomach was done emptying, I sat on the dirty wooden bench, doing my best to wrap my head around what had happened. It was clear to me that I'd been used to commit the murders. Perhaps even the white fog I'd seen had been the killer leading me by the nose to the perfect clue to further the plot. It had to be Dragan. When the moment had come, he'd turned on me, pointing the finger at me. That wasn't the act of an innocent man. He'd stolen my letters from Papa, keeping them from me. And then there was the fact that I'd seen him split his ora. I hadn't known it for what it was then, but there was no other explanation.

But how to prove my innocence? I needed to know how he'd done it, and I needed to know why. Then I needed someone, preferably Nevena or Simeon, to catch him in the act. But how the hell was I supposed to pull all of that off?

If there was one thing I knew, it was that I wasn't going to figure it out sitting in this cell. I needed to investigate. But I couldn't leave. Could I Project?

I lay down on the little bench, letting my legs dangle off the end. I closed my eyes and tried to drift out of my body. But try as I might, I couldn't tug my ora out of my body. It stayed firmly fixed.

I huffed. Damn it. Some small amount of the verbenia must have slipped into my system, despite me vomiting up the liquid. How long would it take to wear off? I didn't know how much time I had. Despair flooded me. There was nothing to do but wait.

* * *

I WOKE to the sound of keys jangling softly in the lock. My back protested something fierce as I sat up with a groan.

Dragan stepped inside the cell, every perfect angle of his face limned with lantern light. We regarded each other for a moment before I let my eyes fall. I didn't want him to see the verbenia hadn't taken hold.

"Are you well?" His voice was soft, touching all the places inside me that had once hung on his every word. The eager, hopeful, breathless corners that gobbled up every hint of his affection. I couldn't reconcile him—the Dragan in Nevena's chambers, casting aspersions at me—with the Dragan who had been my most constant ally. Which was real?

"What do *you* think?" I finally responded.

"It grieves me to see you like this."

"Then maybe you shouldn't have put me in this cell," I bit back. "Why are you even here? To gloat?"

He crossed the narrow space and came to sit on the bench beside me, trying to take my hands. I pulled them back, whirling away from him. Nothing addled my thoughts more surely than his nearness. And I needed all my wits about me. I retreated into the far corner, my arms crossed tightly beneath my breasts. "Why are you here?" I asked again.

"I want to help you."

I scoffed. "*Help* me? I think you've done enough."

"You're not well, Adrijana. Despite the concerns I shared with the queen, I don't think you have ill intent. You're a good, kind person. I think something's happening to you, inside you. If we can figure it out, maybe we can fix it."

"*Fix* it?" Incredulity hit me like a slap in the face. I studied his features, as if I could will the truth from his cool countenance. Did he truly believe I'd had some sort of a mental break? What had Dragan once said? *"Men speak lies not just with their oras, but with their words, their deeds, their mannerisms and tells."* But was he lying now? I couldn't tell, and it frustrated me to no end. Were his lessons even to be trusted? If he was a liar, maybe he'd lied about everything. Maybe it was all hopelessly muddled, back to the very beginning.

He stood and approached once again, each step slow and deliberate. The cold of the dungeon walls bit into my back as I found myself cornered. I couldn't help but breathe in the spicy scent of him, take in the electricity of his nearness, even as my eyes darted about, searching for a safe place to land. The polished leather of his boots, the silver buttons of his jacket, winking in the firelight. The warmth of his breath caressed my cheek as he spoke, eliciting a shiver from my body that might have been fear, or desire, or revulsion. Or maybe a potent mix of all three. "I care about you, Adrijana, truly. Our monarchy hangs by a thread. If Nevena is not up to the challenge of facing the Vruks, if anything should happen to her—"

I looked up sharply at that. "Is that a threat?"

Dragan took my chin in his hand, but I looked away, refusing to meet his gaze. "Of course not. It's an acknowledgment of the seriousness of the situation. In just days, we will be at war. If Nevena dies, it will be up to me to protect this nation. To steer it on a true course. And there's no one I would rather have at my side than you, Adrijana."

"What—What are you saying?" This was the last thing I expected to hear from him.

"Nevena and Simeon care deeply for you. If they realize your actions were caused by a mental break, they won't execute you. They'll want to rehabilitate you and get you well. If you just admit what you did, we can focus on defeating the Vruks."

Disbelief welled in me. He wanted me to take the fall for everything. Queen Ksenjia, King Petar, Aleksi, all of them. Ioseph, the king's guards. To say I'd killed them all. But why? Because he wanted me to throw suspicion off him for long enough to finish off Nevena? I had to know. With one shaking hand, I reached up and took his. "And then what, Dragan? After the war, what happens?"

His deep voice dropped even lower. "Gods forbid anything happens to Nevena, you would rule at my side. As my queen."

I stiffened as desperate confusion warred within me. My traitorous heart trilled at his offer, even as my mind played out all the ways it could be a trick. All the reasons I shouldn't trust him. "I need some time to think." I finally said. I couldn't do that with him here, so close. When he was near, I *wanted* to believe him innocent. If I didn't know it was impossible for one Mesmer to influence another, I would have thought myself Compelled.

"Of course. We will sort this out Adrijana, I promise." He stepped in and planted a firm kiss on my forehead. "Think on my offer. And get some rest."

I kept my eyes fixed on the rough stones beneath me until the cell door clanged shut, and then I sagged to the ground. I still didn't understand what was really going on, but if I *did* accept responsibility like Dragan suggested, then Nevena would still be in danger. That was unacceptable.

I wasn't sure how long I sat in the dark before the lock jangled at the door. I looked up in alarm. Had Dragan returned?

Someone slipped inside the cell, their form too shadowed to make out. Fear tugged at my gut. "Who's there?"

"Shh!" The figure crept forward; when I saw the glint of gold on wild curls, I sagged in relief.

"Georgi?"

"I've come to spring you out." He unshouldered a pack and set it on the floor before kneeling down to rummage inside.

"Are you insane?" I gawked with disbelief. He was going to disobey the queen? His own cousin?

"Simeon told me what happened. I believe you, Adrijana. This isn't you. You aren't a murderer." He had retrieved a pair of my boots and a cloak, which he handed to me. "You're going to run. Until you figure out how to prove your innocence. We can't let him get away with this."

"Who?"

"Dragan! He's the one who did this, right?" Georgi pulled something out of his pocket. It was the little jar of salve that Hristina had given me for my cut.

I gasped. "Did you discover what's in it?"

He nodded. "Valerian root and monkshood. A combination of a

sleeping herb and toxin that can be fatal, even in small doses. If Dragan gave this to you, you're lucky to be alive."

My limbs went cold. I'd *known* there was something off about that salve. Dragan *had* given it to me to ensure I was out of the way when Spirodon had been questioned. So he could Compel the man's confession, without me there to see it. He could have killed me!

"Put your boots on," Georgi said. "We need to go. I have horses saddled and waiting."

"You're coming with me?"

"Of course. I can't let you figure this out alone."

A wave of guilt crashed over me. I may not have been a murderer, but I had transgressed horribly against Georgi. I didn't deserve this kindness, not after what I'd done to him. "You don't know me, Georgi."

He wiped a tear from my cheek. "Yes, I do. I don't know what's wrong, but we have to deal with it later. We don't have much time before the guard shift changes."

I shook my head. No more lies. I couldn't let him risk himself if he didn't even know what I'd done. I couldn't live with myself. I wouldn't be like the other Mesmers. Like Dragan. "I Compelled you, Georgi. And something went wrong, and we had to take some of your memories."

Georgi froze for a moment, his hand hanging in the air.

I buried my face in my hands as more tears burst free.

"Why?" came his whispered question in the dark.

I looked up at him. He was so handsome. Earnest and good. Why had I let Dragan lure me in with his captivating poison? Why couldn't I have fallen for sweet Georgi instead? "Why what?"

"Why'd you manipulate me?"

"I wanted to practice, and you said it was okay. But I should have told you it was dangerous—"

"So I let you?"

I nodded, miserably.

Georgi placed his hands firmly on my shoulders. "I don't care. We can figure it out later. But right now, if you don't do as I say, you'll be the end of me because I'll be discovered here, helping you. Do you want that?"

Georgi's comment slapped some sense into me, rousing me from the depths of my self-loathing. "I'm sorry."

"It's fine. So long as you can be sorry while putting your boots on."

I did as Georgi instructed, and soon I was ready to go, my pack on my shoulders. Georgi let us out of the cell and into the empty dungeon. "Where's the guard?" I asked as we hurried into the servants' hallway that led to the kitchen garden. I unthreaded the bells from my hair as I went.

"I told him there was a gold piece in it for him if he left me alone with you. I think he thought I meant to take advantage of you. Foul man."

My eyes narrowed.

"Don't worry. He'll be punished for his part in this."

Georgi had planned it all flawlessly. Two sleek mares were waiting for us in a quiet corner of the garden, with full saddlebags.

"How did you do all of this without anyone seeing you?"

"I'm frequently underestimated and much loved by the servants. It's a powerful combination, when needed."

A ghost of a smile crossed my lips. *I* certainly had underestimated him.

The icy mist held us close as we slipped beneath the blanket of fog that muffled all sound. Papa's words surfaced in my mind, spoken that first day we came to Selojia. *"That fog has hidden more foul deeds than a man could conceive of."* The truth in those words pained me now, as did my foolish dismissal of them. I wanted to see Papa again.

We led our horses until we were outside the palace walls, and then we mounted, the clip-clop of the animals' hooves the only sound in the echoing, quicksilver sea around us. "We should go to see my father," I finally whispered, when the silence had stretched too long.

"That's the first place they'll look for you."

I bit my lips. He was right. "There are caves near my father's fields, places we can rest."

"Wouldn't Simeon know of them? From your childhood days?"

"Most of them," I admitted. "But there's one that only Papa and I used. It should be safe. Just for tonight."

Georgi's face was obscured by the mist, though he was just feet from me. "That's heading toward the Vruk army. I'd rather not be in their path."

"In truth, I'm certain the Vruks hold some of the pieces to this puzzle. Please. I have a feeling." Even as I said the words, my thoughts stumbled over all of the feelings I'd been terribly wrong about. Dragan first and foremost. I'd been certain I could trust him. I'd been sure it was the Vruk ambassadors behind the queen's and king's deaths.

And now I didn't know anything.

# CHAPTER 35

$\mathcal{W}$e emerged from the mist about a mile from my village. The first haze of dawn was painting the eastern sky with brushstrokes of goldenrod. My body was weary, but my mind was sharp once again. I was fairly certain the verbenia had worn off, and I could Project, but I didn't want to risk doing it on the back of a horse.

The wideness of the open land felt threatening. I knew at any moment Dragan could Project this way and find me. I couldn't stop looking over my shoulder, searching the sky.

We turned off the main road and followed a game trail through sparse woods of birch and alder trees. Relief welled in me when we found the clearing with the jagged entrance to the cave, tucked under fern fronds and mossy tendrils. It had been years since I'd been here, I wasn't sure I'd be able to find it.

We both dismounted and led our horses into the mouth of the cave. Hidden in the back was a small pile of stacked firewood, a folded blanket, and a full waterskin. My heart seized. "My father's supplies. He would wait here if he got caught out in a storm. We're close to our verbenia cliffs."

Georgi laid a hand on my shoulder. "I know you want to see him, but it's a bad idea."

"I know. I just hope he knows to evacuate before the Vruks march through."

"I'm sure the Adrjssian army will be warning people in the Vruks' path," Georgi assured me, but his eyes were distant, as if he doubted his own words.

I couldn't think about that right now. I wasted no time lying down on a blanket on the hard ground, and relief welled in me when I slipped out of my body with ease. I looked down at myself briefly and wished I hadn't. My hair was tangled and my cheeks were striped with dirt and the stains of dried tears. I looked like a bedraggled killer.

Dragan had the answers I sought, of that much I was certain. So it was to his chamber I would visit first. I barreled toward Selojia, wishing the cursed mist would dissipate so I could determine if anyone was on our trail. But I might as well have wished for the moon.

I didn't know if Dragan was inside his chamber, so I made my way around the outside, to float outside his window and peek inside.

But as I neared the palace walls, a shadow swooped behind me, silvery against the mist. My heart seized. If it was Dragan Projecting, I was done for.

A silhouette materialized, and I nearly laughed in relief. Simeon's star-bird. I searched my memory for her name. Xaranti. I slowed to a stop, floating in the air. "Hello."

Xaranti flew in a tight circle around me, almost as if she wished to land. I held out an arm automatically before realizing how foolish I was being. I was Projecting. She couldn't touch my ora. I smiled at her, about to tell her she would be disappointed, when her talons *connected* with my arm.

I floated in shocked silence for a moment, lost in the depths of her obsidian eyes. Her weight strained the muscles of my arm, even as her talons pricked at the delicate skin of my forearm. "You are something," I breathed as I flipped through the *Bestiary* book in my mind. Nothing in its pages had even remotely suggested that star-birds had the ability to connect with a Projecting Mesmer. But maybe the authors hadn't known. The book had said the birds were mysterious. And couldn't the karakals see our spirit form? The chiton blocked Mesmer powers... Perhaps all the great beasts of the continent had some hidden connection to the powers of Mesmerism.

Xaranti seemed to be waiting for something, and so I said, "Please tell Simeon I'm sorry I left. But I need to prove my innocence."

The feathers of her crest rose, and I swore she nodded at me. She gathered herself and launched off my forearm, digging her sharp talons into the flesh of my arm. "Ow." I cradled my arm to my chest as the mist swallowed her like a specter.

I looked down at my arm and watched as the puncture wounds from her claws magically closed, leaving my spirit skin unmarred. *Valko, why couldn't you be here?* He would have been astounded by what had just occurred. The irony was not lost on me that I only missed him now that he was gone.

Shaking away the strangeness of Xaranti's visit, I headed back toward the windows of Dragan's room, praying he was inside.

He was!

I ducked down instinctively and then floated back up ever so slightly, just far enough to see through the window. Hopefully, the mist outside disguised my own milky form.

Dragan was pacing the length of his room, talking to himself. He looked angry. Frustrated? What was he saying? I needed to hear. I needed to get inside.

I considered the objects in the room and settled on the armoire. A flash of memory overcame me—the feel of his mouth on my skin, his hands searching and finding every sensitive spot with master precision as he undressed me on that huge bed. My eyes narrowed. He'd used me in the worst imaginable way. Tricked me into loving him and then *worn my body* as his own. I would make him pay. If it was the last thing I did, he would pay.

I rounded through the hallway and floated through the thick wall into the armoire. There, amongst the coats and boots, I could just peek out through the crack between the doors. Perfect.

His hair was disheveled and his amethyst eyes were wild and shadowed, as if he hadn't slept a wink. "You were impatient and reckless. We agreed not to go for Nevena so soon. We were going to let the Vruks finish her off. Now you've jeopardized everything!"

We? Who was we? Was he truly two people? Two personalities? He'd suffered enough trauma as a child: his flight from safety on Lozian lands, his mother's sacrifice and torture, his sister's death. Nearly dying at the hands of the Vruk forces. Perhaps he was truly mad.

He stopped pacing, his hands on his hips. "Do not—" He huffed in apparent exasperation. "Grateful? That's rich. Will you—" He spun around. "Will you just come out here? I can't carry on a conversation like this."

The silver form of an ora separated from Dragan, a cloud of fog that I recognized instantly. It was the fog that had led me to all those supposed "clues." But then the fog began coalescing—taking human form. My mouth dropped open. A *female* form.

What in Ovyato's holy name was going on?

"You should be grateful because now I've taken care of our little Adrijana problem. She's out of our hair, and the suspicion is once again off of us," the female said. She was lovely and willowy, her hair and dress undulating around her as if she floated in the sea. She had a pert nose and wide expressive eyes, framed by thick, arching eyebrows. But her beauty was marred by the snarl twisting her features. Who was she?

"The suspicion is pointed directly at us! She all but accused us of the crimes. And I had to give up too much information. The queen's no fool. She'll realize that if one of her Mesmers could split her ora, the other could just as easily as well."

The woman waved a hand. "That was a foolish thing to say. It gave away too much."

"They were never going to believe Adrijana murdered the king and queen in cold blood. Nevena is wrapped around Simeon's finger, and Simeon is wrapped around Adrijana's! You saw it yourself. It wasn't until I suggested that she didn't know what she'd done that they'd even considered her guilt."

My shock was palpable. I didn't understand what was going on here, who this woman was, or how she'd been hiding her ora inside Dragan's body, but it was clear to me that she was the real killer. She and Dragan had planned it all.

Dragan resumed his pacing. The woman's ora lounged on the bed, watching him with an expression of amusement.

"We have it all in hand. Will you quit worrying, brother?"

My mouth dropped open. Brother? But Dragan's sister was dead. She'd died when she was a little girl...

If I had a body, I would have gasped. Dragan's warning to me after Ioseph came at me on the Firebird came into stark relief. *The oras of the dead are attracted to Mesmers.* They are drawn to them and can seek them out. If the worst happened...the soul of a dead Mesmer could attach to a live one.

"Silviya, I will fix this, but I want no more interference from you. No more killing. The Vruks are coming. We need to let the war unfold. We're so close to everything we've wanted. We can't let impatience ruin it now."

Silviya. So, it was his sister! Dear Ovyato, had she connected herself to Dragan when she'd died at the age of what, five? They'd been living with two oras in one body ever since? It was a miracle Dragan wasn't mad. Or maybe he was.

Silviya uncoiled herself from the bed and stalked to stand before him, nose to nose. "I will wait. I will bide my time. But the minute it looks like they are settling things peacefully, I will take matters into my own hands. We swore, Dragan. We swore that we would avenge Mother. That we would take vengeance on the country that had rejected her. On the king and queen who'd closed their borders to all the Mesmers who'd needed help. And on the savage beast Vruks who'd plucked her eyes out. We swore we wouldn't stop until Adrjssia, and the Vruks, and the Tsarian line were in tatters. I've been waiting over twenty years. I'm all out of patience."

Dragan held up his hands. "I know. And we've achieved so much. But remember, I still have a head, and I would like to keep it on my neck when this is all complete. We have to be smart."

"I promise you, brother. When this is all over, you'll still have a head. And a crown to sit atop it."

A sharp rap sounded on Dragan's door, and I jumped in surprise. When I looked back, I found that Silviya was gone, and Dragan was smoothing his hair back, donning his expression of arrogant aloofness that I knew so well. How the hell had I been deceived by him so completely?

The open door blocked the messenger, but I heard the words clearly. And Dragan's answering snarl. "Adrijana Mironacht has escaped."

Time to go.

I flitted back to my body as fast as I could move and sat up with a gasp. My hands were shaking, my body chilled. My mind rebelled against the horror of it. My arm ached, and I realized with shock that blood was oozing from a row of perfect puncture wounds in my forearm.

Georgi was at my side in an instant, his gentle hands on my shoulders. "Are you all right? You're bleeding!"

I couldn't speak. No. I wasn't *all right*. My arm was the least of my concerns. Dragan's sister's ora *lived inside of him*. I had no doubt that she'd been inside of *me*. I had so many questions. How was it possible? How had she become like an ethereal fog? How did she look older than the age at which she'd died? What was it like living with another person inside of you? Could they speak while she was in Dragan's body? Was she always in there? *Had she been in there when he and I had...*

A shiver of disgust wracked my body and I pulled my knees against my chest, wrapping my arms around my legs and burying my face in my knees, not caring if blood smeared my dress. What I had once thought of as the most beautiful and pleasurable moment of my life was painted over in a dark wash. I wanted to bathe, to wash this unclean feeling away. I wanted to shove the memory so far down in my mind that I'd never feel the creeping disgust and humiliation that now accompanied it. Could a Mesmer Compel themself? Make themself forget?

For the hundredth time since this morning, I wished Valko were here. I'd taken his gruffness for cruelty, his sternness for uncaring. But with his last breath, he'd supplied me the answer. He would have known what to do. How to fix this.

My mind circled over all of it again and again, bringing it into sharp focus. From the very beginning.

"Please, Adrijana, say something. Are you all right?" Georgi stroked my hair. He took my hand and gently wrapped my forearm with cloth that looked to be torn from a shirt. I had to tell him. He'd been so kind, in trusting me.

So, my head in my hands, I explained it all to him, even while working it out myself.

Silviya had pushed the queen, starting this whole messy business. So long as Valko and I hadn't been looking, she could do it in plain view of the entire kingdom and no one would know. I wasn't sure who'd splashed the muriatic acid to weaken the stones—it had been before I'd arrived. But perhaps Dragan had done it himself, then planted it in Aleksi's chamber. Or used me to plant it. The first time I Projected, Simeon had found me in the hallway. I'd forgotten, but she'd probably used me then too. And then left me slumped over like discarded garbage.

Silviya was the white mist I'd followed, leading me to the whispered conversation between Aleksi and Teodora. Of course, Aleksi had been an easy target, as his affair with the queen called his credibility into question and provided a motive. When he'd fled, realizing he'd been being framed, it only made him look more guilty. Dragan or Silviya had Compelled his companion, making sure Aleksi was eliminated before he could prove his own innocence.

And then there was the king. I didn't know how Dragan had gotten the asp, but it was clear to me that while he had been showing me the kingdom while we'd Projected, Silviya had slipped into my body and taken the asp to the garden, using her Mesmerism to direct it to the king. Perhaps that was why when I'd seen the snake, it hadn't attacked me. Some lingering sense of its master. Then she'd taken her fog form to draw us in so we could "discover" the king's body. Knowing it would be too late.

And then Valko. Poor Valko. I'd seen him and Spirodon talking in hushed tones—she'd led me right to that too. I frowned. That was a piece I still didn't understand. Why would a Vruk ambassador want to kill the Vruk king? There must be a faction within the Vruk government who wanted their king gone. And then the letters. They appeared real, but Silviya and Dragan had used me to hide them in a clever place—guaranteeing I'd remember *just* enough to "discover" them. I'd played my part perfectly, and Valko had paid the price. And then, for her final coup de grace, Silviya had used me to poison Nevena's pastries, aiming to eliminate the last obstacle to their final revenge. At least I had foiled that plot. For now. They'd only gotten rid of one more person. Me.

Georgi's face grew paler and paler as I laid it out. When I was done, he exploded to his feet and stormed outside. I could hear him thrashing in the forest, hacking at something. Part of me wished I could summon anger, instead of this horrible numbness that froze me where I sat.

Tears slipped free. What the hell was I going to do? Nevena and Simeon doubted me. Dragan had their ear and had the upper hand when it came to experience with political maneuvering. He and Silviya had been plotting and planning for *decades*. What was I? A novice whom they'd played like a fiddle.

I had no proof of what I'd seen. I could never get proof. It would be my word against his. No one could see oras but me and Dragan.

No one except the woman and the man from the Vruk camp. The Wretched.

My head shot up. The old woman had seen me. I was certain of it. I didn't know who she was, or why she could see oras, but she could. Maybe she could tell me how she'd done it. Or at least she could confirm what I was saying. I knew her tent. I could find her.

But would she help? The Vruks were on the brink of war with Adrjssia. Would they welcome someone telling them that the war had been manipulated and staged? Likely not. King Andrej was dying and needed the chiton. There was no averting war. But perhaps I could clear my name. Stop Dragan from ending Nevena.

My eyes widened. Perhaps I could find the person Valko had been plotting with—the one who wanted King Andrej gone. It couldn't have just been Spirodon, the ambassador had clearly been ferrying the letters for someone else. With King Andrej gone, just maybe the war could be avoided.

The answers I needed were in the Vruk camp. I had to go. I had no other choice.

# CHAPTER 36

*I* had a semblance of a plan. I couldn't go into the Vruk camp in physical form—they hated Mesmers and were immune to my powers. But in spectral form, I could speak to the woman I'd seen and be safe.

"What about me?" Georgi asked. "I can't just sit here and do nothing."

"You should return to Selojia and warn Nevena," I suggested. "She may not believe I'm innocent, but they need to know to take precautions. Otherwise, Dragan or Silviya could finish the job."

The corner of Georgi's mouth curled down. "They probably know I helped you escape…but you're right. Nevena must be protected at all costs."

I wracked my brain for some other option but found none. "I don't want you to put yourself at risk."

"Nevena won't execute her own cousin without thinking twice. It's a risk I'm willing to take."

"Still—"

Georgi surprised me by pulling me into a hug.

I buried my face in his shoulder, breathing in comfort that I didn't deserve. "I'm so sorry for dragging you into all of this. And for messing with your mind."

"You never meant to hurt me, Jana. I know that. You're a good person."

"So many people are dead because of me." The plush fabric of his velvet jacket lapped up my tears.

"None of this is your fault." He shushed me, smoothing my hair.

I pulled back, wiping my eyes. "Please be careful, Georgi. I couldn't bear it if something happened to you."

"Likewise. Don't leave this cave." He kissed my head and turned and walked into the forest. I sat for a moment after he had gone, my heart aching. I didn't deserve a friend like Georgi. But I was grateful for him, just the same.

When the forest outside the cave was quiet, I lay back down, closed my eyes, and Projected.

The Vruk camp had moved since Dragan and I had visited. My alarm grew as I saw how close they had come to my village: just over the ridgeline. I prayed the people would have sufficient warning to flee.

I headed for the blind woman's tent, nestled in the shadow of the royal tent. I found her just outside, walking beside a warrior with his head completely shaved, but for a braided patch in the back.

She drew to a halt at the sight of me, causing the man walking next to her to stop and turn. "What's wrong?"

"I—forgot there is something I need to attend to," she said. "Go ahead and start without me." She gave me an infinitesimal nod and turned on her heel. I followed her inside her tent, my nerves pinging.

As soon as we were inside, she turned on me. "Who are you? What are you doing here?"

*What should I tell her? How should I spin it?* The truth, I supposed. I had no resources except the truth. "I'm Adrijana. I'm an Adrjssian Mesmer. I work for the queen."

"Spying, are you? Well, you're doing a poor job of it."

I was glad I was in my ethereal form so I couldn't blush.

"We were spying, the first day I saw you. Now, I think I need your help."

The woman settled into a chair. Despite the purple blindfold over her eyes, she moved confidently. Like she could see. "My help? Why would I help the Ostrovs? They didn't lift a finger to help me when I was handed over to this lot."

This wasn't going as I'd hoped. "How do you see me? Are you a Mesmer? Do you have some other ability?"

"Do I look like a Mesmer to you?" She gestured to her eyes. "I'm nobody. I'm a Wretched."

I perched on a little stool across from her. "You *were* a Mesmer, weren't you? But the Vruks took your eyes. How can you still see?"

She stood abruptly. "That is a dangerous suggestion. No one can see without their eyes, especially a Mesmer. You need to go."

"But you *can* see," I retorted, bewildered.

She ripped the blindfold off of her eyes, revealing blackened holes where her eyes had once been, crossed through with faded white scars. "Get the hell out of here, or this will be your fate! Now go!" My stomach would have turned over at the gruesome sight, had I been in my body.

I scrambled out of the tent, my spirit form flowing through the fabric flaps. She didn't follow me. "Fool girl," came her muffled voice from inside.

I stood like the fool girl she'd called me, confused and frightened. What was going on? Why was she so desperate for me to leave? I was certain she had answers, but why wouldn't she share them? I played our conversation back over in my mind, searching for clues to help me understand. I seized on something she'd said. *"Why would I help the Ostrovs? They didn't lift a finger to help me when I was handed over to this lot."* Iskra Juric—the woman who'd written the journal—she'd been handed over to the Vruks. And Spirodon had mentioned her, like she was still alive. Was it possible she was the same woman? Still here, serving the Vruks? Still alive? But why would they have left her alive if they knew she could still see? Still utilize her Mesmer powers?

A realization struck me, and I heaved a deep breath as it clicked into place. "The Vruks don't know." I strode back into the tent.

She whirled. "You? Again? Too stupid to learn a lesson the first time?"

"Iskra Juric? Are you her?"

The woman froze, then lowered herself onto the little cot with infinite slowness. "Once, I was called that, yes."

"The Vruks don't know, do they? That the Wretched can still see. Can you still Compel?"

Her thin mouth twisted. "You think we would still be here, if we could? No, the entire West Adrjssian population drinks verbenia. It's in the water. In the ale. But we can still see. It has to be enough, for us."

"How is it possible? Without your eyes?"

"Do they neglect your theory so much these days? Mesmers do not see with their eyes. They see with their crown Node. That they can only take from us in death. If the Vruks weren't so prejudiced, they might have learned a thing or two about the magic they hate so much."

"Does no one know?"

"A few. A few who can be trusted. If the rest found out, if Andrej found out…" She shook her head. "We'd be dead. All of us."

"How many Wretched are there?"

"Around a hundred, give or take."

I leaned back, stunned. I'd had no idea it was so many. So many Mesmers disfigured—forced into a half-life. "I won't tell."

"Then what do you want from me?"

My mouth opened and closed. If Iskra testified to seeing Silviya, perhaps I could convince Nevena that Dragan had masterminded her parents' deaths, not me. But would she agree? It would put all of the Wretched at risk. Perhaps there was a way to get her to testify secretly. I needed to make her see. "One of the Adrjssian Royal Mesmers assassinated the king and queen."

"Why should Adrjssian politics concern me?"

I blinked. "Because he made it look like the Vruk ambassadors were to blame. He's fanning the flames of this war."

She shook her head. "This war is inevitable so long as Andrej is alive. Whether the Vruk army overtakes the throne of King Petar or Queen Nevena, it matters little."

How to get her to care? I found myself babbling. "But...he framed me. They believe I committed the crimes, when really his Mesmer sister, who is trapped inside his same body, embodied my form when I was Projecting."

Iskra drew in a sharp breath. "I didn't know that was possible."

"I didn't, either. I can prove it, but only to someone who's a Mesmer. I need someone to convince the queen. Or people will die. Lots of people."

"Including you?"

"Yes, me first of all."

She looked at me and crossed her arms. "If what you say is true, it's dark magic being used. The same type of thing that marred the names of Mesmers before the war. But I still don't see how it concerns me."

"If you would testify to Nevena that you too can see this other Mesmer form—and hear her confession—maybe Queen Nevena would believe me. Maybe we could capture the real culprit."

"She won't believe a blind, old Vruk slave. I'm not unsympathetic, but I'm not willing to risk exposing a secret we've all kept for twenty years just to save your hide. I will not trade one hundred lives for one."

I deflated. I didn't blame her, really. "What about another Wretched? Would anyone help...?" I trailed off. No Wretched could help without risking their secret. I dropped my head into my hands. "I just wish Nevena could see what I see. It would solve everything."

"Now there's a thought," she said. I looked up hopefully to find her tapping her fingertips together. "Have you heard of Shadow-singer?"

"King Andrej's dagger, right?" Matija had mentioned it when his fingers had been tight around my throat. My eyes widened as I followed Iskra's train of thought. It was said to contain the power of countless Mesmers—to give the user the power to see oras. "A blade imbued with the power of Mesmers it killed. Does it truly work?"

"Only Andrej knows for certain. But he treasures it like his own son. He never takes it off."

"How would I get it, then?" This sounded like a fool's errand.

"Even kings need to sleep."

"Could you get it for me?"

"Me?" She sputtered in laughter. "No. You're on your own. But I can tell you that the best time would be just after midnight, when the guard shift changes."

If Nevena held this dagger, if its power was true—then she could see Silviya. And she would know that Dragan had been lying to her. It was a solution. Not an easy one, but more than I'd had when I'd arrived here. I stood. "I swear on my life, the secret of the Wretched is safe with me."

She inclined her head.

I turned to go but remembered there was one more mystery I was trying to unravel. "Do you know anything of a plot to kill King Andrej? I think our Prime Mesmer was working with someone. If I could find that person, perhaps we could work together to stop this war."

Iskra stood in a proud sweep, advancing on me. "That is a subject that could get me killed. I will not speak of it with you."

I backed up hastily. There would be no more answers here. "Thank you, for speaking with me."

"You can thank me by ensuring that I never see your face again."

A tug at my stomach jerked me back a step. My confusion coalesced into a horrible realization. Someone was trying to wake me up. Someone had found my body.

# CHAPTER 37

*I* awoke with a jerk. When I saw the features blinking down at me, I wasn't sure if I was still dreaming. "Papa?"

It had been so long since I'd seen his weathered face—his sorrowful eyes and his unruly, gray hair. "Is it really you?"

"I could ask you the same question." It sounded like him. "When I found you here, I was certain you were dead."

I sprang at him, encircling him in a crushing embrace. His familiar scent of verbenia and wood smoke filled my nostrils and my heart swelled so big, I thought it might burst. "I wasn't sure I'd ever see you again." My words were muffled in his coarse cloak.

"Nor I you, my sweet girl. When you never wrote back...I feared the worst."

I pulled back and swiped away an errant tear. "The Para-Mesmer —Dragan. He kept your letters from me. I never got them."

His face darkened. "Why?"

I heaved a sigh. "It's too long an explanation. It doesn't matter. What are you doing here?"

"The Vruks are on the march. The whole village has evacuated. I thought I could lie low here for a few days while they passed by."

"Maggya?" I prayed Simeon's mother was safe.

"She left some few weeks ago. She said her family was drawing near, and she needed to meet them. Can't say I fully understood what she was on about." Papa shook his head.

I wondered how she had known? Nevena had said that the Mora fleet was sailing for Vrilaand, the Vruk capital. I hoped Maggya had found them.

"What are you doing here? Hiding out in a cave?"

"I was arrested for the murder of the king and queen. I escaped."

"What? Again?" Papa exploded to his feet, nearly toppling back over before he got his cane under him. "I thought you were cleared of that crime. Who would spread such lies?"

I rubbed the spot between my eyes, as if I could banish the memories. "Dragan framed me."

"That blond Mesmer? I knew he was trouble. I told you, Jana. I said that Selojia was a place of liars and scoundrels—"

"Papa!" I held up my hands, and to my surprise, he fell silent. "I've learned that lesson very painfully, very personally. Please, no lectures." I didn't think I could take it.

"My sweet Jana." Papa dropped back down, taking my face in his gnarled hands. "You were too good for that place. Too pure. I never should have left you alone."

"I sent you away." A lump grew in my throat. "I didn't even say goodbye. I'm so sorry—"

"Hush." Papa pulled me into another embrace. "Hush, my girl. I deserved what you dished out. I never should have lied to you. I should have trusted you could handle it."

I pulled back, Papa's face twisting through the lens of my watery tears. "Papa, did I really…?" My voice cracked.

"Really what?"

He was going to make me say it. "Dragan said I killed Arabel." My heart—raw and abused and battered as it was—was cracked open at the thought of what I'd done. Was I a killer? Dragan and Silviya may have used my body, but would they have found so willing a host, if not for my natural predilections? I was the perfect subject. I'd killed before. It was nothing to kill again.

He put a shaky hand before his mouth and looked down. Then up. Anywhere but at my eyes. "No, my darling. I am to blame for Arabel's death." He shook his head as his shoulders seemed to curl in like a wilting flower. "I should have watched you both. You were little girls. I'll never forgive myself for leaving you in the yard alone. You two ran off to the lake to swim, and she went too deep."

The day was a curious blank spot in my memory. I'd never been able to remember what had happened. "But you're saying..." I sorted through it. "You don't think I forced her into the lake? With my Mesmerism?"

His head shot up. "That is a foul suggestion. No, of course not. You were young and headstrong, but you loved your sister. You never would have harmed her." His fire quickly dimmed. "It was a tragedy brought on by my negligence."

It was as if a great weighted yoke had cracked, slipping from my shoulders. "I feared it was me." I whispered the admission.

Papa shook his head, wiping a hand across his brow.

It had been a lie. Another one of Dragan's lies. Designed to make me doubt myself, to believe I deserved what he and his despicable sister had done to me.

I stood and walked to the mouth of the cave, my emotions at a rolling boil. The cold air kissed my skin, and I welcomed it, bid it to steal the flush of anger from my cheeks.

Dragan and Silviya had manipulated me. Used me. Convinced me I'd been seeing things—imagining things. He'd made me fall in love with him, he'd used my body, all for his twisted ends. He couldn't just *get away with it.*

Mist shrouded the forest, hanging from the tree branches like dripping moss. In the distance, the steady pulse of drumbeats quickened my pulse. The Vruk camp was close enough to hear. Someone could be standing just feet from me, and I'd never see them. The thought sent a prickle of unease through me, but I did my best to squash it. The Vruks would be enjoying their warm fires and horns of ale tonight, not tiptoeing through strange forests.

My time speaking to Iskra seemed like a distant memory. But I was determined to steal Shadow-bringer, the king's enchanted dagger. Nevena didn't have the proof she needed to move against Dragan, and without me, she'd never get it. So many lives they'd taken—the king and queen, Aleksi, his companion Ioseph, Simeon's poor guard friend, likely the crown prince too. Valko. My anger roared hotter. Dragan had stood just feet away as Valko had been executed. Valko, who'd been his mentor—who had saved his life as a child. And what was worse, Dragan had orchestrated Valko's execution.

My eyes narrowed in the dark. For some reason, the comment Matija had made in the dungeon flared bright in my mind. *"You truly are a sheep among wolves, aren't you?"* There was no doubt I'd been acting like one. Meek and pliable and complacent. Dragan had taken me under his wing. Sheltered me—kept the full strength of my powers from me, under the guise of it serving my own good. He'd kept me weak and dependent upon him—and I'd let him. Hadn't doubted it. Lapped up his esteem and scrabbled for the crumbs of his affection like a starving waif.

But I was more than that. I was a Mesmer. I could continue fearing that part of myself, or I could use it for my own ends. Use it to take him down. I smiled grimly into the dark. I knew which choice I preferred.

* * *

I HAD no idea how I was going to sneak into an enemy camp filled with Vruk warriors dosed with verbenia, but my course was laid out before me. The only way to convince Nevena that Dragan was the true enemy was to show her Silviya. She needed to see the dead Mesmer with her own eyes.

As I headed toward the sound of the drums, I opened my crown node and quested out around me, searching for oras of spies or scouts. I couldn't use my Mesmerism to manipulate their emotions, but I could at least know where they were located. As I drew closer to the edge of the woods, the quiet sounds of men and horses emerged—

muttered voices, the crackle of a cooking fire, the soft clank of a lead line.

I wiped my sweaty palms on my dress and put my hood up, threading my way through the trees toward madness.

I knew the dagger was in the king's tent. Would it be possible for me to get inside without drawing attention though?

I paused as the line of trees ended. Iskra had said it would be best to go during the guard change, but I had no idea what time it was. Just feet from me were the first tents. If I went in there, there was a high likelihood I'd be caught. And Vruks weren't kind to Mesmers. But I had no choice. If I wanted to ever be free, if I wanted Dragan to face justice, I had to do this.

My heart galloped in my throat as I crossed the open space between trees and tents and pressed myself into the shadows behind the nearest tent. I skirted along the outside, toward where I knew the king's tent to be. After a few minutes, I'd made good progress, but I'd delayed long enough. I needed to push into the main part of the camp.

I looked down at myself. Even with my brown cloak, I stood out. My attire was different than the coarse wools and furs of the Vruk camp followers. Delicately and quietly, I unthreaded and pulled a fur off the side of one of the tents and draped it around my shoulders. It wasn't much, but hopefully, it would keep people from looking too closely.

Then I moved forward. It was a deadly maze, sidestepping around open areas where men congregated and cooked, keeping to the dark alleys formed between tents.

I stumbled around a corner and nearly crashed into a couple wrapped around each other in the dark.

I froze. So did they. Then the tattooed man grinned a leisurely smile, revealing browned teeth. "Wait a minute, love. I'll be finished here and ready for another round."

The woman cuffed him over the head and I scurried past, oily panic running sluggish through my veins.

I came to a halt in the shadows between two tents. The king's tent loomed in the distance, large and elaborately decorated. It was set apart from the rest, with a wide swath of trampled grass between it and the nearest other tents. Two guards were stationed at the door.

I chewed my lip. I could go around back and sneak in the side? But the fabric sides appeared to be staked tightly down; it didn't seem like I could slither under.

I needed a distraction.

I didn't think. I just acted. Every moment I stayed here was another closer to getting caught. I sat down quickly and slumped into a ball, separating my ora from my body. I floated into the middle of the campfire nearby, where men were talking and drinking, waiting for a fragrant pot of stew to be finished.

I dashed into the middle of their circle, praying no Wretched was nearby to see me. I focused my energy as I had back at the palace and pulled one of the legs of the tripod holding the pot above the fire.

It tumbled to the side with a clamor, splashing hot soup over several of the men.

They all rose with a shout, cursing and shouting. I was back in my body in a blink, watching the guards' reactions. They were looking at each other—yes! Going to investigate.

It was my only chance. Keeping low to the ground, I dashed along the outskirts of the tent and inside the king's tent, fighting the nausea washing over me in waves.

I crouched down by the door, my chest heaving, my eyes scanning the interior. My head swam from the energy I'd expended while Projecting, but I was stronger than I had once been. I thought I could keep it together. Loud voices carried on outside, but they were distant, by the fire. It seemed no one had seen me come in.

A rattling snore sounded from across the cavernous space, and I froze. I peeked up and saw a distinct lump in the bed. The king was here. Asleep.

The thought terrified me, even though it was exactly what I'd been hoping for. I sent a fervent prayer up to Ovyato for silence and stealth. I couldn't be discovered.

I gingerly straightened my shaky legs. I had done it. I was in. I didn't know how the hell I was going to get out without being seen, but that was a problem for five minutes from now. After I found Shadow-bringer.

I looked about the king's tent as my eyes adjusted to the darkness. A writing table and chair sat in one corner, a chest covered with furs in another. A suit of armor hung on a stand, gleaming dully in the low light. Where was the dagger? He would have taken it off as he'd undressed... I crept closer to the bed. Maybe it was on the ground?

As I continued scanning the space, my gaze snagged on a distinctly dagger-shaped item resting on a little table next to the bed. I took a step closer.

"Well, aren't you clever?"

I whirled around and hissed in a breath. "You!" I whispered. It wasn't the Vruk guards, come to arrest or kill me.

It was worse.

It was Silviya.

She crossed her arms before her and cocked her head. "You know who I am, don't you?"

"Of course I do," I hissed, my eyes fixed on the king. Another loud snore ripped from him. "You're the cause of all of this. You and Dragan."

She took a leisurely step forward. "I told Dragan not to underestimate you. But men can be shortsighted sometimes, especially when they aren't thinking with their heads."

"You're a monster," I spat. "A murderer."

"The *Vruks* are monsters." Her face grew ugly. "King Petar was a monster. He let hundreds of Mesmers be tortured or killed. And for what? So he could secure power? Political alliances? What the Vruks did to my mother..." Silviya tightened her fists. Her eyes were wild, manic. "I was there, you know, Projecting. When they tortured her. Do you know what it's like as a five-year-old? To see men do that to your mother?"

"No," I admitted, and then I hardened, stalking across the room until I was right before her. I whispered, "But I do know what it feels like to be violated. To have my body worn like an old cloak. Used like it was nothing. What *you* did to me...you and Dragan...you're just as bad as them. Worse."

"We did what we had to. We never hurt you."

"*Never hurt me*? Even setting aside Dragan's emotional manipulation, you poisoned me with that stupid salve! I've been imprisoned twice and watched good men die." I spat my words like venom. "You don't get to say you never hurt me."

"It was necessary, Adrijana. For the greater good. For all Mesmers. You'll see some day. Dragan and I are creating a safe place. A kingdom where they can flourish."

"Your utopian kingdom didn't feel very safe for me. Or Valko." Why was I even talking to her? She wasn't really here. She couldn't stop me. I spun on my heel, stalked back across the furs, and seized the dagger in its leather sheath.

"That'll do you no good," she said. "The legends are false."

"You're lying."

"Am I? I could frolic before King Andrej naked and he'd never see me, even holding that dagger. They made up the stories. I've spent enough time in the palace at Vrilaand to know."

I hesitated and then banished my doubts. Why would I believe a word she said? If there was even a tiny chance that this dagger was the answer I needed, I had to take it. I started for the entrance.

In a blink, she was standing in front of me, floating close. I could see the same long nose that Dragan had, the same curve of her lips.

"You can't stop me," I said. "You're nothing but an angry ghost."

She bared her teeth and barreled through me, sending a gasp and a shiver through my body. I whirled to find her standing by the suit of armor. "Can't stop you, can't I?" She placed her hand on the suit of armor—and pushed.

The armor toppled to the ground with a deafening crash.

The king came to with a roar, standing on his bed, towering over me. He was a huge man, his bare chest covered with tattoos in dark, twisting lines. His blue eyes gleamed manic in the dark.

He seized my wrist in an iron grip and wrenched the dagger and sheath from me, holding it above his head. "Who are you?" he bellowed. "This is the assassin they send for me? I will break you like a twig!"

My mind scrambled in circles, searching desperately for a way out. So fixed upon my predicament that it hardly registered when Silviya circled behind him, a feverish glow in her milky eyes. She grabbed the dagger and pulled it from its sheath, held in King Andrej's hand.

I realized her intent too late. "Look out—" My warning turned to ash in my mouth as the silver blade flashed across the king's throat.

His eyes went wide and his hands flew to his neck, as if to hold in the cascade of crimson lifeblood flowing from the slash across his skin. He fell heavy to his knees before me, and Silviya tossed the knife to the floor between my feet. Her smile was gleeful. "Have fun explaining that one," she said before turning into smoke and swirling from the room.

The tent flap opened, and half a dozen Vruk warriors, bristling with weapons, poured into a semi-circle around me.

I lifted my hands slowly.

Have fun explaining, indeed.

# CHAPTER 38

*I* spent a cold, miserable night in a set of Vruk shackles, chained to a thick post in a dim tent. Sadly, I was getting used to being in irons. At least this time they didn't need to dose me with verbenia. The whole Vruk population was dosed, meaning there was little harm I could do here.

When the weak light of the sun came up, I was surprised to find a familiar face greeting me. Iskra looked down at me, a frown etched beneath her blindfold. "That was ill-advised, Adrijana. They think you are an assassin, sent by the Adrjssian queen. Instead of proving your innocence, you've managed to become the most condemned woman on the entire continent."

I snorted a tired laugh, my nerves raw and jangling. So much for being a wolf. "I don't suppose I can convince you that it wasn't me who killed the king?"

"It's not me you need to convince."

The tent flap opened and a tall young man ducked inside. He was handsome in a severe way, a scar nicking one dark eyebrow above his sky-blue eyes. His head was shorn completely, like the king's had been, though a neat, dark beard covered his angular jaw. The leathers he wore were finely-detailed with intertwining knots and patterns.

"You will bow before King Elian," Iskra said coldly, standing up.

I did my best to bow from my chained, seated position. So this was the prince who Andrej had wanted to marry off to Nevena. Now made king, in the wake of his father's death. They had wasted no time.

"I'd like to speak to her alone." The king spoke in perfect Adrjssian, his voice a pleasant bass.

Iskra curtsied and left us.

I licked my dry lips, doing my best to shift from my awkward position. My shoulders ached, and my hands were numb.

The king sat on the stool Iskra had vacated, leaning down to brush some dirt off his boot. "Adrijana Mironacht, you have done me a great service."

I blinked in surprise.

"It is little known, but my father was ailing. Rather than thank Zamo Idvo for the fruitful years he had been given, he conceived this invasion as a way to artificially prolong his life. But my father's time had come. Clearly, you were the instrument of Zamo's will."

I was dumbfounded. He was glad his father was dead? I supposed it made sense. A prince eager to start his rule wouldn't wanted his father to obtain the chiton that would allow him to live an unnaturally long life span. But if the prince was so eager to get rid of his father, why hadn't he just...? My mouth opened and closed. "It was you, wasn't it? You were corresponding with the late Prime Mesmer. Plotting to end your father." The letters Spirodon had been ferrying about killing a king—securing the marriage alliance with Nevena—they'd been between Valko and Crown Prince Elian.

The king rested his chin on his palm as he examined me. "It pleases me that you're not just a pretty face."

It seemed that was all the affirmation I would get. "I didn't kill your father. There was another Mesmer Projecting into the room. She's been working with Dragan Vulpe, the current Prime Mesmer. She seized the blade and killed him. She framed me."

"Hmm." He nodded slowly, then pulled a dagger out of a sheath at his belt. My mouth went dry. It was the dagger I'd tried to steal—

Shadow-bringer. Fear skittered up my spine like a flock of tiny spiders. Was he going to cut my eyes out?

"The one with the long hair and big eyes?" he asked.

My mouth dropped open, my distress forgotten. "You know of her?"

"She haunts our camp like a ghost. Yes, my mother has mentioned her many times."

"Your mother?" My mind spun. The Vruk prince—no, king—knew about Mesmers Projecting into his camp? "Who is your mother?"

He furrowed his brow, nodding back toward the tent flap. "Iskra."

I slumped back against the wooden post behind me, dumbfounded.

"I see she did not tell you all. In the days before and after the war, my father was quite enamored with the Mesmer Iskra Juric, even as he hated her for her power. He cut out her eyes and took her for a slave. She fell pregnant and gave birth to me. For many years, I was also treated as a slave. But my father married twice, and both times, no heirs were born. I was fourteen when my father officially took me as his heir, as I am his only child."

I swallowed. "Why are you telling me all of this?" Was this man a Mesmer? His eyes were blue, not the green of a verbenia-soaked Mesmer. But hadn't I learned that there was plenty I didn't understand?

"It's common knowledge." The king continued to twirl the dagger in his hand. "And to answer your other question, no. The gift didn't pass to me. Father never would have allowed me to live, if it had."

"So you know your mother can still..." I trailed off. If he wasn't a Mesmer, and Iskra had told him about seeing Silviya in camp, then he must know Iskra could still see. Even so, I was hesitant to say it. Iskra had impressed upon me the importance of the secret.

"Yes, I know the Wretched can still see." He shook his head, his full mouth twisting in a grimace. "I detest that name and plan to phase it out during my reign. My people have hated and feared Mesmers for too long. I plan to slowly introduce them back into our society—have my people tested and trained."

"So you will reveal that the Wretched can see?"

"Eventually. It must happen slowly. Be managed carefully. Or there will be a backlash that I fear could be violent."

I shook my head. "I can't believe it. I never expected to find a Vruk so tolerant of Mesmers. Least of all you."

"My father is responsible for fanning the flames of prejudice. Growing up, I felt the pain of being an outcast. I saw how my mother was treated, for nothing more than a gift she'd been born with. She could no more help it than I can help having blue eyes. Besides, Mesmers are powerful weapons. Once, they rode into battle alongside our warriors. I will have it be so again."

That could be trouble for Adrjssia, but it was a far-future problem. "What happens now?"

"Queen Nevena has called for a meeting to discuss the possibility of a peaceful resolution."

"Will you attend?" It sounded like this had been Andrej's war. Perhaps now that his father was dead, Elian would retreat.

"Indeed. I should like to take her hand in marriage. West Adrjssia and Adrjssia should be one again."

I licked my lips. Best to let Nevena deliver the bad news herself. "And what about me? Am I free to go?"

He raised an eyebrow. "Free to go? You are wanted for the murder of not one, but two kings."

A cold sweat broke across my skin. "But I didn't do it. I didn't kill Petar, either. It's the Prime Mesmer, Dragan Vulpe, and his sister, Silviya. They're the killers."

"I'm afraid we have only your word of that."

"And the sighting of Silviya! You said yourself, she haunts your camp."

"But that information cannot be shared, or it would risk the lives of my mother, and all the other Wretched."

"What about the dagger? You could see her through Shadow-bringer's power."

Elian flipped the dagger in his hand. "I'm afraid Shadow-bringer's powers are a myth. Made up by my father to prevent Mesmer spying."

"But your people don't know that—"

"Enough of his trusted warriors do. They would know I lied. And I can't have that, especially when I'm trying to solidify my power."

I shook my head wildly. This wasn't happening. This wasn't right. "You can't just execute me. You know I'm innocent."

"I will not be executing anyone. Nevena has demanded you be handed over to her for sentencing. You will be my wedding gift to her."

# CHAPTER 39

*I* was led to the outskirts of the Vruk camp, where a large, open-air pavilion tent had been erected. I recognized the Adrjssian purple before I could make out the faces.

As I drew closer, I squared my shoulders, though my legs were quaking beneath me. This couldn't be happening. I needed a way out. There must be a way out—something I hadn't seen yet.

Nevena looked serene in a dress of aubergine velvet. The Adrjssian crown, studded with diamonds and pearls, shone atop her glossy, brown hair. Simeon stood at her side, not in his guard uniform, but wearing a finely-tailored jacket of navy blue trimmed with silver, white pants, and black boots. The colors of the Mora.

Georgi stood on Nevena's other side, wearing a tunic of emerald green and brown pants tucked into supple leather boots. The clothes of a Durvo tribesman. His karakal, and Nevena's, stood between them. I was grateful beyond belief to see him safe, and to know that Nevena hadn't jailed him for his part in my escape.

I understood what was going on as I saw Dragan next to Simeon. He wore a white shirt wrapped with a colorful silk belt, and a long, golden coat over the top. He was dressed like a Lozian clansman, rather than the Queen's Prime Mesmer. Together, the four of them represented four of the five tribes of Adrjssia—a show of solidarity and a subtle challenge.

A half dozen guards stood behind them.

The Vruk forces included young King Elian, blindfolded Iskra, and four other men clothed in furs and outfitted to the teeth. I eyed the dagger that hung on the king's belt with a pang of regret. If only the legend of Shadow-bringer had been real. This could have all ended differently.

A Vruk guard booted the back of my legs and I tumbled to the ground, barely catching myself with my shackled hands. I stayed on my knees, though I straightened. Perhaps I would die on my knees, but I wouldn't grovel. I looked up at Dragan, trying to catch his gaze. His features were arranged in a perfect approximation of sorrow and anger. How masterful an actor Dragan was, that he looked upset by the predicament he'd squarely placed me in.

I willed him to look at me. I didn't know why, but I needed to look him in the eyes one more time. Make him see that *I* at least knew what he'd done. That I hadn't bought into his twisted tale that I was a killer who didn't even know myself.

"Queen Nevena," Elian said. "Welcome."

"Isn't it I who should be welcoming you?" Nevena said curtly. "As this is my land."

King Elian smiled and inclined his head. "There has been much bad blood and misunderstanding between our people in our fathers' times. But we two are different people, and things are changing. I hope that we can find a way to work together, in peace."

"It would be easier to believe your words if you had not brought your army to my gates."

"But I am not my father. That was his doing. But now that we are here and have seen your lovely country, I think an alliance is more desirable than an invasion."

"What do you propose?" Nevena asked. She hadn't moved an inch from where she stood.

Elian strode forward and reached for Nevena's hand.

At that moment, a shrieking cry sounded from above, and a great, white shape swooped into the pavilion.

Elian stumbled back away from Nevena, buffeted by the backbeats of Simeon's sky-bird, Xaranti, who came to land on Simeon's outstretched, leather-clad arm.

Simeon drew the bird in close to his chest, stroking its silvery crest once before turning his attention back to Elian.

For the first time since I'd met him, the Vruk king struggled with his composure. "Is that—"

"A star-bird, yes," Simeon said.

"But they—"

"King Elian, allow me to introduce my husband and king consort, Simeon Windrider, of the Mora clan, second of the line of Calysto."

"Your husband." Elian blinked.

I pursed my lips together to keep from smiling. Regardless of my situation, it was satisfying to see Nevena completely outmaneuver the arrogant Vruk.

"If I'd only known, I would have provided a suitable wedding gift."

"Our nuptials were quite recent. Your breach of etiquette is excused."

I did smile then and looked up to see Dragan glaring at me. He must have been furious when he'd discovered that I'd married Simeon and Nevena, solidifying Nevena's political power and securing her a new, powerful ally. I glared back. Good.

Nevena continued. "My husband's people did grant me quite a wedding gift. One hundred Mora ships, fully crewed with warriors. They're currently anchored at the mouth of the Bastiav River."

To his credit, Elian barely reacted to the news that a hostile armada was stationed only a few miles downriver from his capital. "An impressive gift indeed."

Nevena leaned over and gave Simeon a long kiss.

King Elian cleared his throat and motioned to me. "We have your assassin." One of his guards grabbed me by the hair and tossed me forward, onto the grass between the two lines. I pushed up to hands and knees, leaning back on my heels.

"She's not *our* assassin," Nevena said. "This is the girl who killed my parents."

"I thought you blamed us for your parents' death," Elian said. "In fact, one of my ambassadors died in your dungeon for it."

Nevena winced. "That was an unfortunate incident, but we are not to blame. He killed himself."

The king stepped forward. "Lies. Spirodon would never have ended his own life. It is not the Vruk way." Yet another life Dragan and Silviya had taken. The toll was staggering. All under our noses.

Nevena frowned. "I'm willing to discuss…reparations for the death of your ambassador. And your other ambassador is here with us. I will release him into your charge, if we reach an agreement today."

Elian nodded thoughtfully. "Now you are convinced this girl is the killer instead?"

"Did she not just kill your father as well?"

I wanted to scream in protest, but I didn't know what good it would do. Most of the people here knew, or at least believed, that I was innocent. But it didn't matter. Elian needed a scapegoat to blame for the death of his father. He was content for it to be me. Georgi didn't have enough evidence, and Dragan certainly wasn't coming to my defense.

Elian inclined his head, conceding the point. "I had thought to let you execute her as a gesture of goodwill, but…"

"Do you no longer desire my goodwill?" Nevena asked sharply.

Elian looked from Nevena to me. "No, I believe I still do. Though we've come a long way, and my men are hungry for a fight."

"Then they're hungry for death, and the deaths of their families back home as well," she snapped. "I'm disappointed. I thought you were a better man than your father was. But perhaps I was wrong."

King Elian said nothing, his shrewd eyes taking in Nevena, then Simeon. Dragan and Georgi. Me. And then he let out quiet laugh. "I would be willing to call off this battle and turn my men around. But I cannot force them to leave empty-handed."

"You are king."

"Vruks do not follow like sheep. Not like you Ostrovs."

"Insults aside, I would be willing to consider terms. What do you want?"

"Land. You have plenty, lying fallow. Many of my people want to farm."

"You think I will let you effectively move your borders?"

"If we are ever to live in peace, we need to begin to trust each other. Integrate."

Nevena looked down, pondering. When she met his gaze, her eyes were clear. Resolute. "I will allow leases of land, with the option to purchase. Leases subject to revocation upon the first sign of Vruk aggression."

It was the king's turn to ponder. "I think we could work out something along those lines."

My shoulders slumped in relief. Nevena had done it. She'd stopped the war and secured protection against the next Vruk attack. Vruk farmers would petition hard against any aggressive move by their leaders, if it meant they would lose their land. It was a savvy move.

"And what are we to do with this one?" Elian nodded at me. "She must pay for her crimes."

Georgi spoke up. "Doesn't Adrijana get to speak in her defense?"

"What is there to hear? Does she deny her guilt?" Dragan asked.

"I do." My voice was dry and croaky. "The true culprit stands there, beside the queen. Dragan Vulpe, the Prime Mesmer. Along with his sister, Silviya. This was all their doing."

"What proof do you have of your innocence?" Nevena asked. If she looked surprised by my mention of Dragan's long-dead sister, she didn't show it. Her expression was guarded, but I thought I recognized a flicker of pleading in her eyes. *Give me something.*

But I had nothing I could share.

As I looked at Dragan, a silvery form split from him. Silviya—her hair waving in a spectral breeze. She wore an expression of savage delight on her face. Dragan looked ill, but he clearly couldn't tell her to return to hiding, not before all of these people.

I longed to tell Nevena to seize the Vruk king's dagger, to see the true villain. But the dagger was no more than a fable told to frighten King Andrej's enemies. It would do no good. She would never be able to see the truth. "I have proof only a Mesmer could see. She stands right there, before all of you. Mocking you, even as she plots the end of the Tsarian line."

"Nevena, this is wrong," Georgi murmured to his cousin, but she waved him away.

Elian was unbothered. "If you have no proof, in light of the weight of the evidence against you, I feel we have no choice but to find you guilty. Queen Nevena, how do you find?"

Nevena paused, looking sidelong at Dragan for the first time. Once, she had asked me to spy on him, had admitted she didn't fully trust him. But now, she gambled everything on trusting him over me. On believing I lied, and he spoke the truth. Hadn't she learned from what happened with Valko? In her haste, she'd executed an innocent man. Nevena cleared her throat. "In Adrjssia, accused have the right to a semblance of a trial. We will return to Selojia—"

Elian interrupted her. "Vruks do not have trials, not for those guilty of murdering our monarch. She was found in his tent, standing over him as he took his last breaths. I'm afraid I cannot abide my father's killer leaving here alive. Not if you want peace between us."

Nevena licked her lips and my heart sank. Elian had her cornered. He wanted me gone, so I couldn't speak the truth about his plot against his father, or the Wretched, or his plans for the Mesmers of West Adrjssia.

Nevena nodded, once. "Very well."

Simeon looked ill and cradled Xaranti to his chest. The star-bird swiveled her head, looking at me with bead-black eyes. And then she turned her head toward Silviya and let out a shrieking caw.

I looked down at the scabbed puncture wounds on my forearm and an idea burst through me like a comet, leaving a tail of desperate hope. Xaranti had touched my ora. She could touch Silviya. My eyes widened.

"I will carry out the sentence, unless you wish to do so?" Elian unsheathed his sword. A wave of nausea buffered me. My mind worked furiously. If I told them Xaranti could touch Silviya, the phantom woman would simply slip back inside Dragan's body. I needed her close to Simeon, close enough that Xaranti would feel threatened and lash out.

If I didn't figure out how to accomplish that feat, I was going to die. Killed by a man who knew I was innocent.

"I would be grateful if you did the deed," Nevena said.

Silviya started to laugh. She skipped over to me, crouching down beside me. "We couldn't have done it without you, Adrijana. Without your body, I should say. War may be averted for now, but we'll find a way to ensure they destroy each other. Dragan will be king, and these fields will run with blood."

I ground my teeth, glaring at her. I needed to goad her. "They'll stop you. Simeon sees the truth. He may not have the evidence to take you two down yet, but he will. You won't get away with this."

Nevena and Simeon exchanged a look.

"She's gone mad." Elian shook his head with feigned sorrow.

Dragan watched his sister with wild, violet eyes, the muscles feathering in his clenched jaw. Silviya stood and strode to stand before Simeon and Nevena, sneering at them. "I want you go to your grave knowing that your sweet queen and your beloved Simeon are not long for this world."

Simeon's star-bird exploded off of his leather-clad forearm, launching herself at Silviya. Xaranti's wings beat at her, talons shredding the specter's face and arms as she shrieked, flailing her arms to fend off the bird.

My mouth dropped open in amazement. Holy Ovyato, it had *worked!* The bird was *connecting* with Silviya's ethereal body. Actually hurting her.

"Xaranti!" Simeon gave a sharp whistle and held his arm out. The bird gave a final peck at Silviya's face and returned to its perch, her gossamer feathers ruffled.

Silence hung thick in the pavilion for a moment and then a muffled groan drew my attention. Dragan! He was bending over, his face cradled in his hands. A drip of blood escaped through his fingers, onto the grass.

Silviya was straightening, brushing her hair out of her face. The silvery gashes on her cheeks were closing, as her ethereal form healed. But Dragan—he was truly injured. Xaranti's wounding of Silviya had injured Dragan, her host.

"Now you see," I said, in delighted disbelief. "The bird attacked Silviya, the true murderer. She haunts this field like a ghost."

"Prime Mesmer, are you quite all right?" Nevena was examining Dragan, her sharp eyes flicking from me to Dragan to Simeon's starbird.

"I...have something in my eye..." came his muffled voice. He was still doubled over, hiding his face. "If I may excuse myself—"

"No. You stay." Nevena's voice cracked like a whip. "King Elian, I have changed my mind. I would like to swing the sword myself." Nevena marched over to Elian and seized the sword from his hand.

Wait, what?

"Nevena—" Simeon pleaded. "Hold a moment. Something is not right."

The queen positioned herself on my other side. "No more delay. We end this now."

"What are you doing?" I demanded, trying stand to my feet. A Vruk guard shoved me back down. "Nevena, there's your proof right there. You saw the bird attack her. You're executing the wrong person!"

"Nevena, she's right." Georgi stepped between us, his hands up. "Don't you understand what happened?"

"Get back, Georgi," Nevena snapped, "or it will be *your* head. My family has waited too long for justice." Nevena's lavender face was inscrutable; it held none of the warmth I remembered from our long nights playing cards and drinking wine. Now, she was a queen. Distant and cold. "Dragan, come here. Hold her still."

Georgi backed away slowly.

"Don't you touch me," I hissed as Dragan, his face still hidden behind his golden hair, came around behind me. "You don't get to touch me ever again!" I shrieked and flailed against the Vruk guard who held my other arm. This could not be happening. In the last moment of my life, I would not be subjected to his touch.

But Dragan gripped my other forearm, smearing blood across my skin. He and the guard on the other side forced me down, so I was bent over my knees, my neck exposed. Hot tears spilled into the grass beneath me. How I despised him.

"I'm sorry, Adrijana," Dragan whispered to me, ever so softly. "It was never supposed to end like this."

Silviya started to laugh like a madwoman.

I looked up, my voice cracking. "Nevena, please. I didn't do any of this. You and Simeon are still in danger—"

"Have some self-respect in the end, Adrijana." Nevena cut me off, and her words shattered the fight left in me. It was over. The siblings had *won*. That thought would chase me to the grave.

"Hold her still." As Nevena raised her sword, I looked down. I fantasized for a brief moment of attaching my soul to Dragan's so I could haunt him for the rest of his days, to drive him mad for what he'd done to me.

But I didn't want to be trapped inside his pitiful self with Silviya. I wouldn't let him have control over me any longer.

It was time to set myself free.

So I closed my eyes.

I heard the wind whistle as the sword fell.

Felt a spray of warm blood splatter across my cheek.

I opened my startled eyes in time to see Dragan's headless body fall to the grass beside me.

# CHAPTER 40

or a single moment, all was quiet and still.

And then the sound came crashing in—the harsh rasp of Nevena's breath in and out, the chatter of birds in the nearby trees, the hum of shocked exclamations.

I opened my eyes a crack and came face to face with Dragan's glassy, violet eyes. His head had been severed clean off his body.

I vomited noisily into the grass, doing my best with my shackles to crawl away from the pool of blood spreading toward me.

Wiping my mouth, I looked up. And saw them.

Dragan and Silviya, in spectral form, stared at each other in surprise. As if they couldn't quite believe what had happened. "You fool," Silviya snapped. "You colossal, massive fool. Look at·what you've done!"

"What *I've* done?" Dragan cried. "This is *your* doing. You couldn't wait. You couldn't be patient and do things my way!"

They were levitating off the ground, drifting toward whatever great beyond we went to after we died. Silviya seemed to realize their predicament. "Dragan!"

Her face went feral and she lunged toward me. But I was ready. She'd taken everything from me—and now, she was done.

I slammed up walls around my ora, shutting her out. She scrabbled against me, but something was pulling her from behind. A silver thread tied to Dragan, tugging her into the sky.

"Nooo!" she screamed as she was swept away.

My eyes met Dragan's as he slipped past. His expression was weary. Resigned. I thought, just maybe, there was remorse there, too.

And then they were gone.

It was as if a great weight had lifted off me. I was safe. The country was safe. Everyone I loved was safe. I raised my shackled hands to my face and started to cry—ragged, relieved sobs that shook me to the core.

I didn't know how long I sat there, slumped on my knees, crying. A gentle hand on my shoulder made me jump. "Simeon?"

He took me by the arm and pulled me to my feet. The Vruks had retreated, leaving only the Adrjssian delegation beneath the pavilion. Simeon unlocked the irons about my wrists. He must have taken the key before the Vruks had left. I rubbed my sore wrists when my hands were free, rolling my shoulders.

I faced Nevena, sidling away from Dragan's prone body. I couldn't bear to look down at it. "I can't say I understand what just happened. But I am grateful."

"Georgi happened. And Simeon. And you. Georgi explained your side of the story, but we didn't have proof. Simeon was certain of your innocence as well. But after Elian claimed you killed his father, I didn't see how I could demand your release without plunging us back into war. Until I saw what that bird did to Dragan. Your story, as wild as it seemed, was clearly true. Even Elian couldn't dispute the evidence."

*Bless Xaranti.* That bird had saved my life. Perhaps all of our lives. "It was Dragan's sister who killed the Vruk king."

"What were you doing in his tent?" Simeon asked. "That was beyond foolish."

I blew out a heavy breath. "I know. It was said that Andrej owned a dagger that allowed the bearer to see like a Mesmer. I thought to take it and give it to you so you could see the truth of what I'd said for yourself."

Nevena looked thoughtful. "Shadow-bringer. I've heard of it. Did you find it?"

"Yes, but it's a fake. It has no real power."

"Good to know. So we will be able to safely spy on our new allies?" Nevena winked at Simeon.

"Not exactly. I have much to tell you. About the Vruks, and Elian." I swallowed as the odor of blood that filled my senses. "But perhaps we could talk somewhere else? I don't think I can stay here a moment longer."

"Yes, let us go home," Nevena agreed. "My ministers can work on negotiating the terms of the peace."

Home. I was buffeted by an overwhelming desire to curl up in my old bed, to fall asleep to Papa's rhythmic snores and the gentle crackle of wood on the fire.

"Your Majesty," I said. "Might I request a boon? I would like to go home and visit my father. And stay a while." I didn't want to face the corridors of the palace yet. The Mesmer workshop, my bedroom. Dragan's memory would be everywhere there, as if he were still waiting. Watching.

"I have need of you," Nevena protested.

Simeon wrapped an arm around Nevena's shoulders and whispered in her ear.

Her lavender features softened. "Until the Planting Season begins. Rest and heal from your ordeal. Then I need you back in the palace."

A few weeks. If that was what she was willing to give me, that was what I would take. "Thank you."

"And you will take a guard as escort. Simeon will select the best man for the job. You are too precious to be unguarded."

I swallowed my objections and nodded. With Vruks still near, it was a wise precaution.

Georgi stepped up. "May I accompany you home? Just for the journey?"

My heart squeezed. Sweet Georgi, who had always been true,

despite what I'd done to him. I'd be dead if not for him. And I didn't have the strength to argue. "If you wish."

Simeon found a horse and a guard, Yacob, for me, and we were on our way. I hoped Papa was still in the cave. I would find him, and we could go home together.

We rode in silence for a short while. A sticky lump was lodged in my throat. I wanted to cry, to fall apart, but Georgi and Yacob's presence held me together. Just barely.

"I remember." Georgi turned to me.

"Remember what?"

"The memories Dragan took from me. They came back as soon as he was gone."

A wave of wretchedness chilled me. "Oh, Georgi. I'm so sorry. Of course, I'm glad you're whole again. I just wish you didn't have to recall my magic twisting you so."

"I'm glad I remember that kiss." His green eyes were keen, fixed on me. "It was incredible."

My cheeks heated. "And then it got all twisted—and you felt terrible, and I felt terrible." I looked at my reins. My emotions were too ragged and raw to discuss this with any sort of objectivity. I held up a hand and shook my head. "It's too much, Georgi. I almost died—I can't think about this right now."

"Of course. Just know that I am your humble servant, always. Whatever you ask of me, I shall give it willingly."

I looked up sharply at his words. Georgi rested one hand over his heart, and it didn't take my magic to see the adoration shining in his face like the midday sun. It seemed his memories weren't the only thing that had returned.

I didn't know what I would ask of him in the future, but there was true comfort in knowing I hadn't lost my most steadfast ally. And friend.

\* \* \*

WE FOUND Papa in the cave where I'd left him, pacing like a caged beast.

I slid off my horse and ran into his arms, catching him as he stumbled, his cane catching a tree root.

"My fool, brave girl," he said into my hair, his wiry arms a welcome crush around me. "I thought I'd lost you." His voice caught.

"You didn't, Papa. I'm right here." Tears sprang free as the memory of the flashing blade filled my mind. He didn't need to know how close it had been.

We rode the short way home, Papa behind me in the saddle. I leaned back against his chest and let the great weariness overtake me.

Dragan was dead. It hardly seemed real. Surely, he was too crafty to let a simple beheading stop him for long. I kept expecting to see his spectral form, floating just out of reach, watching me with that same impenetrable look he'd worn when alive.

But no, he was truly gone. The killing was finally over. Selojia was safe. Nevena was safe. My relief was a palpable thing, potent and powerful. But that wasn't all I felt. There was something more. Something I barely dared articulate, even to myself. I'd never met anyone as enthralling as Dragan Vulpe, and some broken part of me would mourn him. Not the man he'd turned out to be—twisted and conniving. But the man I'd thought I'd found when I'd gazed into those violet eyes. The man he could have been, if it all had been different.

I tucked the feeling deep inside myself, shutting it into a dark, little box. He had occupied my mind for far too long. No longer. I would not waste my tears mourning Dragan.

"You did it, Jana," Papa murmured into my ear. "Rest now."

My eyes fluttered closed. And I did.

# CHAPTER 41

*A* bluebird sky stretched over the tapestry of tan buildings. Temple bells rang from the azure-tiled domes, declaring the start to Lruzina's season. Every inch of the city was festooned with white and red ribbons marking the end of the long, misty winter. They fluttered from tent poles and lintels, mastheads and bridles. It didn't hurt that the queen had announced the Equinox festival would also be a celebration of her recent marriage. Revelry was in the air.

I untied my cloak and draped it over my saddle as I rode up the sharp-angled streets leading up to the palace. My guard, Yacob, trailed behind me like a silent sentinel. He and Papa had hit it off, playing Royals and trading stories after supper by the fire. But with me, he was always quiet and respectful—standoffish, even. It was fine. I wasn't in the mood to talk.

I had spent the last weeks inside my head, trying to sort out the snarl of emotions Dragan had left for me. The shock had worn off; the tide of fear was slowly receding. But left in its wake, the beachfront of my mind was strewn with detritus. Guilt and shame, regret and doubt.

I was returning to claim the mantle of Prime Mesmer. I wondered how I could advise Nevena on important political matters when my judgment was so clearly defective. I hadn't seen Dragan for what he was. And *so* many had paid the price.

The palace gates smiled wide as I rode into the courtyard, struck by a sense of déjà vu. It looked the same as it had when Papa and I had trundled in with a load of dried verbenia for Queen Ksenjia half a year ago. Yet everything was different.

I found Nevena in her sitting room, writing at her desk. I knocked on the open door frame.

"Adrijana! You are a welcome sight." Nevena strode across the room and embraced me. She pulled back, examining me. "You look well. Are you rejuvenated?"

I offered a false smile. "As well as can be expected."

She took my hand and led me to the little table by the window. An image of twisted pastries covered in powdered sugar flashed to mind. I blinked it away. I had thwarted that plot. It was over.

Nevena's karakal, Roja, jumped into my lap, startling me. She padded in a circle before lying down. I fought back the emotion as I stroked her soft fur.

"You're back in her good graces." Nevena shook her head softly. "It seems Roja knew the truth all along."

"If only she'd been able to tell us."

"Speak plainly, my friend." Nevena looked up. "Are you ready to resume your duties?"

I breathed out heavily. "I don't trust my judgment. How can I advise you when I didn't see the truth of who Dragan was? He fooled me so completely..." I broke off. So completely that I still missed him. That I woke tangled in sheets, his words ringing in my mind. *"Rule at my side. As my queen."* Had he meant it? Or had it been yet another lie? Some plot within a plot I couldn't even fathom?

Nevena laid a hand on mine. "He fooled us all, Adrijana. My parents, our ministers. Even Valko."

I let out a wooden laugh. "I almost think he told me, once, in his own way. *'Handsome men can be villains too,'* he said."

Nevena shook her head, her face darkening. "The man was a monster."

"Yes." I could never tell her that sometimes I wondered how much had been Dragan, and how much had been Silviya. I wondered if any of his feelings for me had been real. I would never know.

"Do you imagine I don't doubt my judgment at times?" she said. "That I don't lie awake at night haunted by my poor choices? I doubt my path. Every day. But I do my best because that's what Adrjssia requires of me. I don't need you to be infallible. But I do need you. I cannot do this without you."

I responded, running over familiar territory we'd traversed in our letters these past weeks. "But I didn't even complete my training. There's so much I don't know—"

Nevena held up a hand to cut off further protestations. "I trust you, Adrijana. And after everything that's happened, I value integrity over experience. If I can do this, so can you."

I looked into Nevena's earnest, brown eyes. She was a good woman and would make an excellent queen. She was asking me to try my hardest. That, I could do for her.

I nodded. "Of course. I will serve you as best I can."

"Thank Ovyato." Nevena crossed back to her desk and returned with an object. She handed me a long, silver necklace, threaded with a pendant shaped like a wide eye. "Valko's amulet." I rubbed a thumb across its surface with a wistful smile, remembering the first time I'd seen it in the throne room. How terrifying he'd seemed.

"*Your* amulet. It belongs to the Prime Mesmer."

I hesitated, that unblinking eye boring into me.

"Put it on, Adrijana. It's yours now." Nevena's words were gentle, but a clear command.

I did so. The pendant nestled between my breasts, heavier than I'd expected. I hoped I'd grow used to it, in time.

"Perfect." Nevena nodded. "I'm glad that's done because we have much to discuss. We have an ambitious new Vruk king with a secret Mesmer army to outsmart."

I blanched at the thought. Elian had said he planned to train the Wretched to fight for him, once his people got used to the idea. It was hardly a comforting thought. "A few against a hundred. Hardly fair."

293

"Perhaps more. We've put out a call throughout Adrjssia for all who have any sign of Mesmer ability to come to Selojia to be trained. Your first pupils have already arrived. Two young Mora Mesmers who were traveling with the fleet."

I yelped. "*My* first pupils?"

* * *

THE MESMER WORKSHOP SAT UNTOUCHED, hushed beneath a thin layer of dust. I stood for a long while, taking in the familiar sights. Sorting through the emotions they brought up as best I could. Finally, I went and sat in Valko's chair behind his desk. My eyes traced the stacks of parchment with his cramped notes, the piled books haphazardly stacked, one cracked and lying face-down on top. A life interrupted.

"I was too late to save you," I whispered, my hand clutched around his amulet. "I'm sorry. If I'd put it together faster, if I'd studied more..." I shook my head. If I hadn't been a lovestruck fool, maybe I would have pieced it together. Found and understood Valko's under-lining in the book before his execution. I should have found a way to talk to him. I should have Projected into his cell, knowing he couldn't come to me. The million things I should have done differently were a hailstorm that hammered at my bruised and battered psyche. There was no shelter from the onslaught.

"I thought I might find you here."

I looked up to find Simeon in the doorway, a lilac tunic clinging to his muscled frame. I ran over and threw my arms around him in a hug. His presence was a welcome relief. "She has you in purple, does she?" I arched an eyebrow as I pulled back.

Simeon rolled his eyes. "I feel like a flower."

"Oh, come now." I grinned. "You know you'd wear blossoms in your hair if it made Nevena happy."

"Gods help me, I would." Simeon put his hands on his hips and surveyed the workshop. "So this is yours now?"

"I suppose. It feels like...wearing a dead man's clothes. I can't shake the feeling that they're everywhere. Valko and Dragan." I shivered.

"You'll make it your own. Get all of this junk out of here. Start fresh."

I retreated back to Valko's chair and sank into it. "A daunting task."

Simeon perched on the desk. "You'll need the space for your new pupils. My aunt says they're eager to learn."

I massaged my temples. "I hardly feel equipped to teach others. What will I tell them? We're surrounded by liars and cheats, trust no one, not even me?"

Simeon chuckled. "That would be a bit harsh for a first lesson. Maybe save that for weeks two or three."

"I'm serious, Simeon! I don't know how to . . . *be* anymore. I don't know how to trust myself. Nevena's relying on me and I'm going to screw things up—"

"Hush." Simeon lay a hand on my shoulder, and I fell silent, swiping at a sullen tear.

"That man is guilty of many crimes, but in my estimation, one of his worst was making you doubt yourself. You are smart and compassionate and capable."

"I don't feel like any of those things," I admitted.

"You will, in time. Do you want to know how I see it?"

"Please."

His tone was soft as lamb's wool. "Your only wrong in this was believing Dragan was good. And that's not a crime, Jana, it's a gift. Don't let him take that from you. Just..." He waggled his eyebrows. "Keep your eyes open to the alternative next time, all right?"

Simeon's words resonated deep in the hidden places in my soul, touching a tender nerve. Perhaps that had been my crime. Believing Dragan was good. I *still* believed that some part of him was, and it was eating away at me. I hated myself for missing a monster. But that wasn't all he'd been. No one was all bad, or all good. Not even him. We were all complicated bundles of desire, and emotion, and thought. We were all contradictions. "That helps, actually."

Simeon took my hand and kissed it. "Good. I am a wise king, after all."

I leveled a gaze at him. "Don't you mean a know-it-all *king consort*?

He winced. "Right. Please don't tell Nevena I called myself a 'king.'"

I grinned. "I'll keep your secret, for a price."

"A steep price, no doubt."

"It seems I have a lot of interior decorating to do." I gestured around me. "I'm going to need a strong back."

"Can't you make your new acolytes do that?" Simeon asked. "Or Georgi? He's smitten enough to move an entire palace of furniture for you."

I ignored his comment, and the tendril of warmth it sent through me. "I'll also need some loose purse strings. Furniture doesn't come cheap."

"Already extorting the crown." Simeon groaned and tapped the pendant around my neck. "You've taken to your role as Prime Mesmer in record time."

His jest landed lightly, and I stood and put my arm around his waist, walking with him to the high window that looked over the glistening Vokai Sea. His arm rested comfortably atop my shoulder, as it had once had when we were children.

The harbor was studded with blue-sailed Mora ships that gleamed like sapphires beneath the spring sun. "Did you ever think we would find ourselves here?" I asked. Simeon, married to a queen. Me, the most powerful Mesmer in Adrjssia.

"You know I didn't," Simeon remarked.

I didn't feel ready for it, not in the slightest. But I wasn't alone. I had allies at my side. Nevena. Simeon. Georgi. And Papa. They believed in me, even if I didn't believe in myself just yet. And that was enough.

# FROM THE AUTHOR

Thank you so much for taking the time to read the *The Mesmerist*! I hope you've enjoyed reading about Adrijana's adventures as much as I've enjoyed writing them!

If you're interested in receiving updates on the Mythical Alliance series, participating in giveaways, and requesting advanced copies of upcoming books, sign up for my mailing list at http://claireluana.com.

As a thank you for signing up, you will receive a free ebook!

Lastly, reader reviews are incredibly important to indie authors like me, and so it would mean the world to me if you took a few minutes to leave an honest review wherever you buy books online. It doesn't have to be much; a few words can make the difference in helping a future reader decide to give the book a chance. Thanks!

# ABOUT THE AUTHOR

Claire Luana grew up in Seattle reading everything she could get her hands on and writing every chance she could. Eventually, adulthood won out, and she turned her writing talents to more scholarly pursuits, going to work as a commercial litigation attorney. But it turns out that's not nearly as much fun!

Since returning to her more creative roots, Claire has written and published five fantasy series: The Moonburner Cycle, The Confectioner Chronicles, The Mythical Alliance, The Knights of Caerleon, co-written with Jesikah Sundin, and The Faerie Race, co-written with J.A. Armitage.

She lives in Seattle, Washington with her husband and two dogs. In her (little) remaining spare time, she loves to hike, travel, binge-watch CW shows, and of course, fall into a good book.

Connect with Claire Luana online at: http://claireluana.com

## OTHER BOOKS BY CLAIRE LUANA

Moonburner Cycle

Moonburner, Book One

Sunburner, Book Two

Starburner, Book Three

Burning Fate, Prequel Novella

Moonburner Cycle, Box Set

Confectioner Chronicles

The Confectioner's Guild, Book One

The Confectioner's Coup, Book Two

The Confectioner's Truth, Book Three

The Confectioner's Exile, Prequel Novella

Confectioner Chronicles, Box Set

The Knights of Caerleon, with Jesikah Sundin

The Fifth Knight, Book One

The Third Curse, Book Two

The First Gwenevere, Book Three

Gwenevere's Knights, Box Set

The Faerie Race, with J.A. Armitage

The Sorcery Trial, Book One

The Elemental Trial, Book Two

The Doomsday Trial, Book Three

The Faerie Race, Box Set

The Mythical Alliance: Phoenix Team

Phoenix Selected, Book One

Phoenix Protected, Book Two

Phoenix Captured, Book Three

Phoenix Trafficked, Book Four

Phoenix Revealed, Book Five

Phoenix Betrayed, Book Six

Mythical Alliance: Phoenix Team, Box Set

Orion's Kiss

Writing as Jae Dawson:

Moonlight & Belladonna

Heartbeats & Roses

Snowflakes & Holly

Made in the USA
Middletown, DE
03 March 2022

62112978R00182